HEART OF
THE DEVIL

Praise for Ali Vali

Beauty and the Boss

"The story gripped me from the first page, both the relationship between the two main characters, as well as the drama of the issues that threaten to bring down the business...Vali's writing style is lovely—it's clean, sharp, no wasted words, and it flows beautifully as a result. Highly recommended!"
—*Rainbow Book Reviews*

Balance of Forces: Toujours Ici

"A stunning addition to the vampire legend, *Balance of Forces: Toujour Ici* is one that stands apart from the rest."
—*Bibliophilic Book Blog*

Calling the Dead

"So many writers set stories in New Orleans, but Ali Vali's mystery novels have the authenticity that only a real Big Easy resident could bring...makes for a classic lesbian murder yarn."—*Curve Magazine*

Blue Skies

"Vali is skilled at building sexual tension, and the sex in this novel flies as high as Berkley's jets. Look for this fast-paced read."—*Just About Write*

Carly's Sound

"Vali paints vivid pictures with her words...*Carly's Sound* is a great romance, with some wonderfully hot sex."—*Midwest Book Review*

"It's no surprise that passion is indeed possible a second time around."—*Q Syndicate*

Acclaim for the Casey Cain Saga

The Devil Inside

"Vali's fluid writing style quickly puts the reader at ease, which makes the story and its characters equally easy to get to know and care about. When you find yourself talking out loud to the characters in a book, you know the work is polished and professional, as well as entertaining."—*Family and Friends Magazine*

"Not only is *The Devil Inside* a ripping mystery, it's also an intimate character study."—*L-Word Literature*

"*The Devil Inside* is the first of what promises to be a very exciting series…While telling an exciting story that grips the reader, Vali has also fully fleshed out her heroes and villains. *The Devil Inside* is that rarity: a fascinating crime novel which includes a tender love story and leaves the reader with a cliffhanger ending."—*MegaScene*

The Devil Unleashed

"Fast-paced action scenes, intriguing character revelations, and a refreshing approach to the romance thriller genre all make for an enjoyable reading experience in the Big Easy…*The Devil Unleashed* is an engrossing reading experience."—*Midwest Book Review*

Deal with the Devil

"Ali Vali has given her fans another thick, rich thriller…*Deal With the Devil* has wonderful love stories, great sex, and an ample supply of humor. It is an exciting, page-turning read that leaves her readers eagerly awaiting the next book in the series."—*Just About Write*

The Devil Be Damned

"Ali Vali excels at creating strong, romantic characters along with her fast-paced, sophisticated plots. Her setting, New Orleans, provides just the right blend of immigrants from Mexico, South America, and Cuba, along with a city steeped in traditions."—*Just About Write*

By the Author

Carly's Sound

Second Season

Calling the Dead

Blue Skies

Love Match

The Dragon Tree Legacy

The Romance Vote

Girls with Guns

Beneath the Waves

Beauty and the Boss

Forces Series

Balance of Forces: Toujours Ici

Battle of Forces: Sera Toujours

The Cain Casey Saga

The Devil Inside

The Devil Unleashed

Deal with the Devil

The Devil Be Damned

The Devil's Orchard

The Devil's Due

Heart of the Devil

Visit us at www.boldstrokesbooks.com

HEART OF THE DEVIL

by
Ali Vali

2018

HEART OF THE DEVIL

© 2018 By Ali Vali. All Rights Reserved.

ISBN 13: 978-1-63555-045-0

This Trade Paperback Original Is Published By
Bold Strokes Books, Inc.
P.O. Box 249
Valley Falls, NY 12185

First Edition: January 2018

Credits
Editor: Shelley Thrasher
Production Design: Stacia Seaman
Cover Design by Sheri (graphicartist2020@hotmail.com)

Acknowledgments

Luck is defined as good fortune, and that is certainly what happened to me the day the Casey Clan popped into my head. They've led me on a great adventure that has definitely brought me good fortune in the people I've met and worked with. Thank you, Radclyffe, for your support, advice, and for the gift of joining the BSB family. Thank you to Sandy Lowe for the great job you do every day, and for the idea of this book.

Thank you to Shelley Thrasher, my editor. This certainly isn't our first book, but no matter the number, you always teach me something new. All those lessons are invaluable.

Thank you to my first readers Cris Perez-Soria, Connie Ward, and Kim Rieff. Your comments and help were much appreciated, but your friendship is the real treasure.

Thank you to the BSB team that does such an amazing job and works so hard so that every project is a success. Thank you to Stacia Seaman for the final polish to every book, to Cindy Cresap for your dedication, and to Sheri for another great cover.

Thank you to all the readers who have loved these characters enough to want more. Your support and emails are very much appreciated. As always, every word is written with you in mind.

Thank you to C for reminding me that there is beauty and joy in this world if you only bother to look. You're always ready for the next big adventure, and for that I love you. Verdad!

For C
Thanks for believing.

Para Mami, Papi, y mi hermano
For giving a sense of adventure and memories to last a lifetime.

CHAPTER ONE

The pain fades, my love," Therese Casey said as she pressed her hands to Derby Cain Casey's back. It was the first anniversary of the death of Cain's father, Dalton, and she had yet to get over the sudden, violent loss.

"Do you really believe that?" Cain turned, put her arms around her mother, and kissed her forehead. "The only thing that'll make me feel better is ripping the throat out of whoever did this."

Nothing made the loss more tangible than standing in the marble mausoleum they'd had built for the family in the old cemetery in uptown New Orleans. The place was cold even in the summer, and it focused the permanence of his absence in her life. She was the heir to his title—a job she'd prepared for all her life, and he'd guided and taught her to be successful, but she still had a million questions she hadn't asked him. That future together had ended abruptly and savagely, and for that, someone was going to pay dearly.

"Right now you need to take care of your family. You can handle the bloodlust when you're sure." Therese kissed her fingers before placing them on Dalton's name. "You've got to get Billy under control before he's beyond our reach."

"He's no angrier than I am, so it's hard to tell him anything." Her little brother had handled their father's murder with his fists. Billy had beaten the crap out of every one of their enemies that had crossed his path, but the fighting only seemed to make his anger grow.

"If he gets any madder you'll have a war on your hands, and we really can't afford that. Your da never wanted to bother me with the business, but I don't live with my head in a pot. Now's the time for level-headedness and a firm hand. Remember his lessons on anger and how it clouds your judgment. It's time to remind Billy of all those wise things your da taught you and soothe that beast clawing at his heart."

"So you're trying to tell me to aim Billy a little?" They walked out into the heat, and the guards glanced around before they moved through the cemetery.

"Your brother's a hothead with a bad case of shortsightedness." Therese slipped her hand into the bend of her elbow and leaned against her. "I'm his mother, so you know I'm right."

"You're my mother too, so God only knows what you're saying about me when I'm not around." She laughed when her mother slapped her arm.

"It's been a year, and I'm proud of how you've handled yourself. The clan's yours, and every Casey alive and gone is thrilled that this load has landed on these broad shoulders. But you've got enough going on without adding to that already impossible burden. Talk to him and lift a little of his fog before something happens to him. I can only take so much loss in this lifetime, and your da's passing is enough."

She opened the car door for her mother and kissed her cheek. "I'll go pick up Marie and meet you at the house later for dinner. I'll talk to Billy tonight."

"Don't let her talk you into too many treats. You're a soft touch, and your sister's got your number."

"One milk shake. I promise."

Therese kissed her hand and shook her head. They both knew she'd give Marie whatever she asked for. Her little sister really was the soft spot in her otherwise hard demeanor. But her and the family's survival depended on her staying as unforgiving as she could manage, and that wasn't a stretch since all she wanted to do was open fire on the world. She didn't care how much blood ran in the streets. It'd been a year, so her revenge was about as cold as she wanted to let it get before she served it to whoever had killed her da.

"You want to put off the meeting with the Liam brothers?" Merrick Runyon asked. The African American guard who'd been at her side for a couple of years was enjoying her new position as the head of Cain's security.

"The Liam brothers need us more than we need to do business with them. Da trusted them, but I've got something else in mind for now."

"Are you sure you want to rock the sturdy ocean liner your father built?"

"The future has to be part mine or I won't make it. Da was the first to say that you only move forward by hacking through the brush yourself. If it's mine, then the pressure to make it succeed will keep me sharp. Don't worry. I know what I'm doing."

"I realize that, but just make sure you're not so sharp you cut yourself off from what works."

"If I close my eyes I can almost imagine Mum is still here."

"Way to make a girl feel incredibly unspecial."

"I love my mother," she said with a smile.

"No doubt, but maybe I have other ideas that aren't motherly at all."

"The last thing you should get is ideas, babe. It's like one of the bullets that took him from me sliced through my heart." She pointed back toward her father's grave and closed her eyes. "Hold out for something better."

❖

Emma Verde tapped her pen on the blank page of her notebook, too nervous to think of anything to write. The new semester hadn't started with much good news, but she was hoping to salvage it by meeting with the head of the university's financial aid.

"Miss Verde," the elderly woman behind the oak counter said. "Go on in."

"Thanks, Miss Betty." Everyone in the office knew her, so if any help was available, they'd give it to her. "Hey, June." She shook hands with the new and incredibly young dean.

"Hey, Emma." June flicked her shoulder-length red hair back with what seemed like impatience. "I appreciate you coming in."

"Please tell me you have good news and all this is a big mistake." The notice she'd received in the mail had sent her into a mild panic. She was barely surviving with her scholarship and her student job. Losing one or the other meant she'd be forced out because of Tulane's expensive tuition.

"The manager of the bookstore loves you—don't think it has anything to do with that." June pressed her hands together and seemed to try to keep her face impassive. She was failing miserably.

"I'm really losing my job?" She didn't need to ask the question because the answer seemed plain and done. "Why? How much can the school save getting rid of me?"

"I've only got so many slots, Emma, and sometimes life is as unfair as it gets. One of the state senators has a kid starting this year, and he's getting your spot."

"Does he even need my job?"

"I might incriminate myself by answering that, so let's skip it. I also want to make sure you're okay, so while I don't want to intrude into your personal life, I have a question for you. Can your parents help out any?"

Emma shook her head while she pressed her hands against her stomach. "No. That won't be possible."

"All I need is a few years of tax returns. We can start with a grant. If not, you might qualify for some more student loans in addition to the ones you've gotten on your own."

Her mother Carol's voice saying that going to school was a waste slammed around in her head. Calling for any kind of help would be admitting defeat. "That's not going to happen."

"Do you want to talk about it?" June asked gently, as if knowing there was more to the story.

"No, but thanks. So am I out right away?"

"I got you two weeks, and I'll do my best to find you something."

"Thanks, June, and I understand. Sometimes it's out of your control, but I appreciate your honesty. I like you, so thanks for the couple of weeks." She packed her bag and tried to keep her smile.

"You'll be training the senator's son, so don't thank me just yet. I feel like an asshole, but I thought it'd be better than nothing."

"There might be an asshole at work here, but I doubt it's you."

She walked outside and dropped her bag to keep from flinging it into the bushes. The urge to get really angry was getting strong, but her buzzing phone made her smile again since she knew who it was. Once a week her best friend from back home called to check on her. The phone was the one extravagance her father had insisted on, in case she needed to call for help and so he could reach her no matter what.

Maddie and her husband Jerry were the only two people who seemed as excited as she was when Tulane offered her the scholarship. Actually, she'd had her choice of three schools, but the city of New Orleans had lured her to Tulane. It was the complete opposite of the small Wisconsin farming town she'd grown up in, and all she'd wanted was to experience the world her mother had tried to keep locked away from her.

"Hey," she said, sitting on the lawn and turning her face up to the sun.

"What's wrong?"

"How the hell do you do that?" Maddie was a year older, but they'd been inseparable during high school, and their closeness hadn't changed much, even after Maddie met Jerry and decided on the life a lot of their friends had chosen.

"You grew up with Carol as a mother, and I grew up knowing that when you sound overly chipper you're covering up something upsetting. Considering that it happened on an almost daily basis, I got really good at it."

"You're a riot." She wanted to stay positive, but it was hard. She could stay in school without some dead-end job if she gave up eating and living in her crappy apartment. "And I'm unemployed."

"Honey, I'm so sorry, but if you show up here without a degree, I'll never forgive you."

"I've got two weeks to find something, so I shouldn't think the worst, I guess."

"And if you don't, you know we'll be happy to help."

"I love you, but I want to try to make it on my own. If I don't, I'm only proving her right," she said, referring to her mother.

"Emma, Carol gave birth to you because she wanted to. You don't owe her a lifetime of misery for the favor. She may think that and find plenty of passages in her Bible to prove that to herself, but it's all bullshit."

Her mother was the most pious person she knew and used the scriptures in her well-worn Bible to point out everything she was failing at in life. Carol's biggest disappointment so far had been her choice to come here. Carol probably wouldn't have wasted high school on her, much less college.

Good Christian women married and hung on every word their husbands and the Lord said. Every Christian woman except Carol, that was, because Emma was sure her father would agree she had no problem stating her opinion.

"I'm not giving in." She lay back and rested her head on the nice leather bag that had been a gift from her father. "You caught me right after I found out. I liked the bookstore since I got to study as much as I worked."

"Why not try what you did here when you had a problem to solve?"

She laughed. "I'd need a ride out of town to find a cow pasture, much less a lake."

"I was thinking more of a walk some place you love. You've been there long enough to have found a favorite spot."

"Thanks, Maddie, and I love you for making me feel better." She hung up, brushed off her jeans, and said to herself, "She's right. You've got to suck it up and think."

She headed to her tiny apartment, wanting to forget the report that was due and everything else, at least for the night. Whatever happened next, it would point her toward her future, or at least give her something to talk about in her later years, as her grandmother used to say.

"Good Lord, no need to be so dramatic. All this will lead to is a barista job somewhere, and my memories of it will be hilarious some day when all I have to worry about is grading papers."

CHAPTER TWO

I'm not sure how you're bringing it now, but I've got better routes and a better deal," Jake Kelly said loudly while pacing in front of Cain's desk. "Word on the street is your father got lazy and just took what someone offered him. Aren't you tired of getting screwed?"

"Jake, stick to what you're here for and leave my da out of it," Cain said, low enough that he had to stop. "We don't know each other yet, so you should realize I've come close to shooting people for saying less about him." She glanced back at Billy, surprised he'd kept his word to stay quiet. The switchblade he was twirling through his fingers made her think he wasn't as out of control as her mother thought since it wasn't sticking out of Jake's chest.

"No problem, and I apologize." He held his hands up and sat heavily in one of the empty chairs. "I'm just jacked about this deal, so forget I said anything."

"Let me think about it." She looked at Merrick, prompting her to open the office door. "But I've got another meeting if you don't mind."

"Don't think too long. I won't be in town that long, and I have other offers."

"If I'm holding you back, then feel free to deal with whoever you want."

Merrick pointed to the door when Jake stood up and took a step toward her desk. Jake seemed to think about it since he stopped and stared before waving the guy he'd brought with him out.

Once the door closed, Billy got off Cain's credenza where he'd been sitting and put his hands on her shoulders. "Please tell me we're not doing business with this guy."

"Not now, brother." She reached for his hand and looked at him. "Lou," she said to the big guard that was with her most days.

Lou ran a scanner through the room and pointed to the right side of the doorjamb. "You ready for that meeting, Boss?" Lou asked when he gestured to her desk.

"Billy, you free?" she asked, shaking her head when Billy went over to rip both of the bugs off and smash them under his heel, she guessed.

"Come on. I could use a beer."

The car her father used sat in the big warehouse, but she pointed to the big Suburban with tinted windows. She liked being higher than the sedans the feds were partial to, so Merrick and Lou got into the front, and Billy joined her in the back.

"Who's this fucker and where'd you find him?" Billy said, once Merrick gave them a thumbs-up.

"He found me, and we're going to keep leading him on until I find what I'm looking for." She glanced out at the port as they drove out.

"What the hell are you looking for? To get screwed?"

She had to laugh at Billy's ability to get right to the point. "Who comes to the office with good deals and bugs?"

"Are you kidding? You let the feds in to help you out on a deal?"

"Give me a little more credit than that. I'm trying to figure out if anything's changed since Da died, so I'm playing dumb for now." She squeezed the side of his neck. "Where were you today? Mum waited for you, and when you were a no-show, she got worried."

"I can't stand thinking about him in that box. If I'd been there I might've been able to save him." He tried to pull away from her, but she didn't let go. "I wasn't there when he needed me most. I'm nothing but a fuck-up, so it's hard to face her."

"Stop blaming yourself. You know Da. He didn't like hovering, so he would've run you off after an hour. None of what happened is your fault, and Mum loves you, so don't go pushing her away."

"I know, but I'm sure it was that fat bastard. You give me the word, and I'll take him out. I'll do it myself and make sure he sees it coming." He punched his palm with his fist, making Cain wince. "The coward that killed Da didn't give him the satisfaction of facing him."

"Billy, you have to promise me that you'll hold off until you get my okay. We've got to show the other families we're not going to go back on our word when it comes to our alliances."

"The others wouldn't ask permission, Cain. They'd kill that son of a bitch and celebrate afterward."

"Lou, head to the house," she said, and sat back to think about the best approach. Her mum was right in that she had to find a way not only to reach Billy, but to defuse him.

"Drop me at the club then. I'm not ready to go home."

"You're not going anywhere. I have another meeting, and you're going to be there."

"You're the boss now, so deal with whatever however you want. I need to blow off some steam." Billy leaned forward and slapped Lou on the back. "Drop me at the corner. I'll find my way from there."

"Lou, if you stop at the corner, go ahead and get out with him."

"I don't need a sitter, sister. My guys will take care of me."

"You get out of this fucking car, and both of you are out. You better pray Lou and your guys can take care of you, because you'll be on your own."

"Yeah, right."

"This isn't the time to test me. You're my brother, but I'm not going to fight battles from every direction. Especially from some place I shouldn't have to worry about. You either accept that I'm the boss or get out. I'm not going to argue about it."

The rest of the ride was quiet, but Billy wasn't giving in. She wasn't about to think that, but she was tired of lecturing too. She didn't want to honor her father with this type of legacy.

Their mother was waiting but Cain discreetly shook her head, so Therese just hugged Billy and stayed outside when they entered the study. She'd invited her father's brother Jarvis and his only child Muriel.

"Thanks for coming, Uncle Jarvis," she said embracing him, then Muriel. "It's time to settle some stuff so we can move forward."

"What's to settle? We all know and accept who Da's heir is, and none of us dispute it. Right?" Billy asked, staring at everyone there as if daring any of them to contradict him, even if he'd done it himself in a way.

"Billy, sit please," she said. "Today's the first anniversary of Da's death, so it's time to decide how we move forward."

"What do you have in mind, Cain?" Jarvis asked, his demeanor and gestures, just like his looks, exactly like her father's.

"You and Da wanted Muriel away from the family business, and I agree, but we need to make one big change. Muriel, you should start establishing your own firm. It'll give you the distance you need from me, but I still need you close to give counsel."

"I'd be honored to," Muriel said.

"Uncle Jarvis, you'll keep your place at my side as my advisor, like you were for Da. You need to come with me for the long-overdue meeting with the other families."

"Vincent and Ramon wanted to give you the space to grieve, but they'll be happy for some normalcy." Jarvis stood and covered her hands with his. "You'll never have a moment to doubt me."

"I know that because I know what family means to you." She smiled at Jarvis and stood up, ready to finish. "Could you all give Billy and me the room?"

Billy seemed restless once it was the two of them. "So you're cutting me out?" he asked after a few minutes of silence, and the allure of the bottle on the small table finally won out.

"Put that down, or I'll shove the decanter and every single matching glass up your ass." She moved around the desk and sat on the edge. "No one's taking anything away from you, but we're not leaving here until we get some stuff straight."

"If you're worried about me accepting how things are—don't. I know what Da wanted."

"I know that, but I still have two questions for you."

"What?" He could only keep eye contact for a brief time before he turned and faced the wall.

"What can I do to help you? And what's it going to take for you to remember who you are?"

"Everything we learned together doesn't make any sense anymore. Da was the strongest man we both knew, so how did this happen? It's been a whole fucking year, and I still don't understand it. If they could get to him, then I don't know if I can protect you, and you and I both know we're screwed if something happens to you."

"Forget about that right now, and think about one important thing."

"What?" He faced her, and she was glad to see his smile again—not forced or fake, but finally that relaxed expression that set off his handsome face.

"Your name is William Dalton Casey, and Dalton Casey expects you to remember the legacy of your blood. We need to be the strongest bastards in the city, and only then will we bring our heel down and smash every enemy we have." She put her arms around him, and they both finally came to accept their reality. "You're the only one who understands what we need to do and why. Neither of us can let him down."

Billy clung to her and started crying until he was sobbing. Her tears fell silently, but their pain was the same. When he was done, she kissed his cheek and poured two drinks. "To the future, brother. It will always belong to us, and we'll make Da proud by how we shape it."

"Damn straight, and you won't ever have to worry about me again. He taught you to lead, Cain, and he taught me to always have your back. We both learned those lessons well."

❖

The report on early American poetry was roughed out, so Emma shoved a few bucks into her pocket and headed for the streetcar stop near her studio apartment. She'd made a few friends in town, but everyone was busy with rush week, so she rode down to Canal Street alone.

One of the things she'd done on her first weekend off when she'd moved here was find the Hotel Monteleone. She wanted to stay and teach in New Orleans, and maybe write some, so the Monteleone had some impressive writing ghosts in its past. Hemingway, Faulkner, and Tennessee Williams had written and drunk there, so she enjoyed walking through the Carousel Bar and imagining her future here.

Right now it was a dream, but she wanted to settle either here or somewhere like it. No way did she want to end up in Wisconsin with her mother. She'd miss her father, but she had to get out from under the weight of her mother's disapproval and judgment.

Barry, the bartender at the Carousel, greeted her when she sat next to one of the windows. "Hey, Emma. School's only been going on a week. You need a break already?"

"I'm walking and thinking."

He smiled and poured some ginger ale. "Here, so you look like every other lush in here."

"Thanks." She immediately started chewing on the straw. "Know of any coffee shop hiring right now?"

"Try the ones by campus. You don't need to be going home late at night by yourself from the Quarter."

"I'll start my hunt tomorrow, but eventually I'll have to find some place, even if it's in the Quarter."

"Then I'll keep my eye out."

She finished her drink and headed toward the river, window-shopping as she walked. The bar a few blocks away made her stop and listen to the loud singing pouring out the open door. Inside, the patrons looked like young attorneys and engineers, but every one of them seemed to know every word of the Irish song the small band was playing. The place was packed and fueled by plenty of beer and whiskey.

"Good God, it's Monday," she said as she watched the wait staff work the room. The tips they were pulling in seemed to be triple what she made at the bookstore.

"Sing, drink, or hit the road, missy," the bartender said.

Glancing at him made her notice the Help Wanted sign. "I'm here about the job," she said, not thinking about what she was saying.

He wiped his hands on the bar towel and smiled. "Sure you are, little lady. Are you even old enough to be in here?"

"I'm in college, so way old enough, and I'm not kidding."

"Maybe you should try some other place. The hours here are brutal, and if you're in school that'll be a killer. I need someone who'll show up and keep up."

"You give me a chance, and I'll prove that I'll be good. Come on. I need the job to stay in school." She stood and stuck her hand over the bar. "I'm Emma."

He stared at her hand before finally taking it. "Josh," he said as he shook her hand. "Here." He gave her a card with his name and number. "Can you be here at four tomorrow afternoon?"

"I'll be here earlier if you want."

"Four, and you're working until ten and not a minute later. That's my deal, so decide now so I can get back to my pouring."

"I'll be here, Josh. No problem."

"I'll spend a few hours going over the ropes before it gets like this, and believe me, it's like this every night of the week. You've worked as a waiter before, right?" She smiled as she shook her head. "Of course you haven't. Okay. Get out of here before I change my mind."

"Thanks." She slapped her hands together, happy with her lack of caution. Here was her chance, and she hadn't even noticed what the name of the place was. The card said Erin Go Braugh. "What's it mean?" She pointed to it.

"My boss said it expresses allegiance to Ireland, which makes sense. She's big on loyalty, so don't make me look bad."

"No way, and the boss will think I'm the best. Trust me on that."

❖

Therese had prepared a large meal for everyone, so Cain enjoyed some of her favorite food and the stories they all shared about her father. Her sister Marie sat next to her and laughed when she poured a sip of her beer into her glass. Cain knew it made Marie feel like she was participating equally with everyone else without getting her tipsy.

Once dinner was over, Marie held her hand as they went upstairs. Marie was an adult, but only because of her age. Her mind would never progress past that of a child, which made the world consider her mentally challenged, but Cain only saw the pure and true happiness Marie brought into their lives. Others might've also seen Marie as a burden, but no one in the Casey family ever thought that.

"Cain, do you think Da can see us from heaven?" Marie asked, swinging their hands between them.

"Da will always be able to see us. Don't worry about that."

Marie's room had a wall of bookcases full of all the stories she'd read over and over, like the Nancy Drew series. "He's probably got the biggest wings, huh?"

"Probably so, and I bet he loves flying around keeping an eye on us. I miss him though." She got Marie's nightgown and pointed toward the bathroom so she'd remember to brush her teeth.

"I miss him too, but I'm not sad."

"Why not?" She folded Marie's clothes as she handed each piece over.

"Father Andy said he's somewhere nice and he's happy, so we shouldn't be sad that he's gone. I didn't know I wasn't supposed to be sad." She nodded and went into the bathroom with Marie. Once Marie finished, Cain pulled the covers back so her sister could get comfortable. "Does that make me bad that I miss him?"

"You're the best person I know, so you couldn't be bad even if you tried real hard. Da's somewhere nice, but I think he still misses us too."

"Okay, and Father Andy said we'll see him again," Marie said before kissing her cheek.

"Don't rush that, okay?" She leaned over and tapped the end of Marie's nose. "We have plenty of time for that."

"Are you happy, sister?" Marie peered up at her with her usual beautiful smile.

"I'm happy because you love me." She took Marie's hand and wished for some of Marie's outlook on life. In Marie's mind, no monsters were waiting to hurt you, but she knew better. She also knew one of her jobs was to keep Marie from ever finding out that truth.

"I love you, so you never have to be sad."

"I know, sweet girl, so get some sleep, and we'll go for snowballs tomorrow. What'll it be tonight?"

"Can you read *The Secret Garden* again?"

She read until Marie fell asleep, then quietly closed her door. Father Andy might've convinced Marie that their da was sitting on a cloud somewhere strumming a harp, but Marie's faith fractured somewhat at night. Ever since Dalton's murder, Marie couldn't and wouldn't go to sleep unless she was holding Cain's hand and listening to her read.

Therese was waiting at the top of the stairs and held her hand out. "Come on. You can put me to bed too," she said with a sad-appearing smile.

"We'd all be better off seeing the world like Marie does." She entered her parents' bedroom and could swear she could still catch a hint of her da's cologne.

The cleaning staff did a great job of keeping the place spotless, but they didn't move his things from his nightstand. The loose change added up to two dollars and sixteen cents, and his old watch still kept time because her mother wound it religiously. The ring he'd worn for most of his life was there as well, and one more piece of her inheritance. After the funeral home had handed over all the stuff in his pockets, she'd brought it back and put it where he used to drop it every night.

"Your way of seeing things is exactly what it needs to be." Therese poured two small glasses of the sherry she liked. "Sit and talk to me, Derby, and tell me a tale like your da used to."

"What do you want to know, Mum?" They sat in the semicircle of the picture window that overlooked the big yard. The rose garden her da had planted for Therese was in full bloom and something her mum never tired of enjoying from this view. Her da had even lit it so Therese could see it no matter the time of night.

"When I met your da, I fell for that charm of his, but I made sure he knew I realized he was charming me. That's what kept him coming back." Therese laughed and took a sip of her drink. "He knew he had to be on his toes around me because I wasn't taking any of that bull he fed all those pretty girls he'd been with before. If he wanted me in his life, he had to make promises first, and he had to keep them."

Cain smiled and thought about all the nights her parents had spent in this spot talking about their day. Her da had always told her those talks while watching her mother's face enjoying those roses was the best part of his life.

"Someone shot the man I love from a car window like he was a dog, and I want to know why. Dalton was no saint, never pretended to be, but he was a good man. He deserved better than that, and he deserves for that not to go unpunished."

"Mum, I wish I could tell you the truth and believe in my heart it was. I haven't been able to figure out who ordered the hit, much less who actually pulled the trigger, but I've got my suspicions."

"Billy keeps telling me this was the work of Giovanni Bracato. What do you think?"

"You know Da would haunt me from the grave for acting without being sure. If I do that, I could put all of you in danger when someone retaliates. Billy believes that, but he's leaving out one thing. Big Gino loves to brag more than anyone I know, and he's been silent on this for a year. If he ordered it, that's a miracle."

"Okay. Now tell me what you've been doing." Therese took off her shoes and wiggled her toes. She'd always been the prettiest woman Cain knew, and age hadn't changed her opinion. "It's been a year and you haven't changed anything."

"Billy's pissed he couldn't protect him, but I feel the exact same way."

"Billy's a good boy, Derby, but he needs something to believe in. You have to give him a reason to let go of his guilt and be proud of himself again."

"I'm trying, Mum. This is more than killing Da. It's a message that his family couldn't protect him." She took a deep breath. "They not only wanted to kill him, but the rest of us along with him."

"So the street, our territory, is in danger?"

"Vincent and Ramon have helped us keep the peace, so no." She sighed and fought off a yawn.

"It's time to wake up and remember your father."

"I'd forget my own name before I forgot Da."

"Then start keeping all your promises and stop just going through the motions. You're a Casey, my heart, and more importantly, you were his, but only for a time. This is your time now, and you need to remember that the clan is yours now. You need to claim your birthright. We'll follow you to hell if it comes to that, so stop holding back."

"Thanks, Mum. Tonight was my first step." She stood so she could kneel in front of Therese. She enjoyed her mother's arms around her and her kiss on her forehead.

"I know, and I want your promise that you'll become twice as powerful as your da." Therese rubbed her head before letting her up. "Find yourself someone to love while you're at it. Grandchildren are the new start this family needs."

"There's a couple of barrels of oats I haven't even gotten to, so don't go clipping my wings yet."

"Between you and your brother, you'll fly around the world five times with those wings of yours before you're through." Cain laughed as she glanced at the nightstand. "Go ahead and put it on. He'd want it on your finger."

She picked up the gold ring that was a replica of one that had been in her family for years. "It should be worn, but someone needs it more than I do."

"Make sure he doesn't lose it and that you're a good girl, Derby."

She laughed and gripped the ring in her fist. "Now that's something no fed or cop has ever been guilty of saying about me."

❖

Barney Kyle drove through the Garden District neighborhood, slowing when he was close to the corner of the estate he was interested in. The house still had some lights on, but the yard was lit enough to see the guards roaming around outside through the wrought-iron front fence.

"Are you hoping to spot something?" Special Agent Logan North asked as he studied the scene as well. "The Caseys have been laying low since the old man got killed."

"I came to this hellhole of a city to take down organized crime. With enough arrests I can go back to DC as the head of my own national division, so don't be such a simplistic thinker."

"That's what's in the record. Dalton Casey got killed, and the wheels came off the train. The operation will probably implode without our help."

"So we should just give up and wait it out, huh?"

Logan straightened up and shook his head. "No, sir. Do you have something in mind?"

"We need to talk Annabel Hicks into twenty-four-hour surveillance. The old man's death can come in handy, and if we can get one, we can get them all."

"Did you have Benton transferred? I waited for him all last week, and no one will tell me anything."

Barney pulled over across the street and turned off the ignition. "I asked, and he volunteered for an undercover assignment. Since he's unavailable, I need a new number two. You interested?"

"Yes, sir. Can you tell me what he's up to?" Logan asked in a way that telegraphed his ambition.

"It's on a need-to-know right now. I want you to concentrate on Casey for now. If we can get something on her, the only way out I'll give her is to flip on Ramon Jatibon and that fucker Vincent Carlotti."

"You tell me what you need to get that done, sir, and I'm on it."

He restarted the car after scoping out a few spots that surveillance vehicles could use. "I've got a meeting set for tomorrow so we can all be on the same page. I don't want any screw-ups on this."

"Not to worry, sir."

He pulled away and took one quick glance back. "We're getting ready to come down hard, so we'll see if Casey is up to the game."

CHAPTER THREE

Y ou still want to head out?" Cain asked Billy when she came back
downstairs.

"Let's head to Emerald's and have a few drinks. I know the owners,
so I promise a good time." He winked as he put his shoes back on.

"You're a riot, and you need to wear more jewelry."

"What? You want me to look more like a pimp?" He combed back
the thick strand of hair that had fallen over his eyes.

"I think a ring won't turn you into an asshole, especially this one,"
she said, holding up her father's ring. "I want you to wear it."

"That's yours, Derby." He didn't often use her given first name,
but he seemed to want to make a point. "It's past time for you to put it
on. That's what Da would've wanted."

"I want you to wear it. I'm his heir because I was born first."

He topped her by only two inches, but he was bulkier and stronger,
so when he put his arms around her, she smiled at his kindness. "No,
you're his heir because he trusted you with the family. He always
recited that family motto to remind us of where we came from and how
much he loved us."

"You're mine, but only for a time," she said. It was engraved
around the ring in Gaelic.

"Well, you're my sister forever, and you're my clan leader. I'll
follow wherever you take me. I'll do that proudly, and I'll kill anyone
to keep you safe or who tries to take what's rightfully yours."

She pointed to his finger and he put the ring on. "It's home again,"
she said.

"How about if I wear it until you have a son? Your kid can be the
next one to have it."

"We'll both be ancient before I have a kid, Billy boy. Come on. Let's go show the world that the Caseys are still alive."

A couple of years before, Dalton had given them the money they needed to open the high-end nightclub Emerald's. It hadn't taken long for them to pay him back and bring in a good monthly profit.

The club was one of their legitimate businesses and had been so successful Cain had opened a smaller and very different place about a mile away. Between Emerald's and the Erin Go Braugh, she had two venues to clean the cash inflow from the real family business. They'd built their fortune bootlegging booze and cigarettes, but what good was money if you couldn't have a good time every so often, her da would say.

Lou pulled up to the door of Emerald's, and she was glad to see the line of people waiting to get in. A popular place in the French Quarter was worth more than a boatload of gold, so two of them were going to help fuel what she had in mind. It was time to start spending on more than just a good time, but that could wait until the morning.

"Let's go find some lucky women, Cain." Billy was already out of the car waiting for her.

"Let's go, Casanova."

Merrick and Lou followed them in and stood in the VIP section, where Vinny Carlotti, Vincent's son, was waiting for them. "The old man sends his condolences. He didn't forget what day it was," Vinnie said to both of them.

"Papi sends the same," Remi Jatibon, Ramon's daughter, said when she came up from the bar.

"Thanks, guys." Cain waved a waitress over. "How about we lift a glass of good whiskey to Da."

Each of them grabbed a glass and said, "Dalton." It was the first of many that night, but it was a time to celebrate. They were alive, and because they were, they'd beat the shit out of whatever and whoever stood in their way.

"Papi said to come by whenever you want. He might have some answers for you," Remi said when they stepped into the soundproof office.

"So he found out who it was?"

"Wait for the meeting, Cain. No sense driving yourself crazy until you've got all the facts. You need to be careful though." Remi dropped onto the sofa that faced the double mirror overlooking the dance floor.

These two strong women would take their families forward, but that wasn't the only thing they had in common. Remi also shared her love of women, but they were too alike to end up together.

"I've had my head up my ass since last year, but I've tried not to be sloppy. Thanks for picking up the slack. You and your family are good friends." She sat next to Remi and exhaled. "It's time to step up and take responsibility for my business."

"Give yourself a break, and you don't have to thank us. Your father helped us make it here. We'll never fully repay that debt."

"Da considered that debt paid years ago, and you know it. Ramon has been a good friend, and our friendship is even stronger since we grew up together." She handed Remi a glass. "To the future, and everything that goes with it." They tapped their glasses together and smiled.

Remi finished her drink and pointed to Billy on the dance floor, surrounded by four women. "Think he needs help?"

"He's going to run dry by the time he's thirty."

"With any luck, we all will. Papi said to enjoy it while it lasts. Once you settle down to only one, all you'll have left is the memories of nights like this."

"Let's go add a few to our memory banks then."

They laughed and headed out to the club. Billy took two of the girls by the hand and twirled them in their direction. Cain didn't feel like dancing, but this was as good a thing as any to get her mind on something else.

"Did you invite that asshole?" Billy said right into her ear, then laughed to cover up the serious question. "At the end of the bar."

Jake Kelly was sitting with his elbows on the bar, drinking and staring at them. "You can't believe that. He's like an untrained puppy who's trying way too hard."

"You want me to pound some Gaelic into his jaw?" Billy asked, lifting the hand he'd put the ring on.

"Not tonight, so set him up with some drinks and keep him by the bar. I'm not in the mood to deal with business right now." One of the girls put her hand on her inner thigh and moved closer. "At least not his kind of business."

"Then let him buy his own damn drinks."

"Don't alienate him now, brother. He might not want to play when the time comes. And for what I have planned, he needs to think he's the smartest guy in the room."

❖

"So do you think you can remember the nicknames for all the beers we went through? We sell plenty of different kinds of booze, but beer and ale are our bread and butter, so try to concentrate on that for now." Josh poured Emma a soda and let her ask as many questions as she wanted. Despite his insistence that she get here at four, she'd arrived an hour early to prove to him he hadn't made a mistake hiring her.

"I think so, but I'm a fast note taker, so I'll write it all down."

It was early in the afternoon, but people were still in there drinking, so she did what Josh asked and followed one of the girls around for the next hour. The place felt like it'd seen its share of fun times and parties, and from what she could tell so far, the employees seemed to be a tight-knit group.

"You're doing good, but remember to hold that tray with both hands until you learn how to navigate the crowd in here," Josh said when she gave him her order.

"Okay, and the guys over there want to run a tab." She pointed to the group that had just walked in and pushed three tables together. "Do I need to get a credit card or something?"

"The guy in the nice khakis is Mano Jatibon. He's a good friend of the owner, so don't worry about it. Just ask when you're not sure, but you'll start to get to know the regulars."

Josh loaded her up with the ten drinks she'd called out, and she took a deep breath before she picked her tray up. It was heavy, but she smiled as she lifted it and turned to head to the table. She made it two feet before the load shifted off balance and slid into a huge mess on the floor.

"Sorry…sorry." She held her hands up and threw the tray over the glasses on the floor so no one would get hurt. "If you point me to the mop I'll take care of this."

"You sure about the job, Emma?" Josh asked, staring at the puddle of spilt booze.

"I promise I'll get better, but I really need this job. Please. I'll try harder."

"Josh, stop giving her a hard time and put the spills on my tab, along with the glasses," the man Josh had said was Mano yelled from his table.

"Carry them in two loads, okay?" Josh repoured and sent her off with five beers. "Tell him not to worry about that first set."

It was the first of her many screw-ups that night, but Josh simply shook his head and kept encouraging her. Like the night before, the crowd was getting thicker, and the room was getting harder to navigate. Once the band arrived it was nearly impossible to get around.

"Emma, pick up for table five." Josh had explained that everyone had to pitch in when it got this busy. "Try your best to keep it on the tray, okay."

"Don't worry, Josh. I think I've got the hang of it now. This place's so crowded it takes a miracle to make it to the tables without spilling something."

She headed toward the table, and an image of her mother popped into her head for some reason. The thought of her mom finding out she worked in a bar made her want to laugh hysterically. That knowledge would drive the ultra-conservative religious zealot to an early grave.

The funny musings came to an abrupt end when she crashed into someone, tipping her tray up and out. The tall woman was now wearing every drop of ale she'd been carrying.

"I'm so sorry. I didn't see you." She used her hands to try to skim some of the liquor off the thick, heavily starched linen shirt, but it was no use. When Josh suddenly appeared at her side, she guessed it was one spill too many.

"Josh, where'd you find this one?"

The woman had the deepest voice she'd ever heard a female have, so she took a chance and looked up.

"I'm sorry, Cain. Emma's training day hasn't been working out quite as planned."

"Emma, huh?"

Emma nodded and held her hand out, even though it was now sticky with ale, but her target took it anyway. "Emma Verde. It's a pleasure to meet you." She grimaced at how wet her hand was and because of the strong smell of ale.

"Cain Casey, and the pleasure's all mine." Cain didn't let go of her, and everyone walked around them, seeming to be careful not to run into them. "Where are you from?"

"Hayward, Wisconsin."

Cain's laugh, like her voice, was a low rumble that seemed to start deep in her chest, and it made Emma's ears intensely hot.

"Any bars in Hayward?"

"Just a diner, but they only serve beer at night."

Cain winked at her before glancing over her shoulder at Josh. "Don't mind me, Josh. I think this hayseed's a keeper."

"Thank you," Emma said, wondering who this was. "I appreciate you not getting mad."

"Don't worry about it. This gives me a chance to go home early." Cain plucked her wet shirt away from her abdomen. "Josh, send a round over on me before I head out, and, Emma, I don't mean the *on me* literally."

Emma and Josh watched Cain head to the table before she said anything. "Who is that?"

"That's the owner, so remember that's the boss. You want to take her order over?" He tapped his watch. "Then it's time for you to head out."

"I can stay later if you want."

"We had a deal, so ten o'clock's your witching hour."

She made two trips but didn't have any more accidents in the half hour she had left. Whoever Mano was, he handed over a hundred-dollar tip when she told them it was the end of her shift so she was getting one of the other girls to serve them. The total of her tips amazed her, because even if they were less than this every night, she wouldn't have to work as many hours as she had been.

"Thanks, Josh." She waved to get his attention before heading out. "Can I come back tomorrow?"

"You sure this is for you?"

"I'll be able to afford school and my apartment without getting any deeper into debt, so if you don't think I'm a total klutz, I'd like to stay."

"See you tomorrow at the same time. We'll work on your balance skills." He handed over a ten. "Is that enough to get you home in a cab?"

"I'll take the streetcar, so don't worry about me. Thanks, though." She accepted her purse and gave him his money back.

"I got it, Josh," Cain said. "We'll give you a ride home."

"I appreciate you guys, but I'll be okay."

"You owe me one for bathing me in ale, so no arguing," Cain said, pointing to the door. "See you, Josh."

"Night, Boss."

A big SUV was waiting outside, and an attractive woman opened the back door. "Cain, I thought we could have a drink," the big guy on the street yelled when he spotted them.

"Jake, I thought you were coming by the office next week? Give me a call, but I don't have time tonight." Cain moved so Emma could get into the car.

"I'm starting to get the impression you're avoiding me like I'm a fucking leper."

"And you're making me wonder why I'd want to do business with you. Is talking like this in open spaces a habit of yours?" Cain turned to her and smiled. "Sorry, Emma, but I don't want to lead this guy to your door. Merrick and Lou will see you home."

"What about you?" She didn't know what was going on, but she thought Cain shouldn't stay behind alone.

"I'll be fine, and welcome to our little family. Let me know if you need anything."

"Thanks, and thanks for the ride."

"Call it an employment benefit."

"That'll be a first for me. This sounds like an interesting place to work."

"That's one way of putting it. I don't know about interesting, but I can promise different. See you soon."

The car pulled away and she glanced back. "That's a promise you've already kept, because tonight has certainly been different."

Chapter Four

The early class was the most boring on Emma's schedule, so her mind wandered to her first day of her new job. She'd waited until she was in her apartment to count her tips and was still amazed that it was what she made in a week at the bookstore.

Beatrice Weller leaned over and whispered, "You want to grab a coffee after this?" She'd known Bea since the first day of school, when they'd bonded over their dislike of math. The short, energetic brunette was also on scholarship but had grown up in Chalmette, a smaller town right outside New Orleans.

"It's the only way I'll make it through the day."

The professor had mercy on them and let them go fifteen minutes early. They walked to the student center, catching up on what they'd done during their break.

"Did you go home?" Bea asked, pouring what seemed like a pound of sugar into her cup.

"I spent a month helping my dad around the farm. That was the best part, but it's like I don't belong there anymore." It was hot outside, but the hot coffee and milk tasted good. "I think I lost five pounds walking those fields to get away from my mother."

"How is the pope?" Bea laughed, having heard all about Carol and reciprocating by sharing stories about her very Catholic mother and grandmother.

"Doing her job, she said, so she's as disappointed and outraged by me as ever. I doubt she has enough hours in the day to pray for my soul now that it's rotting by the minute in this den of iniquity."

"You are a heathen, but so am I. At least we'll have more fun." The huge muffin Bea had gotten looked good, and she nodded when Bea offered her half. "When did you get back?"

"My dad gave me the rent money for the summer so I got to explore, beginning in early July. It was fun, but I was ready for classes to start." They waved to some of their friends passing through but were glad to return to the conversation. "After that, I got notice that I was losing my job."

"Jeez, I'm sorry, Emma. What are you going to do?"

She laughed, knowing Bea would freak when she told her about her new job. "I was thinking some job like at a coffee shop or something, but I ended up doing something crazy."

"Wait, let me guess. You're now a sex operator for one of those 900 numbers?"

"Okay, slightly less crazy than that." She leaned over and slapped Bea's arm. "I started working in a bar."

"Now I know you're going to hell, but I don't mean that literally. It's more like you're going to be in hell when Saint Carol finds out."

"You're crazy if you think I'm admitting that to my mother, but I made as much in one night as I did in a week at the bookstore. If that keeps up, I'll be set for the semester without a problem."

"Wow, that's pretty good. Where's the gold mine?"

"It's the Erin Go Braugh in the Quarter." She dusted her hands of crumbs and couldn't guess what Bea was thinking when she lost her smile.

"The place Cain Casey owns?" The way Bea asked made her even more curious. Bea didn't go out enough to know who owned every bar in New Orleans.

"Yeah, that's the place. I actually met her last night." The memory of Cain soaking wet made her smile. "I smashed a ton of glasses of ale into her chest, and she was pretty nice about it."

Bea took her hand and squeezed it. "Please tell me you know who she is."

"She owns a bar, didn't fire me for soaking her, and gave me a ride home. Well, her staff gave me a ride home and walked me to the door of the building. That's my rundown of facts as they happened, Counselor."

"I'm sure she was all that, but there's plenty more, so don't go getting real cozy in that job." Bea moved closer so she could speak in a much lower tone. "She's also the head of one of the city's mob families."

She laughed loudly and shook her head. "No way that's true. She was really nice."

"You're not from here, so listen to me, and be careful. Maybe you should keep looking and go with your original plan. A coffee-shop job might not be as lucrative, but you'll be better off."

"I'm telling you, she's like a big teddy bear." A big, really good-looking teddy bear with beautiful blue eyes and a great ass. Cain Casey was the first person that had made her notice something like that.

She'd never had the urge to date in high school and had gone out only a few times here, but that kind of lightning-quick attraction had never happened to her until last night. She didn't want to admit it, but she wasn't about to let Bea bad-talk Cain. That didn't make sense to her either.

"A big teddy bear with a reputation. I'm only saying it because I'm your friend and I don't want you to get hurt." Bea let her go and smiled. "That's my two cents, and now I have to run. I have a meeting with one of my professors about the project he's assigning."

"Thanks, and call me. Maybe we can get dinner this week."

"It's a date."

Emma waved and decided to stop at her campus job and give them her notice. She had only two weeks left, but she'd go now if they really didn't need her. Someone else could train her replacement, because she wasn't wasting her time. Her boss appeared relieved she didn't make a big thing about it, so she headed home to finish her homework.

Tomorrow she had a full day of classes, so she read and finished all her assignments to save time. When she was done she decided to read for fun, then took a nap. The story Bea had told her made her think, but she wasn't going to pass up the opportunity to work for Cain.

"Maybe it's time to take a few chances," she said as she headed for the shower after she woke up. "Playing by the rules hasn't taken me very far when it comes to getting what I want."

❖

Ramon Jatibon had run a casino in Cuba before the revolution and had whisked his young family off the island right as Castro entered Havana to claim victory. He'd arrived in New Orleans with enough cash to rent a house and buy food for a month.

He met Dalton before that month was up, and it had been the beginning of a friendship lasting until Dalton's death. Dalton's money had seeded much more than his business, including a bond between the two men and their children. His twins Remi and Mano had grown up with the Casey children, and they were as close as family.

They had no debts between them anymore, but Ramon had helped Cain and Billy keep the peace and what was rightfully theirs at Dalton's death. Cain knew he would've done it without complaint for years if that's what she needed.

"Cain," Ramon said when Remi showed her into his office. "It's good to see you again." He stood and pulled her into a bear hug, letting her enjoy the scent of good cigars that always seemed to permeate his clothes.

"Thanks, my friend. I finally climbed to the top of the deep hole I got dumped into, so I'm ready for whatever comes next."

"No matter what you have in mind, you know you've got good friends to count on. Dalton was my brother, so you simply have to ask if you need something."

"It might come to that, but for now I plan to start the hunt for every single person responsible for Da's murder. I want to strengthen my family's territory and assure you and your family that the ties between us will be honored."

She held her hand out. She should've made the move before now, but she thought Ramon would forgive the timing. Dalton, as if he wanted to cover all his bases, had tried to guide her in case something happened to him. He'd told her to sit with Ramon and with Vincent if something ever happened to him, so that their friendship would be cemented for the next generation. Not that Dalton doubted that possibility, but he wanted Cain to show his two old friends the respect they were due.

She had grieved so long because he'd even thought of that scenario. Some might've considered her father a tyrant, but he'd been a guiding force so strong it had devastated her peace of mind when he suddenly wasn't there.

Ramon took her hand and nodded. "The future will allow you to avenge your father, and you'll do that with friends standing with you. We're beside you, as always."

"Thanks, Ramon. I have a lot of work ahead, so I'll let you know if I need anything."

"Remi mentioned a few things." He steepled his fingers and glanced at Remi. "I haven't found anyone in particular taking credit for Dalton, but I have enough money on the street that I'm starting to hear some rumors. Nothing I've verified, but at least something's starting to shake loose."

"Anything you want to share yet?"

"Give me some more time, but you'll be my first call when I have something solid. Believe me. Everyone who matters in this town is looking for what you want. Dalton wasn't only a great father, but a good friend to so many people."

"Da was one of a kind, for sure," she said, then pressed her lips together.

"I'd never pretend to take Dalton's place, but allow me to give you some advice if that's okay. Once we have the answers we're looking for, we'll stand with you to get that job done. Until then, though, you need to be careful, especially with the scum FBI. I've heard from a few people that they've brought in someone new, who has all of us in his crosshairs."

"You're right, and I'm planning a few things that'll move us forward and flush out the watchers. Between me and you, Da's death was close to paralyzing. If anyone sees that as weakness, I want to prove them wrong." Her father had said that at times honesty was the way to go, even if it made you sound weak.

"If something like that happened to Papi, I don't think a year would be enough. In my opinion, the time you took is a testament of your love and respect for him. He deserved no less because, like Papi, Dalton was a great man. We were both really lucky when it came to our parents."

"Thanks, Remi, and you're right. I'm fortunate in so many areas, and I'm grateful I have you on my side."

"Never forget that," Ramon said, standing when she did.

"No worries there. Thank you both for seeing me, and I don't mean to run, but I have another meeting."

"Need company?" Remi asked.

"Eventually what I'll need is snake eyes, but let me figure out a few things first." Snake eyes was the nickname Remi and Mano had on the streets when they got together to solve special problems—the kind of problems that, at times, needed a permanent solution.

Her next planned stop was the Ninth Ward neighborhood and one of the convenience stores that was part of their network. The little mom-and-pop places didn't seem like much, but they were profitable in their totality and overlooked because they were indeed so small.

The FBI always thought people like her only raked in profits from big operations, so places that were the lifeblood of their neighborhoods never hit their radar, it seemed.

"Lou, stop at the office. I want to make sure we don't have company for the rest of the day."

"You got it, Boss."

"Do you want Billy to come with us?" Merrick asked.

"Depends on what he's up to. I'll take care of it." She entered Billy's office and waved Merrick off. Until she had a solution for the bugs in her office, she'd use Billy's space and the conference room.

"Lou, come in."

"You need something, Boss?"

"Did you take the new waitress home last night?" Lou's expression never seemed to change much, but he did crack a bit of a smile when he nodded. "Good. You know where she lives. Get over there and give her a ride to work."

"That's not going to scare the hell out of her?"

"Let's see if it does, but she made me curious as to where she comes from." The door opened again, and Billy walked in with a jacket on to hide the harness with the two pistols he was partial to. Merrick liked the same kind of rig, and between the two of them, they could take out any threat stupid enough to make a move.

"I'll give you a call when I'm done," Lou said as he left.

"What have you been up to?" She sat and ignored the ringing phone.

"I took Mum and Marie back to the cemetery. Hopefully Da forgives me for being a day late." He sat and fiddled with the ring as if he wasn't used to it being on his finger yet.

"Thanks for doing that. You made Mum happy, if I have to guess. I went by and saw Ramon and Remi, but we need to get down to the Ninth Ward for a visit."

He tapped the bottom of his heel as if he was ready to go. "Something up?"

"The guy wouldn't say on the phone, but someone is muscling into the neighborhood and causing some problems."

He stood and paced back and forth in front of his desk a few times. "Who would be stupid enough to do that?"

"That's what I'm going to find out, but I have got a clue. Someone's trying to squeeze us out. We need to pay attention to anything or anyone new in our life." She got up and walked over to him. "We need to be stronger than Da. You with me?"

"Come on, Boss. Let's go hunting."

❖

Jake Kelly opened the door to his right after putting his pants on. They'd stayed out late the night before, hoping to make at least one deal. One, even if it was small, would line up the big fish, but so far they had nothing.

"Atlanta called," Bradley Draper said, even before the door closed. "Hey, man, sorry."

The woman walking out of the bedroom paused before getting her shoes off the floor of the small living room.

"Don't worry about it. She was leaving. We're done," Jake said, heading to the kitchen and the bottle of whiskey already open on the small tile table. "What did Atlanta want?"

"You're starting a little early, aren't you?" Bradley said, waving off Jake's offer to join him.

"It was a late fucking night with nothing to show for it. My head feels like someone's pounding on it." He poured another two fingers and downed them in a gulp. "Tell me already."

"Maxwell said nothing's happening there either, but he's ready to go whenever you give him the word. He did say all hell broke loose at the club of one of our biggest buyers. The place will be closed until they can put it back together."

"Who's responsible for that?" He washed his face in the sink with cold water, trying to make his head stop hurting. "Does he need anything from us?"

"Nothing we can do but wait until he's back up and running. As for who did it, none of his people recognized anyone."

"We need to force Casey to the table then. There isn't any reason for her not to deal with us, so I don't get it. After somebody killed the old man, her operation is on life support. Going cheaper for the same thing is the smart move."

Bradley nodded as he opened the refrigerator and looked inside. "Maybe she's not as bright as we give her credit for."

"Keep thinking like that, and you'll be dead before the month is out."

"You want me to come back tonight?" the woman asked, using his glass to pour herself a drink.

"Call me later and we'll set something up." Jake waited until she was out the door before saying anything else. "Give that black bitch of Casey's a call and see if she'll move up our meeting. I want to get going on this."

"Merrick is harder to get through to than Casey, but I'll give it a shot."

"We're on a deadline, so don't take no for an answer."

Bradley lifted his hands and spread them out. "Casey seems to be on her own timeline, but she hasn't shared that with me yet."

"If she doesn't want to play, we might have to give her a shove in our direction."

The comment made Bradley close the stainless steel doors and sit down. "That's a bad idea. You're the boss, but it's a bad idea."

"If we end up where we need to be, then who the hell cares?" He stretched, ready for a little sleep before another long day started. "Don't get bogged down in the shit that could go wrong, and concentrate on your job."

"That's what I'm doing, but it'll be hard to get any work done with a head full of bullets."

"Casey doesn't have that kind of personality, so stop making excuses." Jake leaned over and slapped Bradley's shoulder. "Man up, and let's teach this big dyke a lesson for putting us off."

"Just as long as she doesn't end up leading the class and cutting our nuts off, sure. I'm all for it."

CHAPTER FIVE

It's about time we get out by ourselves," Billy said as Cain drove them into the Ninth Ward in the crappiest car she'd ever seen. They'd taken the longest route possible, and neither of them had noticed anyone following.

"When was the last time you were down here?" she asked, giving the car some gas to keep it from dying at the traffic light.

"Right before Da died. Merrick told me she had it under control, so I didn't worry about it. If you want, I'll start coming every day." He took one of his guns out and checked the clip.

"It was under control until last week, from what I understand, so let's see what the problem is before you commit to anything." The neighborhood kids were out playing for the afternoon as she parked a block from Mendel Saint's small grocery. Huge supermarkets weren't the norm here, and Mendel's grandfather had been the first to run this place.

"Cain," Mendel said loudly as he came from behind the counter and hugged her. "Thank you for coming. Good to see you too, Billy."

"How are you, Mr. Mendel?" Billy hugged him as well and waved to his wife. Both of them weren't an inch taller than five feet.

"Not good. We had some problems last week, and they threatened to come back if we didn't cooperate."

"Let's go out back and talk about it." Cain glanced at the empty shelves. A major problem seemed to have arisen in the last week but wouldn't be solved anywhere that fast.

"Who came to see you?" Billy asked, sitting on a box.

"A young guy—I've never seen him before. He waited until we were getting ready to close to come in and take out our liquor section.

All he said after that was that his boss would be stopping by to talk terms," Mendel said, wringing his hands the whole while.

"Terms for what, exactly?" she asked, sitting close to Billy so Mendel wouldn't have to strain his neck looking up at her.

"Protection from something like that happening again."

"I'm never going to charge you for protection, but you're going to get just that. I'll take care of restocking those shelves too."

"You know I hate to ask for that much, and I feel bad about calling you at all. After what happened to your papa, we don't try to bother you."

"Mendel." She reached for his hand. "How long have you known us?"

"You've been coming here since you were shorter than me," he said, and laughed. "The years have been long between us, but that doesn't mean I want to burden you. I'm glad you're here though. The more this idiot gets away with, the more he'll be back here and everywhere else in the neighborhood."

"No one's coming back without some consequences, my friend. You have my word." She smiled when he kissed both her cheeks. "Anyone else having problems?"

"Big Chief had the same thing happen, but he didn't want to call after what happened the last time. I don't know what that meant, and I don't want to know."

"Nothing for you to worry about, but thanks for telling me. I'll get someone today to watch over you, but promise me you'll call no matter what. You and Ethel are important to me, so take care." She stood and embraced Mendel again.

"You have my word, and thank you. I know Ethel will sleep better tonight, as I will."

They walked out, and Cain smiled when Ethel handed over a small bag filled with soft caramels. The candy was one of Marie's favorites.

"Tell her for after dinner, okay?" Ethel said, kissing Cain's cheek when she bent down.

"She'll love them. Thank you."

They headed back outside, and Cain took her time getting to the car, wanting to look around for anything suspicious.

"So Big Chief next?" Billy asked once she started driving.

"Big Chief is a necessity down here, but that bastard is someone I trust about as far as I can throw that big ass of his."

"I'd like to think he learned his lesson after Da literally took a chunk from him."

Big Chief was actually a short, overweight, bald Irish man who'd tried to make more of a profit off what Dalton was selling him. Like her, Dalton had been fair and generous in his business dealings, but neither of them tolerated a thief or a liar. Their usual deal with people like Mendel was to set the liquor prices so as to not attract unwanted attention from the feds or the local police.

The price was lower than that of most outlets but still provided a good profit for the shopkeeps they sold to. Big Chief had broken that deal by acting as a middleman for some of his friends in the bar business—friends Dalton didn't know, hadn't okayed—and one of them had gotten busted in a raid for serving minors.

Everyone involved had clammed up when Dalton had met Big Chief at his house and removed all the fingers of his left hand with a rusty pair of pliers. The bar owner had gladly served his time, knowing his family wasn't going to pay for Big Chief's mistakes, so he'd pled guilty with no confession.

"True, brother, but some people are born perpetually stupid. If he's holding back anything, he's going to pray all I do is take the rest of his fingers."

"You have to admit, Da was talented when it came to getting his point across."

She laughed and nodded.

It took Big Chief less than five minutes to point them in Jasper Luke's direction, so Cain made that their last stop of the day. Jasper was another old friend, but their businesses were miles apart since Jasper was a dealer of things much stronger and more illegal than booze and cigarettes.

"You two are a sight of joy for these old eyes," Jasper's Aunt Maude said once they made it down the heavily guarded private street.

"Thanks, Maude, and we wanted to thank you again for coming to Da's services. Mum was grateful for all those meals you've sent."

"Your father was one of a kind and a good friend, so no need for thanks. I'm hoping, though, that you're here to help my boy before something bad happens and he gets hurt."

"That's why we came, and I'm disappointed you didn't pick up the phone, Jasper."

Jasper Luke was a tall, bald, brick wall of a guy who had a big smile on his face most days. If you were ever in a brawl, this was who you wanted backing you up.

"You've had bigger things on your plate than me, but Aunt Maude's right. It's good to see you."

"What's wrong?"

Jasper gave her a rundown of the hits to his business, from the loss of a major shipment to five dead crewmen. "I've got extra guys out, and it's like I'm pissing in the wind. Whoever's responsible has put my blood in the water, and the little sharks looking for a bigger piece are circling. It's starting to fuck with my head, but I'm not making any headway."

"Ramon put some feelers out, but he said he's only gotten rumors back."

"We did the same thing, and the only consistent thing is Callie Richard. Only fucking thing is, who the fuck is Callie Richard?" Jasper said, rubbing the top of his head.

"Never heard the name before, but let me do a little digging. Thanks for the info, and call if things get any worse. You'd do the same for me, and you know it."

Merrick picked them up once they were done and headed for the house. "What do you want to do about all this?" Billy asked.

"Exactly the opposite of what someone wants me to do."

❖

"Afternoon, Miss Emma," said the big man who'd dropped Emma off the night before as he opened the back door of the Suburban for her. She hesitated as she studied his face, her mind going totally blank. "Lou, ma'am."

"Hey, Lou. Sorry. I just wasn't expecting you." She didn't move from the sidewalk in front of her building, all the things Bea had said going through her mind.

"I figured," he said softly. "But the boss insisted, since she wants to make sure you get back and forth safely. I hope that won't be a problem. Cain's pretty mule-headed when she gets insistent."

"Have you ever called her mule-headed to her face?" She willed her feet to move and got in. She didn't see anything sinister in offering someone a ride.

"No, ma'am, so our little secret's okay?"

"Sure, and thanks for picking me up. If I'm there early I can practice my tray skills."

"Don't knock your skills. They certainly got you noticed. It's not often the boss goes home drenched in booze." Lou drove them down St. Charles Avenue to the Quarter at a slow pace, so she decided to enjoy the view and the conversation.

Something about him made Emma think small talk wasn't a talent he used often. "That was more klutz than luck, but it turned out okay. I'm glad the boss is a good sport."

"Cain's the best when it comes to bosses." He stopped at a traffic light and glanced back at her. "You new to town? Josh mentioned you were in school."

"I've been here almost three years from Wisconsin. He's never seen me because I've usually got my head in a book, or I was working at the campus job I got let go from a few days ago." She smiled back, wondering if there was any more to the interrogation she was sure Cain had asked him to perform. "Once I'm done, I'm hoping to stay and get a teaching position either at Tulane or Loyola."

"Tough gig to break into, from what I hear. What are you studying?"

"At the moment, a lot of poetry, but eventually I'd love to be an English professor. I don't much care what kind. With enough time and tenure, I can be pickier later in my career."

The drive over Canal Street brought them into the French Quarter, and she noticed Lou acknowledged a few people they passed. He stopped in front of the Erin Go Braugh and quickly hopped out to get her door.

"Good luck to you, Miss Emma, and I'm sure I'll be seeing you around."

"Thanks, Lou. You can call me Emma. And please tell the boss I appreciate the cab service, but I don't mind getting myself home if I'm putting you out."

"Don't worry about it, and good luck with the tray skills."

Josh waved and handed over an apron in exchange for her purse that he placed under the bar. "Decided to come back, huh?"

"Of course. Once I took a power nap this afternoon I was good to go."

"One of the girls called in sick, so I'm glad you got plenty of rest. The bigger band is playing tonight, so I hope you took a vitamin too. By seven, this place will be hopping and full."

"Think the boss is coming tonight?" She tied off the apron and grabbed an order book from the stack by the antique cash register.

"We never really know, and I wouldn't ask a whole lot of questions, Emma. Just my two cents. Cain has a kind of phobia about them."

"I only wanted to thank her again, so if I miss her can you tell her for me?"

"Will do. Now get to work."

Josh hadn't lied, and at seven thirty she said a prayer every time she had to wade into the crowd. The bar seemed to have an endless supply of beer in the multitude of taps Josh and the other three guys helping him were pouring out of, and the crowd knew every word of every song.

At some point she thought she'd spotted Cain, but she was too busy to think about taking a break. "Emma, you want to take a minute," Josh asked not long after.

"I'm good, and I'm afraid I'll completely lose track of everything if I stop now." She accepted the soda he handed over while one of his assistants filled her latest order. "If I haven't mentioned it, thank you again for giving me a chance. Can you believe last night I made what I did in a week at my campus job?"

"One more week and you can retire," he said and winked.

"No way. You're stuck with me now, and I can stay later if you need me. I hate to leave you guys at ten if it's like this."

"We can have the same conversation every day if you want, but you know the rules."

"Thanks. And now back into the fray."

"You realize what I'm asking, right?" Cain said to the smallish guy sitting nervously in front of the desk Josh used in the tiny manager's office.

Therese had promised to put Marie to bed when she said she had a long night ahead and wanted to get started. These meetings were the last of the ones Merrick had set up for her, and she hoped to God none of the new people she'd talked to was the one who'd bring her down from the inside. So far no one had given her pause.

"Yes, ma'am. I do."

She glanced down at his name, Bryce White, wondering what his whole story was. He wasn't leaving until she had it, so it was time to get on with it. "Bryce, I've got to say, you sound awfully calm for someone being asked to set up what I want."

"If you think I'm playing you, I'm not. Everyone probably tells you this, but I'll do this for free if you want. Just as long as you let me do it, we'll be square."

"It sounds like you have a story in there somewhere, and if you do, now would be a good time to spit it out." She tapped her fingers on the desk in a random rhythm, and she figured it was bothering him since he was staring at her hand.

"I was up at LSU working on a degree when my older brother got in some trouble and was busted. It was some petty shit, but the campus cops, the local sheriff, and the DEA were looking for a couple of guys to make examples of." She stopped tapping her fingers when he gripped the edge of the desk, appearing genuinely upset. "Sammy was small-time. He was dealing so both of us could stay in school."

"You two were on your own?" She laced her fingers together, curious as to what he was going to say.

"My father ran out on us years ago, so Sammy and me tried to do our best to bring in money so we could stay with our mom. Since she'd never worked, all she could get was menial stuff."

"How much time did they give him?" She glanced up at Merrick, and the guard nodded. His story was easy enough to check out.

"The judge gave the DEA what they wanted, and he got fifteen years at Angola."

"For a first-time offender? That's harsh, but I'm not familiar with drugs and the punishment for selling them. We don't deal in them at all." He was pressing down on the front of the desk so hard, the tops of his hands were white. "You okay, kid?"

"He didn't last a week before someone stabbed him in the middle of the night. What should've been probation almost turned out to be a death sentence, so like I said, I'd do this for free."

"Damn. I'm sorry for such a crappy deal. Give me a day, and we'll work something out."

"Thanks, and I'll never give you a reason to doubt me."

"Let's hope not."

Bryce left, and she leaned back in the old chair to glance up at the ceiling. The old New Orleans beadboard looked ancient, so she was sure it was original to the building. The wood grain had a lot of history in it, so she was glad no one had messed with it. To forget your history for something new and seemingly exciting was a good way to lose your way.

"Check out his story, and I mean all the way to the womb," she said to Merrick when she returned. "I hate adding people, but this situation needs someone like that kid and his skillset."

"Muriel and I'll take care of it, and that's all for tonight. You want to head home?"

"Not yet. I might help Josh pour a few rounds, so take off and get started on all this. Big Lou's right outside, so I have a ride home." She stood and waved Merrick out the door.

"You sure?"

"Positive, and don't forget about our talk with Jasper. I need to have a meeting with whoever this Callie Richard is. If she's responsible for Mendel and the others' losses, it'll be a short conversation."

"You got it, and stay out of trouble," Merrick said and laughed.

The bar was packed, and Cain hummed to the song the band was playing. The old folk story was one of her da's favorites, and she could almost picture him sitting at the bar with her mum singing louder than the band. Dalton Casey was a hard worker, but he also knew how to have a good time and romance the girl he'd loved for years.

"Hey, Boss, you grabbing a shift?" Josh asked when she joined him behind the antique carved oak bar.

"I'm here to earn my keep, so put me to work." She glanced around the room and smiled when the pretty blonde from the previous night headed toward them.

"Here comes trouble," Josh said, chuckling.

"Hey there, hayseed," she said when Emma put her tray down. "You enjoying yourself?"

"I am, thank you, but obviously you don't trust me."

She tensed, raising her eyebrows. "How so?"

"You put the bar between us." Emma knocked on the wooden surface. "I figured you were afraid I'd spill something on you, but you can ask Josh how great I'm doing."

"Let me be the judge of that. What do you need?" She leaned over the bar a little, getting Emma to do the same.

"I need eight black-and-tans."

"Coming right up." She grabbed some glasses and opened the tap, knowing Emma's eyes were on her. She'd had so much on her mind she'd forgotten about her beautiful new waitress, but maybe it was time for some fun.

"Thanks. This should wrap up my night since Josh is heavy-handed with the rules." Emma seemed to concentrate as she picked up the tray, then paused when she turned around with it. "Be right back, so try to talk him into letting me stay longer. Might be fun."

Emma walked away, filling out the snug jeans she was wearing, and Cain enjoyed the view. One of the guys at the table Emma was placing drinks on must've appreciated the sight as well when he put his hand on her butt. Since Emma had more drinks to serve she couldn't do anything about it, but she was trying her best to move away.

Cain swung over the bar and grabbed the guy by the wrist without really thinking about what she was doing. The idiot immediately stood up and took a swing at her, missing badly because of his inebriated state. Lou was next to her impressively fast, but she held him off. This kind of behavior pissed her off, but she'd show restraint not to scare Emma away.

"How about you pay the young lady and get out of here? If you're smart, you won't come back." She grabbed his fist as he took another swing.

"How about you mind your own business, asshole? I don't see her complaining." The idiot staggered a bit when she pushed him back hard enough to get him away from Emma.

"Hey, man, she's right," one of the other guys said, throwing some money on the table. "Sorry for the trouble, Ms. Casey."

"I'm not fucking leaving because I didn't do anything wrong. If you touch me again, I'm going to fuck you up."

Why did drunk people get louder than necessary? "Emma, would you mind waiting for me by the bar?" Emma put her tray down and took off. She waited another moment, never taking her eyes from the big guy. "I'd listen to your friend, but if you want to stay, then stay."

"Fucking right I'm staying—" Whatever else he was going to say died abruptly when she punched him hard in the throat. The blow made the guy double over while holding both hands to the front of his neck.

Lou's presence must've made the rest of the group wary enough not to move to help. "Take your buddy and get out of here. I see you in here again, and you're going to wish this is all I do to you." She grabbed the idiot by the hair and pulled his head up. "The next time you grab any woman's ass without permission, think about this. You do it in front of me, and I'll feed you your balls, and once your friend explains to you who I am, you'll know I'm not kidding."

"You fucking bitch," the guy wheezed out, not taking his hands from this throat.

"Lou, could you see the gentlemen outside right after they empty their pockets? That," she pointed to the money on the table, "doesn't look like enough to cover the tip."

"Sorry again, Ms. Casey. Our pal had way too many."

"Sometimes something like that can be dangerous to your health. You happened to catch me in a good mood, so leave before that changes."

"See them out, or see them out?" Lou asked, grabbing the drunk idiot and hauling him almost off his feet.

"The sidewalk should do it, but you might still get your shot. Brains here doesn't have much of a learning curve if I had to guess." She glanced at the pile of money and smiled. "Thanks on behalf of the young lady, and remember to keep your hands to yourself from now on. Manners beat the hell out of getting beaten."

"Words to live by, Boss," Lou said.

"Or to die by if you don't catch a clue," she said, and only Lou laughed.

Chapter Six

Emma watched as Cain punched the guy hard enough to double him over. It was a night of firsts since she'd never been pawed, and she'd never had anyone defend her honor. That Cain had done it answered the question of if she'd remembered her, but maybe she did that for everyone who worked for her.

She automatically put her hand out when Cain held something out to her. The stack of money seemed substantial unless it was all ones, but at the moment she didn't care. Being the center of Cain Casey's attention was like standing under the hot sun.

"Thank you, but you deserve this more than I do," she said, trying to give the money back. "I appreciate what you did, since that guy really creeped me out."

"Don't ever let anyone manhandle you like that, and let me know if someone gives you a problem." Cain folded Emma's fingers over the money and shook her head. "You earned that, and Josh tells me you need it for school."

"I do, but I don't mind sharing." The band starting up again made her step closer to Cain, and on instinct she took hold of the hand Cain had punched the guy with. "Are you sure you're okay?"

"I'm fine, but it's time for you to leave. School is more important than anything that happens here, so get moving." Cain didn't let her go, so she frantically tried to think of a reason to stay.

Honesty was the best way to go. "Are you sure you want me to?"

"When's your first class tomorrow?"

"Eight, but I took a nap before coming to work today. I'm good to go for another couple of hours." She gently pulled on Cain's fingers, wanting to get to know her.

"How about a compromise?" Cain led her to the bar and asked

Josh for her stuff. "Put your money away, and we'll stop for a snack before I take you home."

"Are you sure? We can stay here if you want."

"I'll come by tomorrow if I can and see your progress, but I'm not in the mood to scream at you all night over this crowd. If you want, it can be a quick trip home."

"A snack it is, so lead the way."

Lou followed them out and held the door like he'd done the couple of times he'd driven her, and what she was doing suddenly seemed surreal. Her life had never been this exciting or different, but Cain appeared to be at ease not only in her own skin, but in having someone drive her around.

"What are you studying?" Cain asked.

After Lou closed the door, the quiet in the back of the vehicle was sudden and enveloping. She was thrilled to be alone with Cain but also incredibly nervous. This, whatever it was, she had no experience in, so the opportunity was probably a one-shot deal. She rubbed her hands along the top of her thighs and tried her best to exude calm.

"You okay?" Cain put her hand over hers briefly as if to stop her anxiety from spiraling out of control. "You sure you don't want to simply go home?"

After taking a deep breath, she said, "I'm sorry. I'm really bad at this, but I'm glad you invited me along. That's why I'm acting like a birdbrain."

"I don't meet a girl who uses the term 'birdbrain' every day." Cain smiled, speaking softly. "And what exactly do you think you're bad at?"

"Oh, geez. I got this all wrong, didn't I? I'm so embarrassed."

"Hold on." Cain took her hand again and didn't let go. "How about we start over?"

"What do you mean?" She spread her fingers so Cain's palm fit nicely against hers.

"We can change snack to date, or to whatever makes you relax enough to breathe. Is that kind of what you're talking about?"

"I'm okay with dating. But I don't have much experience so I'm bad at it." She turned in the seat a little to look Cain in the eye. "I get the impression that starting my dating life with you is like learning to swim at the Olympics."

"Too much too fast?"

"No…well, a little fast, but I'm glad you asked. Hopefully you're patient."

"If you ask anyone, patience isn't one of my virtues, but maybe we can help each other out. Relax and answer my question. What are you studying?"

She gave Cain a long, rambling answer, but Cain listened with an attentive expression, nodding a few times. When Lou stopped and turned the engine off, she stopped talking. The restaurant wasn't familiar, and she had no idea where they were since she hadn't glanced out the window once after Lou started driving.

"Is Chinese okay?" Cain asked, tugging her hand gently.

"I love Chinese."

"Lou, go in and eat. We'll be okay on our own."

The restaurant was still pretty busy despite the hour, and the hostess showed them to a private table. From what she could see, Cain wasn't as eager as Josh to get her home by ten.

"What made a girl from Wisconsin end up here?" Cain asked, resting her elbows on the table.

"My answer should be the great scholarship, but that's not all of it."

"So small-town girl wanted to have a little fun, huh?"

She laughed at Cain's teasing and pointed at her before shaking a finger. "I'll have you know Wisconsin has some big cities."

"So you grew up in a big city?"

"No. I grew up in the middle of nowhere with a big bunch of cows. I came to Tulane to experience something new, and New Orleans certainly is that." The waitress served hot tea she hadn't ordered, but Cain seemed to enjoy it so she tried it. "It's been a fun three years."

"I bet, but how did you end up in my bar?" Cain leaned back as their "snack" turned into a feast with a large variety of food.

Cain handed over a serving spoon so she could get started. "That's simple. It was a completely happy accident. I was getting laid off, so I walked to my favorite place to think of what I could do to stay in school and actually eat every so often." She told Cain what had happened with her campus job, too embarrassed to talk about her mother and her thoughts on her being in school here.

"Would you like that campus job back instead of the one with me?"

"I've only been there two days, but I really like it. I'm also making a lot more money, so I might be able to take a day off every so often. Josh might've hired me, but thank you for being so understanding for bathing you in beer."

"So I'm guessing my bar isn't your favorite place," Cain said and appeared pleased when she handed over the plate she'd just filled.

"You weren't on my radar since I seldom went past Royal Street, so I've done all my ginger-ale drinking at the Carousel Bar."

"You have a little Irish in your blood now, so your life will never be the same. I'm glad you wandered off the path a bit." Cain waited for her to fill another plate before taking a bite, which made her friend Bea come to mind. If what she'd said about Cain was true, the mob boss at least had manners.

"Do you mean it, or is that something people say?" She had no idea where all this out-of-character stuff was coming from, but her gut told her Cain would only be interested in someone bold. And the truth was, meek had never gotten her anywhere.

"Did you like playing with matches when you were surrounded by cows, hayseed?"

The way Cain smiled suddenly made her want to put her hands over her chest when her nipples got stone hard.

What the hell was happening to her, she wondered as Cain's eyelids dropped halfway. "My best answer is, I just recently found my matchbox."

"Used to the safe and comfortable, are you?"

"I've been predictable, but sometimes life has a way of showing me something I didn't know I wanted until it's dropped right in front of me." Flirting wasn't exactly one of her talents, so she was shocked to be holding her own. At least she thought she was, since they were still here, and Cain was still responding.

"I'll go easy on you and not ask what you want. Not today anyway," Cain said and winked.

They enjoyed the meal, and Cain had them pack the rest for Emma to take home. It would keep her in leftovers for at least a week and was an incredibly sweet thing to do.

"Do you often feed poor college students, Ms. Casey?" she asked as Cain carried the bag and they followed Lou out the door.

"People also say there's a first time for everything." Cain opened the car door for her this time, making her smile at the chivalry. "But I guess it makes me appear less monster-like either way."

"Excuse me—what?"

"If we're going to be friends—"

"I think we already are."

"No. We're not quite there yet." Cain had put the take-out bag between them so they couldn't get closer. "Friendship is built on trust and honesty."

"And Josh said loyalty."

"And loyalty. My family is full of interesting people, so maybe instead of friendship, you'd be better off as my employee and acquaintance."

"Do you make it a habit to think for people? If you do, that might be a problem." She seemed to be having an out-of-body experience in that she'd released her fear. "A friend told me about your interesting family, but I'm having trouble squaring what she said with this." She plucked the top of the bag and looked Cain in the eye.

"Even the devil has his good days, Ms. Verde."

"So what did you mean by 'either way'?"

"If you believed your friend, tonight hopefully showed you I'm not all about the rumors and stories circulating out there." Cain closed her eyes for a breath before giving her a melancholy smile. "If you're a young and pretty Quantico graduate, hopefully the same explanation applies."

Lou stopped the car, and Emma wished they hadn't been so close to her apartment. "The only weapon I'm familiar with is words, so that would make me a lousy cop of any kind. Consider that fact before you decide I'm not friend material."

Cain walked her to her door and only kissed her hand when she placed the bag right inside without going in. The move, however chaste, had made her stomach physically clench in an unfamiliar way. If she had to define it, the only word that fit was *want*.

"Unbelievable," Emma whispered, leaning against her locked door. "Maddie was right in that it hits you like a Mack truck."

It was a good thing her truck was this good-looking, since it had mowed her down with those incredible blue eyes.

"You're going to let me in if it takes me a lifetime of trying, Cain."

❖

"Agent Kyle, what can I do for you?" Special Agent in Charge Annabel Hicks said after giving him only a brief glance. It appeared that the file she was perusing had more of her attention than he did.

"Ma'am, as you know, Washington sent me down here for a specific reason, and that's to curb organized crime. This city seems to be a hotbed of activity that has nationwide implications." He sat across from her. How had some stupid bitch like this managed to score a managerial assignment as sweet as this post? He'd worked his ass off but wasn't any closer to a directorship somewhere so easy to build a reputation in.

"I can both read and comprehend what's in your file, so I know why you're here. I'm a real bitch when it comes to the rules, so be very careful when you start your operation." She did look at him then, and the intensity of her glare made him uncomfortable. Hicks seemed to see right through him and into his head. "The Wild West is dead. Remember that well when you cowboy up, as they say."

"I intend to follow the law, ma'am, but the only way to move forward is to start applying pressure. Nervous people make mistakes. Once they do, the rest of the big fish will be easy to reel in."

"What do you want?"

This would be easy. Hicks tried to hide her enthusiasm about possible arrests after so many frustrating years, but he could almost taste it in the air around her. "I need approval for twenty-four-hour surveillance on one of the major players."

"Which one?"

"The easiest target is the Casey family, but once we flip the new head, the rewards will be the Jatibons and the Carlottis."

"The Bracatos seem the easiest to me."

"The easiest doesn't always reap the greatest reward. You can hunt giraffes, ma'am, but there's no sport in it." Hopefully he wouldn't have to go over her head.

"This has nothing to do with sport, Kyle." Annabel sounded close to shutting him down before he even started.

"Getting Casey comes with a ready reward, ma'am. Bracato will come down with time, but he's not part of the network the other families seem to be a part of."

"So twenty-four-hour surveillance will drive Casey to run into your arms in a talkative mood?"

He never appreciated sarcasm, especially from women. "You okay my team and my operation, and we'll see how talkative I can make her."

"You'll be the first man to get her to do that. I'll give you six months, and we'll review after that."

"Thank you, ma'am." He left before Annabel had a chance to change her mind. "I'm going to eventually shove the indictment down your throat," he muttered once he was outside.

CHAPTER SEVEN

I'm going to check on Mendel's place today," Billy said when they sat down for breakfast. "I want to make sure Oliver knows we're not messing around."

"Take some of the guys with you," Cain said while she glanced through the papers Muriel had sent over. "The world seems to be gunning for us, and we can't lose anyone else."

"Don't worry. I gave up Oliver to watch over Mendel and his wife, but the rest of my guys treat me like I'm made out of spun glass." He piled a tremendous amount of food on his plate, and she laughed. What would happen to him when his metabolism slowed down?

"Good, but try to make it back by five. If you've got time, run by Emerald's tonight and go over the books."

He stopped chewing and put his fork down. "Is there a problem?"

"It's more like a preventative measure. I put Blue in charge since he was next up, but I don't completely trust him. We need to make regular rounds before he gets the idea he can skim without losing some vital part." She reached the last page and smiled at Muriel's assessment.

"You got it." Her explanation gave him the go-ahead to finish eating. "Where are you going today?"

"To see Uncle Jarvis and Muriel. Then I might stop by Tulane and check out the sights."

"Ha," Billy said, barely keeping his eggs in his mouth. "Lou told me what homework you have in mind. Who is she?"

"Our new server at the Erin Go Braugh, and I'm not studying. I'm curious." She finished her coffee and kissed him on the top of the head on her way out.

She entered the large study lined with books and antique bookends, and Merrick waited in Jarvis's den. Her first glance of her uncle always took her by surprise since he resembled her father so much. Being with Jarvis would be in a way like watching her father grow old.

"Cain." Jarvis stood and hugged her close. "Welcome."

"Thanks, Uncle Jarvis." She kissed his cheek before he let go. "And thanks for making some time for me." She sat in one of the old leather chairs that had come from her grandparents' place.

"I always have time for you, and I've been anxious to know how you're going forward."

"I've had my head in the mud for the last year, and there's no excuse for it. You and our friends have done an excellent job keeping the peace." She leaned closer to him and took his hand. "If you're anxious about what your spot is going to be—don't worry. I meant what I said. You'll keep doing exactly what you did for Da."

"You know Dalton, Siobhan, and I were as close as siblings could be, but not seeing him every day makes me want to smash someone's head in for stealing him from us so soon."

"We'll get to that, and we'll do it in a way that'll earn us the gratitude of the rest of the families."

"What do you need me to do first?"

"Work our people and find two different but important things."

"Was one of those things Emma Verde?" Muriel asked when she came in. "You've had some strange requests, but this one was odd."

"So you didn't find anything suspicious down on the farm?" She laughed.

"That's why I wrote she's more likely to milk you than spy on you. Why are you checking out college students?"

"Whenever someone throws herself in my path, I'm naturally suspicious. She's our newest employee."

"Uh-huh," Muriel said, shaking her head. "I found some new real estate for my new firm, so I'll give you a tour once I'm fully staffed."

"I'll look forward to it." The way Muriel smiled at her made her want to laugh. "Get going, and I'll finish up with Uncle Jarvis."

She gave Jarvis her wish list, and they discussed the way to get it done. The meeting was over, but Jarvis held his finger up to keep her a couple more minutes.

"I found something I thought you might like," he said, opening the top drawer of his desk. "Da took us all to a fair by the lake when I was eight. Dalton was ten and all worked up to win some prizes at the game section, and had Siobhan excited for a teddy bear."

"He did give new meaning to the word competitive."

"There's an understatement." He laughed as he gripped something in his hand. "I saw this, and he used almost all his money when he realized how much I wanted it. He had just enough for that teddy bear but nothing for himself."

She held her hand out when he gave it to her. The cherry-tomato-sized piece of amber had what appeared to be a bumblebee at its center. It was easy to see how it would've fascinated a young boy.

"It's probably dumb, but I really wanted that thing, and he won it for me. He told me our bond was like that bumblebee in there. It was set and solid, and nothing could ever change it."

"That's how I want us to be, so thank you. Are you sure you want to part with it? It's pretty cool."

"I still love it, but he was so proud to get it. It'll be a good reminder that no matter what it takes, do whatever you need to do to win."

"That's easy when I have you and the rest of the family behind me. Da might be gone, but our sting is still lethal."

❖

"Go ahead and break into groups. The assignment is due next week, so take the rest of the time to split up the work," the professor said as the members of the large class picked their partners.

Bea was already sitting next to Emma, so they took the opportunity to talk since they'd already done most of the work. Emma was still smiling from her experience the night before.

"Okay. I've been dying to ask," Bea said, poking Emma with the eraser side of her pencil. "What's got you smiling so much today?"

"I had the best time after work last night." She told Bea what had happened with the drunk guy and how Cain had handled it. "She had a chat with the jerk, then had him tossed out. It was the end of my shift, so we went out and had dinner."

"Girl, did you forget everything I said?"

"The person I've met isn't at all like what you're describing. I'm sure she's no Girl Scout, but she's been nothing but nice to me."

"Promise me you'll at least be careful."

"I'll be fine. Heck. I had more trouble with the guy who thought it was okay to grope me." She put the sections of the paper Bea had done in the correct order and placed it back in the folder to review later.

"I've never met her, so is she as good-looking as they say?"

"It's weird," she said, taking a deep breath. "I never have noticed anything like looks, but those blue eyes can make me forget everything and everyone." She laughed when a thought popped into her head. "What do you think my mother would think about that?"

"I'm sure there aren't enough rosary beads in the world to cleanse your soul, buddy. You might want to keep your new exploits to yourself."

"That won't be a problem. If you want, I'll read this and give you a chance to review the whole thing tomorrow." They started packing their stuff and followed their classmates out.

"I'm pretty positive you've made an impression on the person you most want to notice you," Bea whispered even though they were in a crowd.

"What are you talking about?"

Bea discreetly pointed to one of the benches, and the sight made Emma want to run off. "Makes me think she either really likes you, or she's really a caring boss."

"I'll call you later, okay?" She shouldered her bag and waved.

"Have fun, and I'd be doing the exact same thing now that I've seen her this close."

"She certainly has woken up things in me I didn't even know existed." She turned and faced Bea and bit her bottom lip. "And thanks for getting this assignment done early."

"What kind of friend would I be if I didn't do everything I could to get you laid?"

"Not exactly my plans," she said, her ears getting hot as she waved again. "But it'll be fun to find out if she's even interested in me." Cain smiled at her, and she walked faster. "That might not be hard to guess."

❖

Cain thought about the years she'd spent on Tulane's campus. Her grades were good enough to have gone anywhere in the country, but she'd stayed and lived at home. Tulane had taught her the mechanics of business from books written by professors who thought they had all the answers. She stayed home, though, for the other half of her education that she could never learn from any book.

Her father had been the best professor she'd ever had, and he'd given her all the lessons she'd need to crush anyone standing in her way. Overall, she'd enjoyed her time on campus, but this was the first time she'd ever sat on one of the benches in the common area waiting for a girl.

People poured out of the building, signaling the end of class, so she hoped Muriel had gotten the right schedule. She smiled when she saw Emma walking toward her with a leather satchel strapped to her back. For someone who tried never to question herself, she suddenly wondered if this was a good idea. She didn't want to scare Emma off.

"Are you here because you heard I have leftover Chinese food?" Emma asked, standing close enough their knees were pressed together.

"I'm here to invite you to lunch, but only if I'm not keeping you from anything." She reached up and took Emma's hand. "But if my being here makes you uncomfortable, then be honest. We can keep it to ale followed by a snack."

"This lunch you mentioned, is it a date?" Emma pressed closer to her, which made her think Muriel's check of Emma was correct. No agent, no matter how badly they wanted the collar, wanted to get a reputation of sleeping with the people they were charged to bring down. Unless she was way off, this was blatant flirting.

"Yes. In my opinion, it's a date."

"Then I'll be happy to go," Emma said, tugging on her hand to get her up.

"Not until I check your bra for a wire," she said, trying not to smile.

"Think again, Ms. Casey. I'm not sure what your norm is, but country girls from Wisconsin don't show their bras until they have plenty of dates on the ledger."

"You should know I can be rather persuasive, and I love a challenge. Something tells me this might be one." She stood and took Emma's bag.

They walked to the car with Emma's hand wrapped around her bicep, and Cain tried to ignore the lingering stares they were getting. Emma slowed when they reached the car and seemed to notice Merrick.

"Emma, this is Merrick. She works for me."

"Hello," Emma said slowly, her eyes zeroing in on Merrick's weapons under the light jacket. "Your family members aren't the only interesting people in your life, are they?"

"Hayseed, I have to say you're taking all this pretty well." She placed Emma's bag in the back and then opened the door for her.

"Well, not really, but I have your full attention, so we'll forget for now why you need an armed group of people all the time." Emma sat sideways again so they could face each other. "But why are you, who could obviously have anyone, interested in me?"

"I met with my uncle this morning and told him I've had my head in the mud for a year now." The coming talk probably wasn't a good idea, but Emma made her believe in new beginnings. She was beautiful and untouched by anything in Cain's life, so it was time to let the pretty girl go before that changed.

"Don't you mean your head in the sand?"

"We don't have a lot of sand in New Orleans, but we do have plenty of mud." She stared at the hand Emma had taken and turned over so she could run her fingers along her palm.

"Why did you do that?"

"My father was killed a year ago, and the suddenness of it put me in a fog. Something happened, though, and it woke me up." She closed her hand, trapping Emma's fingers.

"I'm glad," Emma said smiling at her. "What was it?"

"A beer bath." She winked at Emma. "You shocked me into thinking again, so a lunch date to thank you is the least I can do."

"After lunch you're hitting the road?"

They stopped at one of Cain's favorite restaurants in one of the worst neighborhoods in the city. The abandoned, boarded-up buildings and burnt cars on the street had come long after the Uglesich family had opened their place. The founder had been a friend of both her da and her grandfather and loved it when her mum came for lunch.

"Emma, believe me, I'm doing you a favor by taking you out of my orbit before you're really noticed." She brushed Emma's hair back and allowed her fingers to linger on her neck.

"Maybe I don't want to let go, so promise me you'll think about it before you disappear on me."

"You make it hard to be good."

"That's the first time in my life anyone has ever said that about me," Emma said and laughed. "Now feed me."

The place wasn't in any way fancy. Three guys behind the counter were shucking oysters, the menu was scrawled on a board next to them, and the walls were lined with wooden soft-drink crates. Every dish was named after someone in the family, but every table was packed with New Orleans elite.

They ordered after Emma met everyone working, and they held hands while the owner Anthony cleaned off a table for them. "I'm sorry about your dad," Emma said, leaning in so their heads were close together. "That's a horrific thing to have happened to him and your family."

"Da was the rock that centered our family, so it's been tough."

"I'll be happy to help you however I can, but I don't want you to dwell on it if you don't want to."

"Thank you, and I appreciate you listening. In my line of work, you don't want to advertise weakness." The owner's wife Gail brought their root beers and a basket of garlic bread. "That isn't something I've ever admitted to anyone."

"We might not know each other well, but if you tell me something, it's between us."

"I appreciate that as well." She picked up a piece of bread and handed it over. "Are you working tonight?"

"Considering how much I made in tips last night, I could take the week off, but I don't want my boss to think I'm a slacker." Emma closed her eyes when she took a bite of the toast. "You're going to make me gain weight."

"I'm sure you'd look good no matter your weight, but save room for the trout dish you ordered. These guys are some of my favorite cooks in town."

"Can I ask you a question?"

"Sure. What do you want to know?"

"Do your other employees like following you around, or do you need constant companionship?"

She laughed and thought about the friend Emma had mentioned. "Did you not believe anything Beatrice told you? She grew up around here, so she's familiar with the main parts of what people think they know. The cops and the feds refuse to believe I'm only a barkeep."

"Bea and everyone else can believe whatever they want, but I'm going by what I see and how you treat me. So far, if you want me to believe you're a horrible person, you're not doing a very good job." The food came out, so Cain took her jacket off and tucked her napkin in her collar.

"Some people do think I'm a horrible person, so maybe stop seeing only what you want to see."

"Is it at all important to you what I want?" Emma lost her smile as she took a bite of her fish.

She reached over and took Emma's hand. "What *do* you want?"

"Saying it out loud will make me sound stupid, so I'll do whatever you want. If that's only seeing me every so often, I guess I'll have to accept that."

Emma ate her lunch like she'd be judged for leaving anything on her plate. She answered only yes or no to any question Cain asked, and after trying more than once to encourage her to talk, they finished in silence. Cain stood on the corner when Emma refused a ride back, preferring to take the streetcar.

"Are you ready to go back to work?" Merrick asked.

"You in a rush to spin your wheels?" She kept watching until Emma was on a trolley. "If I'm boring you, I can always take someone else."

"The girl saying no makes her extremely dull-witted, so try not to dwell on it and move on. Happens to everyone eventually."

"The girl thinks I said no, so keep your opinion to yourself. Let's get back to the office." She turned toward the car, but work was the last thing on her mind. "This round goes to you, hayseed."

Chapter Eight

Callie "Cal" Richard had slept until eleven but had already showered and dressed, wanting to be ready when her crew arrived. She'd come a long way from the public-housing kid who'd been sent to sit outside most afternoons and nights when her mother turned tricks in their apartment to feed her crack habit.

The teasing from other kids had made her and her twin brother Boone stick together from an early age, and they'd learned not to take shit from anyone. The weak became either suckers or slaves, or died trying to run, but the strong ruled the neighborhoods. They'd done everything possible to prove their strength and their cruelty to anyone who even thought of crossing them.

She'd once read everyone was a product of their upbringing. If that was true, it wasn't exactly her or Boone's fault they'd become what society thought of as psychotic. That's exactly what she was planning to give as an excuse if either of them got caught.

Harold Allemande, one of her top crewmen, arrived first and offered to make coffee for her. They'd been out late the night before trying to take over Casey's territory. So far only the fat little freak, Big Chief, had bought into what she wanted.

"The guys said the first place we went has some guy sitting inside with the two old fuckers who own the store," Harold said, pouring two mugs of coffee and taking extra time with hers to make it exactly to her liking.

"That means the old guy called Casey. Could be good for us if that's what it is." She put on the cowboy boots she'd treated herself to after their last big job. The alligator-skin boots had set her back a couple of grand, but she needed something to make people remember her while she was kicking the shit out of them.

"Cal, if that's true, she's going to expect something. We've done good because we've laid low. I don't want anything to happen to you."

"Take a few guys with you, and go in like you're there to shop. If the guy's still there, put a bullet in his head and tell Mendel he's next if I have to go back there to talk to him again. He makes me do that, and I'm going to start with his wife and make him watch, so that'll be the last thing the old fucker sees before he dies too."

"You want me to go?" Boone asked when he came in from the bedroom closest to the kitchen. "I'll kill them all and send their heads to that big bitch. I don't know why everyone shits their pants when it comes to her."

"I need you with me today. We have to meet up with the boss in a few hours. He's got something in his head that he wants us to do, and if we fucking manage it, he'll give us whatever part of the city we want."

"He's going to let us run our own stuff? You sure about that?" Boone asked, scratching his naked chest.

It was as if at birth each of them had been given equal but opposite physical traits. Boone was a mountain of a guy with sandy blond hair, square jaw, and a deep voice that seemed to resonate to the middle of your skull when he spoke. She was a smallish brunette with a more round face that resembled their mother's, a fact that pissed her off more than anything. Boone liked to joke that their slut of a mother had probably gotten pregnant by two different guys on the same night.

"He owes us, so it's going to happen with or without his help. The debt he's already got with us is big enough that he can't say no." She tilted her head and pointed Harold out of the room. "You can't wimp out on me now, Boone. We're going to make it work because we got surprise on our side. Not one of these motherfuckers knows who we are, so we're going to take what we want. You don't want to go back to hustling tourists in the Quarter, do you?"

"You're smarter than me, Cal, but these people you think are chumps didn't get this powerful by being stupid. You move wrong or fast, and we ain't going to be around to hustle nobody." He spoke softly as he scratched his chest again. "Think about the long play and not just about what you want right now."

"I got it all under control. No matter what our play is, we aren't ever going to be out pounding our chest to get noticed. That's how we're going to get everything we ever wanted."

"All I want is to not go back to the streets. That's it."

"You're getting that and so much more. All you have to do is believe me."

"That ain't a problem, Cal, but believing something and having someone cut your nuts off because you're fucking with them ain't always too far apart."

❖

"She asked for the night off to study," Josh said. "One of the other girls wanted to pick up a shift, so I didn't think it was a big deal to tell her it was okay."

Cain sat in her study at home and glanced out the window. She'd spent a majority of the afternoon reviewing inventory, but Emma was never far from her thoughts. Her walking away with a case of hurt feelings seemed genuine. Emma didn't seem the type to play her. "It's not a problem. I was just checking. Keep on your toes, though. I think we're in for some kind of shit, but I haven't narrowed down the source yet."

"I'll call if I spot anything out of the ordinary."

She hung up and called Merrick. "Take off if you want some time to yourself, but I'll be ready to go in a couple of hours."

"Any place special I should plan on?"

"Maybe dinner or an early night. Depends on the girl, I guess."

"I'm sure she won't be hard to convince, but isn't this one like hunting a caged animal? She seems like an easy target."

"I have a feeling that easy might be a stretch on this one, so get going if you need to get anything done before then."

Cain took a shower and went a bit more casual, with a dress shirt and slacks, but figured it'd put Emma more at ease. If she was successful in getting a dinner date, she wouldn't be home again to put Marie to bed, so she went looking for her. Marie was in her room coloring a picture she'd drawn of Therese's rose garden.

"That's beautiful," she said, sitting on the chair close to the small desk. "You want to finish it or read something before I have to go?"

"You have to go out again? You work too hard, sister." Marie put her crayon down and held her hand.

"I'm not working tonight." She smiled as she tapped the end of Marie's nose. "I met this girl and wanted to ask her if she'd go out with me."

"Is she nice?"

"She's nice and pretty like you. I had lunch with her, but she left because she wasn't too happy with me. Tonight I thought I'd make it up to her." Marie tugged her along to the window seat so they could be closer.

Marie bumped shoulders with her and laughed. "Do you like her?"

"She's someone I think I could like a lot."

"Then you should do something nice for her. Come on." Marie clapped her hands together before she jumped up and called out for Therese.

The three of them went down to the garden, where Marie, with their mum's help, cut a bouquet of roses for Emma. If it was true that every color of the flowers held a meaning, the variety Marie had put together had a lot to say.

"This is the first time I've ever seen you leave here with flowers," Therese said. "Must be quite a girl."

"She's an *interesting* girl, and she's managed to make herself unforgettable. Tonight I wanted to see where that might lead me."

"Try romancing this time instead of charming, my love. Romance got me plenty of happy years."

"Thanks, Mum, and you too, Marie. The flowers are a good idea."

"Will you tell her about me? Maybe we can be friends if she's your friend."

She kissed Marie's cheeks and hugged her. "I bet she'd love to be your friend no matter what."

Cain drove herself this time, but Merrick and a few others followed close behind. She had privacy, but this wasn't the time to get crazy by being out completely alone. To give Emma what she thought she wanted would take plenty of time, but maybe a taste of what she was in for was the cure-all for what was best for her.

She parked a few houses down from Emma's building and motioned for Merrick and the others to stay put. It was dusk, so hopefully Emma was home. The stairwell to the second floor was dark and drab, making her wonder if this was a safe place for someone like Emma.

The music playing inside stopped abruptly when she knocked, but Emma didn't immediately answer. A full three minutes later she heard the chain and the deadbolt come undone before Emma opened the dark-gray door. Like that in the stairwell, the paint was drab and peeling in more than one spot.

"Hey," Emma said, standing so that she was blocking the entrance.

"I'm sorry for earlier," she said as she held up the flowers and waited.

"What exactly are you sorry for?" Emma asked, not taking her gift yet.

"Two things, actually. I upset you by thinking for you, and I didn't do anything to keep you from walking away." She dropped the hand she held the flowers in and sighed. Maybe she'd get her wish of making Emma not interested in her, just not how she wanted to do it.

"You're used to getting your own way, aren't you?" Emma asked but didn't sound upset.

"I'm not usually disappointed, but it happens." She shrugged, amazed at her own patience.

"Thanks for the flowers," Emma ran her hand down Cain's arm until she reached her gift. "And for saying all that."

"How about you put those in water, change, and meet me downstairs, and we'll go to dinner? I promise this meal will end much differently than lunch."

"You can come in."

"I don't mind waiting. Eventually you'll start believing some of my reputation, and I want you to know that part of me will never touch you."

She went back down and sat on the rickety-appearing bench in the yard. The building might've been old and poorly maintained, but it was in a quiet neighborhood. During the thirty minutes Emma took to get ready, she noticed the strange-looking cable van that wasn't there when she arrived.

The sight was almost humorous, but it was also a change in procedure. The feds checked often but not constantly. They didn't have any reason to be here unless something had happened to make them hypervigilant.

"You ready?" Emma asked, breaking her attention on the van.

"I am, and you look beautiful. Are you sure I'm not keeping you from anything, like your big test?"

"I'm ready for that and so much more," Emma said, taking the hand she held out.

❖

Oliver O'Malley sat in the corner of Mendel Saint's store watching the old man bag groceries for an elderly African American woman.

Judging by their conversation, they were old friends. The liquor section was full again, courtesy of Cain, and each bottle on the shelves hadn't cost Mendel a thing.

The hours hadn't exactly been riveting, but since Billy had asked him to sit and watch, that's what he intended to do. Billy's grandfather had hired his old man, who then went on to work for Dalton. Every Sunday he'd get a lecture on loyalty and following orders so he'd move up like he had. Billy wasn't Cain, but he made a good living making sure he was loyal and followed orders.

"Oliver, you want a soda or something?" Ethel asked like she did every hour.

"No, ma'am. I'm okay." He made sure the magazine on his lap covered the gun in his hand. He saw no reason to scare customers while he was keeping the Saints safe. "If you or Mr. Mendel need to bring any more heavy boxes from the back, let me know. We can lock up for a minute, and I'll carry them out for you."

"You're a good boy, Oliver," Ethel said, and he smiled as he heard a car door slam really hard right outside. Another slam brought him to his feet.

"Miss Ethel, hurry to the storeroom," he said, motioning her back. "Mr. Mendel, get down," he said in a normal voice. The two guys heading inside didn't look like neighborhood types, and if they were, they had to be stupid to mess with a Casey-protected property.

"Can I help you?" he asked when they came in and stopped by the door.

"I need some cigarettes," the smaller guy said, glancing around. "Where's the old man?"

"He's taking a break, so try down the street if you need a smoke that bad." Oliver kept his gun behind his back but was ready to fire.

"Old man ain't going to like you turning away business, and I don't like motherfuckers like you telling me what to do," the guy said and reached in his jacket.

Oliver waited until he had his hand on his gun before firing. He hit the guy in the chest and in the head, splattering blood on his friend. "Get on your belly if you don't want to add some decoration to the walls and floor," he said to the bigger guy when he spread his hands out in front of him. "Now, dumbass."

"Okay, relax," the guy said.

"Mr. Mendel, you got twine back there?" Oliver asked, putting his foot on the guy's neck. "Good," he said when Mendel held some up. "Tie this guy's hands and go make sure Miss Ethel's okay."

He called Billy once the guy was bound and told him what had happened. The Saints locked the doors at his instruction and turned out the lights. Billy had made it clear the police wouldn't investigate this situation, so the guy who was still breathing wouldn't like what came next.

Billy arrived less than twenty minutes later, and the guys with him had the place clean and the body gone an hour later. They gagged and took the guy with him away as well, so the place appeared normal again when the lights came back on.

"You okay with all this, Mr. Mendel?" Billy asked as they sat in the back having a small shot of whiskey. "Normally I'd let the police handle the body and the knowledge that it was self-defense, but this time isn't normal. I need to figure out who these guys are more than the police do."

"You do what you have to. That animal got what he deserved, so thank you for having Oliver here." Mendel poured them a little more and finished his in one gulp.

"Oliver's not going anywhere, and he'll have company until we find whoever's doing this. If you need something before then, you call me."

"Thank God for your family, Billy," Ethel said.

"Thank you, and tomorrow, it's business as usual. Having the store open might draw more of these guys out."

"Whatever you want," Mendel said.

"I just want you two to be okay and really go back to business as usual with no threat hanging over you." Billy hugged them both before leaving out the back after his guys made sure the area was clear.

"Come on. I'll drive you home," Oliver said, since it was their regular closing time.

"You think that other guy will come back because of what happened to his friend?" Ethel asked while Mendel set the alarm.

"That guy will never bother you again, and I'll keep you both safe from any of their friends. Cain wouldn't have it any other way."

"Don't think we don't appreciate Cain and her family, but we appreciate you as well. Like I said, you're a good boy," Ethel said.

"I'm a good friend too, so I'll take extra good care of you. You have my word."

CHAPTER NINE

W hat made you change your mind?" Emma asked. "I'm also liking that it's just the two of us."

"Despite my reputation as a monster, I don't like to hurt someone like you intentionally." She turned toward the Quarter and opened her hand when Emma reached over for it. "I also really wanted an answer to my question."

"Which one?" Emma rested her head back and lightly ran her fingernails along her palm.

"The most important one." She pulled over and got out, moving around to open Emma's door. "Let's take a short walk. We've got plenty of time."

Audubon Park was full of joggers and cyclists, but the golf course was empty at dusk, so she headed to one of the benches close to the last hole. She found one under a stand of large oaks and brushed the seat off for Emma.

"What do you want?" Emma opened her mouth, but Cain placed her finger against her lips. "I know what you said before, but there's no such thing as a stupid answer. Tell me."

Her demand made Emma stare at their hands and shake her head slightly. "I grew up in a very small town with very small-town views and beliefs. I didn't feel like I fit or belonged there very often."

"Some people crave the known and the familiar, but I totally get what you mean," she said, leaning back against the tree and putting her arm around Emma.

"I was starting to think something was wrong with me since I didn't feel much differently here. This city is diverse and so different, but I knew something was missing in me."

"What?" She had an idea of the answer, but she wanted to hear it.

"You," Emma said simply, as if it would explain everything.

"Do you—" She wasn't sure what to ask, or if she wanted to ask anything at all.

"I told you you'd think it was stupid. Before you, no one has ever made me feel anything, and it's childish probably to think you'd be interested, but I want to be honest." Emma couldn't look at her, and an overwhelming sense of protectiveness came over her, so strong she almost shivered.

"Emma," she said to get her to lift her head. When Emma didn't, she placed two fingers under her chin and helped her. "I don't think you're childish, and I think this might be new to both of us."

She slowly moved forward and pressed her lips to Emma's. The inexperienced sweetness of their kiss made her want to skip dinner and go back to Emma's small apartment, but they had plenty of time for that. They'd jumped their first hurdle, but Emma's head would have no choice but to catch up to her heart. That fork in the road would either lead to a relationship or make Emma run so far away from her, she'd never see her again.

Emma pressed her forehead to hers and hummed. "That was better than I imagined."

"It was, so from now on, tell me whatever's on your mind. You never know where that might lead you."

They continued to Vincent Carlotti's restaurant and skipped the menus, choosing to let the staff feed them. Emma glanced around the place, then to her, appearing self-conscious.

"You look beautiful, so relax." She kissed Emma's knuckles. "Will you excuse me for a moment?"

"Sure, but stay." Emma stood with her. "Can you point me toward the ladies' room?"

"The waiter will escort you," Vincent said as he folded her napkin and placed it on the table.

He took Emma's seat and shook hands with Cain again. "You doing okay, old friend?" she asked.

"Better now that I see you out with a beautiful woman on your arm. I've missed you, Cain, but you're a good kid. Your papa would be proud of how you've honored his memory."

"Thanks." She took a sip of her Chianti and placed the glass right in front of her. "Did Jarvis stop by?"

"He did, and my answer is yes. Your father was my oldest friend, and what happened to him was in no way honorable." He jabbed his finger into the table to make his point. "What you have in mind is like seeing my old friend at work again. You, like your father, have the patience to lead. I love Billy, but war only for the sake of war is good for no one."

"Revenge isn't rendered any less sweet with time. Right now we've all got other problems that, if left to fester, will infect our ability to operate. That comes first, so I'm glad you and Ramon understand the importance of getting it right."

"You tell me what you need from us, and it's yours."

"I'll be in touch about that. I'm still thinking of the best approach." She saw Emma hesitate before coming closer. "For now though, dinner is all that's on my mind." She stood and held her hand out to Emma.

"I don't blame you for that," Vincent said before he signaled the waiters to start.

"I'm sorry if I interrupted," Emma said.

"A little work out of the way so we can enjoy ourselves now. Thanks for understanding."

Emma glanced in the direction Vincent had walked off in. "He seems nice. Do you know him well?"

"Vincent was one of my father's oldest and best friends. Some people think he's a restaurateur, and others think he's the head of one of the largest organized-crime families in the South."

"That only adds to the menagerie of interesting people in your life," Emma said, holding her wineglass with both hands.

"True, but it should make you want to run for the farm to get away from it. In my opinion, that's the smart play."

"If it is, then you shouldn't have kissed me. That might've blinded me to smart moves or otherwise."

"I hope you don't mind, but as your friend, I'm going to remind you of those smart moves every so often."

"I don't mind at all, as long as you agree that the decisions I make are my own." Emma reached over and fed her a piece of the calamari the waiter had put down.

"I'll never force you to do anything you don't want." She nodded as Emma held up another piece.

The rest of dinner was similar, and for Cain the sweetest part of it was Emma's somewhat clumsy flirting. She was sure she'd improve with practice but was honored to be the one Emma was learning with. Their conversation covered numerous topics, but the ride back was quiet as Emma held her hand in her lap.

She walked Emma upstairs and pressed up behind her as she unlocked the door. Very slowly she ran her hands from Emma's hips to the undersides of her breasts and smiled at the moan Emma let out. This she understood, and she wanted to touch Emma until she begged her to stop.

Emma turned around and raised her head as if inviting her to kiss her, so she did, only this time, it was a kiss meant to ratchet up Emma's need to match her own. She moved her hand higher and felt Emma's nipple harden under her palm.

"Wow," Emma said when their lips parted. "That was wonderful."

"Aren't you going to invite me in?" She kissed Emma's neck right under her ear.

"I don't think…what I mean is…" Emma stammered a bit, so Cain raised her head. "Please don't be mad, but I'm not ready for that yet."

Cain blinked, waiting for the punch line, but Emma appeared dead serious. "You want to say good night now?" she asked, stretching out the last word.

"Yes, but I'd love to see you again." Emma stood on her toes and kissed her cheek. "Thanks for dinner."

Cain was left standing in the hallway staring at Emma's door. "What the hell just happened?" she muttered to no one, since she doubted Emma was coming back out.

"Mum, romance might have its benefits, but charm usually gets you laid," she said as she went down the stairs.

"Ah, oh," Merrick said as she stepped outside as if surprised to see her. "I was coming up to get you. We've got another appointment."

"Let's go then," she said, hoping whatever it was involved her hitting someone. She knew of other ways to blow off steam, but Emma would've been her first choice that night.

❖

"Call Agent Kyle and tell him Casey's not headed home," Agent Logan North said to his fellow agent Ray Clifton. They'd been following Cain around for their first night after Barney had gotten the go-ahead for twenty-four-hour surveillance. Maybe after a night that almost made him gag watching the beautiful young woman with Cain fawning all over her, things would get more interesting.

He moved to the driver's seat and followed at a distance, not to make Casey suspicious. She was headed back toward the Quarter, bypassing the street where she lived, so she was definitely going somewhere.

"He said if she meets with anyone on the list he gave you to call him immediately. If not, he'll wait for your report tomorrow," Ray said from the back. "I'm trying to see if we can pick up the conversation in either car, so get a little closer."

Their little convoy stopped at Casey's pub, and they parked across the street in a spot marked for loading. "No way are you picking up anything in there with all the noise, so let's go inside," he said, rolling his sleeves up to try to fit in.

"I doubt she's doing anything out in the open, so go in if you want, and I'll wait for you here," Ray said, not moving.

"You never know what she's going to do, but from in there we'll at least see who goes back if she's not using the actual bar. I'm in charge, and I want you inside with me," Logan said to the older agent that he thought had too much attitude.

They entered and sat at the opposite end of the bar from where Cain and her people were standing. It was a good spot since it was close to the door that led to what Logan guessed was the storeroom and office. Whoever her appointment was with would have to walk right by them.

"Too bad this is a work night," Ray said, ordering a couple of sodas. "This is a cool place."

"Maybe once we bring this scumbag down, we can come back and have a drink to celebrate."

Cain smiled as she took the phone from the bartender. Whoever was on the line was making her laugh.

"Here we go," Logan said when Cain hung up and said something into the bartender's ear.

"What was the first name on Kyle's list?"

"Some guys called Jake Kelly and Bradley Draper. He said Casey might be cutting some big deal with them, and that was our way in."

There were no pictures of possible Casey business associates on Kyle's list, but they had the ability to photograph anyone without being noticed. Right now, Casey was just having a beer at the bar and seemed to have already forgotten the little blonde she'd dropped off.

Twenty minutes later, Ray said, "Logan, heads up. She's leaving."

They made it outside as Casey's vehicles pulled away, and the spot across the street had a big van with LINEN painted on the side parked where their van had been. The guy unloading bar towels was whistling as they charged toward him.

"Where's the van that was here?" Logan screamed, grabbing the guy by the collar.

"Hell if I know, man, but everyone knows not to park here ever. The businesses on the block are real particular about their deliveries. I'm guessing your ride is arriving at the impound lot right about now. My advice is, bring cash. Those assholes don't take plastic or checks."

"Fuck," he screamed, figuring Kyle would gut him for this.

"Fuck is right. Now you know why you never leave the vehicle unattended," Ray said, looking in every direction as if the van was close by. "We're never going to live this down. You know that, right? This is like the biggest rookie move ever."

"Come on. Let's at least get the damn thing back before we report in." He walked to Bourbon Street in search of a cab. "With any luck Kyle won't transfer us to the middle of fucking nowhere."

"I wouldn't bet on that. Kyle's wound a little tight, and this will go down in his book as unforgivably incompetent."

"Watch what you say," he said, wanting to defend his new boss.

"No one ever gets far in the Bureau by being an ass kisser, Logan, or by reporting other agents. Remember that if you're after a long career."

"Got it," he said, jamming his hands into his pockets. "And I'm not much on advice."

"Good to know, and I'll make sure everyone else is clear on that going forward. Let's just concentrate on getting the van back."

They cabbed it to the impound lot, and Logan sighed when the guy at the gate told them they'd have it right out. "Once we get it, we can use the transponder you placed to get back to work."

"Sounds good," Ray said, then cursed when the guy came back without the van.

"I'm not sure what happened, but we're not sure where the van is. It got brought here, but someone from your office ordered it back to wherever you keep it, so it wasn't here long." The guy glanced at his clipboard again and scratched his head. "Sorry for the mix-up."

"Come on. We might as well take the fucking beating we got coming tonight," Ray said.

"You sure you want to get Agent Kyle out of bed now?"

"You heard the guy. He already knows. Not owning up to it now will make it look like we're just putting off the inevitable."

Logan leaned against the fence and threw up while Ray called for another cab. Ray was right in that they'd be lucky to go back to a desk after this. Whatever kind of career he'd hoped for in the field was short-lived.

"Cheer up, kid," Ray said, standing a few feet from him. "It's not the end of the world if you can take some teasing. I won't lie. Tomorrow's going to be brutal, but it's not career-ending."

"I hope so, since I want the chance to rip that bitch's heart out. Because as sure as I'm fucking standing here, that's who got our ride towed."

❖

Cain entered the room in the basement of the old but massive abandoned building in New Orleans East and rubbed her fingers together. She could almost feel the grime in the place floating around the stale air, and the smell was hard to clear from your nose without actually going outside. It had been a slaughterhouse years before, and the blood seemed to have permeated every surface.

The guy Merrick had told her about was sitting in a chair glaring at Billy, and she could hear his heavy breathing from fifty feet away. She couldn't blame the guy since he looked like a bloody mess, so his pain must've been intense.

"You think whoever you're working for would be this loyal to you?" Billy asked, waving over his shoulder as if sensing her behind him. "No fucking way. Whoever that is would've given your big ass up after the first love tap. Don't you think so, Boss?"

"Knowing what was in store, they probably would've spilled their guts on the way over here," she said, studying the guy's license when Billy handed over his wallet. "The strong, silent type, huh?" The guy just glared at her but then turned his attention back to Billy. "You're not looking too good, so maybe try and make it easy on yourself."

"He's okay. I was just messing with him a little," Billy said, and she laughed at the fact that the guy's nose wasn't exactly in the middle of his face. "I wanted him to be able to talk when you got here, so I barely touched him."

"So, Harold Allemande," she said, glancing at his license again. "What's your story?"

"I already told this asshole, I got nothing to say."

"Fair enough." She walked behind him, and Harold gave up trying to keep her in sight when Billy aimed his gun at his head. "Let's talk about something else."

"Like how my boss is going to pulverize you?" Harold said and laughed. No one else joined in.

"Pulverize. Now there's a word you don't hear every day, but pay attention. We'll get to your boss, but not yet. I was thinking more about this building." He flinched when she dropped her hands onto his shoulders. "When my father was a boy, he'd come here with his mother to buy fresh meat. They'd let her pick it from the big slabs that used to hang on the hooks still located upstairs. All that carving and gutting used to drip on the floor, and eventually it'd come through the cracks down here. I like starting down here, because all the bad stuff happened up there. Being down here gives you a chance of nothing bad happening to you. That's how it works."

"You gonna talk me to death?" Harold said, and Billy cocked his gun. "Cool it, man. Don't you have a sense of humor?"

"I bought this place after my father told me about it, but I only come here for special occasions." She squeezed his shoulders tight enough to make him try to pull away. "The blood and history of the old business is in its walls and floorboards, but it's still got life left in it since most of the equipment still works as well as it did when my da was a boy."

"What's that got to do with me?" Harold asked, the fear so clear in his voice that she could sense he knew what came next.

"It's time for some show-and-tell, Harold. Interesting name, by the way, for this line of work. Sounds like you should be an accountant living in the suburbs with a bunch of kids running around." She watched Lou tie his feet and hands together, and Harold sat compliantly since Billy had his gun firmly pressed against his temple. "If you'd picked the kids route, I bet they'd have loved show-and-tell. I'm older, but I still like it."

"What do you want?"

"I wanted to have a civilized conversation with you, but you said you had nothing to give up." She slapped him gently and smiled. "Remember that, Harold. There's that old saying that everything happens for a reason, and today everything that happens is because you had nothing to say to me."

"Why?" It was hot, but Harold was sweating profusely as Lou pulled him up and together with Billy carried him upstairs.

"Why?" she asked as they reached the industrial meat grinder at the end of the old assembly line. "Easy answer, Harold. You could've stayed downstairs and had a talk in that spot where nothing bad happens, but that's not what you chose." She moved close to him again and shoved his head in the direction she wanted his attention on. "But the real answer to that question for you is the difference between going into that machine alive or like your friend. This thing is really handy when you have something that needs to disappear." She made a circle motion with her fingers, and Merrick flipped the power switch. "The crabs at the lake are in for a treat tonight."

Harold visibly paled when his friend went in feet first. It didn't matter how much bone was involved. All that came out of the nozzle was the kind of ground meat found in packs in any grocery store.

"Kind of puts you off burgers for a while, but it's damn effective," she said when it was done, making Billy laugh. "He had it easy since our man Oliver you met at Mendel's did him a favor by putting a bullet in his head, but believe me, you're going to have a totally different experience. All that grinding and stopping is going to be a bitch, but you've got nothing to say." She signaled Merrick again, and the loud rumble came back to life. "Believe me, when you see your feet come out of that damn nozzle, you'll give up your mother if I ask you to."

"Wait…wait," Harold yelled, squirming to get away from Lou and Billy. "What do you want to know?"

"You sure, Harold? You were so set on staying quiet before."

"Please, what do you want?" Harold started crying, and he wet his pants when Lou moved him closer to the feed opening.

"Who do you work for?" Merrick shut the grinder down as she spoke.

"Boone Richard." Harold tried to move the caster rollers under him to get away from the grinder.

"Any relation to Callie Richard?"

"That's his twin sister, but I don't deal with her often."

Cain nodded and pressed her hands together. "Where do I find Boone and his sister?"

"Let me go, and I'll tell you."

She smiled, and the tension seemed to drain out of him—until Merrick turned the grinder back on. "You think you're holding any cards here? The game is rigged against you, Harold, and believe me, it's no fun to play if you're the one to go into that thing next."

"Boone usually meets with us at Rick's Café in the Marigny. That's all I know, I swear. You killed the guy that knew more than me." He had snot draining from his nose and was shaking like she was running an electric volt through him. "Please. That's all I know."

"You sure you aren't lying?" she asked, to see if he knew any more. Even if he didn't, she had more than enough to get Merrick and Muriel started.

"No. That's it. Please, I told you—let me go."

"It's the least I can do for you," she said, glancing up at Merrick, then Billy. Her brother pulled the trigger as Merrick started the machine.

"See you at home," Billy said as they waited for the machine to finish.

"Make sure the crew cleans tomorrow, and burn your clothes before you all leave. We can't afford to be sloppy now."

"I'll handle it. Go home," Billy said.

"Thanks. Don't stay out late, and before you start complaining, I'm not trying to take Mum's place. Harold only wishes someone had worried about him and given him good advice. He didn't, so now look at him—he's all broken up about his bad decisions."

CHAPTER TEN

Cain glanced at her phone the next morning as she sat to put her shoes on. She had a full day, so if she wanted to talk to Emma, now was the time. Harold had definitely taken her mind off her sex life, but that was a dead subject on a new day, so she put it out of her mind.

"Good morning," she said when Emma answered. "How are you?"

"I'm still in a great mood after my great night. Any regrets?"

"I'd have ridden off into the sunset, so no regrets. Do you have class today?"

"Two this morning, and then I'm taking a nap so I can work tonight. Will I see you at the bar?" Emma's voice was full of sleep and silk.

"Maybe. Depends on if I finish everything I've got going on. Either way, you wait for your ride, okay?" She finished with her shoes and sat back with her eyes closed.

"I will, and I'd really like to see you sometime today, even if it's late."

"Study hard and I'll see what I can do." She got up, knowing she didn't have a lot of time before people would be waiting on her. She put on her jacket and dropped everything she needed into her pockets. "And if you were curious, I had a great night too."

"Even if...you know."

She smiled at Emma's shyness. "I do know, and even then. Everything worth anything is worth waiting for."

"Are you sure? You didn't exactly look happy."

"I was shocked, and I'm sure. You might kill me before you see what you're missing, but I'm sure."

"You'll survive, and I promise to take good care of you."

"That's good to hear." The strangest sensation came over her, and she came close to driving to that small apartment so she could kiss Emma to start her day. "Be careful, and I'll see you soon."

"You swear?"

"I do, and I won't be late."

"Have a good day and don't forget what you said."

"I won't. Until then," she said before hanging up. It was nice to not feel like her heart weighed a thousand pounds. She didn't put a lot of faith in relationships outside her family, but Emma had awoken something inside her. Until now, she hadn't had the sense to realize a piece of her old self had withered when her da died, and she'd never thought it would come back.

Any more thoughts on the subject died when she reached Merrick, Billy, Muriel, and her mother lined up and waiting. "I don't sense a big welcoming committee to an awesome day."

"They'll get ahold of you soon enough, so spare me a moment so you can see your sister off to school," Therese said, taking her hand. "She's been waiting to hear how the flowers went over."

Marie was finishing a bowl of cereal and talking with the cook, but came over and hugged her the moment they entered. "Good morning, beautiful girl."

"Did your friend like the flowers?" Marie held both her hands, waiting for an answer.

"Her name is Emma, and she loved your flowers. She liked them so much she had dinner with me."

Marie's face was truly beautiful when she smiled, and her words had lit her up with joy. "She did? That's great. Do you think I can meet her?"

"I'll ask her when I see her tonight, but right now school's waiting for you. Emma's in school too. She wants to be a teacher." Cain walked Marie and her mother outside to the waiting car. On most mornings Therese volunteered at Marie's school until her sister was ready to be on her own.

"I can't wait to meet her," Marie said before kissing her cheek.

"A girl you're seeing more than once is someone I'd like to meet myself," Therese said, laughing. "You know I cook every Sunday."

"Let's not give the girl the wrong impression right off," she said softly to her mother. "Another date and a Sunday lunch to meet my family are too different animals."

"Uh-huh," Therese said, kissing her other cheek. "May the Lord watch over you, my darling girl."

"Thanks, Mum, and I'll see you two later."

She watched the car drive away before going in to see what all the glum faces were about. The cook handed her a large mug of coffee, and she wondered if it was too early to spike it with something much stronger than cream.

"Go on," she said as they trailed her to the office. "One of you spit it out."

"Mendel's place got hit again last night," Billy said as he sat next to her on the couch. "Someone shot the hell out of it, tearing everything in there to shreds."

"Muriel, you have anything yet?" She'd given up the desk so Muriel could spread her paperwork out.

"Harold and his dead friend, JJ, are some street rats from Baton Rouge, so we sent a few guys to ask some questions. Both these idiots have rap sheets long enough to impress their mothers, but it was all petty stuff." The police report Muriel handed Cain was thick, and the last thing they'd been picked up for was a street-hustle game. "Somewhere along the line they upped their game into extortion and moved into our territory to try to improve that new skill."

"I'd think that has a lot to do with his friend Boone Richard and his sister Callie. Sounds like they're the complete opposite of the lovable twins we know." She handed Billy the paperwork and finished her coffee. "Share that information with Remi, Mano, and Ramon. If they're interested in us, eventually they'll be next on the list, so cut Vinnie and Vincent into the loop."

"Will do," Muriel said.

"Harold knew more than he was saying, so we need another one of their crew to get a better idea of where to head next," Billy said, not bothering to read what Muriel had compiled.

"I don't think we'll have to look too far," she said as she stood. "We've got a date with Jake Kelly and his trained monkey today, but we need to make time for our old friend Big Chief."

"What's that fat bastard got to do with anything?" Billy asked.

"In every battle, there's always a winner and a loser, but the trick is picking a side before the war begins," she said, buttoning her jacket. "Big Chief saw an impending war and got an invitation to join the invading horde. He agreed because, whoever these assholes are, they're not us."

"I'm going to fucking cut his guts out," Billy said, and she put her hand on his shoulder.

"Eventually, but right now all I want to do is talk to him. Big Chief thinks, no matter why, that he's the smartest guy in the room." She checked the time and didn't want Jake Kelly in her office alone. "Smart guys like that love showing everyone their big brains, so why deprive him of the opportunity?"

"If he double-crosses us he needs to pay," Billy said.

"Everyone pays, brother, but some costs are steeper than others. Right now, though, we need to get going so we can make it to the office. Big Chief can wait, but not for long." He put his jacket on to cover his guns and nodded. "Muriel, keep after the Baton Rouge angle and let me know."

The drive to the office gave her time to think about Emma, but she needed to clear her head. Of all the times in her life for romance to take root, this wasn't the most convenient, but her mother would probably hit her in the back of the head for even thinking like that.

Their gates were locked, and Jake and his man were waiting, leaning against their car. "You get the impression this guy is a little anxious to get this done?" Billy asked as Merrick got out and dealt with the lock.

"Let's get through this, and I'll clue you in on who I think this guy is. We'll only listen, like we did last time, and see how worked up he gets." She laughed when Jake rushed to the driver's side and revved his engine. "I should be flattered he's so excited to see me."

Billy laughed as he hurried around to get her door. "It'll break his heart when he finds out you're already in love."

"Who told you that?"

"Who else?" He slapped her back. "Mum loves to gossip more than she likes to hover. And we both know how much she loves to do that."

"I guess my thoughts on the subject don't really matter." She shook her head, then elbowed Billy in the side when Jake entered. "This'll be a half an hour of our lives we'll never get back."

"You finally ready to deal?" Jake asked, shaking her hand with a grip so tight she thought he was trying to bring her to her knees.

"Come inside and let's talk about it."

"Talk?" Jake said loudly. "We've talked this to death. It's time to deal."

"Maybe I'm just slow, Jake, and I need to hear it again," she said, not walking to her office. "If I'm wasting your time, then you're free to go."

"Come on, Cain." He smiled and shrugged. "I'm excited about the money we can make together. With the amount of liquor I hear you move, our partnership can benefit everyone involved."

"Who's feeding you all this bullshit about us?" Billy asked, and she made no move to stop him. "We're going to iron that out first before we talk about anything else."

"Hey. Who's in charge here?" Jake said, staring right at her.

"Deflecting the question doesn't make me any less curious about the answer," she said, standing in the open space of the warehouse. Out here, Jake couldn't leave anything behind like the bug still in her office. Whatever he said now would stay between them.

"Let's go sit down then. We've got to reach a place where we trust each other, if this is going to work."

"What's the matter? You tired? Answer the question or walk," Billy said. "If someone is feeding you all this information about my family, we want to know who and what they said."

The guy with Jake took his phone out and made the motion of answering it. "Jake," he said after listening for a minute. "We've got issues in Atlanta that sound serious."

"Sounds serious," she said, widening her smile. "Does Jake need to reschedule?" The man with him nodded and put his phone away. "Call when you're ready to talk, Jake, and what I mean by that is answering my brother's questions before we go forward. And I mean all of them."

"Look. I'm just ready to go, so I'm sorry for losing my cool," Jake said, staying put when Billy took a step forward.

"Take care of your serious problems, and call me when you're ready for a very frank conversation."

She left Merrick and Billy to see them out and headed to the conference room across from her office. Lou nodded when she glanced his way, meaning she was free to talk.

"Good morning, Bryce."

The young, geeky guy had passed Muriel's extensive background check, starting with their informants in the prison system. Bryce's brother Charlie had served every bit of the time Bryce had said he had and hadn't had a pleasant time behind bars. Charlie, from his first day, hadn't taken up one of the gang leaders' advances, and the pretty boy didn't take rejection well.

"Good morning, ma'am." Bryce jumped to his feet when she walked in and hesitated before stepping forward and shaking her hand.

"It's simply Cain. If you want to work for me, it's just Cain." She took a seat and waited for him to calm down so they could talk.

"Thank you for what you did for my brother. He called and said since he was out he hasn't slept as well as he has the last couple of nights." Bryce folded his hands in front of him and appeared ready to cry. "Thank you."

"Charlie needs help, so it was the least I could do. He'll be okay until we get him out. I've got someone working on that, so don't think you're alone in the world any longer."

"I promise I'll do good work for you even if you don't do another thing for Charlie."

"Good, but Charlie will be fine," she said softly, finally getting him to smile. "Did you get my gift?"

"The equipment is state-of-the-art. These guys are really interested in hearing every word you say and taking glossy pictures and film of it all."

"Should I explain how much I value my privacy?"

Bryce laughed and nodded. "From what's inside, there's only so many frequencies they can work with. Granted, it's more than the average mass-produced equipment, but it's manageable."

He'd brought information on what he was talking about so she looked it over, curious as to where the taxes she did pay were going. The van that had been towed was fully equipped to determine every aspect of her life, only to rip it apart once they'd heard enough.

"What's your plan?" she asked, handing his report back.

"I don't think I can break theirs, but I can put a bubble around you. You can let them in only when you want, if you want. I can do it so they either hear nothing at all or whatever you want them to." He returned to pressing his hands together. "It'll be pricey though."

"You can't go cheap when it comes to this, so don't worry about it. Get whatever you need and spend what you have to." She slid over the contract Muriel had drawn up for her and handed him a pen. "Just one thing left to do."

He saw the salary on the front page and didn't bother with anything else except signing. "Good." He handed the papers to Lou and gave him an envelope. "Inside is enough cash to get you started. Whatever you've got planned will have to go into one of our locations, and I think Emerald's has a perfect spot for you."

"I turned the transponder back on, so they should find their vehicle today, and turned off the one they put on your car. Actually I put it on the closest car to the one I took it off. Some tourists might be driving around with an escort."

"I'd love to be in that staff meeting when those idiots have to explain they lost their ride," she said and laughed. That the ruse had actually worked was still hilarious. "Are you sure you got everything you needed?"

"Yes, and in a couple of weeks I'll have something in place that'll make your life easier—at least when it comes to the feds. I'll try to give you an upper hand with the rest, but I'll have to figure out how to do that."

"Sounds interesting, but if you can do that—what happened when your brother got popped?" He stared at his lap, but her question made sense as they reached the last part of his interview.

"I tried to take every obstacle out of our way by hacking the Baton Rouge police system for their undercover operations," he said in barely a whisper. "Stuff like that only works when someone listens and uses the information."

"So your brother didn't?"

"He thought the reward was greater than the risks I'd laid out for him. I understand his thinking, but I've never agreed with it." He finally glanced up at her and combed his hair out of his eyes. "All I can do is clear the way for you to do whatever you have to, but I'll also tell you when I can't do that. The risk-slash-reward risks are up to you to assess."

"If you're worried that I'm reckless, don't be. You give me all the facts and variables, and we'll get along fine."

"Great," he said, putting all his papers into the backpack he'd brought. "Do you want anyone to go with me to get all this stuff?"

"Are you planning to rip me off?" she asked, and Bryce appeared mortified.

"No, ma'am," he said, forgetting or too scared to use her name. "I just thought you'd want to make sure about me until you're certain you can trust me. What I'm doing for you, and you not really knowing anything about me, is making you wonder if I'm the right guy. Trust and loyalty take time to prove, but every day I'll do my best to show you I belong here."

"Thank you for saying that, and I'm sure we'll get along fine." She looked at Lou and motioned him forward. "Have one of the guys go with Bryce on his shopping trip. Tell Doug to get in touch with him."

"He's at the house, so I'll have him meet you wherever you want to start," Lou said.

"How will I know him?"

"He's hard to miss, so he'll find you wherever you're going," Cain said of the only other computer-savvy guy on her payroll.

"I'll wait for his call before I start."

"Keep me updated, so don't let Lou here or Merrick put you off if you need to talk to me." She tapped the table with her palm and stood. "You need anything else?"

"Do you want me to wear a suit every day?"

"Do you own a suit?" She smiled when he shook his head as if he were stuck in slow motion. "Then forget about that, and stick to the T-shirt and jeans look you seem to like. If you get the urge to dance at the club, then you're not getting in dressed like that."

"I'm not at all a dancer," Bryce said, waving his hands.

"Lighten up, kid, and get to work."

She went outside and climbed into the vehicle with Billy. The day was barely under way, and she was already thinking how much time what she had to do would take. Callie and her brother were at the top of her priority list, but she also wanted to know who was watching from across the street. The empty room directly across from her office had been leased and paid for in advance for the next twelve months. She didn't know who, but the landlord had given her a call about his good luck, as if not wanting to discuss more than that on the phone.

"Where to next?" Billy asked.

"The Liam brothers are in town, so we're going to listen to what they have to say and get on with what we do."

"So why are you messing with Jake?"

Merrick drove out of the warehouse, and she pointed to the place across the street. "Jake might be the key to our new neighbors."

"Who was dumb enough to rent that rat-infested hole?"

"Our new shadows, and judging by the second car on the left, they're a new fact of life. Remember that the next time you're out either having a good time or doing something for me." They both turned around and watched the dark sedan pull into traffic after they turned out.

"They're going around the clock now? What's changed?" Billy kept looking until she turned his head.

"Annabel's probably brought in a new sheriff to lay down the law. We'll be okay as long as we remember how badly they want us to screw up." She glanced back again. "Hope they're patient. Screw-ups aren't in my plans."

❖

"Where's the report, Agent North?" Barney asked in front of the board where they'd started to put together their case on the Casey family. So far most of the pictures posted were highlighted by educated guesses. They still didn't even have an idea about hard evidence.

"It's not done, sir," Logan said, and Ray nodded as if backing him up.

"What part isn't finished, gentlemen? The one where you left your vehicle and the dumbass you were following had it towed?" Barney's question made the other agents in the room start laughing, then just as quickly stop when he put his hand up. "Or is it the part where you don't have a fucking clue where it is despite all the government has invested in your training?"

"Sir, we're working on getting it back now. The transponder came back online today," Ray said.

"You can thank the newbie, Agent Joe Simmons, for finding it for you. It's in the garage, so you're on desk duty until I say otherwise."

"Yes, sir," Logan said, looking at Ray.

"Get back to work and see if these two nimrods got anything useful last night," Barney said to everyone in the room. "At least the transponder on Casey's car is still on, so see where she went last night and where she is now."

"Actually, sir, we checked that out last night and followed an older couple from Florida through the Quarter this morning. Casey's people found it too and moved it to someone else."

"Agent Kyle," Annabel said, and Barney mouthed the word "shit."

"Yes, ma'am."

"In my office," she said and walked away, since she hadn't left any option in her request. "Explain why a vehicle worth more than three million dollars ended up in one of the worst neighborhoods in the city?"

He stood since she hadn't invited him to sit. "I thought putting one of your experienced guys with North would show him the ropes, but that's not what happened."

"That's not exactly the way Clifton explained it. You chose to go with the greenest people out there so you could lay out the rules, and

North got worked up enough to forget protocol." She raised her finger when he tried to speak. "One more incident like this and we'll do fine without your help. I'm still shocked that the damn surveillance vehicle wasn't completely stripped when we found it."

"Yes, ma'am. I'll personally go out with the crew to make sure they follow the rules and procedures."

"See that you do, and make sure you put North back in the field tonight."

"He obviously isn't ready." He twitched his fingers and took a breath before he spoke. "I thought you didn't want a repeat of last night."

"Last night was on you, Agent Kyle. Neither North nor Clifton will have this go in their file unless you're willing to take the blame, and have it go on your, I'm sure, spotless service record. Is that understood?" Annabel glared at him as if daring him to challenge her.

"Crystal clear, ma'am, but you gave me total control over the unit. Shouldn't I decide who to reprimand?"

"Do you need a week, or maybe four, to review the procedural manual, Agent Kyle?" she said almost menacingly. "You can concentrate on the chain-of-command sections. Once you grasp those parts, you can report back to me and explain them in detail."

"No, ma'am." He stopped before he gave her reason to transfer him. "Is that all, ma'am?"

"Yes, and keep in mind that Casey isn't your average criminal. Last night should prove it. One more stunt like that, and the morale out there isn't going to recover."

"A criminal is always a creature of habit. Smart or dumb doesn't matter—they all eventually can't help themselves."

"And the people charged with bringing them down can also step off the road of proven investigative methods if only to make a name for themselves because they can't help thinking their way is better. Only then, when you're in the deep and tall weeds and off that proven road, do you figure out that you're in danger from all the predators that live in those dark places." She leaned back in her chair and smiled, but the expression didn't soften her appearance. "Once you're in their sights, you'll wish you had the backing that comes from making good relationships with the people you work with."

"I guess only time will tell which of us is right."

CHAPTER ELEVEN

O ur father did business with yours for years, Cain," Shawn Liam said as his brother Royce poured coffee. "I'm glad we made the trip to talk face-to-face. I think with a good conversation we can have the same kind of relationship."

"And build on it," Royce said.

"I've got no plans to change anything that's not broken, but you've got to admit your prices have risen steadily and steeply in the last couple of years." Cain accepted a cup from Royce and rested it on her knee. "Our fathers had a good relationship built on respect and fairness, but they both stepped away from the everyday running of the business about the same time the prices started going up."

"You waited an awfully long time to complain," Shawn said, shrugging. "You've paid the increases without a word up to now."

"I haven't purchased anything since Da died since we had enough inventory, but I'm saying something now before we go forward."

Shawn was the eldest brother and, from the sound of it, the most vocal about his new position at the top of the Liam business. "We can't completely absorb the costs of safe shipments along with the booze itself, and if you were on this side you'd have done the same thing."

"The shipments leave your place in my care, so what safe-shipping fees are you talking about?" She put the cup down and sat back. "I paid only because of Da's request not to insult a friend. If your father really needed the money, he'd pay, but the numbers have nothing to do with your father, do they?"

"The numbers are the numbers, Cain. I can't do anything about that," Shawn said, spreading his hands. "This is, you have to agree, an exclusive business. It's not like you can call just anyone to supply what you're looking for."

"That's really the answer you're going with?" Cain shook her head in Billy's direction when he moved to stand up.

"If you want to part ways," Royce said loudly, "then so be it. We might not need your business if you're going to be nothing like your father."

"Careful, Royce. You wouldn't want to trip and lose all your teeth," Billy said.

Royce seemed to want to move toward Billy, but Shawn waved him off. "This was supposed to be a friendly meeting so we can plan the future, Cain, not a pissing contest," Shawn said. "I'm sure we can work out something if we put our egos aside."

"Ego has nothing to do with how I conduct my business. Your current terms are unacceptable." She stood up and Billy did the same. "From what Royce said, not accepting your terms is a nonstarter to our future. We'll be happy to part ways here, so have a good trip home."

"You're seriously thinking of cutting ties with us?" Shawn laughed as if she'd told him a great joke. "Don't tell me you fell for Jake Kelly's bullshit."

"Shawn, don't ever give me advice about my business or who I do business with. Concentrate on your own small piece of the world. Don't take your eyes off what you think is safe."

"I'm not the one who's had their head buried up their ass for a year, so take your advice and stick it up there if it'll fit alongside your denial." If he was going to say anything else, he stopped when his hands shot up to his face. The coffee cup on the table had hit and broken over his eyebrow. She'd thrown it hard enough to break skin, and he appeared pissed as blood trickled into his eye.

"Shawn, don't do anything stupid like make light of my grief. You do and it's Billy's turn next," she said as Billy put his hand in his jacket. "He won't bother with the dishes, so keep that in mind."

"Get the fuck out, and pray this doesn't come back to haunt you," Royce said.

Billy took a step toward Royce, and Shawn didn't do anything to stop him. "Another word and your father will spend the rest of his life wondering what the hell happened to you."

"If you're smart, this is where we part ways. You push something that should come to a natural end, and you're not going to enjoy our next conversation," she said before walking out the door and having Billy slam it behind them.

"I agree that those two are assholes, but hopefully you've got a plan B," Billy said when they got into the elevator.

"It was worth a shot to get them to come down on their rates, but I was expecting Shawn's response. Royce is a follower with a slow streak, so he shouldn't be hard to find if it comes to that. He'll be right up Shawn's ass, so you might get two with one shot." She smiled and went out the back through the loading dock. She didn't have any reason not to test their new friends with the drab suits. "Trust me. You won't go thirsty."

❖

Emma walked out of her afternoon class and stared at the bench where she'd found Cain the day before. Unfortunately, two guys were occupying it, so she probably wouldn't see Cain until she got to the bar that night. This was her late day at school, so she wouldn't have a nap in her future, but she was too wired to sleep. All she'd done since she'd woken up was relive the kiss she'd shared with Cain and pray Cain hadn't found some reason they couldn't do it again.

"Looking for anyone in particular?" Emma heard someone ask from right behind her. That low-pitched voice slightly tinted with a Southern accent made her smile. Maybe Cain was ready to move forward.

"You're late," she said, turning around and enjoying the thrill of seeing Cain standing there.

"I'm actually early," Cain said, reaching for her backpack and kissing her hello. "You just got out."

"The kiss was enough for me to forgive you." She took Cain's hand and, when they started walking, glanced up at her.

"Do you need to change?" Cain walked them to St. Charles Avenue, where her car was parked, and the vehicle behind it seemed to be watching them.

"Even though, compared to you, I look like a bum, this was the most comfortable thing I have to work in." She waved down her body to the long-sleeved Tulane T-shirt and jeans.

"You're fine, so you want to have a snack with me before you go in?" Cain opened the door for her and put her bag in the back before getting in and waiting for her answer.

"Is this a snack or a date?" She took Cain's hand again and kissed her palm.

"I'd think by now, snack is synonymous with date."

"Then I'd love to."

Cain drove them toward the back of the Quarter to a beautiful old home with a small bed-and-breakfast sign on the gate. The place was gorgeous, but the bed part of the sign concerned her. Cain chuckled when she glanced her way.

"Don't look so worried. It's only for the privacy," Cain said as she drove up to the front. "If you find you can't control yourself around me though, there is a bed in the room."

"You're a riot." She bit the tip of Cain's index finger before she got out to open her door again. "This is a beautiful place—do you come here often?" She couldn't disguise the fact-finding question.

"I've had dinner here a time or twelve," Cain said and winked. "I can't hide from my past, not that I want to, but if you ask me something, I'm always going to answer you honestly. Especially if you want to know something in particular about me."

"I'm sure your interesting past includes plenty of stories involving dinners at places like this, but right now I'm just interested in the fact that I'm here with you." She walked up the stairs on Cain's arm and stayed quiet as the woman who greeted them handed Cain a key.

"You're not at all what I imagined when it comes to a young woman from Wisconsin."

Cain opened the door to the room on the first floor, and Emma wasn't expecting the large suite on the other side. All the doors were closed, and the table by the windows was set with a large candelabra at its center, even though it was still light outside.

"What were your thoughts when it comes to a girl from Wisconsin?" She sat when Cain pulled out her chair and glanced at the beautiful garden. The only strange thing outside was the older man seated directly across from them, seemingly staring into their room.

"I'm not really sure how to answer that, but you seem almost too…accepting, I guess." Cain held up a bottle of wine and she nodded. "If that makes sense at all."

"I grew up on a dairy farm, with a mother who loved the Lord and used her knowledge of the good book to try to steer me in the right direction. That means that I seldom left the dairy farm except to attend the church I was forced to go to." She stopped to take a sip of the excellent wine Cain had poured, deciding the truth was the best way to begin.

"If you want, you can stop there," Cain said, holding up a finger when someone knocked.

The waiter rolled in a cart and served two small filets and two lobster tails with a variety of sides before leaving with a generous tip from Cain. "Don't you want to know?" Emma asked. "Or was this about getting me into that bed next door and moving on?"

"It's about giving you the option of not telling me. That story doesn't sound like it has a happy ending. Why would I want to make you relive it if you don't want to?"

"I wouldn't describe it as a happy ending, but my upbringing did give me a sense of…" Emma tried to find the right phrasing. "I refuse to be boxed into something that I don't choose. I grew up having someone force-feed me someone else's rules and faith, but for now I've decided to have some faith in myself."

"So you went from the convent to what a lot of people would consider the devil's lair? That's the ultimate of not being boxed in, Miss Verde." Cain raised her glass and held it in the middle of the table. "To new adventures that will definitely have nothing to do with religion."

"And the bed?" she asked after tapping her glass against Cain's.

"We'll see about that since you didn't say you weren't interested." Cain smiled, and she couldn't help but smile back in reply.

"You certainly aren't like anyone I've ever met," she said, and Cain's smile grew wider. "Which makes me wonder why I'm here. I'm obviously not what you're used to either."

"So much has happened in the last year, not of my choosing either. Pain has a way of making you see things more clearly, and one of the things I happened to see was you." Cain pointed to her plate as she took another sip of wine. "Maybe we both need something different and should wait to find where that takes us."

"I'll drink to that," she said, holding her glass up.

"Not to sound like a spoilsport, but you might want to look outside before you do."

The older man was still sitting there and still staring at them. "Who is he?"

"If I had to guess, he's an FBI special agent. I'm not so sure what's so special about them, but they get upset if you leave that part of their title out. They've been part of my existence for a long time, but they seem to be my new shadows around the clock now."

Emma glanced out at the guy again and tapped the crystal glass with her nail. "Any particular reason?"

"Maybe my last name, but I doubt that's going to change any time soon. Think about that fact before you decide anything."

When Emma stood up, Cain slouched back in her chair, probably thinking she'd leave. She walked behind Cain and pulled the lever for the plantation blinds, making them come down and block the guy's view.

"Maybe we both need something out of our normal. We might just find something better than what we've experienced so far."

"We'll take it nice and slow so that the newness doesn't completely freak you out," Cain said, taking her hand. "And if you ever want to finish your sad story because you need to talk about it, I'll be happy to listen."

"Thank you, and the same goes for you. You seem to be strong all the time, so I'll be happy to give you a place to relax."

"Only, and I'm guessing here, it won't be a bed, right?"

"The farm girl won't completely disappear overnight, so no beds for a while. Are you okay with that?"

"I'm disciplined enough to handle it." Emma lifted her hand and kissed the tips of her fingers. When Emma smiled, Cain added, "With plenty of cold showers."

❖

"The Quarter is packed tonight, so tell me if you need help in your section," Josh said when the crew that arrived at four stood by the bar donning their aprons. "Tonight, unless I say so, go ahead and get a credit card for the tabs. We don't want to be giving free booze away. Anyone have any questions?"

"The day crew is staying?" one of the girls asked.

"All but a couple. This place has been a madhouse since noon, so thanks for all the hard work, everybody."

The night did get extremely busy, and when the band started, the bouncers began limiting the number of people coming in. Emma had handed her tips over to Cain for safekeeping by nine, glad to have her so nearby. Cain was pouring drinks like an old pro and winked at her as she pocketed the large wad of cash.

"What can I get for you guys?" Emma asked the group that had just gotten a table close to the bar. They looked familiar, and then she recognized the guy who'd grabbed her. "Wouldn't you be more comfortable somewhere else? You'll find plenty of bars close by."

"What kind of place runs off paying customers?" one of the men asked, and the others laughed as if the question was hilarious. "Besides, it's a free country, and we can drink anywhere we want to."

"Ms. Casey asked you not to come back. Did you forget that part?" Emma asked, starting to back away.

"Ms. Casey can kiss my ass, and I'm back to kiss yours," the guy who'd touched her said, burying his face in her crotch. "Let's start in the front though."

It happened so fast that Emma had trouble processing it, but just as fast, the guy's nose was bleeding profusely. He didn't have much time to recover when Cain hit him again, and he howled. The uppercut seemed to have slammed his teeth together with his tongue in the way.

He spat a large amount of blood on the front of his shirt as two of the bouncers dragged him toward the office. The rest of his group lost their bravado when Cain grabbed the biggest one of them by the hair and whispered something in his ear.

"I see you here again, and I'm going to make new earrings for my wait staff out of parts of your anatomy I'm sure you're particularly fond of." She pulled the guy's head down farther, and he went compliantly. "Do you understand?" They all nodded.

"What about Martin?" another one of them asked.

"Is that the idiot bleeding in the storeroom?" Cain asked, and they all nodded again. "You're worried about him now and not when he was sexually assaulting someone?"

"Come on. It was just for kicks. He didn't mean anything by it," the smallest of the foursome said as he backed away from Cain and the guys now holding his friends.

Cain cracked the bones in her neck before kicking him so hard between the legs she thought he'd throw up. "I see your point. When you do things simply for kicks, it's pretty liberating."

"Do you know who the hell I am?" the guy wheezed out.

"You're Jonas Belson's son, so I'm going to throw you out of here without breaking all your fingers. If you're smart, you'll leave Daddy out of your problems, but you aren't the type, are you, Jonsie?"

"Cain," Emma said, taking her free hand. "The police are here."

"Thanks." Cain squeezed Emma's hand before letting it go. "Get behind the bar with Josh, and I'll take care of this."

"She attacked our friend for no reason, so I want her arrested," Jonsie Belson said, pointing at her but keeping one hand on his crotch.

"Cain, you okay here?" one of the beat cops asked.

"The trouble is over whether these guys decide not to come back. Thanks for stopping by, guys. Tell Josh to give you some coffee or soda, whatever you want."

"You're leaving?" Jonsie screamed. "What the hell is this?"

The police left as Cain motioned to her security team to take out Jonsie's two sidekicks that were still standing. Cain grabbed Jonsie by the hair and pulled him into the storeroom where his friend was still bleeding. She pushed Jonsie to his knees and handed him her cell phone.

"You wanted to call your father, so do it. And don't forget to leave anything out." He didn't take the phone, so she shoved it into his hand and squeezed until he grimaced. "Call or you're going to have trouble punching in the three numbers that'll save you from me."

He watched her as he dialed and seemed surprised when he heard his father's voice. "Jonas, your son needs to talk to you."

"You know my father?" Jonsie took the phone, and his hand fell limply to his side.

"Have a talk and then tell him our deal is off."

Jonsie put the phone to his ear and listened as she watched him. She doubted the esteemed state senator would tell him about being addicted to prostitutes and beating the crap out of them after he screwed them. She knew his whole repertoire since she had five of his encounters on DVD. In exchange for some favors, she'd given him her word his little secret would stay in her vault.

"I'm sorry," Jonsie said as he handed the phone back to her. "He'll send a check for the damage, and I promise never to come back."

"You think it's that easy, Jonsie? You waltz in here like some little tough guy, throwing your daddy's name around, and you're going to walk out of here with an 'I'm sorry'? You're wasting your daddy's money on that expensive Tulane education if you think that, you little piece of shit."

"Please. My dad will pay. He said so." Jonsie was crying now, pressing his hands together as if he were praying. "We really were just having fun."

"Maybe I should have a little more fun with you before I send you back to your mama. How about it? It'll all be in good fun." She took a step toward him and he cried harder, but he calmed a little when she grabbed him by the jaw. "You're never going to know, little man, when I'm going to make you pay for your disrespect. You'll never know, but you will pay, and your daddy doesn't have enough money to save you from me."

"Cain," Merrick said, and when Cain glanced up she saw Merrick had Emma with her.

"Get out of my sight," she said to Jonsie, unmoved when he stopped and apologized to Emma. "Merrick, get this guy somewhere he's not bleeding on my floor."

"Are you okay?" Emma asked her.

"That's something I should be asking you." She opened her arms, and Emma immediately moved into them. "I'm sorry that happened again after I told you it wouldn't. Are you all right?"

"I'm disgusted that guy put his hands on me again, but you took care of it. Thank you, and that's exactly the second time someone has ever defended my honor. The first was when he touched me before, and you took care of that too." Emma pressed the side of her face to Cain's chest. "As an English major, I've read about that sort of thing plenty of times, but it's good to know it can really happen in everyday life. Dashing knights really do exist."

"That's putting a good romantic spin on it," she said, holding Emma tight. "Maybe it's time to take off the rose-colored glasses and take a long look at my world."

"You keep trying to get rid of me but follow that by beating up a bunch of guys for disrespecting me. Make up your mind because you can't have it both ways." Emma lifted herself up on her toes and kissed her. "And if you're thinking of going, know that I'd rather you stayed."

"Come on. This has been enough excitement for one day. Let me take you home." The idea was almost humorous, but looking at Emma this closely, she thought of a few romance stories herself. Emma made her want to prove herself a worthy partner, even if the smarter move was to let go.

"Not before you tell me you're not going to disappear on me." Emma reached up and held her face so she couldn't glance away.

"Cain," she heard Billy say.

"I promise." She gave Emma her answer as well as her word. "Now turn around so you can meet my brother. Billy, this is Emma," she said, smiling in his direction.

"Pleasure to meet you." Billy took Emma's hand and held it. "I'm sorry I missed all the fun, but Josh tells me my sister took the trash out with no problem."

"She did great, and it's nice meeting you too." Emma peered back at her and closed her eyes for a moment. "I'll just get my things."

"Take your time, and don't forget I've got some of your tips." Emma nodded and waved at Billy before she left. "Expect a call from Jonas Belson," she said to Billy. "That little pipsqueak you probably saw leaving with Merrick is his son Jonsie."

"How do you want me to handle that?" Billy took her hand and looked at her knuckles. They were starting to bruise, but she felt good.

"I haven't decided yet, but this'll cost him more than he's willing to pay because I'd like to skin little Jonsie and make a wallet out of him before I send him back to that pompous ass for his disrespectful behavior."

Billy nodded before releasing her hand. "If it's any consolation, I'd have busted my knuckles over her too. She's pretty."

"She is, but I don't think she's completely realized what she's getting into here." She stared at the small pool of blood the asshole had left on her floor and sighed. "I'm almost at a point where I don't really care."

"Good." Billy hugged her and kissed her cheek. "You deserve to be happy and loved. If she feels the same way, there's no harm in it. She might know exactly what she's getting into if that entails you."

"It's that simple, huh?"

He laughed and hugged her tighter. "Hell no, but you deserve only good things, and that girl seems like a really good thing."

"We'll see, but I agree that she is something."

CHAPTER TWELVE

Emma was glad Cain chose not to drive and was sitting in the back with her. Josh had hugged her before they'd left and told her to take a few days off. The last thing she wanted was to act like a weak female, but the night was so far out of her norm that the solidness of Cain comforted her.

"Are you sure you're okay?" Cain's voice seemed to touch something deep in her that made her think of home. She'd never experienced that sensation. While she was growing up, she'd dreamed of nothing but leaving and going somewhere else. Her childhood felt like it'd lasted three lifetimes.

"The stuff that happened tonight should freak me out, but knowing you weren't that far away made it okay. We've known each other only a few days, but I was certain of it." She pressed closer and put her arm around Cain's middle. "Me saying that doesn't freak *you* out, does it?"

"No, and I'm glad you have that kind of faith in me." Cain kissed right under her ear, making her shiver.

"No one without honor would spend their time trying to talk me out of being with them. Having faith in you is the easiest part of this."

The car stopped, and Cain carried her bag up for her and kissed her. It took all her willpower not to invite Cain in, but this situation was moving too fast. If Cain was serious, then waiting wasn't a problem.

"Have a good night, and call me if you need anything. No matter what, you call me, okay?" Cain pressed a card into her hand before kissing her knuckles. "Tonight someone might've noticed you, so I need you to know that I'll take care of you."

"I just want to get to know you better. You don't owe me anything." She circled her finger around the button on Cain's shirt at eye level.

"Please, Emma. You haven't really taken me seriously, but a certain danger comes from being with me." Cain lifted her head by gently putting her fingers under her chin and kissed her again. "I don't want anything to happen to you because of me, so no arguments."

"Josh wants me to take some time off, but does that mean I won't see you?"

"You can't think that," Cain said, hugging her. "Get some sleep, and don't worry about things you don't have to."

"Thanks, for dinner, too."

"Remember one thing," Cain said, and she nodded. "If anyone in a boring suit shows up, don't give them my phone number." She pointed at the card in Emma's hand.

❖

Cain went downstairs and studied the cars on the street. The panel van parked three cars up from where Merrick was had also been outside of the bar when they left. The surveillance was heavy handed, but the feds didn't seem to mind showing that it was more than blatant. Instead of taking the car, she walked to the sidewalk and headed toward Audubon Park, since it wasn't too far from Emma's place.

The guys watching her would either have to leave their little haven or drive slowly behind her. She smiled, taking her time as the van crept up to new spots as she made her way. That wouldn't work once she entered the dark park.

She heard a door open as she made it past the big pillars by the entrance. The guy behind her didn't bother her, so she kept up the same pace until she was halfway in. She walked through a gate in the middle of the brick wall along a stretch of the park that led to the grand homes on the other side and locked it.

Billy was waiting in the second driveway, and unless the agent scaled the wall, he couldn't see them leave. "Thanks, brother."

"You're so popular, I'm shocked you have time for me," Billy said, laughing.

"Did you find Big Chief, funny guy?" She sat back as he made his way back toward St. Charles Avenue, parking before he got there. Billy left the old car he'd picked her up in and moved them to a newer one with tinted windows.

The intersection where he'd turned would take them right by

where she'd last seen the panel van, but that's the route she'd asked him to take. Billy drove by and glanced in the rearview mirror without moving his head. The van stayed parked, and no other tail took its place.

"Merrick stopped by his place today, but he was in the wind. He must've gotten nervous after Mendel's store got blown to shit."

"So he's gone?" she asked with her eyes closed.

"Mr. Know-It-All needs lessons on how to hide, if that's what he's trying to do." Billy patted her knee. "He's bunking in his storeroom."

"Anyone we don't know watching him?"

"He's only got a bottle of Jack for company. From what Merrick said, the destruction at Mendel's scared the crap out of him because he knew it'd piss you off." Billy drove and parked about four blocks from Big Chief's place. They made their way through the backyards of a couple of homes and could hear the blare of the television as they neared the idiot's store.

"Maybe someone should also give him some pointers on not making this much noise while hiding out," she said as Billy picked the lock and quietly slipped into the storeroom. They didn't have any reason for all the stealth, since the television was so loud they could've driven through the wall.

"What the hell?" Big Chief screamed, spilling some of his drink over his naked stomach when Billy tapped him on the top of his head with his gun.

"Not yet on the hell part, but tonight might not be a good time to try my patience." She sat and had a hard time looking at the almost-naked, disgusting little man. "I was telling Billy about wars and picking sides. Some brave souls in every conflict pick a side before the battles begin. Is that how you see yourself, Big Chief?"

"Cain, come on. Anyone would've taken the opportunity to make more money. You would've done it if you were in my place."

"From where I'm standing, your place doesn't look all that great." She picked up the whiskey bottle and poured what was left over his head before holding it by the neck and smashing it against the table next to him. It had broken in jagged edges, and she pressed one sharp piece to the bottom of his eye. "You're going to tell me all about Callie Richard and her brother, and you better start praying I believe you. If I don't, I'm going to carve out every round thing in your body with this." She held up the bottle right in front of his eyes. "Stop and think of all four things in your body that are round."

"Please. I don't deserve this." Big Chief tried to lean back away from her, but it was no use. Cain was in front of him and Billy behind him.

"You're already a disgusting piece of humanity, so spare me what you don't deserve." She cut slightly into this cheek, then pressed her fingers against his lips to keep him quiet. "Remember. Make me believe you."

"They came to see me and the deal sounded really good, so I listened. There was no crime in that, but then they threatened me. They said they'd tell you about it and that you'd kill me." He blinked rapidly as he heard Billy cock the hammer on his gun. "I tried to tell them to forget it, but then I was in too deep."

"See, Billy, this is one of those brave souls."

"You're right. I told them you were the one I was doing business with, and only you. You have to know that."

"So what about the great deal makers? Do they magically appear and offer all this wonderful stuff?"

"They call me when they need something, and that's all I know."

She cut deeper and waited for him to stop screaming. "I don't believe you."

"Wait. One of the guys with them said they're new to town."

"Let me explain the next part. I already know everything you've just said, so with or *without* you, I'm going to get the information I need. You really ought to concentrate on that *without you* part."

"I'm telling you, they're crazy about their privacy, so I don't have a way of calling them. The big guy Boone shows up when they need something from me." Big Chief put his hand over his cut, but it was still bleeding.

"Like I said, *Carl*, because only you would pick Big Chief as your nickname, I don't believe you. The Richards aren't taking over my territory by having limited contact with bastards like you." She cut into the other side of his face but didn't make it too deep. "They've kept you close so you'll go out and get other dumb bastards like you to buy into what they're doing."

"Goddamn." His other hand went up and he put his head down. "A guy comes by every day to collect and talk. He's usually here by two, but I only know his nickname. He goes by JJ."

"And what does JJ look like?"

Big Chief gave her what she wanted and raised his head to look at her. "You didn't have to do this shit, Cain. I've been loyal to you from the beginning."

"How did JJ know to send his goons to Mendel's place?"

"Shit, man, they offered commissions, and I thought the old man would appreciate the extra money."

"Who else was on your list, Carl?" she said before sighing. He told her the names of five more places, three of which weren't hers. "I somewhat believe you, but how you got in with these people is total bullshit."

"I swear, that's all of it."

"No, Carl, it's not," Billy said, as if he'd lost patience with the whole conversation.

"You sold me and my family out for a few bucks, and you're hiding back here because you knew what I'd do to you," Cain said.

"Callie said they're watching you all the time, so you can't kill me. You gonna go down for killing some low-on-the-totem-pole peon like me? You know you can't touch me."

"Want to make a bet?" Billy pressed his gun right to Big Chief's forehead.

"Wait, just fucking wait." Carl screamed, but he had to know no one was coming. He frantically searched next to him in the cushions, but Billy drove his head back as Cain grabbed Carl's hand.

"Thanks for saving us the trouble of finding it," she said, yanking out the .357 he was going for. "You know what sucks more than anything in life?"

"Your mother?" Carl said sarcastically.

"Reverting to your childhood in this situation isn't perhaps your smartest move, little man." Cain pulled the trigger, hitting Carl square in the chest for his non-funny response. "My answer is getting killed with your own gun, so you were way off," she said as Carl gurgled as if he had a mouthful of blood. Billy moved and she fired again, opening his head like a melon. "The only thing worse than that is getting killed in some ratty underwear while having all your shit go up in flames."

They opened a few of the bottles of booze in the boxes close to him and doused the area around Carl's chair and the boxes of paper products he had stockpiled for the store. Billy started a few fires around the room as she wiped the gun and dropped it on Carl's chest after she poured a bottle of bleach on it as well.

They were almost back to their car when they heard the first sirens in the distance. The fire seemed so big and hot that Big Chief's place would be a total loss, so all the firemen could do now was salvage the places next door.

"See who Merrick sent to Baton Rouge, and join them to shake some trees. Have more of our guys sent into the neighborhoods to keep an eye on things, and put enough money on the street to flush out JJ. If he exists, I'd like to talk to him."

"We'll find him, but it'll be easier to just find Callie and Boone." Billy parked one last time so they could use one of the large SUVs the feds were used to seeing. "You think they're working with someone else?"

"That's why I'd like to talk to them. If they give me the chance, I'll show them the same hot time we gave Big Chief."

CHAPTER THIRTEEN

The house was too quiet as Callie walked down the hallway to the kitchen for her morning coffee. It had been too quiet for too long, so Harold came to mind again. Harold was always around, so eager to please, or at least a phone call away, but he'd disappeared. She'd sent Harold and JJ to take care of the unbending old man with the corner grocery, and that'd been the last time she'd seen either of them.

She tried Harold's number again, but it went immediately to voicemail. After the beep prompted her to leave a message, she said, "Where the hell are you?"

Boone's door was open, but she wasn't worried about him since she'd spoken to him at midnight. He'd found some bitch to spend the night with, he'd said, then was headed to Rick's Café to meet with his crew. It didn't thrill her that he'd decided on such a public location, so she hoped no one paid attention.

The house phone rang, and she found herself hoping it was Harold. "Yeah?"

"Today at eleven. Don't be late. The man wants a face-to-face."

After the short message the phone went dead. They were making a lot more money, but she was starting to get the impression she was a trained seal expected to perform on a whim. "Hey," she said when Boone answered, sounding groggy. "We have a command performance at eleven, so skip Rick's and meet me here."

"What now?"

"The guy who called didn't go into specifics. Don't make us late," she said, ending the call so she could get the door. She opened it to Ryan Douglas, another one of their crew. "Have you heard from him or found him?"

"It's weird, Boss." Ryan came in and locked the door behind him. He was tall and muscled to the point Callie thought he had a steroid problem. "He took JJ with him to see that Mendel guy, and he's like smoke in a high wind. We drove by there and the place's open, so I don't even know if Harold made it over there."

"Nothing was different?" She started the coffee and pulled the tie on her robe tighter. Ryan seemed to be staring at her ass when she turned around, which was brave.

"People from the neighborhood coming and going like usual, so nothing seemed off to me."

Her robe was made of a satiny material, and he seemed to be enjoying the way it clung to her body. "Did you send some guys like I asked?" She leaned back against the counter, making the robe pull tight against her breasts.

"That's all we been doing, but no one saw nothing. If something went down, it was a good cleanup."

"I guess Harold's dead and whoever did it got JJ too." She walked up to him and put her hand on his crotch. From the feel of him, maybe he wasn't juiced up. It was going to be a long, stressful day, so maybe Boone had the right idea. A good fuck would relax her. Ryan appeared almost shocked by her straightforwardness.

"You okay, Callie?"

"You turning me down?" She squeezed harder, and he took a deep breath as he sat up straighter. "I didn't think so, and this is just about fucking, so don't get any cute ideas."

She led him to her bedroom and dropped her robe while he shed his pants and boots. He lay down when she pointed to the bed and climbed on top of him. No way would she ever be pinned by another man, and this position prevented any kissing.

They were done and dressed by the time Boone made it home to shower and change. Since Ryan was still there, he drove them to their meeting, but Boone told him to wait outside.

"What the fuck am I paying you two for?" Giovanni "Big Gino" Bracato screamed when they were led into his office.

"What do you mean?" Boone asked, his voice tight and controlled. One move against this fat fucker and they'd never make it out alive, but any more bullshit, and Boone appeared ready to take his chances.

"Big Chief's place burned down last night with that stupid fucker inside. I thought you said he was working with you?"

"He's dead?" Callie hated asking the question since she realized it made her sound like some dumbass punk deaf and blind to what was happening on the streets. "If he is, we didn't have anything to do with it."

"He's fucking dead, and he was your fucking responsibility, so you might as well have pulled the trigger." Big Gino pounded his desk and spit over the surface as he spoke. "You might use this to our advantage, though, and threaten some of those other people with the same thing. Tell them there's a fire waiting if they don't get with the program."

"We'll start with the next weakest link and build from there," she said. "It didn't take that long to flip Big Chief."

"You got another week to finish a block," Big Gino said, lowering his voice as if for effect.

"We get too heavy-handed and someone's gonna call the cops," Boone said.

"You come down hard enough and no one's calling for help. You're big enough to make them all understand that, so just do it."

They left and glanced at each other over the car. "What do you think he's going to do if we don't deliver?" Boone asked.

"Try and wipe us out, but we haven't made it this long by bowing to guys like that. He comes after us and we'll hit him hard. That's what guys like Big Gino understand."

"Let's hope he understands, because nobody wins if we have to try to take each other out."

"Big Gino's talking tough because he knows what we've done for him, and he's going to use it against us before we can return the favor." She held Boone's hand as they took off. "He's got to know, though, that what we did for him needs to stay quiet for both our sakes. That's a secret we all need to take to the grave."

❖

The peeling paint on the bench in front of Emma's building was noticeable since Cain felt the rough edges through her pants as she sat waiting. The unkempt appearance seemed to be prevalent throughout the entire building. She flicked a piece off her knee as she wondered how long Emma would be. They'd spoken that morning and Emma had said she'd be home by eleven, but it was fifteen after.

In a totally uncharacteristic move, she'd walked through the

French Market to shop for flowers before going to Emma's. The elderly woman who'd helped her had recommended the bouquet next to her on the bench, so she carried them away, probably confusing the fed trailing her. It was only fair since she was a little confused about all this herself.

She saw Emma turn the corner and smiled when she started walking faster. The happy expression on Emma's face made her glad she'd stopped for the sappy gift.

"Hey." Emma dropped her bag on the bench and put her arms around her neck when she stood. "I didn't think you were coming."

"It was too nice a day to be inside, so here I am." She handed over the bouquet of sunflowers, now thinking the roses like she'd brought before would've been a better choice.

"Oh, my God," Emma said with a beautiful smile. "Ever since I was little I've grown these every spring and summer. They've always been my favorites since they make me happy. Thank you."

"You're welcome, and I'm glad, since you make me happy."

Emma really brightened and kissed her again. "Are you serious?"

"Yes. I seldom kid," she said, trying not to laugh.

"You're so funny." Emma pulled her toward the front door. "Let me put these in water and drop my stuff inside."

"If you're not tired, let's take a walk and have lunch."

Emma hugged her for the suggestion and almost shyly handed over her bag to carry up.

"Do I need to change?" Emma asked, but she stayed right outside the door when they got to the apartment.

"You're fine, so take your time."

She watched Emma comb her hair back and pull it into a tie. She'd had plenty of women in her life, but this was so new to her. Emma was either a good actress, or she really was this fresh, untouched beauty who had completely captivated her.

The phone rang and Emma seemed ready to ignore it.

"Go ahead. I'm not in a hurry."

"Hello," Emma said, and her face became a mask of misery. Her expression was so pained that Cain wanted to go in and hold her, so she did. "I lost my job, so I had to find another one so I could stay and finish."

Standing this close to Emma, she could hear the woman on the other end. "Why am I just hearing about this?"

"Because I've been busy with my new job, and I have a full course load this semester. I haven't had time to phone, so I'm sorry you found out by calling the bookstore."

"Emma, don't take that tone with me. Every moment you stay in that pit, the more likely we'll lose you to the devil himself."

"Mama, all I want is an education, so I'm working to get one." Emma leaned back against her so she tightened her hold. "I haven't asked you or Daddy for anything, so that should make you happy."

"You're an ungrateful child, Emma. I didn't allow you to use any of our money because I wouldn't be part of the mistake of sending you there."

"I know you don't agree with what I want, but I'm going to do whatever I have to so I can finish." Emma's voice was soft, as if she was mortified this was happening. She could see and feel the heat of Emma's blush, so she pressed a kiss to Emma's temple. "All I've ever wanted was for you to be proud of me," Emma whispered.

"No. All you've ever wanted was to get away from what you know is best for you."

"Believe what you want, but I really don't want to argue about it. I'll call you and Daddy soon." Emma slowly put the phone down and exhaled loudly. "I'm sorry you had to be here for that."

"Don't apologize for something that's not your fault. You shouldn't feel bad for saying the things you said, as long as they're true." She turned Emma around, and the tears tracking down Emma's cheeks drove her to want to make Emma feel better. "Never apologize for standing up for yourself, especially if what you're doing is right."

"I try my best, but I'm never going to be what she wants."

She combed Emma's hair back and framed her face with her hands. "Maybe you should ask yourself what *you* want."

Emma peered up at her and seemed almost pained. "I never—"

The way Emma stopped made her think she was somewhat lost in her own life and didn't know how to ask for what would make her the happiest. She wanted new things, but she was still walking the maze of pain her mother had made for her. "We don't know each other well yet, but maybe we need to stop running and take a look around as to where we are. Blinders can keep the pain out, but they keep you from seeing everything else too. We both carry our unique set of problems, but together we can work through them."

"You make it sound so easy." Emma slid her hands up Cain's arms until they were on her shoulders.

"It can be as easy as telling me what you want. Forget about pleasing anyone but yourself for once."

"I want this," Emma whispered. "It's new, and I hope you don't mind that I don't have a lot of experience, but you're what I want."

"Then forget the rest for now, and let's concentrate on that." She kissed Emma, and some of her well-built defenses fell away. The sensation was liberating.

"Thank you for all that." Emma hugged her and sounded happy again.

"Come on. You'll feel better with some food in you."

They walked down St. Charles Avenue to the Magnolia Grille. The old New Orleans favorite only had a lunch counter, but Cain liked the simplicity of the menu and the waiters with their unique form of entertainment.

Emma seemed to like the banter and the singing, so the lost hours of work were worth it to Cain. "Do you want to split a piece of pie?"

"I'd love to but you pick."

"Are you an apple fan?"

Emma nodded, so she ordered and pointed to the guy preparing their piece. He cleaned the grill, dropped a hunk of butter onto it, and placed the slice in the melted pool it made. Once it was crispy on both sides, he plated it and put ice cream on it.

"Everything on the plate except the butter is homemade."

"You're dangerous to me fitting in my jeans," Emma said, then hummed when she took a bite.

"That's okay. I'd rather you be out of them." She smiled when Emma blushed and slapped the side of her arm.

"You like keeping me off balance, don't you?" Emma scooped up more pie and fed it to her.

"We're even then, since you're doing the same thing to me, but I can't wait for you to keep me on my best behavior as we navigate all this."

They finished and walked back so she could leave Emma safely at home. She would've taken the day off, but she had some appointments to keep. Besides, she hadn't held someone's hand this much since grade school.

"Will I see you tonight?" Emma asked as Cain unlocked her door.

"I've got a thing, but I'm all yours after that." She pressed Emma against her door and kissed the side of her neck. "What would you like to do?"

"Can we go somewhere quiet so we can talk?"

"We can do that, so finish your homework and I'll call you later," she said. She'd never expected to say that again after high school.

Emma grabbed her lapels as she started to move away, but that's as bold as she seemed to be as she clung to her. She kissed Emma, making her moan when she took possession of Emma's mouth. Emma's response turned her on, but Emma caught her hand as it crept too close to her breast.

"You're killing me, but I'll call you later so you can torture me some more."

❖

Cain opened her eyes when the car stopped inside her warehouse, her daydreams abruptly ending. Lou had picked up Paul Sardine and driven him in the car with the darkest tinted windows they owned. Paul had been in a few of her classes at Tulane, and they'd reached an agreement back then.

Paul's brother Victor ran their legitimate business, but without Paul's side, they wouldn't be living the rich lifestyle they had grown accustomed to as children when their father and uncle ran the business in the exact same way. Her father had agreed to this arrangement before his death, but she'd given him her word that she'd talk to the Liam brothers first. Even Dalton had figured there'd be no compromise once Roger Liam retired.

She had trusted Paul from the very beginning of their friendship, and he'd sounded eager when she'd called the month before. She smiled when she saw him standing by the office entrance waiting for her.

"You look good, old friend," Paul said, pulling her into a bear hug. He was six inches shorter than she was, but she hadn't forgotten his affectionate nature. "My family has kept you in our prayers, considering what happened. Your father was a good man, and he raised exceptional children."

"Thanks, Paul, and you were always too generous with the compliments." She led him to the conference room and poured them a drink. "Are you and Victor enjoying your time at the helm?"

"My little brother and Papa keep preaching about the work, so it's cut out all my fun. Your call almost sent both of them into a nirvana-like euphoria. We do well, but partnering with you will triple our business." After Paul downed the whiskey in one gulp, he got up and poured the next one. "Are you sure about the numbers?"

"We don't do much business with the Liams, but I want to expand as well, so you lucked out that you'll be filling my orders going forward. The only way to strengthen my position is to open new territory, and I'm working toward that."

He nodded and finished his second drink. "I want the business, but only if you and your family are going to be okay." Paul was so full of nervous energy that he sometimes reminded her of a windup toy.

"We'll be fine as long as we don't have any kinks along the way. Neither of us can afford any on-the-job training or problem-solving once we start."

He offered her a third drink, but she waved him off.

"I've already mapped out our routes and gone over them with Muriel enough times that I dream about them."

"Muriel is even more fanatical about the rules than I am, but you'll thank her when you start spending the money," she said, making him rub his hands together and laugh.

"I might need some of that money for a wedding," he said, covering his eyes with his hands. "Can you believe I finally met someone I'm willing to leave bachelorhood for?"

"More like I can't believe you found some willing soul to put up with you." She stood and shook his hand. "Tell me about it."

"It happens to the best of us, so don't think you're immune. One day you meet one who you can't get out of your head, and before you really think it over, she's living in your house cutting things out of bridal magazines and taking up tons of room in your closet. It helps that her family is sort of in the same business. They've owned a high-end whiskey distillery for years." He shivered, as if thinking about it, but his smile never faltered. "You have to swear to me you'll come."

"When is this happy occasion?" she asked, wondering if Paul's mind wasn't a bit muddled to cut such a big deal with her and not miss something along the way.

"In six months, and you can quit worrying," he said as if reading her thoughts. "Victor's nowhere ready to get married, so he's reviewed everything I've done. I'd never leave you hanging or exposed, Cain. You can trust me."

"I know, and I promise to be there, wherever that might be."

"Don't worry about that either. We wouldn't send you into the frozen tundra of Canada in winter. Daphne agreed to move the party to Bermuda so we could thaw out."

"I'd love to, so let's talk about our first shipment."

They reviewed everything they'd agreed to and how it would make it across the border to the warehouses Cain had empty and waiting. After an hour she was satisfied with the logistics, and he was happy with the money.

"Do you mind me asking what happened with the Liams' deal with you?" he asked as he packed all his paperwork away in the file he held and handed it over.

"Royce and Shawn, unlike you and Victor, never learned anything from their father. The last shipment was off in quantity and way overpriced, but Da didn't want to throw away the years and friendship he'd shared with their father Roger right off." She handed the file to Merrick so it could be placed in Muriel's safe. "We met, but Shawn used the time to beat me over the head with the fact that he's in charge instead of trying to convince me to do business with them."

"Shawn has always been a bully but needed backing to threaten even small children. He's an ass, but be careful. Royce is also a vindictive, sore loser, and losing your account will gut their business. Neither of them will take that lightly."

"There's that and Jake Kelly," she said, scrubbing her face with her palms. She always had too many problems and couldn't afford not to come up with some solutions.

"Who the hell is Jake Kelly?"

"He solicited my business, and he's pretty persistent. He says he's big in Atlanta and wants to expand into the South. Since he heard I'm the biggest buyer in this area, he's developed a crush."

"We've got business in Atlanta, and I've never heard of him. Of course all my buyers are like you in that we don't sell unless we knew your grandparents. We don't usually go after new and especially small stuff."

"Good to know, and I'm still digging into that. You heading back today?"

"I just got here, so I plan to enjoy myself for a few days before it's back to the grind. My lovely fiancée is with me, so how about a private dinner so you can meet her?"

"Do you mind if I make the arrangements and bring someone?"

Paul slapped the table before pointing at her. "Are you holding out on me?"

"I don't see any rings and ceremony in my future, but I did meet someone recently."

"Then I'd like to meet this woman. Please bring her, but dinner is on me after the obscene amount of money you just agreed to pay me."

"You'll have to arrive early so we can keep it private, but I'll have Merrick call you with the details."

Paul left with Lou, and she had a moment of doubt about having included Emma. It wasn't a trust issue, but she was concerned about how the relationship would change if Emma came with her.

"Success isn't built on cowardliness," she said as she picked up her phone.

❖

"Anything else?" Cain asked Merrick when she returned from walking Paul out.

"Danny's here to see you."

"Danny, as in my cousin Danny?" Everyone in her immediate family loved her mum more than life itself, but Therese's family, the Baxters, were a different story.

Alex and Robert Baxter were her mum's brothers, and Cain never could decide which of them was more useless. Her da held the same opinion but tolerated them because of his love for her mum. Dalton had even given them a monthly stipend and her cousin a job. Danny wasn't part of the *family* business and never would be, but he still earned a good living off the Casey coffers.

"That's the one. I left him out in the warehouse since your office is off-limits."

She didn't need to ask what he wanted since he always wanted the same thing. Danny had grown up watching mob movies, and considering his family connections, he wanted in the worst way to be a wise guy. However, he couldn't keep his mouth shut, and he was dumber than a pile of twigs.

"Cain." Danny stood and buttoned his too-tight stained jacket, then held his hand out to her. "Who was that guy? Is that something I could be helping you with?"

"That was no one important, and you already have a job."

Danny had inherited the Baxter red hair but was especially short and freckled, which pissed him off more than his non-wise-guy job.

"The gig at Emerald's is way beneath me, and you know it. I'm ready to move up and carry a gun. We're family, for God's sake."

"I gave you a job at Emerald's keeping an eye on my customers because you're my cousin. It's a job you get way overpaid for, but like I said, you're my cousin, so I do it to help you out. If you don't want that job, then find your own, but it's the only one I've got for you." She moved closer to him and stared him down until he stepped back.

"Don't you want someone that's related to you watching your back?"

"What do you mean by that?" Merrick asked.

"Careful, Danny, before Merrick shoots your hands off," she said and laughed, setting off his anger. "That'll blow your sex life all to hell."

He appeared mad enough to tell her to fuck off but seemed to think about it. "Uncle Dalton trusted me with stuff," he said so loudly that spit flew out of his mouth, landing on her chest.

"That's right. You drove Da for a few days, and the witnesses at the scene said you were hiding like a little bitch while my father was gunned down." She grabbed him by the jaw to keep him quiet. "You finally got that gun you were so hot to get for a few days, but you never fired a shot and could give not even one clue as to who killed him."

"That wasn't my fault, and there was nothing I could do to stop it. Even the cops said it was an ambush."

"Get out of here, Danny, and for once be happy with what you have. You keep bugging me, and I'm going to cut you out altogether, and you can take your father and uncle with you."

"They're your uncles too, Cain."

"I forget that sometimes, since I don't ever see or hear from them unless they need something. Hell, the only reason any of you came to my da's funeral was to make sure the tap of endless money you don't do anything for wasn't turned off at his death." She moved her hand down to his shoulder and squeezed hard. "The best thing you can do is to keep your head down and do your job. Stop trying to be something you're not, and stay as far from me as you can. Do we understand each other?"

Danny obviously tried his best not to appear intimidated, but the sweat beading on his upper lip gave him away. "Yeah. I understand."

"Good. Now get out of my sight and get ready for work."

She headed home and planned to spend the afternoon with Marie, since she hadn't had an extra few free hours in a few days. Therese was out playing bridge with her friends, so she found Marie on the back patio playing checkers with Billy.

"You'd better not have bet money, brother. She's really good," she said, kissing the tops of their heads.

"I already lost ten bucks," Billy said as Marie took two more of his pieces off the table.

"Look, Cain. I'm going to win again." Marie clapped her hands and jumped in her seat.

"You're a checkers shark," she said, sitting with them.

"What's a checkers shark?" Marie asked.

"It means you're really good at it," Billy said. "You all finished?" he asked Cain while he rubbed his jaw as if thinking hard about his next move.

"We're back in business, and I'm having dinner with him and his fiancée tonight." She groaned when Billy moved, opening a chain for Marie to take four more pieces. "You're going to lose another five dollars."

"Why?" he asked, then slapped his forehead when Marie didn't hesitate to go in for the kill. "Man. I didn't see that."

"It's 'cause I'm a checkers shark, brother," Marie said, and laughed when Cain did.

"You sure are, and you're taking all my money." Billy handed over another five dollars. "You want me to go with you tonight?" he asked as Marie set up the board again.

"You're welcome, but I have a date."

"Are you taking your friend Emma?" Marie asked, clapping again after making her first move.

"That's who's going with me." She winked at Billy. "Do you have enough for the doll you wanted?"

"I got this much." Marie held up her money.

"You need a little more than that, so you know what that means?" she said, holding up two fingers.

"Double or nothing, brother," Marie yelled. They'd both taught Marie that phrase years before, and she'd never forgotten it. Gambling on checkers was how she got most of the toys and art supplies she wanted, and it made her happy to win and have her own spending money.

"You're killing me, but I'm winning this one," Billy said, moving the first piece he was about to sacrifice.

"Not against the shark," Marie said, holding up his black checker.

"Let's hope we all score this big tonight," Billy said with a big smile.

"If that's your goal, then stay away from nice girls from Wisconsin."

Chapter Fourteen

"Wow," Cain said when Emma opened her door. She'd been a wreck wondering what to wear until Bea showed up with a few choices from her closet. She'd gone with the simple black dress that stopped right above her knee but was tight enough to make her look good.

"Are you sure this is okay?" She smoothed the dress down for the hundredth time. Her heels were new too, but she didn't think Cain would mind if she hung on to her all night.

"You're beautiful," Cain said, holding her hands out and staring intently at her. "I mean really beautiful."

"Thank you. If this is a business thing, I didn't want to look like a dork." She picked up her lipstick and held it up. "Would you mind putting this in your jacket pocket? I don't have a purse that matches this outfit."

"I'd be happy to, and don't worry so much. Paul is an old college friend and is in town with his fiancée. Billy might join us as well, so be prepared for whoever his date is. I'll make it up to you later." Cain locked her door and pocketed her keys.

"What's that mean?" She held on to Cain's arm, glad she was taking the stairs slowly.

"I love my brother, but he doesn't exactly love a challenge when it comes to dating." Cain got the door for her and opened the umbrella she'd left right outside. The weather had been rough for the last hour, but the rain was starting to slack off.

"And do you like a challenge, Ms. Casey?" she asked right before Cain shut the car door.

"I'm beginning to see the merits of the long-term dating plan. You're a good convincer, Ms. Verde."

"I'm not sure about that. You didn't even kiss me hello." She sat in the circle of Cain's arms, enjoying the flirting and the fact that Cain didn't mind their pace.

Cain kissed right below her ear and took her hand. "I didn't want to mess up that perfect makeup job. Later on, though, if you let me, all bets are off."

"I believe I handed you my lipstick, so you should've taken the chance." Emma scratched Cain's stomach through her shirt, but before she could kiss her, the car stopped. "You missed your shot."

Cain kissed the side of her neck again and raised her hand so she could kiss her palm. When she glanced outside, they were at a traffic light and hadn't reached their destination yet, so their fun wasn't over. "I don't think anyone has ever said that about me, but it's early. I'm sure I'll get another opportunity." Cain moved to her lips but kept the kiss light.

"I think you're right."

The restaurant Cain had taken her to before was fairly near work, and when they stepped out, the van right behind them slowed and parked across the street. "Friends of yours?" She figured it was simply some of the people Cain usually traveled with.

"Remember the guy in the courtyard at the B and B?" She nodded, thinking of who Cain had said the guy was with. "It's more friends of his than mine. We're just having dinner so nothing to worry about. The last time I checked that wasn't illegal."

It was strange to be such a center of attention, but all that mattered to her was that she was on Cain's arm. Cain introduced her to everyone who stopped to talk to her, and she smiled when Billy gave her a hug as he said hello. Like Cain had said, his date seemed somewhat bored and aloof, but her dress didn't leave much to guess as to what was underneath.

"Cain…Billy," an older man said as he put an arm around them. "Welcome. Especially when you come with such beautiful company."

"Vincent, the good thing about you is you never change," Cain said, kissing his cheek. "Emma, you remember Vincent Carlotti, even if I was remiss in introducing him before. He's one of our oldest family friends." She smiled when Vincent kissed both Emma's cheeks.

"Good to have you come by again, Emma, and hopefully you'll become a regular," Vincent said.

"Maybe you should put in a good word for me then, Mr. Carlotti."

"Please, call me Vincent. Let me pretend to be a young man for a little while longer." Vincent led them to a private room where a big man stood by the door as if guarding it. She'd never seen him with Cain, so she figured he worked for Vincent. Old family friend probably also meant old business acquaintance as well. The couple inside broke their kiss when they walked in, and Emma felt almost like an intruder. Cain's old college friend and his girlfriend were a lovely couple.

"Paul, this is Emma Verde," Cain said, holding her hand. It was the last formal thing that happened that night, and Emma enjoyed some of the stories Paul told of his time at Tulane with Cain.

His fiancée seemed to hang on his every word, but she didn't appear to be a pushover. Daphne Sinclair was the heir to a whiskey empire she was helping her father run, but she also seemed to be very much in love.

"What brought you to Tulane from Canada, Paul?" Emma asked as the waiters cleared their entre dishes.

"My mother's from here, and after a lifetime of stories about New Orleans, I wanted to come experience the place she loves so much for myself. It was a good decision since I made some lifetime friends along the way. Cain and Billy are old classmates I might not see often, but they're like family."

"She's easy to like. You have my total agreement on that," she said as Cain kissed her hand.

"Before Vincent's wonderful dessert, Daphne has a gift for you, Cain," Paul said.

"Paul told me how much you love a good whiskey every so often, so I brought you and Billy a case of our reserve. It's not your beloved Irish brew, but we're pretty proud of it." Daphne handed over a bottle from the wooden crate with her family's crest burned into the side.

"It's bad luck not to share," Cain said, cracking the seal. The waiter immediately brought everyone a glass. "To good friends and new beginnings."

They left first after dessert with Billy and his date, but like Cain had promised, they drove off alone to a lounge in the large hotel by the river. The band played soft jazz, and the hostess gave them a secluded table in the corner. Once they were by themselves, Cain ordered a bottle of wine and took her hand.

"I think you're a closet romantic," she said, tracing Cain's eyebrows with her fingertips and enjoying the way Cain closed her eyes, seeming completely relaxed. "You may not show it to many people, but I'm sure enjoying the attention."

"I probably have a reputation, but it isn't for being a romantic,"

Cain said after she'd dropped her hand. "Are you sure none of this bothers you even a little?"

"It sounds like you want it to." She leaned in and kissed Cain on the lips, then on each eyelid. "All I want is to spend time with you. The rest of it, like these people following you around, isn't any different than all that crap I come with."

"You should give lessons in optimism. I don't think our situations are anything alike, but thanks for trying." Cain didn't seem to be able to help herself as she kissed her again.

"Is it a matter of trust? Do you think I'm trying to put something over on you?" She moved slightly away, never really considering that possibility, but then Cain probably wouldn't think of anything but that with any new person in her life.

"I usually live by the rule that anyone who asks me that is trying to get something on me."

Emma moved a little farther away, but Cain held her so she couldn't go too far. "You really think that of me?"

"Concentrate on the word 'usual' and the fact that every rule has an exception. I don't think you're trying to get anything on me, but I don't want to pull you into anything you're not ready for."

She shook her head and smiled. "Remember when I said how romantic you were?" Cain nodded and chuckled. "You're losing points fast."

"Then let me try to make it up to you." Cain stood up and extended her hand to her. "Dance with me."

She put her hands on Cain's shoulders and moved with her, willing to go wherever Cain led.

They ended up dancing more than once, and Emma enjoyed every moment of their night. Since dating had never been part of her life back home, she was glad Cain didn't mind indulging this particular part of what she'd dreamed a relationship should be. She'd never understood her mother's thoughts on the subject, because without the freedom to see someone she might eventually come to love, she wouldn't have a chance to marry and settle down. Then again, her mother probably had planned to pick someone for her who was as Christian and devoted as she was.

"You okay?" Cain asked as they made their way back to her apartment.

"I'm fine. Just thinking of how I can talk you into something tomorrow."

"So all that quiet was you plotting, huh?" Cain turned in her seat slightly, so Emma moved closer to her and put her hand on her abdomen. "That shouldn't be a difficult sell, and since I dragged you out tonight, it'll be just us tomorrow night."

"That means I'll be waiting for hours." The sight of her street was somewhat depressing, but it was getting late, and classes in the morning would be a challenge with so little sleep.

"You'll survive, and I also promise not to keep you out this late," Cain said like she had insight into her thoughts.

Cain walked her upstairs and kissed her in the hallway close to her door. Her body was flushed and hot when Cain's tongue entered her mouth and her hands squeezed her butt. The sensation of wanting to rub herself against Cain was new and different, but she couldn't help herself. Cain must've noticed because she squeezed harder, making her moan, so she broke the kiss to regain some control over herself.

"Thanks for tonight," she said, glad that Cain took the subtle hint and let up.

"I'll see you tomorrow then." Cain's next kiss was gentle before she opened her door and waited until she'd locked it. This was harder than she thought, but her gut told her that giving in would be a mistake if she wanted a future with Cain that lasted longer than a couple of weeks.

"I want her to see me, but hell if I don't want her to strip me bare and touch me too," she said aloud, putting her hands over her rock-hard nipples. "Patience and virtue totally suck."

CHAPTER FIFTEEN

Annabel Hicks decided to arrive an hour early so she could sit in on Barney Kyle's briefing with his team. The ambitious agent Washington had saddled her with thought he could get away with not including her by scheduling his meetings with his handpicked team either extremely early or after hours. He must've thought she was a strictly nine-to-five law-enforcement kind of agent.

"Let's get down to it," Barney said, coming in without really looking up at anyone. He had a thick folder under his arm, so maybe after all the expense of constantly watching Casey, he finally had discovered something. "Did anyone get anything after Casey went home last night?"

"The house went dark, and the team on Billy said he stayed put with the woman he was with," Agent North said as he put more photos on the board.

"Who's the girl Casey's been after for days now?" Kyle tapped the blonde's picture before taking it down.

"We pulled her file from Tulane, sir," one of the young women in the room said. "Her name is Emma Verde. She's an English major from Wisconsin and is working for Casey at her pub in the Quarter."

"That's it?" Barney said, barking at the woman.

"All we could piece together was she's starting her senior year and lost her campus job. It was simply luck that landed her at the pub, but she seems to have only wanted a job."

"So you're saying she's not some cleverly disguised assassin Casey hired who also happens to like poetry?" Annabel asked, making Barney whip his head in her direction.

"No, ma'am," the woman said as a smattering of laughter circulated around the room.

"If you all would put together what you have so far, I'd appreciate it." The agents took her not-so-subtle hint and cleared the room. "From what I can see so far, you've got the makings of a good scrapbook for the lovely new couple," she said as she took down a picture of Cain and Emma holding hands. "The stepped-up surveillance doesn't seem to be having quite the effect you anticipated, does it?"

"You can't think it would just take a week." He laughed and tossed the photo into the trash when she handed it back.

"No. Good investigative work revolves around a team working together to build a solid case one brick at a time. That has been my experience, and it's gotten me plenty of convictions in my career. That is, after all, the goal of what we do."

"Are you saying you don't agree with my methods?"

"It's too early to see if they will bear fruit, Agent Kyle, but I'm not especially optimistic."

He took the kind of deep breath that telegraphed how pissed he was that she was questioning him and his work. Barney Kyle was a typical alpha male agent the FBI produced like IHOP produced pancakes, but she hadn't climbed this high by letting men like Kyle bother her.

"Then why are you here, Annabel?"

"Agent Kyle, if I need to remind you that I'm not some starstruck flunky here to fetch your coffee, then you might find yourself trying to make cases in the middle of the bush in Alaska. You will give me the respect I'm due, even if you have to hold your nose while you're doing it. Is that clear?" He nodded, but the smug smile was enough to make her want to drive his nose toward his left ear and then reassign him. "Before you pat yourself on the back for thinking you've gotten to me, know that I have your transfer order at the top of my stack on my desk."

"I hate to argue with you, *Agent Hicks*." He said her name with the same contempt she reserved for the people they apprehended. "But I'm not going anywhere. I was sent down here to try to curb the problem you've let go way too long."

The insubordination was stunning, but Kyle knew he had the support of her deputy director. "I'm sure you believe that, but shall we review? Let's begin with the towing of one of our vans, losing the subject in a very public park practically empty at the time, and having the same subject mock you every chance she gets. From my perspective, your surveillance sounds humorous and amateurish, and will go over like a comedy with your good buddies that sent you here."

Her threat seemed to hit its mark when he lost his bravado and went on the offensive immediately. "You know the van was a rookie mistake, with one of your guys along for the ride."

"Agent Kyle, you have a short period of time to prove yourself, or you move on. If all you have to show, let's say in two months, is how well Casey romances someone she's interested in, then this isn't going to work out. To me it's not worth the expense."

"So it's all about the money?" He laughed as if she'd given him back the upper hand. "If you decide to remove me from my post, I'll make sure that motive is included in the report as well."

"It'll be twenty-four-hour surveillance with someone else in command. Money isn't my motivation—results are—and from what I see here, you're far from achieving any of those. My suggestion is to clear the board and start over."

"And then will you leave us alone to do our jobs?"

"Then I'll continue to sit in to see if you get anywhere or if you need help clearing out your desk."

❖

Emma stopped with the rest of the crowd at a barricade they'd set up at Tulane.

"It should be clear by tomorrow, but they've shut the campus down for the day," a security guard told them.

"What happened?" Emma asked since she was the closest to him.

"A classroom was destroyed last night, and the fire department's trying to figure out what caused the blaze. They don't want to chance it happening again with students in the building."

Since she had the day off, she called the house number Cain had given her, guessing it was early enough that she'd catch her before she left for work. "I'm sorry, Miss, but Ms. Cain is at the office already."

"Do you think she'd mind if you gave me the address?" The Hispanic-sounding woman told her without any more prompting, so she started walking. St. Charles Avenue was the best place to hail a cab to save herself the at-least-two-mile walk.

The driver stopped in front of the warehouse with no signage in front, but when she spotted the man patrolling the roof with a rifle in his hands, she knew she was in the right place. She wasn't sure why Cain needed constant protection, but Cain didn't seem the type to answer that kind of question, so it would remain a mystery for another day. The large man at the gate stopped her, but when she gave him her name he let her right in.

When she spotted Lou at the large entrance, she waved and walked a little faster. Seeing a familiar face settled her nerves somewhat, since the only times she'd seen Cain was on Cain's terms. In her mind, this was a test.

"Hey, Emma. The boss didn't mention you were coming by," Lou said, taking her bag like Cain did every time she saw her with it.

"She's not expecting me, but I have a rare day off so I thought I'd surprise her. Do you think that's a bad idea?"

"Do you honestly think that'll be a bad idea?" he said, leading the way inside. "She's right through here."

After the façade of the old brick building, Emma didn't expect the posh office. Cain sat behind a large wooden desk with carved panels along the front. When she moved closer, she noticed the carvings were of small harps. The rest of the room contained dark wooden paneling, nice paintings, and a series of family photos on the shelves against one wall. The space almost appeared out of place, like it belonged in a grand home instead of here.

"Muriel, let me call you back," Cain said when she turned and noticed her. "Hey. You're a good surprise."

"Do you like surprises?" She suddenly felt like the room wasn't the only thing out of place.

"If it's a guy holding a subpoena, then no. But I can get used to having you come by." Cain stood and circled the desk to hug her. "You aren't playing hooky, are you?"

"There was a fire…maybe this wasn't a good idea. I shouldn't bother you at work." It was probably silly, but it suddenly occurred to her that Cain was way out of her league. The clothes, the guards, the fancy office were all signs of money and privilege she had no clue about.

"Hey," Cain said, not letting her go when she pulled back. "What's wrong?"

Of all the times for her not to be able to control her tears. "Nothing. I just think I'm bothering you, and I didn't mean to."

"Darling girl, you're not bothering me, and that would be true even if I was in the middle of a meeting with God himself."

"I'm sorry." The tears flowed faster, and now she came closer and buried her face in Cain's chest. The starch of her shirt felt stiff and rough against her cheek.

"Emma, you're going to have to explain, but from where I'm standing, you don't have anything to apologize for."

"You probably think I'm some kind of nutcase." She followed Cain when she walked to the room next door with a long, beautiful conference table. One wall was dominated by an antique map of Ireland and the other by a bar.

"How about you start from the beginning," Cain said, helping her into a chair so she could sit next to her. "First off, are you okay?"

She told Cain about the fire and her day off. "I thought I'd come by and see you."

"And the sight of me made you burst into tears?"

"No," she said, and her brain seemed to freeze. No words were coming to explain what she was feeling. "You keep telling me what a bad idea it is to be with you, and seeing this place makes me wonder if it's because we're so different."

"It's not that I don't want you in my life, but I'm trying to save you from the bad parts of it. We are who we are, Emma, and changing something that's an important part of who we are to make someone else happy doesn't work." Cain caressed her face and smiled.

"Maybe I don't want to be saved, but it doesn't mean I belong with you either."

"So this is a visit to say good-bye?"

"You want me to be safe, and I want to be something better for you. I think you deserve someone you can be proud of."

"What happened to you, lass?" Cain asked, holding both her hands.

The question was like a sharp rake that ripped through her heart. She was tired of not being enough. "It's a long story and really not your problem."

"It can be, but I won't force you to share it with me if you're not ready."

She nodded, grateful Cain had given her an out, but to give up now meant losing her place with Cain. "So what does that leave us with?"

"One afternoon to see if there's something about each other that's worth knowing." Cain stood and pulled her to her feet. "So you have the whole day off?" She nodded again, glad for the contact. "Spend the day with me then."

"I'm not keeping you from anything?"

"The world can wait, but my curiosity can't."

Cain took her jacket out of her office and stopped to talk to the attractive African American woman who seemed to always be around. Whatever she said didn't make the woman happy, but Cain didn't appear upset.

Cain held her hand out and smiled. "You ready?"

"Lead the way."

They left with Cain driving, but they weren't alone. From her count at least three vehicles were following them. The attention didn't seem to faze Cain, so it must've been so engrained in the fabric of who she was it was a given, like having blue eyes. However, she couldn't take her eyes off the company behind them.

"Can I ask you something?" she said, still staring at the side mirror.

"Your friend Beatrice was mostly right."

"Excuse me? What do you mean by that?"

Cain glanced at her and winked. "No one outside my family really knows me, Emma. The rumors and stories are always funny and fantastically overblown, but they're simply that—stories."

"Is that why they follow you around?" From all the movies she'd ever seen, the federal government never followed without just cause.

"They follow me because they think I'm the head of a vast criminal empire."

She laughed at Cain's almost casual answer. "Do you run a criminal empire?"

"That's sort of like asking me my weight and age. From what I hear, it's just not done," Cain said and winked again. "So let's stick to other subjects for now."

"And later?"

"Later isn't something I worry too much about."

They stopped at an old cemetery with a large stucco wall around it. "We're going in?"

"If you want to take those baby steps, then yes. We're going in."

Cain opened her door, and they walked along the broken and cracked pavement until they reached a tomb with the name "Casey" written across the top in marble. The flowers were fresh, and the bench in front was free of leaves and moss.

"Is this where your father's buried?"

"Quite a few generations are in there, but he's the most recent to find his eternal rest here. That's what his good friend the bishop tells me anyway. If you notice the space around it, my family is good at planning for the future. They figured we'd need to expand eventually, and that's how we plan our business as well. Nothing is left to chance."

"Hopefully you won't have to expand here for a long time," she said, not really knowing why they were here.

"Hopefully not," Cain said, then sighed. "But for today, I wanted you to meet the greatest man I ever knew. He was also my teacher, my best friend, and my safety net. You always feel invincible when you know you have someone there to catch you no matter what."

"He sounds like a wonderful man. I'm really sorry for your loss."

"True, but that's not why we're here." Cain took a deep breath and put her arm around her. "My father was the alleged head of our alleged criminal empire. He traveled with that entourage you were looking at, and even with that, someone gunned him down and killed him."

"That explains why you have all the interesting people around."

"No. That explains what I'm trying to protect you from. Some scum got to him even with the interesting people."

"So you really do want me to go?"

"I want you to listen to me and then make up your mind. My family comes with a certain warning label, I guess. I don't let people in easily, not because I'm suspicious, but because of things like this." Cain pointed to the tomb.

"My father's family came from France two generations ago to farm here. He makes his own cheese and butter, and he believes in tradition. He married my mother, and some or all of that gave way to her need to be a good Christian."

"They did something right," Cain said, pulling her closer. "They made one perfect child."

"One is exactly what they had, but I'm far from perfect." She rested her head on Cain's shoulder and stared at the name on the tomb. "Maybe we belong together so we can heal those parts of ourselves that'll fester if we're alone."

"Are you sure? If you get any more into my head, I might not be able to let you go so easily."

"You'll come to see that you won't be able to let me go because, more than anything, I don't want you to."

❖

"Everything is quiet," Oliver said when Billy stopped at Mendel's, walking through the back. "I got Pops sitting on the corner as our first line of defense. Ma appreciates him being out of the house for a couple of days."

"How's Pops?" Billy asked, remembering one of his da's favorite crewmen that even Dalton called Pops. Pops had helped build their network in the neighborhoods behind the French Quarter.

"Pops never changes much. He's enjoying retirement and spends most of his days tending his garden and lecturing me on how to act at work."

"Da was a good one for that too, so I completely understand." This was his fifth stop of the day with nothing to show for it, so he was starting to get frustrated. "Keep watching, and call if there's a change."

"Will do, and Mendel mentioned a few folks talking about what happened to Big Chief. There's gossip and some worry about that, so I thought you'd want to know."

"Thanks, and let me know if someone's really interested in that situation."

"That fat bastard had it coming, but I'll pay attention to anyone too curious."

"Where to, Boss?" Ian Evers asked Billy when he got back into the car.

"Let's head to the office and regroup. Maybe Cain will let us bust some heads to get some action going."

He glanced in the side mirror and noticed the black sedan two cars behind them. If they were tailing him, there was another car somewhere else, since he hadn't seen this one behind Mendel's place. "This is going to get old real fast."

"Yeah. We noticed the other guy while you were talking to Oliver. We got to work something out if we need to do business without an audience," Ian said.

"Slow down," Billy said, resting his head back but still keeping watch. The car behind them blew their horn a couple of times, then passed them. "Start going through some lights and see what happens."

"I think they'll go through them with us to keep up, Boss," Ian said, laughing a little with Gabriel in the backseat.

"I know that, smartass. I just want them to know I know they're back there wasting my time and theirs. Put your seat belt on, Gabriel. You're going to make a nice hood ornament if you don't and this goes bad."

They went another mile before Ian hit a yellow light, and like he'd told Billy, the car behind them kept pace. Billy's plan didn't quite work out when they had to slam on their brakes or risk hitting an elderly man ready to step off the curb. Ian stopped in time, but their tail's reaction wasn't as great. He slammed into them with enough force that they landed in the middle of the intersection. By some miracle, they missed the old guy.

"Come on, man," a guy that ran from the other side of the street screamed as he banged on Billy's window. "You got to get out before this shit blows up."

Billy was dazed from hitting his head on the side window, and Ian was unconscious from slamming his head into the steering wheel, Billy guessed from the way it was bent. He fumbled with the door handle, and the people that had gathered to help unlocked the door and got all three of them out.

"Call 9-1-1," Billy said before he passed out with a smile for the agent standing behind the good Samaritan who'd helped him.

The guy Billy spoke to got his phone out and did as he asked, then told his friend to make sure the two guys who'd caused the accident didn't leave. The man behind him seemed rooted in place, appearing anxious as he looked at the two guys passed out well away from the car that was now on fire.

"Tell Cain to get here fast," Gabriel said, trying not to cry from what felt like a broken ankle. The pain, though, was making him nauseous. Cain's assistant, Mrs. Michaels, took the information but kept him on the line.

"What happened?" Mrs. Michaels asked.

Gabriel told her about stopping so they wouldn't hit the man loud enough for everyone around to hear. He figured the explanation would go a long way in convincing all the witnesses standing around to remember the same thing.

"Sit tight, and I'll have Mrs. Casey meet you wherever they take you. Make sure you have someone call us with that information."

"Yes, ma'am." Gabriel heard the sirens coming closer, and he tried to overhear what the guy in the gray suit was saying. He appeared nervous, but the older guy with him seemed woozy from the large cut across his forehead.

He grimaced when they loaded him, and he glanced back at Ian and Billy. They were both still out, and the paramedics were carefully loading them on backboards. Another car screeched to a stop close by, and he saw Muriel and two guys get out and move past the police.

"You okay?" Muriel asked, but her attention was on her cousin.

"I was in the back so I think my ankle or foot is broken, but I'm better than Billy and Ian. Make sure those assholes don't get out of this because they're feds," he said so only Muriel would hear him.

"Don't worry, and I'll call your family and have them meet you at the hospital." Muriel patted his chest and moved so they could load him. "And, Gabriel," she said from the back of the ambulance, "you don't talk to anyone about anything unless I'm there. Remember that."

"Got it. Stay and make sure Billy's okay. He and Ian are pretty banged up. It's almost like they were gunning for us," he said, almost yelling this time.

"That's a lie," the young guy that hit them said.

"Fuck you, man. You were following way too close, and you never stopped." He smiled when they closed the doors after that remark, and the crowd that had gathered started saying "yeah" as if they agreed with him.

Fuck you and everyone with you. Cain's going to make you pay if anything happened to her brother, and I'm going to love watching her take you down, asshole, he thought before he closed his eyes for the bumpy ride to the hospital.

❖

Cain sat on the blanket Lou had gotten out of the trunk for her and gazed out at Lake Pontchartrain, enjoying the warmth on her bare feet. Emma had read most of her classwork after the sandwiches they'd stopped for and, after twenty pages or so, had fallen asleep with her head in Cain's lap.

She had a huge list of things to do but couldn't find the motivation to get up. Their talk after the cemetery had centered on basically nothing important. She now knew some of Emma's history and took a moment to thank God that Therese Casey, not Carol Verde, was her mother.

She turned her head slightly when she heard someone running toward them. If it was a problem, Merrick and Lou were close enough to take care of it so she didn't disturb Emma. She stopped breathing though, when Merrick stopped by her, appearing almost panicked. The last time Merrick had that dreadful expression she'd told her someone had killed her da.

"What?" she asked, finally exhaling.

"Billy's been in a car accident, and he's at the hospital with Ian and Gabriel."

"What the hell happened?" She threaded her fingers into Emma's hair and gently scratched the back of her neck to rouse her.

"From what Muriel said, the agents following them came close to killing all three of them when they rear-ended them. Your mom is on her way to Mercy, so I told her we wouldn't be far behind." Merrick exposed her weapons as if she'd need them and turned toward the panel van most likely watching and listening. "These guys are out of control."

"What's wrong?" Emma asked, coming to a sitting position quickly.

"My brother's been in an accident, so I've got to go. I'll have Lou take you back." She put her shoes back on and stood up. "I'll call you later."

"Do you want me to come with you?" Emma put her hands on Cain's abdomen, seeming genuinely concerned.

"I appreciate it, but let me see what this is about. You'll be okay with Lou."

Emma tried again. "I could help."

"I know you would, but not this time." She kissed Emma and walked away, resisting the urge to run. She'd learned the lesson of sudden loss well, and it was still too fresh in not only her mind but also in her heart not to want to rush to Billy's side.

Lou nodded as she passed him, and she didn't look back as Merrick sped away. When they arrived, all of Billy's guys were in the emergency-room waiting area, and they pointed her in the right direction. Her relief was so complete when they said Billy was awake and talking, she almost had to sit before going back.

"Hey," she said to Billy when she walked into the small room that smelled of antiseptic and bleach. "Did you piss those guys off or something?"

"Yeah, but too bad for them I've got a head too hard for them to do any real damage. I'm okay, really," he said, obviously seeing the worry in her expression.

"Don't go tempting fate," Therese said, making Marie laugh. "He's got a concussion and they fractured his arm."

She hugged her mum after hearing the clear upset in her voice. "Muriel's taking care of it, Mum."

"This once I'd like for you to be taking care of it, but I know you can't."

"I wish I could grant that wish, but that would be inviting the jackals in to pick us clean." She kissed Therese's cheek before doing the same to Marie and asked Billy, "Can you go home?"

"The doctor said maybe tomorrow, but they want to make sure I didn't get my brains scrambled before they let me loose on the world." Billy lifted his good hand but didn't touch his head. "Sorry for all the worry, sister."

"It's my job to worry even on days when you're not getting your car blown up. I'm just glad everything that happened is fixable." She sat on the bed and placed her hand at the center of his chest. "Concentrate on getting better, and I'll handle the rest."

His eyes grew glassy at what she'd said, and he shook his head as he covered her hand with his. "I love you too, but could you check on Ian and Gabriel for me? They won't let me up to do it."

"Mum, send Merrick if they come to move him. I'll be right back."

Ian was still knocked out from bashing his head into the steering wheel, so Cain spoke to his parents to assure them she'd taken care of everything. Pops clung to her when she opened her arms to him, much like she had when her da had died. Gabriel's family was there as well, but they were waiting for him to get out of emergency surgery to reset the bones in his ankle and foot.

Whatever the hell had happened was serious enough to sideline two of her guys and Billy, since, no matter how much he complained, he wasn't going back to work until a slew of doctors agreed to it. She was headed back to Billy's room when Merrick stopped her and pointed to an empty room.

"Muriel just called again and said the field director of the FBI is headed over here to talk to you. She said to please wait until she gets here."

"Where's Muriel?" She put her hands in her pockets and tried to calm her anger. Her da always said anger and giving in to it was the best way of losing control, then losing everything.

"She said she stayed behind to encourage the NOPD to not let all the FBI credentials being flashed around at the scene intimidate them. They have enough witnesses to point out who was at fault, starting with the old man Ian stopped to avoid hitting."

"Then why the visit to the hospital?"

"Muriel didn't want to talk about it, but I'm sure she'll tell you when she gets here."

They were ready to move Billy when she returned, so she helped her mum and Marie gather his things and follow the gurney to his room. "Make sure someone's always on this door until he goes home," she told Merrick as they moved Billy to the bed. "Let me know if anyone gives you any shit about it."

"You got it, Boss."

Billy closed his eyes, but he was smiling as Therese and Marie sat with him and prayed. The nurse came in often and asked him a series of questions, so he wouldn't get any sleep until they were sure his head was fine.

"You're still beautiful, so you have that going for you," Muriel said when she came in, making Billy laugh.

"Don't tease me. I've got a splitting headache," Billy said, opening only one eye.

"Then I'll talk about you outside." Cain followed her out, and Merrick led them to the empty room across from them. "From what Kevin said, they were thinking about running the light to mess with those guys, but they stopped to avoid killing the old man I talked to at the scene. The next thing they knew they were all being dragged out by helpful citizens because the agents hit them hard enough to rupture their gas tank. The agents tried to get out of it, but the traffic cop cited the driver, so Annabel Hicks would like to talk to you."

"About what? Does she want to exchange insurance cards?"

"She didn't say, and I can't force you to stay quiet, but it's not a good time to antagonize her or anyone that works for her."

She nodded and stepped to the window. "And everything else?"

"It's fine," Muriel said cryptically, as if the room were bugged, and there was a good possibility it was. "Believe me, it's fine."

"Then let's go see Annabel and hear what she's got on her mind."

Three men were standing with Agent Hicks when they entered the hospital-floor waiting room, but Cain barely glanced at them. Annabel held out her hand, and Cain didn't hesitate to take it, deciding to follow Muriel's advice. The man directly to Annabel's right seemed to study her like a bug on a slide, but it wasn't time to acknowledge him yet.

"Ms. Casey, I'm Special Agent Annabel Hicks," the woman said as she released her hand.

"I didn't realize your agency investigated traffic accidents, Special Agent Hicks." Muriel sighed but she was smiling.

"I'm sure Ms. Casey here informed you that two of my agents rear-ended the car your people were in. It was an accident, pure and simple, that our agent takes full responsibility for. We'll handle all the medical expenses, and the damage to the car, but I'm here to assure you it was simply an accident."

She couldn't help but stare at the man now smirking as his boss put her ass in the fire. "Is that your opinion, Special Agent—"

"Kyle, Barney Kyle, and yes—just an accident."

"You've both done your job then, so you're free to go," Cain said, now sure who was across the street from her office, her home, and life in general watching and listening. "Accidents happen, right?"

"Is that a threat, Ms. Casey?" Barney asked.

"No, it's a group of people minding their own business on their way to work almost getting killed in *an accident*. Not everything's a conspiracy, right?"

"Sounded like a threat to me," Barney said.

"Agent Hicks, forget about my family, and concentrate on whether everyone who works for you has had all their shots."

"What's that supposed to mean?" Barney said, taking a step forward, Annabel holding onto him to keep him from getting closer.

Cain stepped forward one pace. "From what I hear, rabies rots the brain," she said, and his face got cherry red. "That's not good for anyone with a badge and a gun."

"Ms. Casey, simply remember that we'll take care of the costs of the accident, and we won't bother you again while your brother recovers," Annabel said, forcibly pulling Barney back. "Call if there's any problem."

"All I'm asking is for you to stay away from my family so something like this doesn't happen again."

Barney jerked away from Annabel and stood extremely close to Cain. "We have a job to do, so you're in no position to request anything."

"Everyone has a job to do, extra Special Agent Kyle, but no one else's job description lets them get away with almost killing three people. You want to do your job, do it like everyone else before you— stay across the street."

"Don't fucking—" Barney said before Muriel stepped into the limited space between him and Cain.

"Agent Hicks, it's time for you to go, and anything else you want to add to this conversation can go through me. Today might've been an accident, but there's more to consider than medical costs and a car. One of our employees is in surgery, and the other is still unconscious."

Muriel, like Cain, didn't seem the least bit intimidated by Barney Kyle. "Once they're able, I'm sure they'll have more demands than what you've offered."

"I'm sure we'll entertain any reasonable requests," Annabel said. "Excuse us for intruding."

"I'm sure it won't be the last time," Cain said, making Barney stop walking, but he didn't say a word when he turned around.

Let the games begin, extra Special Agent Kyle, she thought, smiling at him when he turned around again before leaving. *Whoever ends up with a bullet through the head first loses.*

"How is he?" Emma asked after answering Cain's call as she sat in her dark apartment. Lou had walked her to her door, and it had taken over an hour to recover from her anger at being sent away like a small child.

"He's in the hospital for the night with a fractured arm and a concussion. I'm more worried about the guy who was driving him. The doctors put him in a medically induced coma for a few days because of the swelling in his brain."

"I'm sorry, and hopefully he'll be okay. Will you let me know how Billy makes out?" The feeling of not fitting in with Cain came back full force, and she was sure she'd never break into the circle of Cain's family to have a real future with her. It was good to realize that now, before she cared any more than she already did.

"Am I keeping you from something?" Cain asked, and the noise from her end disappeared as if Cain had moved.

"No. I was sitting here trying to study and was thinking about you."

"Somehow I suspect that's not a good train of thought." Cain sounded tired and totally serious. "I'll leave you to it."

"So you get to decide or conclude what my thoughts are and move on?" She stared up at the ceiling, blinking rapidly to keep from crying. She was tired of crying and starting to see tears as one of her weaknesses. "Thank you for giving me the benefit of doubt."

"Today two FBI agents rammed the car my brother was in hard enough to hospitalize three men. Their only reason or suspicion for following them at all was that my brother was in the car. We're Caseys so we must be guilty." Cain shot off the words like she was firing them from a machine gun and each of them was meant to inflict harm. "I know this won't be the last time something like this happens, so I give no one any benefit of doubt."

"Not even someone who cares about you?" She couldn't stop her tears and cursed her inexperience with relationships. She'd been overwhelmed at having found something she'd searched a lifetime for and not known exactly how to handle it. Wanting something with Cain had gone way too fast, and she couldn't deny just how much she cared. Had she actually admitted it, she would have scared Cain off way before this.

"Don't say things you don't mean or understand."

"I never have in my life, and I'm not going to start now. You can push me away if you want, but don't try to lay the blame on me." She tried her best to keep the quiver out of her voice but was failing fast. "Your brother and his friends will be in my prayers," she said and hung up.

Cain called back a few times, but Emma couldn't handle any more hurt or rejection so she lay on the sofa and cried. Perhaps her mother was right, and God really had abandoned her for her disobedience.

The phone woke her the next morning, and the sound of cows mooing made her smile. "Hi, Daddy."

"Hey, sweetheart. I was calling to check on you," Ross Verde said, his voice always the definition of gentleness. "Your mama told me you two talked and you mentioned losing your job. Do you need me to send you some money?"

"I lost my spot, but I found something else, so don't worry about me." Her neck and back were stiff, so she got up to start a pot of coffee. "I really am, so don't make it hard on yourself, and you know exactly what I mean. Mama won't like it too much if you send me anything."

"Your mother just worries about you," he said, and Emma wondered if he truly believed that. "But anyway, what are you doing now?"

"I got a waitressing job with good hours and pay. Actually, I'm making more now, so I don't have to put in as much time as I did at the bookstore. The owner's really nice too." Everything she'd said was technically true, but she saw no reason to spur her mother south to hogtie her and drag her home by admitting she worked in a bar. The only part she cared about anyway was the last part, but the conversation from the night before meant Cain was probably a memory, or soon would be.

"What's his name?"

"Her name is Cain Casey, and she graduated from Tulane too."

Ross stayed quiet, as if waiting for more of the story, but that's all she was willing to give up. "It's good you're making friends," he said, as if fishing for something to keep their conversation going. "Are you okay? You sound kind of down."

"Just tired from studying all night. Have you gone by Jerry and Maddie's place? She said they had a good birthing season." It was a blatant change of subject, but she wanted to stop any questions about Cain.

"We both lucked out this year, and Jerry was a big help with some of my stubborn ones. He and Maddie still seem to be in that honeymoon stage, so I'm happy he found the time for me."

"She sounds happy whenever we talk, so that's good." She glanced at her small kitchen clock and grimaced. She'd already missed one class and was about to be late for another one. "I hate to cut this short, Daddy, but I have to get going."

"I love you, Emma, so have a good day."

She put the phone down and covered her face with her hands. "I doubt I'll have any good days for a while, Daddy."

Chapter Sixteen

Jonsie Belson walked across campus trying to find his car and nursing a massive hangover from a bender that had stopped early that morning. He'd gotten plastered at home since his state-senator father, Jonas, demanded he stay put until he could smooth things over with that fucking bitch Cain Casey. Now, he was pissed he hadn't stood up to her. She wouldn't have touched him if she realized how much shit his father could bring down on her head. Granted, they knew each other, but she didn't have any experience with Jonas Belson's bad side.

"Hey, Marty," he said, answering his phone. Martin "Marty" Williamson III hadn't come to school after getting his nose broken, but at least his mother's plastic surgeon had promised he'd look the same or slightly better once the swelling went down. "What's up?"

"I'm fucking going nuts looking at the walls all day, and my dad could give a shit that I ran out of pain meds." Marty sounded whiny and nasal.

"You want some weed or something to take the edge off?" He found his car and pulled away from the curb, not caring about his afternoon classes or his father's orders to come straight home. "I have some of that good shit we scored last week."

"Fuck yeah, and hurry. I've got something to talk to you about."

The Williamson estate, one of the largest on St. Charles Avenue, took up almost a whole city block. The lot was large enough for not only the grand main house, but a pool house and a mother-in-law apartment close to the back entrance. Marty had moved there the minute he'd graduated from high school, and his parents didn't mind since he was still close by.

Marty buzzed Jonsie in, and he'd brought his backpack in case he ran into Marty's dad. Getting caught with a bag of weed on the old man's property would get him banished for life. The generation before them seemed to have forgotten all the sins of their families now that they were in charge of the money.

"Come on, dude. We'll sit outside. My mom comes down a couple of times a day, and she'll freak if she smells weed."

They headed to a part of the yard that had high shrubs, a few old statues, and some wrought-iron chairs. "You look like shit, man." He lit up, inhaled deeply, and passed the joint to Marty.

Marty squinted his eyes and flipped him off. The entire part of his face around his eyes down to his cheeks was black, and a large bandage covered his nose. "Fuck you too. My head hurts so bad I can barely think, but I did have an interesting talk with this guy who was waiting to see the doctor yesterday. He had plenty to say about Casey."

"Who was it?" Jonsie didn't come from old money, so his old man had taught him plenty. Jonas loved telling stories about how he was from the streets, and they were only a misstep from landing back there.

"Some fucker who called himself Big Chief, and I talked to him after I eavesdropped on his phone call." Marty took a few more hits before he seemed ready to go on. "Casey double-crossed this dude, and he was working on something to take her out."

"Take her out? Like what, killing her?"

"Stop being such a douche and listen. What do you know about Casey? Your dad must've told you something." As Marty relaxed under the weed's influence, he started to sound less nasal.

"All my dad gave up was that she was a fucking bootlegger. Who the hell knew we still had those?" Jonsie accepted the joint back, took a long drag, and held it in. "Casey's family has made a fucking fortune with that shit though, and she's bulletproof because of all that money."

"What if someone cuts the deal she's about to before she does? According to Big Chief, she's shopping for a new supplier and found one, but they're still hammering out the details." Marty waved for the joint back and stopped talking for another hit. "Somebody pulls that off and all of a sudden Casey isn't so bulletproof."

"Who exactly are you thinking is dumb enough to do that?"

"You and me are going to set this up, and when it goes down, I'm going to fuck that bitch up for doing this to me."

Jonsie stared at Marty, trying to figure out if he was serious and if the blow to the face had knocked something loose that impaired his ability to think clearly. "How in the hell are we supposed to do that?

First off, the only criminal we know sells us weed. I take that back. The only other criminal we know fucked you up and got my father all worked up about something. Besides, deals like that cost big money. It's not like they're going to give it to you on credit."

"You want to hear this shit or not?" Marty flicked what little was left of the joint at him, and he came close to leaving.

"Okay. Spill it," he said, wanting to hear this grand plan.

"Big Chief asked me what I was there for, and when I told him, he asked if I wanted in on his action. Turns out, we were there for the same thing done by the same person."

"Wait. He was there because Cain Casey fucked him up?" No way could that even be possible. The chances of such a total coincidence were as close to impossible as every woman he'd ever found remotely hot but had shown absolutely no interest in him lining up to fuck him, and if Marty weren't so stoned, he'd see that.

"I'm telling you, I thought this old dude was fucking with me, but I believed him when he told me the whole story."

"So what's the deal?"

"If I put up seventy-five grand, he'll set us up. Since the guy Casey deals with knows her and probably won't deal with anyone but her, we tell him we work for her."

"Where the hell are you getting that kind of money?" he asked, hoping like shit Marty didn't plan to ask him for any.

"From my trust, and for every dollar I put in, Big Chief says I get seven in return. Can you imagine? Fuck, we pull this off and I can tell my father to kiss it while I'm drinking beer on some beach." Marty laughed as if he were already retired and rich. "If we could pull off a few of Casey's runs before she figures it out, we're set."

"It's your money, man. You'll be set."

"No way, Jonsie. I put up seventy-five large, and you put up what you can and I lend you the rest. When I heard about this, you were my first and only call. You were the only one who stood up for me when that bitch sucker-punched me, so you're the only one I'm cutting in."

"You sure this fucker's on the up-and-up?" Easy money and a steady stream of it made him want in. All that could happen was Marty lost a little cash, but the upside was escaping two more years of Tulane and his father's constant bitching.

"He fucking hates Casey more than I do."

"I'm in. What do we have to do?" He slapped his hands together, ready to go.

❖

"Remember, total rest for at least the next week, and I'll see you then," the doctor said as he wrote in Billy's chart.

"When's this headache going to let up? And when can I take something for it?" Billy asked as he sat up slowly because of the pounding in his head.

"I wrote you a script for something mild, but if you take it easy, you should be fine in a day or two. If it doesn't get better in about three days, call me."

"Not to worry. We'll take good care of him," Cain said, helping him put his shoes on.

"Thanks, Doc," he said, and stood up with Cain's assistance to get into the wheelchair. "How's it going with my friend Ian?"

"I can't really talk about his case, but his family is in the ICU waiting area if you want to stop before you go. Let me know if you need anything."

Cain waved off the transporter and sat on the bed. "None of it is your fault, Billy."

"I know, but it still pissed me off. That bastard probably didn't even get a ticket." He closed his eyes and took a few deep breaths. The doctor really preferred that he stay another night, but he wanted out of here so Cain wouldn't be an easy target. "You want to push me over there so I can at least see Pops before we leave?"

Ian's family took up half the waiting room, and they were sharing trays of food from Vincent's with the other families waiting to see a patient. "I told Vincent to send stuff over until Ian's home," Cain said as Merrick opened the door for them.

Billy tried to ignore his head as they visited and was grateful when Cain cut it short. The ride home was slow, and he appreciated the smooth route Lou took, and after greeting Marie and their mum, Cain helped him upstairs. Therese followed them and closed the blinds to cut the late-afternoon glare, which he appreciated since his head still hurt like a bitch. The only light in the room was from the lamp by the leather club chair in the corner.

The memory of his da sitting there was still vivid in his mind as Cain sat after Therese went back down to get him something to eat. Dalton had loved that spot for their talks, or his lectures, depending on the day. When it came to following the rules, Billy wasn't as good as

Cain, but he didn't need to be. His older sister was their father's heir, and he thanked God for that.

"Do you ever regret being born first?" he asked, wondering if Cain tired of carrying the burden of being the boss.

"Every once in a while, but I can't do anything about it, so I don't dwell on something I can't change." Cain spoke softly, and the random pattern of her tapping fingers on the bottom of her shoe relaxed him. "Do you ever regret being born second?"

"Not once," he said and laughed. "Even if I'd been first, we'd still be in our same spots, and you know that's the truth. You're a true clan leader, and I'm proud of that fact, sister. Now tell me what's wrong, since it's not the weight of the crown."

Cain laughed, but she wasn't that easy to crack. "Nothing's wrong. I'm just worried about you."

"You're full of shit, but lucky for you, I love you anyway. I also know what it is, so take my advice and call her." He opened his eyes to see her reaction. "I'm surprised she wasn't with you when you got to the hospital, since Lincoln said that's who you were with," he said of one of his guards that had called Merrick.

"I sent her home with Lou." Cain's tone was flat and devoid of emotion.

"Call her," he said again.

"I did, and she wasn't interested, so forget about that."

Cain's answer was too fast and too adamant. "You're the smartest person I know, Derby, so don't change my opinion by being a dumbass."

"I'll let that slide since you have a head injury, but don't make it a habit."

Therese came in with a tray. "Cain, Muriel's here to see you with some kid named Bryce. Don't worry. Marie and I'll keep our boy company."

He smiled when Cain kissed his forehead before she left. Cain *was* the smartest person he knew, but she was too dense to realize she was falling for the little blonde he'd seen her hugging in the storeroom at the Erin Go Braugh. Some idiot had been on his knees bleeding profusely, but his sister was comforting Emma. The only people she would've done that for were Marie, his mum, or him, but he doubted Cain thought of Emma in a sisterly way.

"What are you cooking, Billy Boy?" Therese asked as she handed him a fourth of a sandwich.

"Has she told you about Emma?" He took a bite of Therese's corned beef and suddenly felt better.

"Is that the one we picked flowers for?" He nodded, and Therese held a glass of juice up to his lips. She was never happier than when she got to baby one of them. "Have you met her?"

"I have, and you're going to see why Cain's tied up in knots." He accepted another piece of sandwich and some more juice.

"It's strange," Therese said, exhaling. "I've prayed for you and Cain to find what your da and I had, but it terrifies me just as much for you to actually find it. I knew who and what your da was when I married him, but the days of complete loyalty and that kind of acceptance seem to be long gone."

"You'll probably think I'm nuts, but you need to see Cain with this girl, Mum. She's found someone who will be around for a while, and if hardhead will let her guard down for a minute, she'll see that too." He waved off the rest of lunch, not wanting to get sick because of his headache.

"Close your eyes and relax, my love," Therese said as she moved the tray to the desk. "Do you think we should get Derby to invite Emma to Sunday lunch?"

"That's one of our next steps, but first we need to persuade Cain to call her."

"Maybe you should go about that the same way you did when you were five," Therese said, sitting next to him and gently combing his hair back.

"Bug her about it until she gives in?" He laughed at the memory of how Cain would finally say okay to anything he wanted after he asked about a thousand times an hour.

"Thank God you were so cute. If not, you'd have never survived your childhood."

"I'm still cute, and she can't punch me in this condition." They both laughed, and Therese moved to the chair with her book. "I just want her to be happy."

"With everything Derby will face, she'll need a safe harbor no matter how much the storm rages, so I want that for her too."

"Da told me once that even the devil has a heart, but it took the right woman to bring it to life. When you say your prayers, Mum, ask God to keep the heart of our devil safe and well loved."

❖

"Hey," Bryce said as he stood and fidgeted in Cain's office.

"If using the name Cain makes you nervous, try Boss," Cain said as she moved to her desk chair. "Did you need something?"

"No. I just wanted you to know the system is ready to go." He handed over a sheet that specified in simple terms what he'd done. "I realize the chance you're taking on me, so I thought you can go slow until you're sure about what I've put in place."

"Are you absolutely sure?" She looked at him, and for once he seemed to still at the attention. "Now would be a good time to give me any reservation you even think of having."

"After researching everything available out there and seeing firsthand what they have, what I put together will give you the barrier you need. The only time they'll come in is when you let them." Bryce stepped forward and offered his hand. "You have my word on it, Boss, because I know what failing you means to me and my family, especially my brother."

Cain shook his hand and nodded toward Muriel, who said, "We filed a petition on Charlie's behalf for a new trial with a friendlier judge. Once that happens, I think we can get him out with time served and a promise he'll never do it again."

"Are you serious?" Bryce got so excited he hugged Muriel, almost knocking her completely off balance.

"She's serious," Cain said, smiling. "It's your bonus for a job well done, so get over to Emerald's, and I'll meet you there later. It'll give you time to call your mother and give her the good news."

Bryce shook her hand again and practically skipped out of her office, making her laugh. "If you could make everyone that happy, you'd rule the world," Muriel said, laughing with her.

"I'm only interested in ruling a little piece of the world, so what do you have for me?"

"We've got our first nibble, and the next step should set the hook well enough to land the big trophy fish you're interested in," Muriel said, making Cain shake her head at all the fishing metaphors. No matter what else was happening, Muriel went deep-sea fishing about twice a year in Mexico. It was one of her passions that she sort of shared. She liked fishing but didn't love it like Muriel.

"What will that do to our bottom line?" Reshuffling any deck changed the landscape no matter how careful you were or how much you planned. In this case, it had to happen, and she was trying to pull the trigger but ease any doubt she had.

"The expanded business should take care of any turf problems we'll have, but the territory Katlin is opening up is like virgin snow. We're the first ones in there, and we've triple-checked the folks she's dealing with."

Katlin Patrick was a few years younger than they were and also their cousin. Dalton had put her to work after college but had kept her away from the watchful feds until she got a handle on the business. Katlin made the deals Cain specified and took care of the business they already had, and in the few years she'd been at it, she'd reminded Cain of Billy. He was a bull in a world-sized china shop, but he had a good head for business.

"Good. We'll need the extra capital for our coming-out festivities."

"I can't talk you out of that?" Muriel cocked her head slightly as she asked.

"Your da agrees with me, so go back to your office and put a wall between us for the next month or so." She stood and moved to Muriel so she could hug her. "Da was killed and I won't let that go, so whoever's responsible will have to start paying a price. Once I'm sure, I'm going to wipe their entire family from existence, and it still won't cover the debt of my loss."

"Be careful then. I'm a better business attorney than a criminal-defense one."

Muriel left and waved to her da as he arrived. Right before Dalton died, he'd hit Big Gino for trespassing into their territory, and both Cain and her uncle agreed that the move had cost Dalton his life.

"How's Billy?" Jarvis asked after he'd kissed her cheek when she joined him in the back of the car.

"He's upstairs napping and trying to get over his headache. His arm will take a little longer than that, but he'll be okay."

"I talked to Pops before I came over, and Ian's doing better than they thought, so it might be a quicker recovery than the doctors predicted."

"Good, and it's a real shame the FBI is off-limits. Once he feels better, Billy's going to have to force himself not to beat that little bastard that rear-ended them to death with his cast." They drove to Ramon's bar, the Gemini Club, named, like all his businesses, for his children. The downstairs was a club, but Ramon's real business was upstairs.

The Gemini Casino was a myth to law enforcement, but they'd never gotten the warrants necessary to prove or disprove its existence because of the Casey family connections with the cops. Ramon had used the capital from the Gemini to fund and maintain their legitimate businesses. It was a lesson he'd learned well from his initial investor, Dalton.

"Cain...Jarvis," Ramon said when they walked in. "Come sit and have some café." He pointed to the Cuban coffee the waiter was pouring as the rest of the staff got ready to open.

"Thank you for seeing us, Ramon," she said, taking the demitasse cup the waiter slid in front of her.

"Any time for you and anyone in your family, Cain, and I'm sorry about Billy. Therese said he's doing better, so that's good."

After her da's death, Ramon and his wife Marianna had become especially close to her mum, and their support meant a lot to all of them. "He's okay, and once his arm heals, he'll be good as new. I can't do anything about that situation, so we're here about something else."

"If I can help, you can count on my family."

"I'm sure Da told you about Big Gino's move into our neighborhoods," she said, and Ramon nodded. "Da hit some of his men, and three months later he was dead. Granted, we're in a different line of business, but Big Gino muscled in on not only our street corners, but the shopkeeps. They didn't want anything to do with the crap Big Gino is selling and the crime it was bringing to their neighborhoods, so Da tried to help."

"So what would you like to do? If it's to kill that pig, I'm with you."

"I'm going to finish what Da started and wanted to warn you, in case, because of our friendship, he takes aim at you as well." Vincent arrived as she spoke, so Jarvis caught Vincent up on what had been said.

"Are you asking our permission?" Vincent asked.

"No," she said with the kind of finality that meant she'd entertain no arguments. "I'm here as your friend to tell you, but I'm going to hit back and, no matter how long it takes, prove who was responsible for Da."

"Ramon and I figured that's what this was about, and we can't let you do that," Vincent said.

"Excuse me?" she said softly because Jarvis had put his hand on her wrist.

"We are all successful because we balance each other with different businesses. When one is out of balance, the other two should do what we can to bring the peace back," Ramon said with both hands out in front of him as if to keep her calm. "What Vincent means is, we won't let you take on all the risks alone. This is our fight too, because Big Gino wants to destroy all three of our families."

"I'm sorry for misunderstanding," she said, sighing. The last thing she needed was to go against these guys as well as Bracato.

"Relax, kid, I was just fucking with you," Vincent said, and laughed. "You say when and where, and we'll cut Big Gino's organization down to the size of his dick. That can't be very big."

She laughed and squeezed Jarvis's hand. "Thank you both, and I'll be in touch. If the time ever comes that our family can return the favor, we'll be there."

"Your father's blood runs through those veins, so we don't doubt that," Vincent said. "Make our old friend proud. Dalton deserves that."

"I always try my best, and I won't take up any more of your time. Thank you both for your friendship."

"Don't forget it'll always be there for you," Vincent said before finishing his coffee. "I'll wait for your call."

"Here." Ramon poured her some more as Jarvis walked Vincent to the door. "I want you to join us for our big-money tournament Mano set up. A group's coming in from Las Vegas, and they're looking for some high limits at the craps and blackjack tables."

"That's an invitation I can't refuse." She could almost feel the jolt of caffeine making its way through her body. "I love a good craps game."

"Good. I'll feel better with you there and Mano watching over the blackjack games. Remi will be out of town on business, and I don't want to reschedule since I want Mano to start making contacts for our expansion out to Nevada. Even with all the action there, we can still make money." He stood when Jarvis returned so Cain joined him. "Please bring a date if you want, Cain."

"Maybe, but I'll definitely be here." She put her arm around Jarvis's waist and smiled. "If I can talk Uncle Jarvis into staying up late, I'll drag him over here with me. Twenty-one is his favorite number."

"You take care of yourself and your family, Cain. Vincent was right about your father except the fact that he's already proud. He never failed to tell me that when he and I spoke, and I never minded his bragging because he put up with mine. We are both proud papas."

"Thank you, Ramon. My da was a man with excellent taste and luck in friends."

Chapter Seventeen

It had been a month since Emma had shared lunch with Cain by the lake, and it'd been the last time she'd seen or heard from her as well. After a couple of days she hadn't been able to stand the silence, so she'd called, but none of the messages she'd left had been returned. Cain had effectively cut her out, but Lou still dutifully picked her up and took her home from work.

"Emma," Josh said, loading the last drink on her tray. "You okay?"

"Sorry. You caught me daydreaming in the middle of this madhouse." She moved the tray closer and headed off after scanning the room one last time. She still didn't see Cain. The table next to the one where she left the drinks did have a familiar face, though—Bea. She hugged Bea before taking her and her date's order. "I'll be right back."

Josh mixed their drinks and pointed to his watch. No matter what was going on, he knew when it was a few minutes before ten. "Wrap it up after this one. I know all about the big test tomorrow, so no complaints."

"Thanks, Uncle Josh," she kidded with him as she walked back to Bea's table. "Here you go, guys, and my relief will take care of your tab."

Bea said, "Let's plan for lunch tomorrow after class if we both finish at the same time," and she agreed.

Lou had the door of the car open for her so she got in without any complaints. She'd tried in the beginning, but Lou still showed up no matter what she said. After the first few times she'd started to enjoy it since it was like someone in the universe aside from her father cared that she was all right.

When Lou pulled away, she asked, "How's Billy doing?"

"His head's okay, or so say the doctors, but the cast is driving him a little batty. Unfortunately, he's got at least four more weeks of that to suffer through." Lou drove with his usual patience and seldom glanced in the rearview mirror, so she smiled when she made eye contact with him. "Are you doing okay?"

"You want the truth or the lie I tell myself every night?" She shrugged when he smiled back at her, as if trying his best to comfort a friend.

"If it's that bad, let's go with the truth, and I'll give you some words of wisdom."

"I'm sad most of the time, but every so often I get really mad at your boss. She's so stubborn and refuses to talk to me." She let her head drop back and couldn't believe she'd actually said that out loud to Lou, of all people. It was probably his job to report back all the stupid things she said on these trips. "If you could keep that between us, I'd appreciate it."

"No worries. I'd never break your confidence. Are you ready for the words of wisdom?"

She laughed and straightened herself up. "Sure. Hit me."

"You aren't the only one who's upset, so when the opportunity comes, don't back down. Cain will let you go if you sit back and do nothing. You need to decide if you want this or not. If you do, you might find the solution to that sad part of your problem."

"Thanks, Lou."

"You can thank me by keeping *my* confidence. The boss hears I'm giving dating advice on her behalf, and I'll be guarding the weeds outside the office."

"Don't worry, big guy, and thanks for the ride." She knew better than to open her own door, so she waited for him and took his arm for the walk upstairs.

"Good luck on your test tomorrow, and I'll see you at four."

She waved Lou good-bye and locked her door. The material for her exam was practically written across her brain, so she showered and went to bed. A solid seven hours of sleep helped her concentration, and she finished her test in forty-five minutes. Since she didn't want to spend another day alone in her apartment, she waited for Bea outside.

Fifteen minutes later, Bea asked, "Feel like Chinese?" And since Bea had a car, she went to the place Bea liked. "What's got you in the dumps and acting like a hermit these days? Ms. Wonderful turn out to be not so wonderful?"

"We haven't talked in a month, so I'm not sure about the wonderful part. If it's okay, I'd rather not discuss it."

"Sure, but since you're still working for her it can't be completely over. Just keep calling until she talks to you."

They ordered, and Emma played with the chopstick packet next to her fork. "You were the one who told me to stay the hell away from her, so you should be thrilled."

"I was wrong, okay? Call her and set something up. If you're worried about her hurting your feelings or venting on you, make it somewhere public. Pick some place like this with plenty of people around."

"I'm not afraid of Cain. I just think we're too different for it to work."

"That's bullshit and a total cop-out. What happened anyway?" As soon as the guy delivered her soup, Bea put a handful of fried wonton strips into it. "Tell me already."

"I'm not going to talk about it, so skip it." She took a sip of her soup and, when Bea demanded an explanation, dropped her spoon. "You want to know? It didn't work out, and I wish it had, but it's done, so forget about it."

"Will you let me know if you decide to take my advice?" Bea asked, and Emma was sorry she hadn't gone home alone.

"Sure, but why's it so important to you?"

Bea laughed like her question had been a joke. "I'm just looking out for you and want you to be okay." Bea's syrupy-sweet answer made Emma think that was the last reason Bea wanted that information.

"Sure," she said. Did Cain have a bounty on her head or something? Cain's distrust of almost everything now made perfect sense. "You'll be the first to know."

❖

"One drink," Billy said as he and Cain walked through the warehouse after Paul's first delivery. They were the only two that not only knew where it was, but that it was coming at all. "I just want you to have one drink with me, and maybe that'll chill you out a little."

"What the hell does that mean?" Cain asked, finding the box with the note on it that Paul had told her about. It was a case of the sherry Therese loved, along with a few bottles of Daphne's family whiskey for her home bar.

"It means you're mad at the world, but you refuse to do the one thing that'll make you feel better." Even with his cast, Billy took the box from her and placed it in the trunk of the car. "The next time you tell me I've got a hard head, I'm kicking your ass."

"Why the hell can't you and Mum accept it didn't work out? I barely even know this girl." When she realized she was yelling, she took a deep breath. "I've moved on."

"The hell you have," Billy yelled back. "All you've done is scream at everyone for two weeks straight, so either call her or get laid. Either of those options should make you feel better."

"Get in the car before I break your other arm," she said, satisfied everything was in order.

"You know you only get this pissed when you're wrong." He put his hands up when she took another deep breath. "Forget I said anything, but you're not getting out of the drink, so get in."

"Let me guess. You want to have this drink at the pub, right?" She climbed into the car, not ready to admit to Billy or anyone that she was angry because she missed some woman.

"Sorry, rock head. We're going to Emerald's to run that last test on the system. Bryce is waiting for us, but we need to cruise by the house and pick up some of our friends." He drove out and secured the padlocks on the door, as well as the industrial deadbolts.

"What exactly is the test?"

"It was Muriel's idea, and she wanted to do it before she gets into that court case for this kid's brother. She figured why go through all the trouble if Bryce is some elaborate setup the feds cooked up." He left through the back of the industrial park even though he'd have to drive through a large neighborhood. It was easier to spot something out of the ordinary in this situation than on the interstate.

"So you told him you were conducting a test?" She tried her best to keep her cool if that was indeed the idiotic truth.

"Duh, no. Muriel told him you might come by and have a drink with her and your suffering brother, and you'd check on him." He spoke slowly, as if she were the one having mental issues. "We're going to plan something before that drink, though, and we'll try some of Bryce's supposed foolproof gadgets while we do. Let's see where the feds show up."

He drove the longest route toward uptown, and as soon as they were miles away from the warehouse, he called Muriel, who was standing outside talking to Lou about the weather. "You ready?" Billy asked.

"Are you sure the boss okayed this?" Merrick said, turning her back on the van parked across the street like Billy had asked her to.

"She's sitting right next to me, so yeah, I'm sure. Tell them to move everything to the office. That's the last place those stupid fuckers have ever thought to look. The gate's open, and the guys are ready for delivery," he said and hung up.

"So you're giving them permission to get a warrant for probable cause?" she asked, shaking her head.

"If your wonder boy is on the right side, then no one's showing up at the office, and they'll follow us from the house and watch us have a drink with Muriel." He turned onto their street and stopped to pick up Merrick. "If Lincoln calls, then there might be problems, but not for us."

The van close by started up when Merrick got in, but before it could get into gear, Billy pressed the accelerator and took off. Around the corner, one of their neighbors had the gate open, so Billy turned in and cut his engine. The owner closed the gate after walking away with his dog. If anyone caught a glimpse of him, all he was doing was his nightly chore.

"I thought that only worked in bad gangster movies," Cain said, laughing as they sat in the dark.

"Don't celebrate yet. After this an army will probably follow us around, but let's see where they look for us," Billy said, getting out and waving her and Merrick toward the back of the house. Like at their place, the back let out to the next street, and once Merrick had scanned the area, they took another car and headed to Emerald's.

Once they arrived, Cain went to see Bryce and check on what he had. "Anything new?" she asked.

"The jammers are working from my end, and the daily sweeps are coming back clean. Lou and I will take that job, and I'm researching anything new on the market daily to make sure nothing gets past our system." Bryce appeared more relaxed sitting in front of a bank of computers, and from this viewpoint looking out over the club, she had a good view of the crowd.

The place was full, but none of the people drinking and dancing looked out of place. "Good job," she said, picking up the phone and calling Lincoln. "Are you having fun?"

"Bored as hell, Boss, but I'll call you if the party gets going," Lincoln said.

"The drinks are on me when you're done, but don't move until you hear from Billy." She patted Bryce on the back before going to the office where Billy was waiting. "Anything?"

"You'd think they'd be as vigilant about checking their surroundings as we are," he said as he cued up the recording of the inside of the FBI surveillance van. Lou had left a few gifts no one but she, Billy, and Lou knew about. From what she heard, once Billy had turned the jammer on when he called Merrick to the point where he outran them, their watchers had no clue as to the conversation and where they were.

"Give Muriel a call and tell her to send someone good for Charlie White. We need to keep his brother Bryce happy." She poured them both a drink and tapped her glass against Billy's. "That's one less thing we have to worry about and gives us some room to work."

She finished her drink and kissed Billy's cheek. "Have fun and be good."

"You're leaving already?"

"I promised a drink and I had one, but I have some early stuff tomorrow, and I'm headed home. Don't pout. I feel more relaxed already, so you did a good job on that too."

She left Merrick with Billy and took the car. She'd planned to go home, but everything Billy had said went through her mind, so she made a last-minute decision and headed to Emma's. Maybe she'd been too quick to dismiss Emma, and seeing her again would give her an idea on how to start over.

The street, as always, was quiet, so she parked and sat for a bit. Like clockwork, Lou drove up and walked Emma upstairs. A few minutes later Lou took off, and the light in Emma's apartment was still on. As she put her hand on the door handle, another car pulled up, and the man immediately got out.

The guy stopped and glanced up before going in, so Cain sat and tried to think if she'd ever seen him before, since he seemed so familiar. She waited, and it finally came to her. He was the young agent at the pub who'd left the van long enough for her guys to have it towed. He'd been with Hicks and Kyle the day at the hospital as well.

"What are you doing here?" She glanced at her watch and sat. No fast visit where Emma told this guy to buzz off lasted twenty-five minutes.

That's how long it took for the guy to get back outside, and he didn't linger. But Cain couldn't determine his facial expression because of the darkness.

"What are you up to, Ms. Verde? You can't have made such crappy friends in two weeks."

Now she wanted to see Emma, but romance was the last thing on her agenda. "Why does the story of the Trojan horse come to mind?"

CHAPTER EIGHTEEN

The next day Cain got away from the office early and had dinner with Marie, Billy, and Therese. She helped Marie get ready for bed and left her mum to read to her so she and Billy could go out. She still had plenty of time to make it to the pub before the witching hour of ten o'clock.

"I'm glad you finally came to your senses," Billy said as they arrived and saw Muriel by the door. "Lou told me you called to make sure Emma was working."

"I want to talk to her about a couple of things, so I did need to make sure she was here."

Josh had saved them a table and delivered the first set of drinks himself. Cain sipped the dark beer he'd given her and stared at Emma as Billy and Muriel teased each other about little things. It seemed Emma was trying to build her confidence to come over, and after a deep breath she made her way to their table.

"Hey," Emma said, holding refills for them. "It's good to see you."

She wanted to lash out, but as always, Emma seemed so earnest and shy. All she could do was look at Emma and not say anything, so Billy jumped in to try to save her. "Good to see you too, Emma," he said, and introduced her to Muriel.

"I'm glad you're doing okay," Emma said, keeping Cain's beer on her tray. "Are you seriously not going to say anything to me?" Emma asked like she was speaking to a petulant child.

"Why should I? Does your boyfriend need me to confess to something?" Her back came off her chair, and she spoke with as much accusation as she meant.

"What are you talking about?" Emma seemed mortified at her outburst, and her trembling lip made Cain think she might start crying.

"Don't deny it. I saw that guy last night."

"What guy?" Billy asked instantly, getting angry on her behalf, she guessed.

"He was there for one of two reasons." She was glad she remembered the control in her pocket that engaged the jammers around the building that Bryce had installed. Being played was humiliating enough. She didn't need to make it worse by broadcasting it. "So either he was recruiting you…" she said, and Emma shook her head.

"Don't say it," Emma pleaded.

"Or he was there to get—"

Before she could finish, Emma poured the beer on her tray over Cain's head and ran toward the office. She came close to running into Josh, who was headed to the table when Emma soaked her. Cain slowly stood and pointed at Billy, who was now laughing.

"Cain," Josh said, pressing his hands together.

"Zip it," she said, going after Emma. When she reached the back, Emma was coming out of the employee bathroom dabbing her eyes with some tissue.

"That guy came to my place and asked me to help him spy on you," Emma said, her tears still falling. "I told him I would never do that to a friend, so he told me some stuff about you and your family. I guess it was supposed to change my mind, but it didn't. He threatened me, so I returned the favor and told him I'd call the cops if he didn't leave."

"Why should I believe you?"

"Because I called you and left a message," Emma said loudly. "But for some reason you won't talk to me, so I figured that's why you came tonight. I'm not hiding anything from you."

She didn't think Emma was lying, but she glanced at her phone, and Emma *had* called her and left a message. "I got this all wrong," she said, combing her wet, sticky hair back. "You have every right not to forgive me, but I'm sorry."

"Why did you shut me out?" Emma said, crying harder. "If you say it was to protect me, or because I'm better off, I'm going to pour something else on you before Josh fires me."

"No one's firing you." She took a step forward, hoping Emma didn't bolt. "All this is my fault, and I'm really sorry."

Billy said, "You should take that, Emma, since she's seldom wrong about anything. If you two are going to kiss and make up, I'll head back to my beer, but if you need me to knock her around, I will."

"I think I can handle it from here," Cain said and laughed.

"I was talking to Emma," he said and winked before he left.

"Why didn't you let me go with you the day he got in the accident? I could tell you were upset, and I wanted to be there for you."

"You have to understand who I am…who I was raised to be," she said, wanting to do anything but have this conversation.

Emma took her hand and led her to a row of crates and sat down, not letting her go. "I don't understand what that means, but you're going to explain as soon as I finish saying a few things."

"We can't leave it at 'I'm sorry' and move on?" She got up, but only to grab a bar towel to wipe her face and hands.

"I'm sorry I did that."

"I doubt it," she said and smiled. "I probably deserved it."

"You came in here that first night and answered every question I never thought to ask because I'd never considered the subject. I'd finally found the reason I never fit in back home and why I'm such a disappointment to my mother." Emma held her hand sandwiched between hers. "It's like she knew all along and rejected me for being an abomination, which is what she'll see me as."

"You're no abomination, darling girl." She put her arm around Emma and kissed her temple. "You're no such thing."

"I don't want to change to please my mother, and I want you to stop running away from me." Emma turned and faced her. "Do you think you could do that?"

"I meant that I never show weakness, but Merrick telling me Billy was in the hospital brought back the day my da was killed." She closed her eyes to center herself and felt better when Emma pressed her hand to her cheek. "It almost paralyzed me, and I didn't want you to see me like that."

"I want all of you. Don't you know that?" Emma leaned in and kissed her. "I don't need to know your business, and I'll never betray you, but I need to know *you*. Do you think you can let me in just enough to prove I'm not out to hurt you?"

"I think we'll take your plan of going slow and see where that leads us."

Emma kissed her again. The way she laced her fingers through her hair gave Cain the impression she wanted to keep her in place. "I missed you."

She smiled and nodded when Emma whispered that in her ear. "I missed you too, but maybe we can do something about that."

"Something like what?" Emma tugged on her hair and squinted, as if daring her to say the wrong thing.

"Starting over means starting over, so how about a first date some place you like?" The noise of the pub grew louder, so she glanced back to see who'd opened the door. "It's okay, Josh. I promise not to keep her too much longer if you need her back."

"Can I do anything for you?" Josh asked.

"Not a thing, but if we have such a thing as employee of the month, don't give it to Emma," she said and laughed when Emma pinched her ear. "Think about what I said, and I'll see you later," she told Emma.

"You're leaving? I just now got to see you again."

"Let me go home and change, and then I'll come back and take you home." She stood and kept Emma from hugging her, earning her another pout. "It's bad enough that I smell like someone bathed me in beer. Get back to work before Josh has a nervous breakdown."

"You're coming back though, right?"

"I doubt you'll have time to miss me again."

Emma laughed and kissed the back of her hand. "That was pretty sappy, mobster."

"Mobster?" she asked, laughing with Emma.

"That's what the world keeps wanting me to see, but I'm happy with the view. Besides, who else is going to call you that to your face?"

"Certainly no one I know, so it's a good thing I like you so much."

"Do you?" Emma took hold of her other hand.

"I do, and I look forward to showing you."

❖

"Do you want to go to the pub again?" Bea asked her new boyfriend. They'd been together less than two weeks, but the big guy was terrific in bed and took her out whenever she wanted. "Emma's working again tonight, so maybe we'll score some free drinks. Not that you can't afford it," she said, slapping his ass.

Boone rolled over, and Bea noticed he was hard as stone again. The guy couldn't get enough of her, so she was loving it. "You want to talk me into it?" He put his hands behind his back and slightly spread his legs.

She tapped her chin with her index finger a couple of times like she was thinking about it before she moved down and put her mouth on him. He held the back of her head and hummed as she went down on him. After he pulled her hair, she got on top of him, and as he thrust up while holding her hips, she came with him.

Once Boone was done he jumped up and hurried into Bea's shower, closing the door like he was suddenly shy, but that had been his habit from the first time he'd come over. She put on her robe to wait for him, since she knew he'd come out clean and dressed.

"How's your friend doing with Casey?" Boone asked as he sat next to her to put his shoes on.

"Sounds like whatever they had going on ended. I talked to her at lunch, but little Emma finally has shown she's interested in someone, so that might change." When she got up to take her shower he grabbed her by the back of the belt.

"That's it?" he asked, sounding like her answer hadn't satisfied him.

"Babe," she said, massaging his neck. "Why are you so interested in Emma's love life? She's from some farm in the middle of nowhere, so believe me, it's boring as shit."

"I might want to do some business with Casey. What I asked you to do isn't all that hard. You didn't tell her you were asking for me, did you?" The way he asked scared her because he'd never been anything but nice. "Did you?"

"No. I just told her I cared about her, and we could all go out together if she was serious about her. Like I said, she's inexperienced, so I thought she needed a push. Hell, I had to tell her who Cain Casey is, and I still don't think she believes me."

"Get ready, and maybe you can talk to her again." Boone let Bea go and started putting his socks on. She moved away slowly, glancing back at him, so he smiled.

When the bathroom door closed, Boone reached for his phone and called his sister. He was getting tired of fucking this little know-it-all, but Callie wanted to use Emma to get close to Casey. How Big Gino had gotten the information on these two college bitches was still a mystery, but Callie had agreed it was their best move.

"Hey, where are you?" Callie asked.

"At Bea's, and I'm ready to move on to something better than this," he said, trying to keep his voice down even though the shower was still running. "Has that fat prick told you how he knew about this girl, and the other one, Emma?"

"He said Bea's family does some work for him, but they don't like to advertise it. As far as your coed knows, her daddy's family makes money delivering bread."

"She said she tried to tell Emma about Casey, so she might not be so stupid on the subject as her daddy might think." He grabbed his wallet and keys, feeling naked without any type of weapon. "Let's just hope this shit works. If you ask me, all I need is a day of following Casey, and I'll find a way to finish this crap."

"That's the best way to get either arrested or killed, since the word on the street is that Casey's got the feds up her ass. If she gets killed in some place like the bar she owns, the crowd will give you cover, so calm down. Once you eliminate Bea and Emma, there'll be no one to identify you."

"Next time you get to do this shit."

Callie laughed, and he came close to hanging up. "Come on. Enjoy your little fuck buddy and wait this out. Keep remembering what's at stake."

"Okay, but after tonight, I might try it my way."

"You need to tell me before you try anything," Callie said, her humor gone.

"What the fuck do you think I just did?"

CHAPTER NINETEEN

Cain showed up the next morning wearing khakis and a golf shirt, wanting to make Emma comfortable. After taking over the family business, she'd adhered to her father's unwritten rule of always looking the part. No matter what was happening in his life, her da had always dressed impeccably.

"I really want to play hooky today," Emma said when she stepped out of her building.

"You might want to, but I'm not that much of a bad influence. You're going to school, but I'm going to walk you over there and wait." She kissed Emma and reached for her bag.

"You're taking the day off?" Emma slid their hands together and still dragged her feet, as if wanting to make their time last as long as possible.

"I promised last night and I'm sticking to that. You go to class, and I'll sit outside and do a little homework." Tulane was only a couple of streets over, and she almost laughed at all the slow-moving vehicles behind them. "So you'll have a chance to think of where you want to go for lunch."

"We're going on another picnic, but this time I'm requesting some place a bit more secluded. Think you can manage that?" They were close to the building where Emma's class was, so she stopped at her bench. "Are you sure you want to work out here because of…you know?" Emma pointed to the right as discreetly as she could.

"I'm positive, so go ahead and leave me to our lunch planning."

She watched Emma walk away, sitting when Emma went inside. The jammer was in her pocket, so she reached for it but didn't turn it on, even when Lou and two of her other men were in place with the equipment that would make it work. Instead she took out her phone, as Merrick sat two benches down from her.

"Jake," she said, recognizing his voice.

"Cain, you finally ready?"

"Have you cleared your schedule since we talked last?" She kept putting him off but thought it was time to move on.

"That's why I've been calling. I've got some stuff going on, but I'm ready to sit and show you what we can do."

"That's why I'm reaching out." She turned her face to the sun, now facing the guys following her. "I need you to understand that we're moving on, so feel free to deal with whoever you want."

"What can I do to change your mind?"

"Nothing, and just so you understand—our organization isn't interested in anything you're selling, so good luck."

He stayed silent for a long few minutes, but she didn't feel the need to say anything. She could almost hear his mind working overtime to grasp for something to reel her back in. "You really don't want to cut a better deal than what you have right now?"

"You should remember what Billy said about guessing about things you don't know anything about, so like I said, good luck. Hopefully you'll get what you're looking for, but leave me and my family out of it." She hung up, not needing to add anything else.

She didn't open her eyes when her phone rang again, knowing Muriel was always punctual. "You're not at the office," Muriel said as a greeting.

"I'm playing hooky because I've got a date," she said, stretching her legs out in front of her. "Are you at the office?"

"I'm trying to get unpacked, and no one asked me out, so yes, I'm at the office. There's that and our donation to our decided charity for the year, and I wanted to make sure before I cut the check."

"It's a good cause, but wait before you send them anything until I'm sure it's our best fit." She heard the doors opening and people coming out way too early. "Anything else before I start my date?"

"We were served with a lawsuit this morning by a Martin Williamson III. Does that ring any bells?"

"Not in the least. Should it?" Emma stopped between her legs and blocked the sun.

"It says you broke his nose."

"Respond to his attorney that he can either drop it or you'll represent Emma when she sues this guy for grabbing her."

"Thanks. That might get him to back off," Muriel said, and Cain heard talking in the background, which meant they might be interrupted by the young associates Muriel had brought with her from the old firm.

"Actually, go ahead and file. We need the world to know exactly how we handle idiots like this." She smiled when Emma mouthed, "What?"

"I'll take care of it, and I've got to go, so have fun."

Cain put her hands on Emma's waist and simply stared at her beautiful face, surprised that no one had tried to win her over. "You're done already?"

"The professor handed out grades and some extra work if we need the points, so I'm done until I need to go to work." Emma tugged her to her feet and took her arm as they started walking. "What was that about?"

"The guy who grabbed you is suing me, so you're going to return the favor, with my cousin Muriel's help. If you get something out of it, you won't have to work as much if you don't want to." Merrick pointed to the car parked less than five hundred feet away.

"That sounds interesting," Emma said, taking her hand. "If that'll be a hassle, I don't mind working."

"He doesn't think it's a hassle since he started it, and he really started it by grabbing you. I was simply defending your honor, so I'd do it again."

Emma leaned against her and sighed. "You weren't protecting your property, were you?"

"That's a bizarre question," she said, opening the car door for Emma. "They must do things differently in Wisconsin."

"Some people back home think like that," Emma said, and Cain imagined there might be more to it than that simple explanation.

"If you need clarification, I don't want to own you no matter how long we're together, but I'm not going to stand by and let someone touch you without your permission. I would never do that to you or anyone, so I expect everyone to show that level of respect." They headed toward Metairie but stopped at a small bistro along the way, where Merrick got out and went in. "That attitude unfortunately is engrained, so hopefully it won't bother you too much."

"You're someone I didn't think existed anymore, so it won't bother me at all."

When Merrick returned, they started again, and Lou drove to the back of Longue Vue Gardens. The tourist attraction wasn't usually crowded on weekdays at this hour, but as a precaution Cain had talked to an old friend and had a section roped off to give Emma what she wanted.

Cain carried the bags of food Merrick had ordered and led Emma to the spot her old friend had waiting. The huge crepe myrtle had a blanket spread under it and no one else in sight. "How's this?"

"It's beautiful. Thank you." Emma waited for her to put her stuff down so she could wrap her arms around her. Cain noticed a new boldness in Emma. She wasn't shy anymore when it came to wanting to touch her. "How'd you know I'd pick a picnic?"

"I didn't know for sure, but I was willing to talk you into it since I thought you'd enjoy this spot." She kicked her shoes off and helped Emma sit. "You ready to eat?"

"Not yet." Emma moved and sat on her lap once she'd leaned against the tree. The sound from the nearby fountain and the chirping birds dissolved from her consciousness when Emma kissed her. "I missed you, and I wasn't sure what I would do if you didn't talk to me again." Emma kissed her again, and Cain found it sweet but passionate enough that she could easily fall for this farm girl so different from any other woman she'd known.

"What did you want to talk to me about?" she asked, and surprisingly Emma blushed.

"Promise you won't think it's stupid?" The blush spread to Emma's neck.

"I promise," she said and tried to keep her face impassive because she thought it was important to Emma to be taken seriously.

"I'm sure you worked out who you are and what you want a long time ago." She nodded when Emma stopped. "It wasn't that easy for me, and all I'd figured out pretty early was that I wanted to leave."

"I remember you saying you didn't fit there."

"I didn't, but even after coming here and enjoying the freedom to do anything, something was missing. I thought something was missing in here." Emma placed her hand over Cain's heart. "But you woke me up, and then you were gone. When you wouldn't take my calls, I swore that I'd stop being afraid and, if you gave me the chance, just tell you."

"Tell me what, lass?" She moved her hands so they were slightly under Emma's breasts but then slid them back so she could pull her into an embrace. Emma seemed to gather strength and moved back a little so she could see her face.

"That I want you in my life, and I want to see where this goes. I'm hoping we land somewhere that we can build a long and happy life." The last part of Emma's confession came out in a whisper, but she never lost eye contact.

"Are you sure?" Her mum had always said the falling was easy, but the small details sometimes doomed it to fail. "Take off those rosy-outlook glasses and admit that the average person doesn't have an FBI surveillance team after her for no reason. Maybe I'm some of those things they believe me to be."

"Do you think you could care about me?" Emma was certainly persistent.

"You can't believe otherwise. We're completely different people, but you seldom leave my mind." This time Emma's kiss had an edge of seduction, so she pulled back before they got ahead of themselves, and Emma appeared both confused and disappointed.

"Thank you for giving us a chance, and only time will show that you can trust me. We'll build that a brick at a time." Emma laid her head on her shoulder and sighed with what sounded like contentment.

"There's more to this than trust, darling girl," she said, and Emma jerked her head up. "My family is the most important thing in the world to me, so I couldn't imagine losing them because of who my heart chose. If we get serious, will I cost you something you might come to resent me for?"

"I don't like talking about my parents, not because I'm ashamed, but because I think it's the other way around. Not so much my father, but he's never stood up to my mother and her Bible. If she knew or saw this, she'd disown me."

"Do you want time to think about all this?"

"No," Emma said loudly. "I've lived all this time being what I thought she wanted, and I've been miserable. On top of that misery, I've never come close to pleasing her."

"And your father?"

"I have to believe that eventually he'll be happy for me, but I want to finally feel like I belong with and to someone."

"You're a strong and brave woman, Emma Verde, and you're going to make my mum almost as happy as you make me." She exhaled sharply when Emma slammed her into the tree with an enthusiastic hug.

"Now that you're not tossing me out, I'm starved."

"I can take care of that hunger and so much more."

❖

Logan North sat in the back of the surveillance vehicle with Joe Simmons and reviewed what they'd been able to get so far. The only clear thing was her conversation with Jake Kelly and her cousin Muriel Casey about a lawsuit and a donation to charity. At that pace, all they'd be able to convict Casey on was being citizen of the year.

"What charity do you think she's talking about?" Joe asked, glancing up from his scope pointed at the garden gates.

They'd lost sight of Casey and the blonde once they went in, and since they had no idea where they were, they hadn't caught anything else. "Why would you think that's important?"

"I'm only curious," Joe said, sounding like he was bored with him and this operation. "What kind of charity does an alleged psychopath donate to?"

"You can't believe all those idiots in the profiler unit. Casey isn't a study case. She's just a thug and a common criminal," he said, returning to those two conversations. "It's shocking that she and her family haven't been caught since they don't seem all that smart."

"Maybe because they're not all that common or thuggy," Joe said.

"Just keep an eye out and tell me if you spot something."

Ray Clifton had been relegated to the driver's seat and was currently sitting with his head back like he was a plumber on his lunch break and afternoon nap. "Hey, lovebirds, someone's coming, so how about both of you pay attention."

"Got them, Ray," Joe said, and pointed one of the cameras in the direction they were coming from.

Two large SUVs had turned down the unpaved canal road and effectively boxed them in, one in the front and one in the back. They'd gotten as close as they could without actually kissing the bumper. The guys inside got out and leaned against their vehicles, and every one of them reached inside their jackets.

"Shit," Logan said in a harsh whisper as he unholstered his weapon. "We need to get out of here. These guys are going to take us out."

"Calm down," Ray said without lifting his head. Every single guy brought out a pack of cigarettes and lit up. "Keep cool, but get ready just in case."

"God dammit," Logan said when his phone vibrated, scaring him into almost falling off his stool. "Yes, sir," he said when he saw it was Agent Kyle.

"Got anything for me?"

"Two conversations, but she's just taking the blonde out on a date." The gates opened and Casey's car came out, but all they could do was watch it drive away. "Sir, you're going to have to send another team," he said, explaining the situation.

"First you get towed, and now this," Kyle said in a very unamused tone. "Make sure you three at least transcribe the telephone conversations before you get back."

"Yes, sir." He hung up and slammed his hand down on the shallow metal counter. The noise made the smokers glance their way, but they didn't come closer. "Catching this bitch can't come soon enough."

"That's what the boat captain said in the movie *Jaws*, and look how well it turned out for him," Ray said, and Joe laughed.

"Shut up and start typing," Logan said, slamming his hand down again. "This isn't funny."

Joe opened his laptop and shook his head. "No, but I bet if you ask Casey, she thinks it's hilarious."

❖

Lou drove them back to Emma's apartment, and Cain heard Merrick and him get out, but she didn't want to stop kissing Emma to see where they'd gone. She could've stayed under that tree for hours, but she still had a few things to take care of, so it was time to head to the office.

"You're working tonight?" she asked Emma when they finally broke apart.

"Yeah. Josh said he'd be shorthanded, so he actually might let me stay late."

"Lou will be there at ten like always, so don't let Josh get any cute ideas. If I'm done I'll take you home, but if that's the case, feel free to have all the cute ideas you can come up with."

"Let's hope you're done then," Emma said, tracing her lips with her fingers. It was like Emma couldn't get enough now that she felt comfortable with her. "But if you're not, when will I see you again?"

"I've got this thing I promised a friend I'd go to, but it's kind of dressy," she said, wondering how to ask without making Emma think this was an out-of-bounds move.

"What?" Emma asked, as if she realized her discomfort.

"How'd you like to go shopping with me tomorrow?" Killing

Harold and feeding him through the grinder had been easier than coming up with a way for Emma not to feel like a kept woman.

"Oh," Emma said, sounding distinctly disappointed.

"I want you to go with me, and I'd like to get you something to wear." She kissed Emma's neck. "So stop acting like I'm kidnapping your puppy."

"Why not simply start with that, mobster?"

She laughed at the reprimand. "Because I'm relationship stupid, but I'll learn. I didn't want to make you uncomfortable."

"My Tulane long-sleeved T-shirt is the closest I have to dress clothes, so I'd appreciate the help, and I saved some money so I can pay for them. I'm not after you for your money."

"Good to know, but we'll argue about the bill tomorrow, so prepare yourself."

"Cain." Merrick knocked on the window. "Heads up."

She glanced in the direction Merrick was pointing and found Jake Kelly and his flunky Bradley Draper. "Can you sit tight a minute?" she asked Emma, who nodded. She opened the door and stopped him before he got any closer to the car. "What are you doing here?" she asked, making Jake click his jaw shut. "Was I stuttering when we spoke earlier?"

"No, but I thought about it and figured you were just under the influence of your new friend. I mean, who the hell passes up a deal like this?" Jake snapped his fingers and laughed. "I know, someone who's more interested in getting laid than in making money."

Cain stared at Bradley, and he took a few steps back. "Every so often I wonder how some people get through the day without falling in an open manhole because they're too stupid to look down. That kind of applies to you," she said, and he pointed at her as if getting ready to lay into her for the insult. His finger came precariously close to her chest.

"Wait a fucking—"

She grabbed his finger and pulled up before reversing course and going out. Jake's fingers cracked twice, and he screamed in pain. "Stop pretending to be a big man, Jake, and go back to wherever you crawled out of. I don't appreciate you talking about my friends like that," she said, letting his finger go and jabbing hers up his nose and driving his head back. "It upsets me, and if your boyfriend tries anything, you'll be in surgery a long time while they try to reattach this." She pulled his head back farther.

"Okay," he said, sounding nasal. "I'm sorry. I only wanted to work things out."

"*No* really does mean *no*, Mr. Kelly, so forget about this address. I see you here again, and you and me will have another chat like this one." She let him go, and he immediately cradled his hand with the broken fingers. "Before you decide that coming here really is a good idea, remember that you've got eight more of those," she said, squeezing his fingers again, and he went down to his knees.

"We won't be back, Ms. Casey," Bradley said, both hands up like she was holding him at gunpoint.

"You seem like the reasonable one, so remind him about this in the morning once all the vodka wears off. Repeating myself is one of my pet peeves, so I don't want to have this conversation again."

After Bradley drove away with a moaning Jake, Emma got out. She looped her fingers into the back of Cain's pants, and they watched the car turn the corner. "You must not have a lot of people disagree with you, huh?" Emma asked.

"Sometimes the easiest way to get someone to listen to you is to jam your fingers up their nose and force them to pay attention to the fact you're serious."

"If you say so, honey." Emma held her hand as they went upstairs. "Hopefully I'll see you tonight, but what time tomorrow if I can't?"

"Don't worry. I'll take you home no matter what, and I'm leaving someone outside just in case." She unlocked Emma's door and handed her keys back. "I know tomorrow's your late day, so we'll go after that."

"I need two things before I see you again," Emma said, dropping her bag inside the door.

"Name them," she said, lowering her head when Emma tugged on the back of her neck.

"One, you kiss me," Emma said, opening her mouth when she gave in to her request.

"What else?"

"Wash your hands before I hold your right hand again. You had your fingers in that guy's nose, and that was plenty gross." Emma gave a mock shiver and kissed her again.

Yes, the falling was easy, she thought as she kissed Emma and fought the urge to carry her inside.

Chapter Twenty

Shawn Liam walked out of the bedroom of the suite they'd gotten on their return trip to New Orleans. When they'd gone home and told their father they'd lost the Casey business, he'd ordered them back to fix the problem. What the hell good was it to let him and Royce control the business if he had to second-guess every move they made?

"Did you get in touch with Cain?" Royce asked. His brother was putting together the numbers with and without Casey's business. He wasn't stupid enough to think losing more than a fourth of their sales wouldn't hurt.

"Not yet," he said, picking up the sheet Royce was working on. "The old man said to fix it, but he didn't say how to do it, so I'm going to do it my way. No fucking way am I going back to Casey and beg her for anything."

"That's not what Poppa said. He wants that business back, and he said to remember the Caseys are the reason we've been able to grow this much. When he finally checked the books, he wasn't happy. He was pissed that Dalton died with the deal you cut."

Royce was always the one who gave in, but with that attitude they'd never make the kind of money he wanted. They needed to dominate the supply chain.

"Stop hyperventilating, Royce, and listen to me." He threw the page at him and moved to the window. "Poppa won't be around forever, so you'll eventually be stuck with me. It's time to start backing me up."

"What exactly do you want to do?"

"I'm going to find another buyer, so we'll advertise the fact that we have an opening in this particular business." He looked out over Canal Street and the five police cars that sped by with lights flashing. Whatever had happened obviously needed plenty of backup. "We have more than one way to expand, and we're going to find someone who'll think our pricing structure is totally acceptable."

Royce stood but didn't move from the desk. "What about what Poppa said?"

"Poppa might've built his business with the Caseys, but we're moving in a different direction."

"Do you honestly think Cain's going to let someone set up with the same size or larger operation right under her feet?" Royce threw his pencil on all the papers and sighed. "The smart play would be to try to talk to her."

"The smartest play is to do what I tell you, or did you forget who told her to get lost in the first place? I did you a favor by not telling Poppa, so now you're going to listen to me. Casey won't be a problem if she's not around to bitch about anything." He closed the curtains and shrugged when he faced Royce.

"Now I know you've lost your mind. You kill Casey, and you'll bring down the wrath of the entire Casey family on us. Billy alone will wipe us all out, including Poppa."

"You and Poppa need to have more faith."

"I have faith, but I also have a need to not make problems when we don't need to."

"Trust me, Royce. We're not going to take the fall for killing her, and once we get going, the only problem you'll have is how to spend all the money we make."

❖

The professor finished giving out the assignments for their midterms, and Emma was thrilled when he finally stopped. Bea had arrived late so she wasn't able to sit with her, but she was glad about that too. With Bea in the front row, she wouldn't be stuck in some long conversation about Cain or anything else. She waved on the way out the back door, knowing Cain was waiting for her in front of the administration building.

"Emma," Bea said from the top of the stairs. "Wait up."

"Sorry. I've got a date," she said and kept going.

Cain was standing outside the front SUV of the two parked out there, staring down the street as she spoke on the phone. She seemed to have a way of knowing Emma was around since she glanced at her and smiled when she was still a hundred yards away.

"Hey, beautiful," Cain said, meeting her halfway and making her believe the compliment.

"Hey." She kissed Cain and put her arms around her under her jacket. "I didn't keep you too long. Did I?"

"Not at all, but let's go before one of these campus cops gives us a ticket for parking illegally." As always, Cain took her bag and walked her to the car door. "You ready to shop?"

"I'm spoiled for picnics, but I'll take you however I can get you." She pressed herself to Cain and liked the way Cain put her arm around her. "Hey, Lou," she said, and Lou nodded.

"Picnics are becoming my favorite too, but too much of a good thing, lass, might bore you," Cain said and pulled her closer. "I'll be happy to show you the pleasure of variety in your life."

"I bet you would." She laughed with joy about where she was at the moment. "So what are we shopping for?"

"We've got a date in a few days, so something that'll go with black tie."

"Are you sure you don't want to take someone else?" she asked, never having attended anything like that. "You know, someone used to black-tie things."

"I promise plenty of picnics and nights at the pub having fun, but sometimes life isn't about jeans and T-shirts. When those days come, I want you with me too." Cain held her and kissed the back of her hand. "I'll never want to make you uncomfortable, though, so if you really don't want to go—you don't have to, but I'm not taking anyone else."

"I want to go, but I don't want you to think I'm a bumpkin in heels either. I don't want you to be ashamed of me."

"Don't ever think that again. You're a beautiful woman, and I'm one lucky bastard that you're with me," Cain said with passion.

"Okay, and I only wanted to give you an out without feeling bad about it."

Cain laughed and pinched her side. "Isn't that what's made you mad whenever I've done it since we've met? Let's agree that no matter what it is, I want you to come with me."

"Okay." When Lou stopped in front of Saks downtown, she took a deep breath. "I've never been in there, even to look."

"It's like any other store, except for the sometimes snooty people who'll wait on you." Cain opened the door and held her hand out to her. "Come on. I'll try to make it fun and painless."

"I don't think I have enough tips to pay for anything in there."

"I asked, so you're not paying. Think of it this way," Cain said, holding the door open for her. "You've had all these birthdays that I've missed, so I have the afternoon to make that up to you."

"I can't accept that much from you. We really haven't known each other that long, and this isn't what I expect." She pointed to the corner of the shoe department so they could have a semi-private conversation. "Can I just borrow something from Bea?"

"Sure, but I really don't mind."

"I know you don't, and I'm sure plenty of people are with you because of what you can give. I just don't want you to think I'm like that. I don't mind paying my own way."

"It's a gift freely given. If you're worried about the label of a kept woman, don't. That only applies when you have to pay me back with something you're not ready to give."

"Thank you," she said, not wanting to feel like she was proving her mother right by caving in to the first temptation that came along.

"Let's just look, and then you can make up your mind." Cain took her hand, and when she turned around, the woman named Merrick was standing close by with a phone in her hand. "Sorry. Give me a minute."

Cain's conversation was short and didn't seem pleasant in any way. "You want or need to reschedule?" she asked when Merrick disappeared with the phone.

"I'm sorry, but I need like two hours, so stay and look around."

"Without you?" She thought of being thrown into a very deep pool full of hungry alligators.

"You won't be alone." Cain called one of the salespeople over and had a short talk with her. "Have a seat, lass, and I'll be back as soon as I can."

She sat and looked at the display of shoes nearest her. They were all beautiful but probably cost more than she made in a month. "Ms. Verde," a handsome, well-dressed man said when he stopped in front of her.

"Hello," she said, wondering who this was. Sometimes she thought her naïveté was tattooed on her forehead.

"Kevin, ma'am. If you'd like some assistance navigating the store, I'll be happy to help. I'm a personal shopper and friendly ear if you need a friend." He had a gentle and kind manner, and he seemed completely sincere. How many times had Cain used him for this?

"If you don't mind me asking, how long have you known Cain?"

"I've never met Ms. Casey. Of course I've heard of her, and she comes in every so often for her own shopping needs, but she asked for a personal shopper you'd feel understood you."

"I'm not exactly sure what that means, but I appreciate your help." She stood and groaned, realizing that her bag and money had left with Cain. "Maybe we can just browse, and once I get my money back we can decide on something."

He looked at her as if she'd grown a horn-sized pimple in the middle of her forehead. "My boss told me you wouldn't have to worry about that, but you evidently didn't get that memo, did you?"

"No. Cain mentioned it, but I don't want to be like all the women in her life, if that makes any sense. Like you said, you may not know her, but you've heard of her. I'm sure reputation has to be a part of that."

He shook his head and then snapped his fingers. "Since I'm new, and we're stuck with each other, want to test your theory?"

"What do you mean?" She looped her arm around his and followed him to the third floor.

"If we're going to be friends, you have to swear to keep this between us," he said, and she nodded as he opened the door that led to what appeared to be the offices. He dragged a chair into his cubicle and brought up Cain's account.

They both reviewed the list of purchases, but not one thing on it indicated any purchases for what could be considered another woman. Cain had good taste, according to Kevin, but most of her purchases were personal, with a few notations for Marie, Therese, and Billy Casey.

"Judging from this record," Kevin tapped the screen, "she's being nice and totally out of her shopping character."

"Thank you, and since we're promising to keep our secrets, I have to be honest and say I'll never completely fit into Cain's orbit." He glanced back at her after shutting his system down, and his surprised expression probably meant he had the wrong impression. "Not the rumor part, but the clothes and experience part. I grew up on a dairy farm in Wisconsin."

"Miss Emma, it'll be my pleasure to prove you wrong on that one. Shall we?" Kevin stood, bowed, and offered her his arm again. "The clothes and accessories are my specialty—the rest is up to you, but I'm confident you'll do fine."

"That makes one of us."

❖

"So who do you work for?" Jake asked when he opened his door after a few minutes of pounding.

"We're here for Cain Casey," the guy who appeared to be in his early twenties said.

The kid looked like he'd gotten hit in the face with a bat. Casey had gone to extremes to convince Jake she wasn't interested in dealing with him, so that he and his friend were here at all was confusing as hell.

"Cain Casey sent you here for what? To fuck with me?" He turned his back on them but didn't shut the door. He poured himself a shot and took one of the pain pills the ER doctor had prescribed. The doctor had splinted his fingers but said they'd have to wait for the swelling to go down before they decided if he needed surgery.

"Hey, you want us to leave?" the shorter guy said with the kind of attitude he was way too small to pull off well.

"Calm down and tell me who you are," he said, knocking on the wall to get Bradley up. He'd spent the night since the ER visit had taken so long. "I said calm down," he repeated when the little guy reached for something in his waistband. He opened the drawer closest to him and held them at gunpoint in case these two had a learning disability. "Start talking."

"I'm Marty and this is Jonsie," the taller guy said. "Obviously Cain can't deal with you directly, so it's us or nothing."

"Why can't she?" he asked.

"Man, you know the five-o is all over her ass. So you want to deal or not?" Marty asked.

"How much of a deal?" Bradley asked when he came out wearing only his jeans and holding his gun. "Same as usual?"

"We're like the two low men on the totem pole, so how the fuck should we know what's her usual." Marty spoke but kept glancing at Jonsie as if for backup. "How do you want to do this?"

"Give me a number, and I'll think about it," Jake said.

"This is only a trial run, so a hundred grand," Jonsie said, and Marty nodded. "If there's no problem, we'll up the numbers, but she really doesn't know you from nobody."

"Why send you two if, like you said, you're peons?" he asked. It was too early for this shit.

"She didn't really explain herself, but if you want my opinion, if you can pull this off, the big stuff should be easy as shit," Jonsie said as he leaned against the counter, obviously trying not to act like being held at gunpoint wasn't making him twitchy. Jake wasn't fooled since the kid's eyes were open wide and didn't leave the end of his hand.

"Do I get to talk to her?"

"Call her, she said, and the deal's off. Her words were, you could go fuck yourself," Marty said and motioned for Jonsie to get going. "Sounds like you're not interested, so fuck off."

"Hold on," Bradley said, moving between them and the door. "A hundred grand is a small order, but sure. We'll do it. We just need some guarantee that she'll deal with us exclusively from now on."

"I don't think that's going to be a problem," Marty said. "How much time do you need?"

"Give us a week and we'll be good to go. How do I get in touch with you?" Jake was thinking this was some kind of setup, but maybe that was why it wasn't. Cain had gone out of her way to show the feds she didn't want anything to do with him or anyone. In a fucked-up kind of way, maybe this was the way she'd go about giving him some business.

"We'll be back in a week with the money, so don't disappoint us," Jonsie said, and they pushed Bradley out of the way.

"You buying this?" Jake asked when the two tough guys slammed out of the apartment.

"It's not like anything I've heard Casey doing. She's a control freak when it comes to everything in her life," Bradley said as he poured himself some orange juice and smelled it. The move made him laugh since he couldn't remember when he'd bought it, so it was probably bad. "Her father was careful, and that's what he taught her to an extreme that might make this our only chance to do business with her."

"So is this bullshit or reverse psychology?"

"She's probably laughing her ass off thinking about us overanalyzing this situation, so tell me how you want to handle it," Bradley said, putting his full glass in the sink.

"We've come too far to choke now, so set it up." He took another small drink and held his broken fingers against his chest. "This is going to be sweet."

"Or we'll spend even more time in the emergency room piecing you back together."

❖

"That's right," Cain said to Billy on the phone as she headed back to the mall to get Emma. "Stick with the information Lincoln found. If you uncover anything, promise me you won't follow up alone."

"Are you kidding, and have you, Mum, and the guys after me? I don't think so. Go have fun, and we'll touch base when you get home. I'll probably still be up."

She hung up and hoped what Billy's crewman Lincoln had found in Baton Rouge would lead them somewhere. Muriel had called her about that and the start of the distribution of their first shipment. Billy had set it up, and after checking their routes numerous times, their guys had started for their new delivery locations. She'd wanted to be there to make sure they didn't have any compromised spots in their new setup, and so far everything was running smoothly.

"You want me to go in with you?" Merrick asked once they stopped.

"The only thing in danger is my credit card, so wait here." She headed in alone and paged Emma to try to find her.

"Hey," Emma said five minutes later as they met at the bottom of the escalator. "Are you sure you don't mind paying?"

"Did you find anything?" she said with a smile.

"Sort of," Emma said, and dropped her head onto Cain's chest. "The guy that helped me found more than one thing, but I had him put it all back once I was able to speak after the sticker shock."

"Ah," she said, kissing the top of Emma's head. "You could always wear the clothes with the tags and return them afterward," she said, laughing.

Emma slapped her side but laughed with her. "I'd never do that, and I've never experienced anything like today. He dragged me to every department, and I mean every one."

"I'm not sure what that means, but if that's the case, hopefully you picked something for me too."

Emma glanced up at her appearing mortified. "Did you need something? I can get it if you tell me what it is."

"How about we go upstairs for a few minutes, have a drink, and talk." She walked Emma to the glass elevators outside and rode up to the hotel on the eleventh floor. "Hopefully you had a little fun."

"Do you like to shop?" Emma asked, ordering them two glasses of wine and an appetizer.

"Sometimes," she said, watching a string of barges go by since they had a great view of the river. "My sister Marie is mentally challenged, and she likes coming and getting something for church with my mum." She smiled when Emma kissed her cheek. "She also likes toys and games, so I shop mostly for her."

"That's sweet." Emma kissed her on the lips this time. "Will you tell me about your family?"

"It's basically your story but with more kids. My parents loved tradition, and they tried to teach us to be good people. Marie and Billy are my only siblings, and Billy and I take turns caring for Marie to give Mum a break. She's a sweetie and really wants to meet you." She talked more about Marie and the rest of her family, thinking it was only fair since Emma had talked about her mom and dad.

"It sounds like you all take good care of her," Emma said as she traced her palm, stopping only to kiss a spot on her hand. "Do you really want me to get the dress we found? I think things will change if I let you do that."

She was finding that conversations with Emma were sometimes like wandering through a maze. "Nothing needs to change except that doubt or fear you have that I'm moving on. This is uncharted territory for both of us, but I want you to stop thinking that something like today somehow tallies up a debt between us." Cain took her hand and shook it gently. "That's the last thing on my mind."

"I just wanted to be sure and not screw up anything."

"Did you by chance find something you could wear to Sunday lunch?" She hoped dropping Emma in the middle of her family wouldn't overwhelm her, but it was time for that too.

"I thought you said you spend Sundays with your family?" Emma fed her a cracker with cheese.

"I do, but I'd like them to meet you. It's up to you, like the gifts, to decide if you want to or not. It's your decision, but like I said, from now on, whatever I'm doing, I want you there with me."

"Here," Emma said, holding up a card. "Kevin said to call when I was sure."

"Who is this?"

"Kevin, my personal shopper." Emma shook her head and laughed. "That's something I never thought I'd hear myself say."

"How about you and me make another deal?" Emma nodded since she'd put some of the appetizer into her mouth. "Today was my idea, but whenever you want something, you let me know and we'll do it. Both of us need to be happy or it won't work."

"Dinner at my place tonight—I'll cook. It won't be fancy, but I'll have you all to myself," Emma said as she stroked the side of her neck. "Does me touching you this much bother you?"

"Not a bit."

"Good, since I can't seem to help it. That's never happened to me either."

"Lucky me," she said and paid the bill. They stopped at Saks, and she signed for everything Emma had chosen before heading to the grocery. At the market Emma insisted on paying for the ingredients she needed for the spaghetti she planned to make. The totally domestic day should've made Cain's head explode, but she willingly pushed the cart while Emma added a few more things for herself.

"I figured since I've got help carrying all this stuff upstairs, I'm shamefully going to use you," Emma said and winked while they checked out.

Merrick and the guys waited outside, and in the apartment, Cain followed orders to relax while Emma put everything away. Once the six o'clock news was over, Emma joined her on the sofa while her sauce simmered.

"It's kind of surreal that you're here," Emma said, straddling her lap and combing her hair back.

"How so?" She tried to keep herself in check and not get too turned on.

"It wasn't that long ago that I was spilling beer on you, and now I want to strip naked and have you touch me." Emma was beautiful when she blushed, and now was no exception.

"If you need a second on that plan, I'm all for it."

"Not quite yet," Emma said and kissed her. Before they could get too involved, Emma's phone rang. "Damn."

"Your mother again, you think?" She sincerely hoped not, since Emma was in a great mood.

"I've already had my weekly lecture, so I doubt it." Emma stretched and picked up the receiver since whoever it was didn't want to hang up. "Hello."

"Hey, you ran out so fast today I didn't get a chance to talk to you," a young woman said. Emma was close enough that Cain could hear every word, but Emma rolled her eyes and didn't seem to mind her eavesdropping.

"I was meeting Cain and didn't want to be late." Emma smiled when she laced the fingers of Emma's free hand with hers. "Did you need something?"

"You two worked things out? I thought you promised to let me know."

"You sure are curious," Emma said, stopping for a quick kiss. "Are you interested in her or something?" she asked jokingly.

"No. I want you to be happy, and I also thought we could double date. I started seeing someone recently."

"Let's talk about it later, okay? I'm in the middle of a project."

"Live a little, Emma. Life isn't all about homework."

Emma hung up the phone and unplugged it. "Depends on what you're learning about, I guess," she said, and kissed Cain like she wanted to devour her.

Cain was in serious pain by the time Emma got up to check on dinner, figuring any sins she'd ever committed were somewhat being forgiven for not pushing Emma on relieving the pressure. The place was small enough that she watched Emma put everything together and plate it.

To see the care and time Emma had put in to making her a meal made her think of how much she craved this woman who seemed to have turned her life upside down in a very short time. It was ridiculous, but Emma was the first thing on her mind when she woke up and the last thing she thought of as she went to bed. It was like she'd become a character in a romance novel, but it didn't bother her because the other main character was Emma. Her head might've been wanting to use caution, but her heart was ready to commit.

"Do you like to cook?" she asked, rolling up her sleeves after a few bites. Emma was right in that it wasn't fancy, but it was delicious.

"I do now since it became a necessity. Cooking and leftovers are cheaper than eating out, so I don't go out often."

"Thank you for cooking for me. We're experiencing all kinds of firsts together." She held up her glass of the wine that had been her contribution and tapped it against Emma's. "To the chef."

"Thanks," Emma said, combing her hair back almost shyly. "Maybe we can make this a weekly thing."

"If you don't mind cooking, I'll be happy to be here."

They did the dishes together, but Cain stopped to answer the door, figuring it might be Merrick since she'd left her phone in the car, not wanting to be disturbed. "Delivery for Miss Verde."

Cain signed for it while the guy made two trips and hung the garment bags where Emma pointed out, then put the bags on the bed. "This is kind of a lot, huh?" Emma asked, holding her hands over her mouth.

"Think of it this way," she said, not peeking in any bag even though she was curious. "Once school's over, you'll need some stuff to go out and interview in, so it's a bundle of your birthday and graduation gifts."

"I don't think I could interview in any of this," Emma whispered. "It's all evening stuff since that's what you said. I took advantage, didn't I?"

"Hey." She held Emma and rubbed her back. "The stuff I'm going to say next isn't bragging, okay?"

"Okay," Emma said, her head pressed against her chest like she was listening to her heartbeat.

"When I went to school I never thought about what anything cost. I didn't have student loans, I didn't have to limit anything, and I had my family not only around me but behind me in support. What I mean is, I didn't have to do it alone, and it wasn't a hardship because my family had money."

"I work for you, so I understand the money part."

"What you don't seem to understand, though, is why have all this money if I can't spend it on someone I want to spend it on? I want to share with you what isn't all that important to me in the realm of what's really sacrosanct in my life." She lowered her head and very gently pressed her lips to Emma's. "And you don't work for me. You work for yourself."

"But it's unfair to you in the long run, isn't it? I can't give you that much in return. Not even close."

"Good Lord, you're stubborn," she said and laughed. "You just spent the afternoon cooking for me. No one but my mother had ever done that because I can't cook to save my life, and no other woman has offered. And even if they had, I probably wouldn't have gone because all the rest have wanted what you don't care about—the money."

"Okay, I believe you, and thank you for this. Everything Kevin helped me with is beautiful, and I hope you like it."

"Do you like it?" she asked, making a mental note to add Emma to her account.

"I love everything," Emma said, kissing her chin.

"Good, and from now on you can go without me if you need something. Ask for Kevin, and he'll know how to handle it." She pressed her finger against Emma's lips. "If not, the money simply sits in the bank, and nights like tonight will make us even."

"If you say so."

"I did say it, but it's important to me that you agree."

"You're hard to beat in a debate," Emma said as she hugged her tight.

"My persuasive personality is the secret to my success."

CHAPTER TWENTY-ONE

Three days later, Emma got a call from Kevin since he remembered it was her and Cain's big date she'd gotten the first dress for. "What time is Ms. Casey picking you up?"

"Seven for dinner, then to some place called the Gemini Club," Emma said, yawning.

She'd taken two shifts at the pub the night before, then come home and studied some for her midterm stuff after Cain had dropped her off, since Cain had worked from the pub with Billy. A steady stream of people had gone back to the office, and a few appeared somewhat terrified when they left. The situation was interesting, but she wasn't in the mood to ask what it was about.

"Get dressed and meet me in the shoe department in a couple of hours, if that's okay," Kevin said. "You'll need something stylish but comfortable, and I have one of the girls lined up to do your makeup after you get your hair done."

"It's like I'm going to the prom," she said and laughed. "Do I need to call someone about my hair?"

"A friend of mine is ready at his salon, so don't worry about it. We'll go there first, then have a late lunch before the makeup."

"Are you sure? I don't want to suck up your whole day." She sat up on the sofa and couldn't believe she'd been napping so long.

"My boss gave me the assignment, so no arguments, buttercup," he said, sounding almost giddy. "Did you go to the prom?"

"No," she said, sticking her tongue out at the phone.

Granted, she'd known Bea and a couple of other people longer, but Kevin had become a closer and better friend in less time. He made the day fun and took plenty of notes to go in her profile. She laughed since he was the first person in her life to know her bra and underwear size, but now there was a record of it. He also gave her some pointers about social niceties that had nothing to do with his job and kissed her cheeks when he turned her back over to Lou for the ride home.

Already showered, after some reading she unzipped the garment bag and took out the black dress Kevin had found her. It was sleeveless and form-fitting all the way to the knee but had a high collar. She'd seen stuff like this only in magazines, but this one was hers.

Once she'd stepped into it she realized her problem, but the knock on her door solved it. She checked to make sure it was Cain before opening the door and turning around. "Perfect timing," she said as Cain very slowly zipped her up.

"You look absolutely beautiful," Cain said when she turned around again. "You look beautiful all the time, but you're simply stunning tonight."

"I had to keep up," she said, seeing how good a tuxedo could look on a person. "My date might outshine me."

"No way are you in danger of that. You ready?"

"Without Kevin's help, I'd still be fumbling around, so thank you for that."

"Who's Kevin again?" Cain asked, taking her keys and locking the door.

"My guy from Saks."

"I'm glad he helped, but I had nothing to do with that. He must just like you, so if he's interested in anything else but helping you, tell him you're already taken."

She laughed as she got into the car. "I doubt he'll leave his boyfriend for me, honey. He's good to know since he's more knowledgeable about clothes than I'll ever be."

Cain chose Le Coquille D'Huîte in the French Quarter, since the Blanchard family and the Caseys had been friends for years, and it was also close to where they were going. The food and the romantic atmosphere made Emma give thanks to the universe again for having put Cain in her path. No matter what anyone else believed about her, Cain had been nothing but caring.

"I've never had such a good time," she said when Cain handed the bill back to the waiter.

"You deserve nothing but good things, lass, and since we started over I wanted to make all our time together memorable. So date number four should be different from all the rest."

"Different how?" she asked, thinking Cain really enjoyed teasing her.

"You gambled on giving me another chance, so that's the theme of tonight's date. Did you bring the money I asked you for?" Cain asked with a truly mischievous expression.

When Cain had asked her to bring two hundred dollars, she'd found the request bizarre, but she hadn't argued. "Yes. Do you want it?"

"Not yet." Cain stood and offered her a hand. Merrick and Lou were waiting outside, and it didn't take long to reach the Gemini. The sign on the door said it was a private party, so Cain laughed when the guys in the van behind them kept driving.

"Cain, welcome," a very handsome older gentleman said after they were escorted inside. "Your date is much more beautiful than Jarvis, but don't tell him I said that."

"Thank you," she said, extending her hand to him. "Emma Verde."

"Welcome to my club, Miss Verde. Ramon Jatibon." He lowered his head to kiss her hand. "Hopefully the dice will fall in your favor tonight."

She smiled and nodded as Cain led her up the stairs where the second floor eventually opened up to a nice-sized casino. "Let's get some chips," Cain said, heading to the cashier's cage. "Do you know how to play craps?"

"No, but I'm guessing I'm getting ready to learn," she said, handing over her money.

"Think of it not as a two-hundred-dollar lesson, but as a chance to make fast money." Cain signed something, handed her money to her, and accepted a tray of chips.

"That's if we win," she said, but followed willingly.

"You have to have faith, darling girl." They found a spot toward the end of the table, where Cain arranged their chips, but they didn't bet until a new game started. "Now's the only time you root for the seven," Cain said, putting her bet down and pointing to where Emma should place one of her two chips.

The guy next to them shook the dice and tossed an eleven. "Eleven, winner," the dealer said, placing a chip next to the one she'd put down.

"See, easy hundred," Cain said, kissing her. "Pick that one up and gamble with Ramon's money."

The night went on with Cain pressed up to her back, cheering her on when it was their turn to throw. With Cain's help she'd turned her two hundred into fifty-three hundred, which was more money than she'd ever had. They'd also spent a lot of time touching and kissing, without anyone giving them any kind of problem, and the time seemed to fly by.

"You okay?" Cain asked when she really leaned back against her.

"I'm fine. Just resting my feet." She cocked her head to the side when Cain kissed her neck, and the room got hot. "But I'll keep doing it if you keep doing that."

"I will, but I'd like some more privacy, so one more game and we're out of here." Cain sucked her earlobe in and held her up when her knees got weak. "Lend me seven hundred dollars."

She handed the chips over, even though Cain had a pile in front of her, and took the dice when Cain dropped them into her hand. No one blew on them like in the movies, but she let them fly when Cain put her hand on her ass and squeezed.

"Seven, winner," the dealer said.

"Pick them up, lass, and let the bet ride," Cain said, her hand not moving, but they were so close together no one could see. She threw, and the seven came up again.

"Seven, winner," the dealer said, moving her winnings closer to her.

"You're at six thousand, so you're doing good," Cain said softly in her ear since their table had drawn a loud crowd.

She threw until she'd set and hit a number, adding another couple thousand to her total and a passionate kiss from Cain. If she'd known gambling was this much fun, she'd have defied her mother years ago and moved to Vegas.

"Oh my God," she said when the cage counted out her money. "This is so much." No one had mentioned taxes or signing anything, so she didn't ask. "I can pay you back if you want."

"You can do that by saving that stack for next semester. If you have a rainy-day fund, you won't have to work as much." Cain pocketed Emma's money since it wouldn't fit in her small purse and signed something for her own winnings. "Just don't bank it, since the place you were in is a figment of your imagination."

She smiled and shook her head. When they were alone in the backseat, she said, "My mother warned me about you."

"Your mother couldn't have imagined anyone like me," Cain said and kissed her. The ride home drove her need up, and in her hallway when Cain put her hand on her breast, she didn't stop her. "I want you," Cain said with a hoarse voice.

"I want…" She didn't know enough to finish that statement, and Cain seemed to notice.

"You're going to kill me, but we need to slow down," Cain said, pulling back a little. "Let me help you with this dress before I go."

She stood in the middle of her apartment and held her breath when Cain lowered her zipper. It would be so easy to ask Cain to stay, but she still wasn't sure of herself.

"Go change," Cain said, holding her dress closed, which confused her.

"Do you want to—"

"I do, but not when you've been drinking," Cain said, kissing her shoulder. "Don't give that part of yourself to anyone until you're in love and you want it more than anything. And have a clear head so you're sure."

"I'm thinking straight now," she said, smiling at Cain's generous nature.

"That's your slightly tipsy hormones talking, so go put something on before I forget how honorable I am. You're not the only one with a hormone problem."

Kevin had included a couple of things to sleep in, but those would have to wait for another night. Her T-shirt and sweatpants would do for now. "Thank you for a beautiful night."

"Get some sleep, and I'll come by at eleven thirty to pick you up," Cain said as she put her arms around her. "And no matter what my mother tells you, you're stuck with me."

"Good to know since you're going to have to move to another state if you're thinking of ditching me."

"That's the last thought in my head." Cain kissed her, then walked to the door. "Until tomorrow, lass, and every tomorrow thereafter."

"I'm an English major who happens to love poetry, so you certainly know how to romance a girl with beautiful words," she said, leaning against her door.

"I've been a lifelong charmer, but now, with you, I'm going to listen to my mum."

"What did she say?"

"My da swept her off her feet, and they had a lifetime of happiness and all that comes from that. It's time to romance the girl, so how lucky am I to have found such a good one."

"Words like that are binding," she said, holding her hand out to Cain.

"Remind me to tell you what every Casey baby hears at birth, but not tonight. Get some sleep, and I'll see you in the morning."

"Good night." She locked her door and exhaled. Every tomorrow thereafter sounded like heaven.

❖

Cain arrived half an hour early the next day and seemed happy to sit on the sofa while Emma finished getting ready. She'd woken up hours before, wanting to lay everything out, including the sundress Cain had helped her pick out. It was simple but elegant, and she hoped it would pass the inspection she was sure Cain's mother had planned for her.

"Are you okay in there?" Cain asked, and she heard the rustling of the paper Cain had brought with her. "It's lunch, lass, not the Academy Awards."

"It's lunch with your family, so I want to look like something that didn't fall off a truck. Cut me some slack. I've never done the meet-the-parents thing."

"I've never done that either, so we'll hold hands and get through it together," Cain said, smiling at her. Her tan skin made the white of the thick linen shirt stand out, and that combination made Cain's eyes bluer and more beautiful. "Trust me. Therese Casey is a tough old bird, but she's been waiting for you a long time."

"Me? We just met, honey."

"Okay. She's been waiting for me to come to my senses, cut out all my running around, and bring home a nice girl."

"You weren't interested in nice girls then?" she asked and laughed as she stepped back into the bedroom to put on her lipstick.

Cain followed her and sat on the bed. "I've met a few in my life, but the thought of being with them for more than a month made me antsy."

"And now?" she said, glancing at Cain in the mirror.

"And now, I'd tell you the answer to that question, but I'm not sure you're ready for it," Cain said and winked at her.

"Try me," she said, putting her lipstick tube down and turning around.

"I'm dying to, but you keep turning me down," Cain joked, but stood up and took both her hands. "It's the strangest thing. Right before we met, Mum and I had a talk, and she mentioned it was time to settle down and give her some grandchildren."

Emma backed Cain up until she landed back on the bed so she could sit in her lap. "Try not to wrinkle this dress and go on."

"I don't think we're ready for the grandkids just yet, but I'm ready for you."

"Are you sure? Because while I don't have much experience, when I pick someone, it's going to be for a lifetime."

"I'm sure," Cain said and kissed her. "So finish getting ready and let me introduce you to my family."

She grabbed her bag and held Cain's hand as they walked down to the car, surprised that she was actually not only driving but was alone. She also hoped that Cain wouldn't notice that her hand was clammy.

"Why do you look so nervous?" Cain asked as she opened her door for her.

"Are you kidding? You keep mentioning how important your family is to you, so what if they don't like me?" She took Cain's hand again as soon as she got behind the wheel. "I can especially tell how important Marie is to you, so I want her to like me so she doesn't mind sharing you." She snapped her fingers and kept Cain from putting the car in gear. "Which reminds me, I got Marie something, but I forgot it upstairs. Can you give me a minute to run up and get it?"

"Tell me where it is, and I'll go get it." Cain took her keys and took only a few minutes before she came back with the large bag she'd left by the door. "You could have grass clippings in this bag and she'd love it."

"Do you think I should've gotten something for your mom?"

"Lass, quit your worrying. Marie's going to love you, and so will my mother. You've already met Billy, and he's in the firm like-you column." She squeezed Emma's thigh and smiled as they got under way. They actually didn't live all that far apart, so it was a quick trip to the other side of St. Charles Avenue. "Remember that Marie gets confused at times, but just be patient with her." Two of the guards opened the front gate, and Emma waved, recognizing them from the pub when they accompanied Cain.

"I'll remember." She smoothed down her dress for the hundredth time since Cain had come over. "Are you positive I look all right? I don't want your mother thinking I'm not right for you."

Cain's smile softened her expression. "You look fabulous. At least I certainly think so."

"I just want them to like me," she said, positive that she sounded like a broken record.

Cain got out of the car and walked to Emma's door. When she opened it she crouched down and pressed her palm to Emma's cheek. "Do you think you're right for me?"

"With all my heart."

"That's all that matters."

Before Cain could say anything else, the front door opened, and Marie pressed herself to her sister's back. "Hi," she shyly said to Emma. "We're going to be great friends."

"Hi, Marie, and you're absolutely right," she said, smiling at the young woman who resembled her big sister.

Marie's words proved that Cain was right. Life might have given Marie a mind that wouldn't mature like most, but her heart had fared just fine. Emma smiled and gazed into eyes that were exactly like Cain's, missing only the mischief always shining in her sister's. Emma felt an instant affection for Marie, which crystalized in her mind how positive she was that she was falling in love. It was a good thing Cain had talked to her back at her apartment about how she felt so she wasn't alone on that front.

"Marie, Cain told me how much you like art, so I thought you might like this." She accepted the bag from Cain and handed it over. When she was young, she'd loved the paint-by-numbers canvases and after looking at a few places had found a big one. "I thought it'd be something we could do together."

"I love it," Marie said, clapping her hands before she even took the bag from her. "Thank you, Emma." After accepting her gift and hugging her tight, Marie headed into the house, calling for her mum.

"I should've brought something for lunch. It was rude not to," she said as they followed Marie inside.

"Mum is more likely to send you home with something, so stop worrying before you pass out on me," Cain said and followed Emma's line of sight to the portrait in the foyer and the vase of flowers under it. "That's my da," Cain said and smiled as the older woman who had to be Therese Casey touched the painting as if to straighten it, even though it was perfect. "Mum, this is Emma Verde."

"It's a pleasure, ma'am," Emma said in a voice so high she thought Cain was right and she'd pass out.

"I'm glad you're here, Emma," Therese Casey said with her hand out. After she took Emma's hand she led her toward the back of the house. Cain followed, appearing amused after she'd gazed back at her with a panicked expression. "Tell me about your family."

"I'm from Wisconsin, and my parents run a dairy farm. After high school I got a scholarship to come to Tulane, so I've been here three years studying and working until recently in the bookstore."

"And your parents know about my Cain?" Therese asked as she tore lettuce.

Emma tried her best to answer the question without sounding like she didn't appreciate her parents as people, but she didn't want to lie either. Her story was stilted and hesitant, but Therese had nodded through it, eventually reaching over and covering her hand with hers for a moment. The strain of telling it had worn on Emma, so by the time the end came, she was leaning heavily against Cain. She straightened immediately when she finished, remembering who her audience was.

"Go tend to your sister," Therese said, and the dismissal was only for Cain. "Emma, would you mind helping me finish?" Therese asked, in case her first directive wasn't clear enough.

"Sure." Emma realized that she sounded anything but sure of herself.

"Give us a minute, okay?" Cain took Emma's hand and tugged her to her feet. "She deserves a tour before you put her to work making lunch, Mum. I promise I won't keep her long."

The house was grander than any Emma had ever seen, but every room was comfortable and unpretentious, except for the front parlor with its multitude of family photos, Irish lace, and a bar with the most beautiful crystal glasses and decanters she'd ever seen. She ran her finger along the etching on the one closest to her. Would she ever fit somewhere like this?

"Those have been in my family for generations," Cain said as she hugged her from behind. "My great-great-great-grandmother Rosin Casey purchased them after she established the family business in America. Every generation has enjoyed hearing her story, and we're all grateful for her bravery in laying the groundwork for this."

"They're beautiful," she said, and dropped her hand to her side. "I'd be afraid to use them, considering how special they are to your family. We weren't poor, but we didn't have anything like this. My dad's family has some china they brought from France, but that's about it. My mother never uses it."

"Beautiful things are meant to be enjoyed, child," Therese said from behind them. When Emma turned, Marie was standing close to Cain's mother, smiling at her. "When Dalton was alive, we sat in here at least twice a week and shared a drink."

"That sounds so nice, and so romantic," she said, squeezing Cain's arm. "Now I know where Cain learned it."

"Dalton was the love of my life, and things like sharing a drink out of those glasses with him are the moments I miss the most." Therese sighed and motioned her to a chair. "Cain, take Marie and yourself and wash your hands. Lunch is in thirty minutes or so."

Cain appeared to hesitate for the same reason she'd followed her to the kitchen, but if she wanted to prove she was strong enough to defend the fact that she belonged with Cain, she had to start now. If she folded and had to have Cain fight every battle for her, they'd never have a future together.

"Go on," she said to Cain. "We'll be right behind you." She closed her eyes and smiled when Cain nodded, then gave her a quick kiss on the lips.

"This is a first," Therese said as she sat across from her.

"What do you mean?" She sat and placed her hands on her thighs, trying not to move them. Rubbing them against the material of her dress would be a dead giveaway of the nerves threatening to run amok.

"My Derby bringing someone home." Therese smiled, and while she was an attractive woman, Emma found no resemblance to Cain in her face. "It's a development I really like."

"But you know nothing about this hick, right?" she asked, and Therese laughed. "Like I just told Cain, I grew up with traditions too, Mrs. Casey, only we don't have any beautiful glasses to show for them. My father's a farmer, and he shared with me those things you need to run a successful dairy business."

"Only you don't want a future milking cows, do you?"

"Not until Cain becomes interested in cheese and butter."

"Even if your father's cows could spit whiskey out of their teats,

I still can't picture Derby doing that," Therese said, and laughed again. "The Caseys are a rowdy bunch, but they love fiercely and are loyal to the end."

"It'll take time for you to understand and believe what a gift Cain is to me."

"Derby is my first-born and has so much responsibility resting on her shoulders after her da was killed. I worry about her even though she's never given me reason to. That job goes to her brother Billy, who seems to worry me all the time, but he's your biggest fan and the one who pushed the most when hardhead decided not to talk to you." Therese stood and poured a little of her sherry into two glasses and handed her one. "That boy of mine is a menace, but he loves his sister and seems to think you make her happy."

"I give you my word she'll be safe with me, and more than anything I want a life as long and as happy as you had with Mr. Casey."

"Do you love her?"

"I do," she said without hesitation.

"Have you told her that?" Therese asked with a widening smile.

"Not yet, so I hope I don't lose points for telling you first," she said and laughed. "Cain is my first love, and if I can convince her, she'll be my last. If you hit perfection right off, you don't have any reason to keep looking."

Therese held up her glass and tapped it against hers when she did the same. "If that's true, then Rosin's glasses will be in good hands." Emma nodded at the small approval. "Remember your pretty words, Emma, because if they have no foundation, you'll have to pay a price that might be too steep for you, and one you might not recover from. Do we understand each other?"

"Yes, ma'am," she said, and hesitated. "It's crystal clear."

❖

"You okay?" Cain asked when she got back to the kitchen and caught Emma alone for a moment.

"You have a great mother, and I'm fine," Emma said, putting her arms loosely around Cain. "Don't pout, mobster. She really was nice."

"Okay, but tell me if this is too much for you," Cain said and kissed her as if she wasn't worried they were in Therese's kitchen.

"Ooh, I'm telling," Billy said in a singsongy voice.

"Get out of here, goofball," Cain said, not letting her go. "You're just jealous."

"Emma picked too quickly, because clearly I look much better drenched in beer than you," he said, rocking on his feet.

"You didn't have a chance," Emma said, standing on her toes and kissing Cain's cheek.

"Damn, Emma, you don't have to rub it in," he said and hunched over when Therese slapped the back of his head.

"Don't curse the guest, Billy Dalton Casey," Therese said, pointing to the dining room. "Go sit and try to act like you weren't raised by wolves, the both of you."

"Emma, you want to come sit by me?" Marie said, and Emma gladly took Marie's hand. "I love my present."

"If you want, I could help you."

"Did you hear that, sister?" Marie said, sounding extremely thrilled that Emma seemed to like her.

"I heard, and if Emma helps you, maybe you can make her some cookies and teach her to play checkers."

Lunch was nice, and Emma liked how much Cain's family laughed together. She saw how compassionate Cain was with every one of them, so she meant every word she'd told Therese. She didn't need months to know what was in her heart, so once she'd helped Therese clean the kitchen, she took Cain's hand and walked out to the backyard. On Sundays, Therese let the help have the day off, so she didn't want to leave her to do all the work.

"Oh," she said when Cain led her to the rose garden close to the house.

"Mum's pride and joy. Some of these plants go back a few generations, and all of them came from clippings of the first bushes Rosin and Delaney Casey brought when they purchased their first house in New Orleans." Cain sat on the bench at the head of the garden. "One rainy day I'll tell you the story of my two grandmothers from ages ago who started the family business."

"Sounds like an interesting story as full of history as those plants," she said, pressing into Cain when she put her arm around her.

"I grew up listening to the history of my family, and a lot of it revolved around the relationships instead of what we did to make money. Rosin and Delaney are part of that history, so even though it was years ago, no one ever looked upon them any differently than my da and mum."

She closed her eyes and nodded. "The relationships are the most important. Business is business, but the great loves in our past make those stories you tell your children so special."

"Do you like kids?" Cain rubbed her fingers along the length of Emma's arm, then back down.

"As in having some or in general?" She moved so she could look at Cain's face.

"Both, I guess. All those stories my parents told me didn't really register, since I paid attention only to the business parts."

"But now it's different?" she said, placing her hand over Cain's heart.

"I've never brought anyone home to meet my family, especially Marie. If they didn't come back, she wouldn't understand that it didn't have anything to do with her. But then I've never met someone who I think is a perfect fit—someone who I see still by my side when I'm old and cranky." Cain smiled and pressed her hand to her cheek. "You're the answer to everything I thought didn't exist."

"I love you," she whispered, and Cain smiled so widely she thought her cheeks would hurt if she held her expression too long.

"I love you too," Cain said before she kissed her. "Before we take that next step, though, you and I need to talk about the unromantic business side. You shouldn't commit to what you don't know."

"That will come with time, so let me enjoy the next chapter of the story we tell in the future." She combed Cain's hair back and then traced her eyebrows. "Thank you for bringing me here to tell me. You're right that we haven't known each other that long, but you've completely changed my life. I never thought I'd find someone who makes me this happy, and your family only completes that picture of what life could be like."

"What exactly were you worried about?" Cain asked, and they both turned their heads when the loud laughing inside broke their peace, so Cain moved them to a more secluded spot.

The swing hanging from the old oak branch was covered in pillows and seemed like the perfect nest for an afternoon of reading. "Not being accepted, I guess, was my greatest fear," she said, putting her feet up and resting against Cain when she encouraged it by patting her chest. "There's no one like you back home, and I was tired of living in denial to please my mother."

"No matter what, you should always go with what makes *you* happy," Cain said, placing her hand flat against her upper chest. "If you do everything to make someone else happy, eventually everyone around you, especially you, will be miserable."

"I'll be glad to keep that promise, just as long as I get to keep you."

"I'm more than willing," Cain said and sighed. "Mum should be thrilled as well."

"How so?" She moved a little so she was facing Cain and not hiking her dress up.

"When we had the talk about settling down, I told her I still had plenty of oats to sow."

"You do, mobster. Only now I have exclusive farming rights."

CHAPTER TWENTY-TWO

So what exactly do you want from me?" Callie Richard asked the guys Big Gino wanted her to meet. Shawn and Royce Liam seemed to come as a package deal, and they'd talked nonstop since they'd sat down.

"Casey was our buyer, but Royce and I would like to go in another direction," Shawn said. "If we're not supplying her, then it shouldn't be too long before she becomes vulnerable enough to take out. From my understanding, you're interested in that."

"I don't talk much business with people who come to me out of the blue and uninvited."

Shawn smiled like it was all he had to do to convince her of his sincerity. "We have plenty of mutual friends who'll vouch for me and my brother, so I don't think that'll be a problem."

"So I shouldn't worry my pretty little head over it?" she asked sweetly before taking out her switchblade and pressing it to his neck. "You can't be that stupid, can you?"

"One of our mutual friends did say you took a little getting used to, but I'm as interested in taking Casey out of the game as you. Consider that, and I'm sure you'll realize how beneficial a partnership between us can be."

"What's your beef with her?" she asked, thinking this pretty boy looked like he didn't take too kindly to rejection and that was his problem with Cain.

"We want to do business with someone else who understands mutual respect, and Cain is not that person," Royce said.

Her phone rang, and it was Boone, so she decided to let him wait until she finished with these two fools. "Let me talk it over with my brother, and I'll get back to you."

"When you're ready, we can sit and talk not only buying, but how to turn a profit once you've received your supply," Royce said.

"Casey shared that with you?"

"Not exactly, but our family has been in this business longer and is much more successful than Casey will ever be," Shawn said.

"Sounds like you should do it all yourself then, but you might get those soft hands dirty and callused," she said and laughed. "Respect is earned, and so far I'm not there with you. Like I said, I'll talk to my brother and call you. If that's not good enough, then move on."

"Opportunities like this don't come around often," Shawn said.

"Yeah, that's what every scumbag in the old neighborhood told my mother, and now she's a strung-out hooker. So you wait or you don't. I'm not the one who wanted this meeting." She folded her knife and stood up. "The next time you want to play the tough guy, bring more than your little brother," she said, pointing to Royce.

"You're turning us down?" Royce asked.

"I'm telling you to wait. Go home and I'll be in touch, but forget Casey. She's ours and we'll handle it, but we'll do the same to you if you try to set up in our neighborhoods on your own." She pushed her chair back and stepped behind Royce. "You do that, and I'll be happy to remove your tonsils through your neck."

"Do you ever get tired of the threats, Ms. Richard?" Shawn asked.

"It's the killing that tires me out, but the thrill more than makes up for it."

❖

"I hope you're not a stranger after this Sunday, Emma," Therese said as Cain prepared to take Emma home. "Here's something to help you study."

Emma accepted the shopping bag full of containers of food before handing it to Cain. "Thank you, Mrs. Casey, and I'd like to come back to help Marie with the art project I brought. I promise to call first to make sure it's okay."

"You come whenever you like," Therese said, hugging Emma. "But do call if you need anything before then. If your schedule's not too bad, come by and have lunch with Marie and me. We'd love the company."

"Okay. Let's not smother her right off," Cain said, placing the bag in the backseat.

"You hush, Derby," Therese said before kissing Emma's cheek, followed by a shyer Marie. "It's important for Emma to have someone looking after her since she's so far from home."

"Don't laugh," Billy said, kissing Emma next. "She knows where you live, so you can't escape her now."

"You and your sister behave, and I'd love to come for lunch, Mrs. Casey."

"We don't stand on ceremony here, so call me Therese. I'll see you this week then, and definitely on Sunday."

"Yes, ma'am," Emma said, hugging Therese again. "And thanks for the food."

"You ready?" Cain asked, helping her in the car. Emma waved as they drove off before she grabbed Cain's free hand. "See? They loved you."

"They're certainly different from my family, and easy to get along with." Emma leaned over and kissed her cheek. "Thanks again for bringing me."

"I wanted you to know them and vice versa," she said as she parked close to Emma's building. "Do you have to study?"

"I got everything done ahead of time so we could relax for a while. Do you have to run off?" Emma's soft voice had a way of making Cain want to touch her. "We could watch a movie or something."

"Let me help you unpack the two weeks' worth of food my mum gave you, and we'll do just that."

They walked upstairs and sat on the sofa after everything was refrigerated, leaving them free to get close. "You make me nuts when you kiss me like that," Emma said a few minutes later.

"Do you mean that in a good way?" She kissed Emma's neck and rubbed her hand down to her butt. "Or in a bad way," she said, reversing course.

"It's definitely a good thing, honey. I think you know that already and just like to tease me," Emma said, then groaned when her phone rang. "Sorry. My dad usually calls today."

"Go ahead."

"Hey, Bea," Emma said after she answered. The way she rolled her eyes made Cain think it wasn't a call Emma wanted to stop for. "No. I got home a few minutes ago. I had lunch with Cain's family." Emma grabbed her hand when she got too close to her breast and smiled. "Maybe later. I'll ask her." She paused again and bit one of her fingers. "Okay. I'll call you…or that's good too."

"Something wrong?" she asked as Emma leaned over her and kissed her neck.

"Bea's got this new boyfriend, and she's really anxious to get us all together. It's nuts, but we've both been single for so long that I guess it'll be fun now that we've both found someone."

"You want to invite them to the pub for a few drinks? Sunday's usually our slow day, but the band's pretty good. They take enough breaks that we can talk in between sets."

"I really wanted you all to myself for the rest of the day."

"Don't worry. I won't leave right away when we come back." She stopped to kiss Emma with a little heat. "You can drive me crazy, then send me home to my cold shower."

"Poor baby," Emma said, rubbing her shoulders. "You'll survive."

"Barely, so call, and I'll phone the house and let them know I'll be a bit."

"What? That you'll be out past curfew?" Emma said, kissing the tip of her nose.

"Yes. My guys worry when I'm left to my own devices." While Emma called her friend back, Cain stepped aside to talk to Billy. "Take a few of the guys and sit back. It's probably nothing, but Emma's friend sure is pushing this meeting for it to be only a double date."

"We'll beat you there, so feel free to ignore us," Billy said and hung up.

"It's weird, but you made Bea's night." Emma had put on some more lipstick and handed her the tube. "Do you mind if I leave my purse?"

"I won't need it, and I'm glad to be of service to Bea."

"I promise we don't have to stay long, since I'm not sure what this is about. Bea has never been a shy dater, so maybe this has to do with you."

"How so?"

"It's strange that she knew all about you and warned me at first to stay away from you, but now she can't wait to spend time with you. I really don't want to stay long, but if you really don't mind, it'll get her off this double-date thing."

"You're the boss tonight, lass, so whisper in my ear, and I'll bring you home and whisper some stuff back." Emma kissed her and wiped her lips to get the lipstick she'd left behind. "Did she tell you Mr. Wonderful's name?"

"Not yet, but judging by her little hints, they must be horizontal as much as possible." Emma shrugged and appeared somewhat uncomfortable. "I know it's what everyone does without much thought since it's a totally natural thing."

"Except when you want it to mean something," she said, not liking Emma's bout of self-doubt. "Don't rush something that's special, lass. When you're ready, and the time is right, you'll know it, so stop beating yourself up about it. I'll be happy to tell you that as many times as it takes."

"But you want it, right?"

"I was hoping that when that day comes, I'd be the one you've been waiting on," she said, squeezing Emma's hands. "But if you need me to be clearer, it's a resounding yes. I really want to."

Emma laughed, then filled her in on all things Beatrice Weller. The only Wellers Cain had heard of ran a small rackets operation in St. Bernard, but she wasn't familiar enough with them to know the extended family. It was small-time, but small fish were always interested in fattening up from the scraps of bigger fish, so it paid to be vigilant.

"Hey, Boss," one of the bouncers said when she left the car idling. The guys working the pub's doors parked it for her and would bring it back when she was ready to leave. "Hey, Emma. You sure clean up good."

"Thank you," Emma said, taking her hand. "Wow," she said when they walked in and the band was in the middle of a song. The place was full, but the table in the corner was waiting for them.

"I should've said Sundays were our slow days, but now a day of beer, pretty girls, and singing has been a hit," she said, waving to the bartender. Josh was usually off on Sundays and Mondays, but his backup Benny was as trustworthy. "What would you like to drink, lass?"

"White wine, please."

She gave the waitress their order and pulled out Emma's chair after she'd hugged the young woman hello. It didn't take long before Bea arrived, dragging a large man behind her, and the guy did what she would've in the same situation. He glanced around slowly enough that Cain was impressed with his thoroughness, but he seemed to overlook Billy and his guys.

"Bea," Emma said, pointing to the chairs across from them. They'd be able to have a normal conversation for the fifteen minutes the band was on break. "This is Cain Casey." The introductions between them were done except for the big guy, who didn't seem the coed type.

"This is my new boyfriend Boone," Bea said, and Cain fought her urge to show surprise at the name.

"Boone," she said, standing up and cutting only her eyes toward his chest. The double holster was identical to the one Billy and Merrick wore. "Cain Casey."

"Boone Richard," Boone said, not making a move to sit.

The way he stood with his feet slightly spread and still holding her hand made her think she'd somewhat miscalculated the situation by having Emma this close to what was potentially a bad situation. "Emma, do me a favor and go to the bar for the next round."

Emma had started to get up when Boone opened a switchblade in his other hand. "Sit, and keep your mouth shut," Boone said to Emma as he pressed the knife tip right under Cain's breastbone.

"Boone, what the hell?" Bea said, loud enough to draw attention to them.

"I said shut the fuck up." He took his eyes off Cain long enough for her to grab his hand, but his bulk helped him slice deep enough to make a large spot of blood appear on her shirt. "I wanted to fucking enjoy this, but quick is good too."

Before Boone could do any more damage, Billy knocked him out cold with the butt of his gun. "Take this jackass out back," Billy said to the bouncers. "What the hell?"

"He said the service was too slow and the beer wasn't cold enough," she said, holding her hand over the cut. "Call the cops and tell them what happened with Mr. Boone Richard. I want to press charges."

"You got it, so let Emma take care of you."

Emma had grabbed some clean bar towels from the waitress and put them over the wound. "You need to get us to the hospital," Emma yelled at Lou.

"Emma, I'm so sorry," Bea said, appearing terrified.

"So help me God, if you know anything about this…" Emma said as she wrapped her arm firmly around Cain's waist. "What the hell was that about?"

"We'll deal with it later," Cain said, the ache in her abdomen becoming acute. "Billy, everything by the book."

"Don't worry. I know who's outside," he whispered in her ear as he helped Emma get her in the car. "Get going, Lou, and I'll be there as soon as I'm done here."

"I'm so sorry," Emma said as Lou sped away.

"You've got nothing to be sorry for. This is the part I want you to think about."

"All I want is to concentrate on you and what you mean to me. Stop trying to talk me out of being where I want and need to be, or I swear *I'll* stab you. You said you loved me, so you're stuck with me now."

"Fair enough, and I do love you," she said, wiping Emma's tears. "Your friend Bea, though, not so much."

CHAPTER TWENTY-THREE

Callie called Boone for the fifteenth time after not accepting his call, and now it was going straight to voicemail. He'd left a message telling her about meeting Bea, and then he'd disappeared. If he'd tried to take Casey on alone, he might be dead already.

"When did you see him last?" she asked Ryan as she tried Boone again.

"Yesterday, and he told me to fuck off when I gave him your message."

"So that's it?" She slammed her phone down and bowed her head, trying to think. They had been able to get so much done because only Big Gino and the people he'd introduced them to knew them.

"I don't know about that, but he wasn't happy with the handcuffs he thought you'd put on him. Boone wanted to go into Casey's place guns blazing and finish it." Ryan put his hand on her back as if in comfort. "He thought doing that would make it easier for you to get what you wanted going forward, since it would give you the reputation as someone not to fuck with."

"If he's dead, what the hell good is a reputation? Take some guys and hit all the spots again." She waited until she was alone to call Big Gino and tell him Boone was missing. He and the rest of her crew probably thought she was panicking, but Boone always called her back.

"Your idiot brother's not missing. He's in central lockup for stabbing Casey. It's highly disappointing that the bitch is still alive and fucking strange that she had him arrested."

"No way he didn't call me if he got picked up."

Big Gino laughed, and she would've stabbed him had he been in the room. "You think you're so smart, so think about why he didn't. Maybe he kept his mouth shut so he wouldn't lead Casey to your door."

The reasoning was probably right, but Boone had made a pact with her when they were children to never leave each other alone no matter what. They did it together or not at all, so he would've called because he knew she'd take care of herself and him. "Are you going to help him? I need to know before I waste any more of my time on your ass and any of your friends."

"There's the little public-housing bitch I hired," Big Gino said, laughing at her again. "You and Boone are too deep in this shit to fuck me now, so sit your ass down and wait. If you even think about talking to pull you or that idiot out of a hole, you won't be able to hide from me no matter how far you run."

"I just want him out. No one's talking about anything. You don't think I know we're screwed since I did what you asked." She stopped and took a deep breath, not wanting to sound as hysterical as she felt. "How do you even know for sure that's where he is?"

"I've got friends in the department, so wait it out—he's fine for now."

Fuck you, she thought as she hung up and considered her next move, but she really didn't have anything to think about. If Boone was in a cage, she was going to get him out and they'd take off. They had enough money to last a while as they started over somewhere else. The last thing she'd do for Big Gino was give Cain Casey the information she'd been hunting down on the street. Casey was willing to pay big money for it, and if she did, that would be the most fucking hilarious thing of all.

"Your fat ass should've helped me," she said to the phone. Guys like Big Gino always bullied their way through life, and the only thing that stopped them was a bigger bully. "Cain Casey sounds like the right bully for the job."

❖

"Thank you for coming, Mrs. Richard," the bail bondsman said to Heidi Richard while they both waited for Boone's arraignment.

Heidi nodded, barely moving her head. Her headache was about to make her pass out or throw up, and her body ached, but the only thing that would make her feel better was a hit. The guy who'd picked her up had said that coming here and getting her son Boone sprung would set her up with enough shit for a month, but he needed her to be sober enough to get through the process.

"You remember what you need to tell him and the attorney we got him?"

"Yeah, that Callie sent me, but you know they're going to run the minute he hits the door, so don't blame me for that. Those two only care about each other. It ain't natural, I always said." She scratched her forearm until it bled and only stopped when the guy put his hand over hers. "I get my stuff after this, right?"

"You get through this and don't screw up, and you're set for life."

"Shit yeah."

They stood when the clerk called the court to order, and she waved to Boone when he came in wearing an orange jumpsuit. It didn't take long for the public defender to get a fairly low bond and for Boone to nod when his mother explained Callie had sent her because she couldn't come herself.

They both got into the car with the bondsman, and Boone opened his window when Heidi lit her pipe. "It's good to see you, baby," she said, feeling her pain fly away as fast as the scenery on the interstate. "You don't come around too often no more."

Boone took her pipe and tossed it out the window. "We've been busy, so I sent you some money to get by."

"You know that wasn't enough for what I need." She could sense her words were starting to slur, but she still wanted to rage against the fact that she was still having to hook to get by. Her eyes closed and everything faded away.

"Where the fuck are we going?" Boone said, propping Heidi against the car door and off him.

"After what happened, Callie moved to keep Casey off your ass," the guy said, turning off the highway into an industrial area. "She was pissed, but you'll be okay."

"Why the hell did she call Heidi to do this? Callie fucking hates her." He glanced at the woman, who'd never given a shit about anything but the pipe, and wanted to despise her as much as Callie did, but Heidi was still his mother. She was fucked up, but she'd bought him cookies and sung to them as kids, so it hadn't always been horrible.

"I just paid the bail, man, so you'll have to ask her that yourself." The guy drove through an industrial park, then backtracked a couple of miles until he stopped by a warehouse. "Here you go. She's right inside."

Boone looked at the place and hesitated before getting out. Something was hinky about this, and the guy standing next to Heidi's side of the car confirmed his suspicion. The gun he was holding was pointed at his head, and the guy wasn't alone.

"Get out, asshole, and don't get cute."

"If you're going to fucking kill me, go ahead."

"Kill you?" The guys around the man laughed. "You think I'm going to kill you for cutting my sister? Well, technically, I am, but I'm not wasting bullets on you. Get out or we'll get you out, but if we have to do it, think pain like you've never experienced in your life."

The bondsman took a thick envelope from the guys and drove away after they'd taken Heidi out with him. "What kind of son are you?" another one asked him. "Pick her up and let's go."

The building was dark, but he could make his way with Heidi draped over his shoulder while trying to think of where the best place to fight was. He'd fallen for this shit like an amateur and thought of Callie always telling him not to be so soft, especially when it came to Heidi. She was right in that his hope of Heidi finally doing the right thing for him had overridden the reality of who Heidi was and what she was never capable of. Mainly that was being a mother.

"Put your mama down, big man," said the guy he figured was Billy Casey, pointing to the ground. He did it quickly, figuring it would free him up to make a move, but as he started to straighten back up, Billy popped that bubble. "I know what's going through that pea brain, so think before you try anything. I'm not going to kill you, but I will shoot your knees and feet before you get within three feet of me."

"Okay, now what?"

"Strip," Billy said.

"You asking for my dick, asshole? You just had to ask. I ain't into that shit, but if you're desperate, go ahead. I know what your sister likes, but I didn't know it runs in the family."

"Once you're done, get your mama undressed," Billy said, totally unfazed by his taunts.

He did what was asked, thinking he might make it out since Billy said he wasn't going to kill him. "Okay. I'm fucking naked." He spread his arms out and kicked his pants toward Billy. "My mama doesn't have anything to do with this, so why not let her go?" He picked Heidi up and cradled her.

"Not quite yet. You've got a lot of bonding to make up for before you can begin to forgive her for selling you out for a bag of rocks." Billy threw him Heidi's payment, and as soon as it hit Heidi's abdomen, he was pushed backward.

"Fuck," he yelled, his face pressed up against the little glass window. It wasn't until the door shut that he realized how fucked he really was.

"Don't sweat it," Billy said and smiled. "I left you a lighter and a pipe, so you should be fine."

"Wait." He banged on the door. "You let me out, and I'll tell you something you and your sister want to know bad."

Billy opened the door but stood with his gun cocked and pointed at him. "Let's hear it."

"It's about your daddy. I know who pulled the trigger."

"Sure you do," Billy said, moving back.

"I'll tell you, but after you let me go." It was amazing how cold he was instantly.

"You're not too terribly bright, are you?" Billy spoke loudly as he slipped two padlocks in place, effectively shutting him in the industrial freezer.

"It was me, but I was hired," he said, shivering.

"I know because you bragged to Heidi. Telling your secrets to a junky is how I know you're not too bright, and in the couple of days of being Heidi's candy man, I also know you've been a very bad boy in our neighborhoods." Billy pocketed the keys and stepped close to the glass window. "What you don't know is how imaginative my sister is at punishment."

"Fuck you," he said, his muscles aching badly from the shivering.

"I'll leave with the hundred-and-third thing on my list of stuff I hope never happens to me," Billy said, and smiled again. "That would be someone snapping my frozen dick off and shoving it up my ass, so what you should've said was, fuck me. Because when that happens for little Callie's entertainment, you'll be too far gone to care."

"You can suck my dick."

"Sorry. Small popsicles were never my thing."

❖

"We don't have an inmate by that name," the receptionist said, never looking up from her paperwork.

"I got a call he was here, so check again," Callie said, trying to be patient.

"He isn't here. They released him this morning," the woman said with as much impatience. "He made bail."

"Does it say who posted the bail?" Her instant stab of fear made her have to hang onto the counter to stay on her feet.

"Some woman, I think, but it's not in the paperwork. You need anything else? You're holding up the line."

Callie pointed to Ryan and asked him to take her to someone she figured might've been paid to spring him, but she couldn't believe he wouldn't have called her after getting out to keep some little twit happy. If that was true, she was now too pissed to be scared. She'd go see for herself.

She knocked on the door. "Can I help you?" the young woman asked.

"Are you Bea Weller?"

"Yeah. What can I do for you?"

"Plenty," she said as Ryan pressed the barrel of his gun to Bea's forehead. "Let's start with where my brother is."

"Hey…wait a minute. Who's your brother?" Bea asked, trying to back up fast enough to get away from the threat. "Look. I don't know what you're talking about."

"Sit down and shut up," she said, and Ryan pushed Bea into a chair. "You were with my brother and now he's missing. If he's not here, then where is he?"

"Are you talking about Boone? The police took him away—that's all I know." Bea held her hands out as if it would protect her from what was coming.

"Tell me exactly what happened."

Bea told her side of the story until Boone was knocked on the head and taken away. "He stabbed Cain Casey right there, and I took him there. Do you know what Casey's going to do about that? Is that why he wanted to meet her so bad?"

"Did Casey say anything to you?" She took her switchblade out and sliced through Bea's hand like she was cutting a ripe tomato. Ryan put his hand over her mouth to keep her quiet but almost couldn't because Bea's head was shaking so hard. "Did she?"

"No. She told the guy to call the police, then left for the hospital. I got thrown out after that." Bea held her wounded hand and cried. "If he's missing, I don't know anything about that."

Callie was about to cut Bea again when her phone rang. "Boone," she said, relieved.

"Actually we've got Boone on ice," a man who wasn't Boone said. "But he's been asking about you."

"Is he dead?" she asked, sitting down and pressing her thumb into the center of her forehead.

"No. He's having a long conversation with your mother. Don't take too long to decide if you want to join the family reunion."

"Who's this?" She concentrated, trying to hear anything in the background that might give her a hint of something she could use.

"Callie." She heard Boone's muffled voice. "Callie," he said again, and she punched her thigh.

"Him I think you know," the guy said. "Remember, not too long."

The phone call ended, and she took a few deep breaths before she took her frustration out by stabbing Bea until she was a bloody, mutilated mess. "Fuck."

Ryan wiped his face, only smearing the blood that had landed on his cheeks. "Who was that?"

"Some guy who said not to take too long to make up my mind about coming to get Boone. They're going to fucking kill him, so I want them all dead."

"I'm with you, but we need a plan." Ryan walked to the kitchen and rinsed his hands.

"Make sure you wipe everything you touched." Ryan moved around the room rubbing different surfaces. She called Boone's number, and someone answered on the third ring. "When and where?"

"Wait at the apartment and I'll call you. Use the time to decide how you want to deal with the Dalton Casey issue. Your brother folded before anyone even landed a hand on him, so you shouldn't have pushed him into this life. He certainly doesn't have the balls for it."

"What did he tell you? We don't even know who Dalton Casey is," she said, the word "fuck" echoing through her head.

"That's the fear talking, Callie. Fear doesn't get you any respect."

She hit the side of her head with her fist and couldn't believe how fast everything had unraveled. "I'm not afraid. I'm confused as to why he lied."

"He's not the only one who knows the whole story, and Heidi wasn't as easy to get the story out of as Boone, but she backed him up."

"I need to see him."

"Patience, so sit and wait."

She threw down her phone and told Ryan, "Get every one of the crew to the house and tell them we're going to war. I want everyone in the Casey family dead. They don't know who they're fucking with."

"Is Boone gone?"

"He's alive, and we're going to get him. We'll either free him or kill everyone trying, starting with that bitch Heidi."

❖

"Papa," Bea said, using what seemed to her like the last of her strength to get to the phone. "You need to come."

"What's wrong?" Palmiro Weller asked.

"Remember the name Boone Richard," she said as she closed her eyes. "His sister did this to me. I love you, Papa." It was all she could manage before the phone fell out of her hand.

Chapter Twenty-four

Y ou want some ice or something?" Emma asked Cain, holding a cup close to Cain's mouth.

"Sit right here, lass," Cain said, patting the spot next to her. "I'm okay, so take a breath."

"Who was that guy? He just stabbed you for no good reason," Emma said, taking a bite of ice chips. "Why was Bea with him? She kept asking me to get together with her and that guy. You think she was in on it?"

"That's a good question," the police officer who stuck his head in said. "Do you mind answering some questions, Cain?"

"Hey, Norm. Did you arrest the guy?" Cain asked, holding Emma's hand.

"We did, but he made bond already. He's out and saying it was self-defense."

"That's bull," Emma said, coming close to standing up. "He stabbed her right after saying hello."

"I know, there were plenty of witnesses, but that's the story he's going with. His name's Boone Richard," Norm said, reading his notes. "Do you know this guy, or did he not like you right off?"

"I met him with Emma today, and he went for his knife without explaining what his problem was. He came with Emma's friend."

"Do you have an address for her?"

Emma gave him Bea's address, and Norm thanked them and promised to keep them informed. While he was talking, Therese arrived with Billy, and Cain stopped Emma from moving away. She'd made that mistake once, and she wasn't going to send Emma away again.

"You okay, Derby?" Therese said, kissing her forehead first, then Emma's. "And you, my darling?" she asked Emma.

"We're okay, or at least we will be, Mum." She rubbed Emma's back and glanced at her mum.

"Come with me, Emma, and let's get you cleaned up. We brought you a change of clothes," Therese said, smoothing over the spots on Emma's shirt that had blotches of Cain's blood on it. "Marie was happy to lend you one of hers."

"It's okay, love," she said, kissing Emma. "Right now she might be the best person to talk to."

Therese took Emma out, and Billy took her place on the bed and sat close to her. He took a larger jammer from his pants pocket and turned it on, but even then he whispered in her ear. "We took care of everything so it's waiting when you're ready," he said. "The next piece should be done soon."

"Make sure they do this without being seen. This was only one of our problems, but I doubt if any of the others will just walk in and shake my hand."

"There's a little more." He sighed, which meant it wasn't good. "You know what Heidi said about Da? Well, Boone said he pulled the trigger, so it might not have been some drug rant on Heidi's part."

"It can't be that simple. Some gutter scum comes here and kills Da for no reason? I don't buy it. There has to be more to it, and I need to know who he was working for." She pressed her hand over her wound and shifted on the bed. "Does that big ape strike you as the mastermind that killed Da?"

"In a way, yes, since it was an ambush, but he got the idea from somewhere else." Boone's phone rang, and he held it up for her to see. "Yeah?"

"What do you want in exchange for my brother? I'm done waiting."

"You need to go to this address and wait," Billy said, giving her the address of an abandoned building across the river that had no connection to them. "I'd tell you to come alone, but we both know you're a lying little bitch."

"When?"

"We're ready now, and remember to not give my guys any problems since I assume you want Boone back in one piece and not in a closed-casket sort of way. Think about that as you start spinning ideas in your head."

"You're going?" Cain asked when he cut Callie off.

"That territory belongs to Jasper, so he'll be happy to gift-wrap and deliver."

"He's also pissed about the dynamic duo pissing where they didn't belong, so make sure he delivers her alive and able to talk."

"He promised alive but maybe missing a few teeth."

"Tell him he can work on his anger management on her crew. A little target practice can be rather cathartic."

❖

"He just attacked her—he didn't even say a word," Emma said in the bathroom as she changed out of her bloody top. "I don't understand."

"Come with me." Therese led her to a bright sunroom that had one of Cain's men stationed at the door. "Our family never discusses our business, but I'm sure you've heard the rumors, child. Derby told me your friend Bea talked to you about it."

"Bea can believe whatever she wants—I don't care. After she brought that guy there, we're no longer friends."

"Forget about her, and try to understand that Cain is at times in danger simply for who she is. She's her father's daughter, and she'll carry on in his position until the next generation is ready to lead." Therese took her hands, her eyes glassy with tears. "I lost my love because some fool thought they'd gain by his death, but they underestimated the Caseys."

"I'm so sorry for your loss," she said, hugging Therese.

"My pain will never heal, but I go on for my children. Ask yourself, if you go any farther with my Derby, can you survive days like today and move past them? I look at her and see how she feels about you, but before you commit you need to know and accept all of who she is. You have to accept the things she can't let go." Therese's tears fell, but Emma didn't think they had anything to do with any sadness over Cain's choices.

"Are you afraid I will or I won't?" Maybe Therese found something lacking about her.

"She loves you, so I pray that you will. Derby is kind, compassionate, and loyal. Once she commits to you, she'll give you her all and her heart, but she's also strong and as unbending as her da. Those who hurt her family and those she loves are very seldom forgiven."

"Don't cry over things you don't have to worry about. She could be the devil incarnate and I wouldn't care, because I love her. The heart of the devil is safe with me." Therese nodded, and the raw emotion on her face made Emma cry as well.

"God bless you, my darling," Therese said, kissing her cheek.

"I feel blessed and, more importantly, very loved." She returned Therese's affection and smiled. "I'm not blind to who Cain is, but she loves me despite my faults, so all I can do is the same. Thank you for accepting me."

"Your mother will one day learn there's a price for not treasuring the precious gift you are, so you need not thank me for that. Your strength will make you a good Casey, but your choice, I pray, will bring you as much happiness as mine did so long ago."

"She's not the only blessing I've found," she said, kissing Therese's cheek again. "You and your children are more than I ever hoped for in a family, so let's get back to taking care of them."

"It's a big job."

"True, but I've got a lifetime to get it right."

❖

"Are you sure you're okay to go out right now?" Emma stood in the middle of the den in the Casey home with her hands on her hips, not appearing too intimidated to stand up to Cain. "You got out of the hospital an hour ago. What can't wait until tomorrow?"

"Believe me, lass, if I could put it off, I would." Cain glanced at Therese, but her mum shook her head as if she didn't want to get in the middle of this. "Billy will be doing all the heavy lifting, so I'll be fine."

"Cain," Merrick said before Emma could give her rebuttal. "Can I talk to you a minute?"

"Sure," she said, knowing Merrick never butted in for minor things. Merrick followed her out and told her the news Norm had called with. "Who the hell did that? Wait. Come on so we don't have to go over this twice."

"What's wrong?" Emma asked when she returned, as if she could sense bad news.

"Your friend Bea is dead, lass. I know you might've been mad at her, but I doubt she had any hand in what happened, so she certainly didn't deserve her fate."

Emma rushed close and fell against her. "She's gone? How? What happened to her?"

"According to the police, she was able to call her father with a dying declaration," Merrick said when Cain nodded at her. "The guy who hurt Cain had a sister, and for some reason she stabbed Bea to death. She died before she could say why."

Emma cried for a bit, as if not being able to process what was happening. "Do you think she might've had something to do with you getting hurt and that's why she got murdered?"

"I really don't know," she said, and the doorbell cut her off.

"Ms. Cain, some men are here to see you," Carmen the housekeeper said.

Billy went to the door with her, where Kyle and his little helper were waiting. "You need to come in for questioning," Kyle said, pointing to his car.

"Questioning for what exactly?" She glanced at Billy and mouthed Muriel's name.

"Beatrice Weller was killed, and we have reason to believe you were involved," the young guy said.

"Am I under arrest?"

"I said questioning," Kyle said, placing his hand on the doorjamb.

"If you want, come in and ask away."

She sat next to Emma and smiled when Emma took her hand.

"Do you realize she just got out of the hospital?" Therese said, pointing to the love seat if they wanted to sit.

"According to the NOPD, the girl who died was killed by the sister of the guy who stabbed you," the smaller guy said.

"Her name was Bea, and I didn't know her any more than I did the guy who cut me. It wasn't exactly a stab," she said, hearing the door open again, and Muriel appeared a few minutes later.

"From our viewpoint, that's motive." Kyle paced in front of them. "We know how you deal with anyone who dares go against you."

"Agent Kyle, how long have you been in town?" Cain asked, and Muriel sighed.

"Five minutes, but I can read. Your file is extensive."

"So does it say anywhere in there that I'm a psychic? If I didn't know the guy who cut me, how am I supposed to know he has a sister? All I knew was his name was Boone Richard, because he introduced himself right before he cut me."

"Rumors were going around that you were looking for him. You backed it up with plenty of money," the little guy said.

"I did? I have no idea what you're talking about, so the next time, come with facts and the ability to prove them, but you're free to go if that's all you got."

"This isn't done," Kyle said. "And you should open your eyes and get out of here, Ms. Verde."

Emma didn't say anything as Billy escorted the men out. Cain glanced at Muriel and shrugged for not waiting for her before talking. "You okay?" she asked Emma.

"You were the one hurt, and they're blaming you for Bea? That's crazy," Emma said.

"The FBI has a way of connecting the dots, but sometimes they take a circuitous route to try to force the issue. I'd say you get used to it, but I'd be lying."

"They're really trying to force it now," Billy said, clapping his hands together. "They've got us boxed in from every block."

"Let's stay in then, and eventually they'll move on," she said, looking at her watch.

"I'll start dinner," Therese said, and Emma and Marie went with her.

"There's no getting out?" She cursed when Billy nodded. "Where'd you have Callie put?"

"With Boone and Heidi. We had a short window of time, so tomorrow will be too late."

"You realize if they die, they take their secrets with them," she said, walking to the front of the house. Kyle had really stacked the deck with two vans and a number of sedans waiting for them to go out. "There's got to be a way."

"It'll be hard to shake a tail today."

"Maybe," she said and made a call. "How much are you in for these days?" she said, making Billy come closer. "Damn," she said, and laughed. "Come by in an hour in your official capacity, and I'll pay up before you lose the use of your legs and your pension."

"Dinner will be in a few," Therese said, wiping her hands when she came back. "We're having sandwiches in case you have to run out."

"Excellent idea, and we need to send Emma home with Lou when we're done," she said, heading for the kitchen. "Hopefully we won't have to chip away at our problem to get some answers."

"I'll bring the icepick just in case," Billy said.

Chapter Twenty-five

It's not much, but here you go," Jake said as Bradley counted the money. "You can see we delivered, so when's our next deal?"

"Hell if I know," Marty said as he touched a few of the boxes. "We'll check with the boss and get back to you."

"It's all here," Bradley said, zipping up the small bag it'd come in.

"Good. Tell her not to wait too long or the price might go up," Jake said, taking a bottle of whiskey before he left.

Marty and Jonsie had the delivery made to one of Marty's father's empty buildings and laughed until they cried when they were alone. Even if they doubled their money, they'd be set to make a few more of these deals.

"You have Big Chief's numbers?" Jonsie asked.

"I called him already, and he's sending someone with cash and a way to get it out of here." The building backed up to the river, so that's how they figured it was leaving, but Marty could've cared less. "I say next time we put everything back in and make a bigger score."

"What if he calls Casey and asks how she liked the service?"

Marty exhaled, wishing Jonsie had a little less bitch in him. "We already told him she doesn't want to deal with him directly. He calls and the deal's off. Eventually we'll tell him we're branching out on our own. It's a win-win since all we are is the middlemen."

They heard a horn outside, and Marty opened the delivery door. The white paneled truck backed in, and the driver had them lower the door. "Hey, you Marty?"

"That's me." He shook the guy's hand and waited. He didn't see any reason to waste his time with the help. "Big Chief on his way?"

"He's not coming," the guy said, reaching into the truck for something. When he got it, Jonsie had a gun on him. "Jeez, man. You want your money or not?"

"How much is in there?" Jonsie said, not lowering his weapon.

"Three hundred large." The guy handed over the bag. "What, you don't want it?"

"He said seven to one," Marty said.

"There's a lot of heat on him right now because of Casey, so this is it. You want to pass, I'll call him and tell him. I'm only here to pick up."

"We'll take it," Jonsie said.

"Good. I'll need a couple of hours, so if you want, take off and I'll lock up."

"You want some help?" Marty asked.

"Nah. Go ahead." The guy waited until they were gone before he moved to the back of the truck.

"Fuck, man," Marty said when they were driving away. "If that's all it takes, we need to set up another deal quick."

"Make sure your friend wants to buy some more so we don't get stuck with it."

Jonsie drove them back to Marty's place, where they put the cash in the small wall safe and called Big Chief.

Marty tried his best to sound nonchalant but pumped his fist when Big Chief told them he'd take all they could get. They'd handle the exchange the same way, and they had to keep up the lie that they worked for Casey.

"Man, we can score serious cash when we're done," he told Jonsie after repeating what Big Chief said.

"Who says we've got to be done," Jonsie said, and they both laughed.

"That bitch is going to wonder where all her business went. Then she won't be so fucking tough without backup."

"Dude, let that go. We'll be getting blown on a beach somewhere thinking about how to spend money."

"Some shit a man can't let go of."

❖

"Who is that?" Kyle asked as the front gate opened.

"Not sure, sir," Joe Simmons said as he checked the license plate to verify it belonged to the NOPD. "The car's property of the city," he said as the guy came into view. "That's the guy who came by the hospital to get a statement. Maybe he's back to talk to Verde or he's got an update."

"There's nothing to update. The guy who did it easily got bail, but now his girlfriend's dead and his sister's in the wind. Did any of you connect the Richards to Casey?" Kyle asked as the cop pulled toward the back because of all the cars in the drive.

Logan North spoke over the radio. "Not yet. According to Boone Richard's jacket, the guy's been in and out of jail plenty of times, but they're from Baton Rouge. There's no connection yet."

"Everyone keep your eyes open. You know Casey's up to something," Kyle said.

"It's catching her at it that's been the problem, sir," Joe said, and Kyle tried to ignore the sarcasm.

Norm drove out and headed back toward his precinct in the Quarter, with a black sedan for company the whole way. He kept up a running commentary of the guy's movements the entire time, as directed, and sounded relieved when he parked in the police lot.

"He's gone, guys."

"Thanks for the ride, and don't forget to pop the trunk before you go," Cain said, handing over a thick envelope. "And don't forget to pay up before you head to the track again either."

"You're a lifesaver, Cain. I don't think my wife would've stuck around if I'd told her about this one."

Norm left her lying on the backseat and went inside like she'd asked and called once he had the vantage point of the second floor. When he didn't see anything suspicious, he called her so she could get Billy out of the trunk.

"Norm gives new meaning to protect and serve, doesn't he?" Billy said as he climbed, out, rubbing his shoulders.

The car she'd asked Ramon for was waiting a block away, so they took their usual careful route to the warehouse. She unlocked the freezer while Billy held both his guns on the door in case the cold hadn't completely knocked the fight out of their guests.

Callie was the only one able to crawl out on her own, so Cain watched her while Billy dragged the other two out. They should've been cold but still alive, so she was surprised that Boone and Heidi were both dead.

"What the hell?" she said as Callie shivered at her feet.

"You fucker," Callie said, her face wet with tears. "You killed him."

"Unless he slit his wrists with an icicle, he should still be alive," Billy said.

"He and that bitch smoked everything in that bag. They were both gone when you put me in there."

"Your brother admitted he killed our father, so I'm not exactly sorry he's gone. But I didn't think he'd take the easy way out until he talked to you again," Cain said, standing over Boone's body. "No tears for your mother?"

"That bitch can rot, for all I care, but I'd kill you over Boone if I could."

"Who hired you to kill my father?" she asked, realizing she had very little leverage now that Boone had overdosed instead of facing her.

"The only thing I'm telling you is that Boone didn't kill that bastard."

"I know—you did." Boone might've done it, but the real killer had to be this cold-hearted, deeply flawed woman. "You came here to do it, and you got lucky."

"It was easy, so luck had nothing to do with it. Your old man had a reputation, but he was an easy target."

"Who paid you?" Billy asked.

Callie leaned into the barrel of his gun and laughed. "Fuck you. Go ahead and pull the trigger, because I'm not telling you shit."

"Billy," she said, and Billy shot Callie through the foot. The sudden pain was too much to ignore, and Callie howled. "Who paid you?"

"Shit," Callie screamed, but she turned her face away. Billy shot again, and she still wouldn't give it up. "You can fucking do this all day, and I ain't telling you squat, so fucking kill me."

"I'm not killing you," she said, and Billy holstered his guns. "And since you love your brother so much, I can tell you he'll be out of here in a bit. You and your mother, though, won't be so lucky. You can keep her company in the smoker when I tie you face-to-face."

Billy started the grinder, and Boone met the same fate as Callie's two other guys. "You're a sick bastard," Callie said as she pulled the hair at the sides of her head when Boone's head finally disappeared into the machine.

"All I'm doing is avenging my father. You didn't even know him, and you killed him for a few bucks." She squatted and grabbed Callie by the throat. "You're going to die in this pit, and you'll be forgotten before you hit the ground. No one will think to retaliate, so you'll die as badly as you lived."

Callie beat on her arm, but she couldn't make Cain let go of her. "This will never be over, bitch," Callie managed to say.

"That's optimistic," she said, pushing Callie back. "I also changed my mind. There'll be no slow death for you. You deserve to see it coming."

Billy emptied both clips into Callie, starting at her lower body and working his way up. The why would come in time, so they'd have to settle for the fact that their da's killer was dead.

"You think she would've talked if Boone hadn't fried his brain?" Billy asked.

"They were both hustlers, so I doubt it. Why bargain when you know you're not leaving? And she was smart enough to know she wasn't leaving here alive."

"We'll get our answers some other way, then, but I'm not sorry. This bitch and her brother deserved what they got."

"We won't be finished until everyone responsible for Da is dead. We owe him that."

Billy hugged her and kissed her cheek. "I know, and that's why I love you. You're a closer with the patience of Job."

"I'm no saint, brother."

"I know that. It's why we get along so well," he said and winked.

❖

"She's dead, and I want the bitch who did it. I know she's working for you," Palmiro Weller screamed at Big Gino while pointing his finger at him.

"Are you saying you think I ordered this?" Gino slammed his hand on his desk and got louder than Palmiro. He wasn't used to anyone interrupting his meetings. "How long have you known me—worked for me?"

"Years, Gino, but she was my only daughter, and I'm not going to swallow any more bullshit about Cain Casey being at fault. Callie Richard killed Bea, and if you're really my friend, you're going to hand her over." He wiped his face impatiently as his tears fell. "She was an innocent girl."

"Palmiro, I don't know why this happened, and it's been some time since I've seen Callie or Boone. You deserve what you're asking for, so I'll try to get Callie brought to you."

"If you want to continue our friendship, don't take too long," Palmiro said softly.

"Are you threatening me?"

"I'm telling you the same thing you'd be saying if it was one of your boys. We've worked well together, but now's the time to prove your friendship. If you don't, then you're my enemy. I've already met with the others, and they've agreed to throw you out of our neighborhoods." He spoke in the same soft way and sounded totally serious. "You made things easier, Gino, but never think you're indispensable."

"I fucking get it, so wait for my call."

"You've got until tomorrow, so don't disappoint me."

Gino stood and leaned over the desk. "I understand you're grieving, so I'll let this disrespect slide. But don't push your luck."

He laughed and stood as well. "Kill me or anyone in my family, and the cops get everything they need to cage you like the animal you are. You think I'm bullshitting you, try me."

"I said you'll get what you want, but after that you're going to fuck off."

"After that, things will change. On that you have my word."

Palmiro slammed out of the office, and Shawn Liam stood and buttoned his jacket. "I can see this might not be the time to talk business, Gino."

"You're getting scared because of him?" he asked, laughing.

"Our success comes from staying in the shadows and out of street wars. Until you get things under control, we'll sit out, but we'll be ready once you put your house in order."

Royce got up when Shawn motioned to him. "My house is already in fucking order, so don't sit too long. Your old man was tight with Dalton, but with no one backing him on the street, things might not be so easy, and it sounds like things didn't work out with Casey."

"Try to keep your assumptions to a minimum, and concentrate on finding and controlling your people. If Callie Richard is who you tried to set me up with, maybe all this was a mistake."

"Callie can go fuck herself," Gino said, coming around the desk and opening the door.

"I have a feeling Cain Casey is doing that right now, so hopefully little Callie didn't have any big secrets," Shawn said and walked out after Royce.

CHAPTER TWENTY-SIX

Cain conducted business quietly for months as a war broke out on the streets in the east. The Weller family had actually been a stronger force in St. Bernard than she'd first thought, and the bloodshed had hit both Bracato and the families in New Orleans East hard. No one knew why. After years of what seemed to be mutual and profitable interests, they'd thrown it all away to try to kill each other.

She'd monitored the chaos from a distance to ensure her territory and clients remained untouched. The day-after-day routine of going to the office and deepening her relationship with Emma had thinned the gray-suited crowd outside her door. Evidently boring days and her romance techniques didn't interest the FBI.

"Are you sure you want to keep giving to charity?" Muriel said as they started their weekly meeting. "We're up to three million a pop."

"Still cheaper than our normal supply line. We'll give it another month, then pull our end. Once that happens, the game will change significantly, but not before a significant bonus," Cain said, drumming her fingers on the table in an uneven, random pattern.

"For us, I hope," Muriel said.

"If it weren't, that'd be called a hit, not a bonus," Billy said jokingly, shoving Muriel. "All we're waiting for is you, Boss," he said to Cain.

"Don't worry. I'm paying attention, but if that's it, I've got a few errands to run."

"Do you need help with anything?" Billy asked, wiggling his eyebrows.

"I think I can pick an anniversary gift all on my own, thank you." The day of Emma's first day of work was coming up, and she wanted to find something special to commemorate it.

Emma had become such a constant in every aspect of her life that she almost hated to leave her most nights. It was a comically strange development, considering that a lot of people considered her a psychotic killer. With Emma, though, she didn't have to be strong all the time, and it was a relief to put her responsibilities down for a while and not be judged as weak.

"Hey," Emma said, entering the conference room with one of their new guys, Maurice. Everyone called him Mook, and the young man was here as a favor to Vincent. Mook was a good addition since he didn't appear out of place as he stuck with Emma on campus.

"You all done already?" she asked, standing up and kissing Emma hello.

"All signed up and ready for my last semester," Emma said, having pushed back her graduation one more semester for the internship Cain had gotten her. "You want to go out and celebrate?"

"What? You think I wouldn't have planned something?" she said, trying her best to pout.

"If you're done here, you can tell me all about it over lunch. I'm starved."

"Just one more thing." She kissed Emma again before taking her hand. "Billy." She looked at him and Merrick. "I'm done waiting."

"I heard that," Billy said, and Merrick nodded before they both stood and kissed Emma's cheek as if she were responsible for their upcoming fun.

She led Emma out, and they headed to Blanchard's for lunch. Emma's appearance had changed in that Kevin helped her dress more professionally for her campus gig, but she still wore jeans for her job at the pub. She wasn't there as often but had wanted to keep her primary source of income to pay for the little things she liked buying for Cain.

"Are you excited?" she asked Emma after they'd ordered.

"Excited and nervous," Emma said, playing with Cain's fingers. "I don't want anything to change, but I guess they have to."

"Change how?"

"Not necessarily change," Emma said, sounding nervous now.

"You can tell me anything, lass."

"If I turn out to be just a teacher, I don't want you to get bored. I'm not sure what'll happen to me if I lose you."

"Lose me? My darling, that's the last thing that's going to happen. If I could, I'd have married you by now."

"Really?" Emma smiled as if she'd dropped to one knee. "What do you think our future will be?"

"Whatever we make it to ensure we're happy. It's been, as you love to say, an interesting time, but all those poems you love are right. I've found in you someone who completes a part of me that was empty." She lifted Emma's hand and kissed her knuckles. "You'll teach and I'll do what I do, and we'll build a life full of love and happiness."

"I should ask you questions like that all the time," Emma said, wiping away her tears and smiling. "You're quite the poet yourself, mobster."

"I'm no Byron, but I try," she said, releasing Emma's hand so the waiters could put their plates down. "I want to make sure you don't get bored along the way yourself."

"You're delusional if you think that," Emma said, spearing a shrimp on her plate and feeding it to her.

Their lunch morphed into shopping and then separating for the date she'd promised to celebrate Emma's academic hard work. Cain was planning to add the day they'd met as well, and the fact that she hadn't died of a year of celibacy.

"Honey," Emma said, grabbing her wrist when they sat in her booth at Emerald's and someone took their picture as they kissed. "It's just a picture, not an assassination attempt, and I'd love a copy."

"Sorry. I forgot about that guy." She waved Lou over and took the box he'd been holding for her.

"What's this?" Emma asked when she handed it over.

"I tried to think of something that would show you how proud I am of you and how I feel about you. You're beginning your life, and it's something I thought you'd find useful."

Emma pulled the ribbon and found a very old edition of Lord Byron's love poems. She'd read some of her favorites to Cain, and she wanted Emma to know she'd been paying attention. Emma touched the first page very gently with her fingertips and shed a few tears.

"My life started the day you came into it."

"We sound a bit over the top, so save that for later, and let's celebrate," she said, and Emma laughed. "Thank you though."

They danced, and she took Emma home, promising they'd meet for lunch the next day after Emma finished setting up everything she needed for the new semester.

"I love you, mobster, and thank you for being so good to me." Emma stood in her apartment with her arms around Cain.

"You're easy to love, my darling girl, and you've made falling in love a wondrous thing."

"I'm glad that's something we learned to do together." Emma pressed her ear to her chest, seeming content to be held. "If those guys outside knew what a softie you are, it'd ruin your reputation and they'd leave us alone."

"You might get your wish since it looks like they're getting bored. I only saw the one van tonight." They laughed, and she was happy that the more colorful aspects of her life still didn't seem to faze Emma all that much. The solidness of their relationship was something she now not only trusted but depended on.

"Maybe they're following you to get some romance pointers," Emma said and laughed.

"I'm sure that's it." She kissed Emma and unzipped her dress. It was their sign that the night was over. "It's late, so get some sleep and I'll pick you up tomorrow."

"Do you want to stay awhile?" Emma sounded almost shy and unsure, but they'd come a long way from where they'd started.

"Let's me and you make a deal." She placed her hand on Emma's naked back and gazed down at her. "You know the waiting is only a problem in here," she said, tapping the side of Emma's head. "The day you're ready, you'll know, so you won't have to ask. Until then, we wait. Deal?"

"How will I know?"

"When you can't go another moment without having me not only in your heart but on your skin. It's not a question of giving in to something you think I want from you, but taking the rest of what's yours already."

❖

Emma waited the next afternoon outside the English department with Cain's words from the night before running on a loop in her head. She'd waited at first to take their relationship to the next level because she'd thought Cain would move on, but if she was truthful, that wasn't it. She'd waited because she was so unsure of herself and thought that would turn Cain off.

Assuming that, though, was unfair to Cain, so now she felt foolish for not giving Cain something that had truly belonged to her from the beginning—herself. Cain's declaration had unshackled her from her doubt, and she wanted to plan something special for her.

"What's a beautiful woman like you doing out here all alone?"

She smiled and shut her eyes when Cain embraced her from behind. "I was waiting for my girlfriend, but she's late, so you'll do."

"It's my lucky day then," Cain said, turning her around and kissing her.

Emma glanced around when Cain took her hand, and she could swear they were alone. "No entourage today, mobster?"

"It's a beautiful day, so I left the kids at home so I could take my girl to lunch. I figured no audience watching me kiss you might be a good change of pace." Cain walked her to a motorcycle she'd never seen before and handed her a helmet.

"This is yours?" The thought of sitting with her legs and arms around Cain made her skin tingle.

"A hold-out from my college days."

They took the long route through town until they were out by the lake and the spot where they were sitting on the disastrous day Billy had been in his accident. Today he was waiting and guarding the picnic already laid out, and he kissed Emma's cheek before driving away.

"It bothered me that I was such an ass the day we were here," Cain said, helping her to sit. "I thought it'd be a good place to tell you that I'll never shut you out ever again. I love you, so you have my word on that."

"You're so perfect," she said as she caressed Cain's cheek. "I thank God for you every single day."

"I'm happy you think so, my love."

They enjoyed the food Therese had made, which consisted of some of her favorites, and were content to share the scenery and kiss. "You know something?" she asked, tracing Cain's lips with her finger. "I've read countless romances and love poems, and you've surpassed all of them in the courting stage. I'll treasure this part of our time together."

"Are you going somewhere?"

She laughed and shook her head. "No. When we're old, and I'm telling our grandchildren about how a girl wants to be treated, I'll share this with them."

"You'd like to have children, really?" Cain asked, placing her hand on the side of her neck.

"I'd like to have your children."

"Do you think your father would put a bullet in me if I asked for your hand?"

She laughed again, imagining Cain with her father. "More like he'd faint, but maybe one day you two will become good friends."

"Then right now I'll concentrate on doing my best to get the girl to say yes."

"I don't think that'll be a tough sell, no matter what the question is."

CHAPTER TWENTY-SEVEN

Emma had talked Cain into tending bar while she worked, and she'd enjoyed their flirting throughout the night. Cain was as good behind the bar as she was keeping an eye on her, and for once she got a ride home on the back of Cain's bike and not with Lou.

"Don't forget we're having lunch with Muriel and your uncle tomorrow," Emma said as Cain kissed the side of her neck.

"He's been looking forward to it since Mum has been filling him in on how wonderful she thinks you are." Cain kissed her and sighed. "So let me get going and I'll see you tomorrow."

"It's late," she said, like it was some kind of news flash.

"Don't worry, lass. It's only a few blocks home." Cain walked to the door and pointed to the lock. "Sweet dreams, and lock up."

She leaned against her apartment door, listening to the receding footsteps on the other side. It had been an electric year, enjoying being a part of Cain's life. She was about as far from her father's dairy farm as she could imagine herself but had kept a promise to herself to maintain her independence even though she knew Cain would take care of her in every sense if she'd just asked.

When the hallway was quiet she moved to the window to watch Cain leave, but instead of mounting the bike, she stood near the bottom of the window looking up, apparently knowing she wouldn't have to wait too long to see her again. The now-familiar Casey smile was in place when she peered down. It was the one trait Cain, Billy, and Marie all shared, but tonight Cain's smile undid her. Tonight, she knew exactly what Cain had meant when she'd said she'd be certain when the time was right.

"Do you have to be anywhere else right this minute?" she asked, leaning out of the window.

"I'll be wherever you want me to."

As an answer she dropped her shirt on Cain's head and moved away from the window and unlocked the door. She laughed when she heard the footsteps out in the hall again, only this time she heard more of a run.

Cain opened the door and stared at her standing there holding an arm over her chest, and the fact that she wasn't so sure of what to do next must have been clear to Cain. In all their time together she had never teased Cain too much as she got more comfortable with taking their relationship to the next level. Now wasn't the time to make a wrong move.

"I want you to stay," Emma said as Cain closed the door without ever taking her eyes off her.

Cain moved closer and opened her arms to Emma. "Come here a minute, baby." When she wrapped her arms around naked skin, she felt Emma relax. "Do you mind if we talk for a minute?"

"No." Emma sounded so nervous Cain's libido cooled a bit.

"Come sit with me." Emma went willingly and clung to her as she sat on her lap. She put her fingers under Emma's chin so she could see her eyes. "You need to know a few facts before we go forward." Emma nodded, and she kissed the tip of her nose. "You're the woman I'm going to spend my life with, period. That's my commitment to you. If you want the same thing, no one will ever share my bed or my life until it's over."

"Thank you for saying that, honey."

"There's a reason, and it isn't what you think. Because I want to spend all my life with you, lass, I can be patient. We've had this conversation more than once, but when we make love, it's going to be the right decision for both of us."

"Don't you want to?"

She smiled and placed her palm on Emma's cheek. "More than anything, but I'm willing to wait. I love you, Emma, and because I do, it means I'll wait as long as it takes."

Emma closed her eyes and leaned farther into Cain's caress. "You do?"

"More than anyone or anything else."

"Could you say it again?" Emma asked as she looked her in the eye. "I never get tired of hearing it."

"I love you, Emma, so very much."

"I love you too, and I want you to show me." Emma leaned back a little and moved to sit across her lap, placing one of her hands on her breast.

The move lit a flame in Cain that she knew would never truly go out. It was as if Emma had become a part of her very essence and she couldn't cut her out without permanent damage to herself. She got out of the chair and felt Emma's legs tighten around her waist as they moved to the bedroom. To get Emma to feel even more at ease, she set her down and unbuttoned her own linen shirt and pushed it off her shoulders. They both moaned when skin met skin for the first time.

"Tell me if I do something that makes you uncomfortable, okay?" She watched as Emma lay back and raised her hand to her.

"I want you," Emma said as she lifted her hips so she could get her skirt off. "I need your hands on me." She gave Emma what she wanted and lay next to her. "Your hands are hot," Emma said as Cain placed her hand on her chest.

She moved her hands constantly, never keeping them in any one place too long, which seemed to be driving Emma crazy. "I can't help myself, you feel so good," she said as she stopped short of where Emma seemed to want her most when her hips came off the bed. Emma seemed to freeze momentarily when she sucked on her right nipple until it grew hard.

"Oh my God, please don't stop." Emma clamped her hands around Cain's head and held her in place.

"I want to make you feel good, baby, so relax for me."

"Cain, relaxed is the last thing I'm feeling right now. And if you stop right now I'm seriously going to whack you in the head," Emma said, tugging gently on her hair when she chuckled. "Could you take your clothes off for me? I want to feel all of you."

Cain pulled her mouth away, getting Emma to open her eyes. She wanted nothing hidden in this part of their relationship. "I love you." After she made the declaration, which was a first to anyone outside her family, she unbuckled her belt and shed the rest of her clothes. When she lay back down, Emma moaned as she moved her hand down to her most intimate place.

She took her time running her fingers through the silky wet heat, encouraging Emma to move with her to increase her pleasure. Emma's clit got steel hard as she very gently stroked it, dipping lower with each pass. She wanted to ramp up Emma's need to help ease any discomfort Emma might feel.

"Look at me, lass. This is the first night we give ourselves to each other, but I'm going to take a lifetime living up to the commitment that goes with this honor."

Emma gazed up at her and pulled Cain's head down so she could kiss her. "This is how I dreamed this night would be," Emma said as she slid her fingers into Cain's hair. "I want you to take what's yours."

"This is ours, my love, for now and for always," she said as she very slowly pushed past Emma's innocence and held her hand still, but not her thumb, which was still stroking her clit. "Okay?" she asked when Emma closed her eyes for a long moment, but Emma nodded.

"I'm okay," Emma said as she pressed her hands to her face. "And I love you."

"Look at me, love, and see how much I love you and want you," she said as she started to move her hand slowly.

At first Emma simply held on to her and didn't move much, but then the passion seemed to build enough that she pushed up into her, and her breathing grew deep and unsteady. "Let it go, lass. I promise I'll be here to catch you."

"Oh…oh," Emma said as she clutched at her and pushed her away at the same time. "You're making me crazy," Emma said loudly.

"Relax and let me in."

Emma tightened her hands on her shoulders, and she became taut and rigid as the orgasm reached its peak. "Wait," Emma said, out of breath now. "Wait," she repeated, and she began to pull out, but Emma grabbed her wrist.

"I love you, lass."

"After that, I believe you," Emma said and laughed. "I'm so sorry, honey."

"For what?" she asked, panicked. If Emma felt this was a mistake, she might not be able to come back from that.

"You feel so good, so I'm so sorry I made you wait this long," Emma said and reached up to kiss her. "Do you forgive me?"

"I'll think of some way for you to make it up to me," she said, smiling, and repositioned her hand just a little, making Emma gasp but not tell her to stop. "What's the old saying, love? Good things are worth waiting for," she said and kissed her in a way that was meant to start the fire in Emma again.

"I want to touch you," Emma said, her hips starting to press into her again.

"I'm all yours, so you don't have to ever ask me that," she said and rolled to her back without moving her hand.

Emma started off slowly and almost shyly, but as Cain increased the pressure, Emma reciprocated and slid her fingers over her clit like they'd been lovers for years. The sensations seemed to be multiplied by the fact that she was deeply in love with Emma, so Emma broke through every defense she'd ever put up.

"You have to admit I'm a total idiot," Emma said when she fell completely relaxed against her.

"You're actually the smartest woman I've ever met." Emma lifted her head and peered down at her as if to see if she was serious. "You're so deep in here now that I'll never let you go," she said, tapping over her heart. "If we'd started here first, maybe that wouldn't have happened."

"So you're not sorry?"

"I'm in love and happy, so there's nothing for me to be sorry about. We started in a way that our grandchildren will love hearing about, and we've built to where we are a day at a time."

"I can't wait to see where we go from here," Emma said, lowering her head when she ran her hands down her back.

"Wherever that might be, we'll be together, and that's all that matters."

They spent the rest of the night talking and getting to know each other intimately. Emma sighed as she pressed up against her back and put her arm around her. Cain was right. She'd never walk away from this union unscathed if something broke them apart.

❖

Emma woke first but didn't open her eyes so she could enjoy the sensation of having Cain in her bed and pressed against the length of her. Their first night together hadn't been at all what she'd imagined in that she hadn't been as nervous as she thought she'd be. Cain had let her explore and do whatever she'd wanted at her own pace.

"I love you so much," she whispered, moving closer and putting her hand on Cain's abdomen.

"That's an inspiring message to wake up to," Cain said, tickling her side.

"Faker." She laughed and crawled on top of Cain so she could pretend to hold her in place.

"I'm not faking when I tell you I love you too." Cain hugged her and kissed her chin.

Emma decided then that hugging naked definitely was different and somewhat addictive. "You're probably becoming diabetic by now with all these romantic declarations, so how about I make you breakfast?"

"We're taking a shower and going out for breakfast," Cain said, slapping her ass.

"Are you sure you don't want to stay in?" She kissed Cain before sitting up and straddling her hips. "So much time to make up for."

"You are absolutely beautiful." She smiled as Cain started at her knees and ran her hands up until they were over her breasts. "A lifetime will never quench my thirst."

Cain sat up as well so she could reach her mouth, and Emma got instantly wet. She moaned when Cain put her hand between them and flicked her fingers over her clit. "You need to finish what you started," she said, moaning again when Cain pinched her nipple.

"Believe me. I'm planning to."

They kissed and Cain lay down, taking her with her. She went with it when Cain rolled them over and hovered like a predatory cat. Cain kissed her before starting down her body, stopping to suck both nipples until they were hard and dark pink.

"Tell me what you want, baby?" Cain asked as her fingers moved easily over her sex.

"I need you to go inside," she said, ready to beg.

"I promise I will, but not yet."

She would've complained, but it seemed like a moment later she opened her legs wider when Cain put her mouth on her.

If she had any shyness left, she lost it when she bucked her hips up to encourage Cain to suck harder as she slipped her fingers inside. It was like rattling apart, but Cain was there to drive up her need more than she thought possible. She arched her back and held on to Cain's hair, not thinking it could get any more intense until Cain pulled out and slammed her fingers back in.

The orgasm started, and Cain seemed to know how long to stroke until she stilled her hand but not her mouth. Touching herself never brought this kind of intense crescendo, and she started crying. That didn't seem to bother Cain as she came up to hold her, not needing to fill the void with unnecessary words.

When Cain cradled her a while later and carried her to the bathroom, she went willingly. She didn't want to go outside, but she didn't want to keep Cain locked up.

"I'm done for a few days, so do you want to do something later when you've finished work?" she asked after touching Cain until she came close to ripping her shower curtain off.

"I was planning to spend the day with you, but I can go in if you want some time to yourself. I just have to check with Billy about a project." Cain stood behind her and gently washed her hair for her.

"You're taking the day off for me?"

"I'd planned to, but not because of last night. You're starting your semester soon, so I wanted to enjoy your time off with you."

"Really?" She was thrilled at the thought of Cain's complete attention for that long.

"Really, so don't sound so surprised. How about a short trip now that you've seen me naked?"

She laughed and pinched Cain's butt. "Where would we go for only two days?"

"I've got a place in mind, so pack a couple of shorts and your bathing suit."

Someone came for the bike and dropped off a car so they could store Emma's bag. Cain drove home to pack, but before they could make it inside, a large number of agents blocked the gate and demanded entrance. "Cain," she said, worried when they headed right for her lover.

"Go inside, love, and tell Mum to call Muriel."

"I don't want to leave you."

"Go on. I won't be long," Cain said, and a couple of agents laughed.

"You're going to be forty years to life, so don't give the girl false hope. But maybe they'll let you have some special visits," the closest agent said.

"You'll have to do better than that to get a rise out of me, Agent Kyle," Cain said, all her humor seemingly gone. "But we can't expect much from a guy who has to pay for company. You do know that's illegal, right?"

"Shut up and get in the car. You're coming in for questioning, and it's not voluntary."

"Emma, go make that call, and have Mum pack my bag for later. I promise this won't take long."

Emma nodded and was stopped from coming closer.

"Don't be too late," Emma said, trying to prove she had all the confidence in the world that Cain was right. "I'll be waiting here."

Chapter Twenty-eight

Barney Kyle did all the talking on the way back and finally turned around when they reached the federal building. "Enjoy your last taste of freedom before I lock you up. I can't believe you made it this easy for me."

"What? Nothing to say?" the young agent driving said.

"What's your name again?" Cain asked, drumming her fingers on her knee and trying to not lose her temper.

"Agent North," he said and laughed. "It's going to look good alongside Agent Kyle's on the warrant for your arrest."

"Or the direction of your transfer once we're done," she said, smiling. "It's a toss-up at this point."

They led her to an interrogation room and left her alone, staring at the two-way mirror until Muriel joined her. She locked eyes with her cousin and didn't say anything when she arrived. This wasn't the time for talking, and all they could do was wait. Muriel took the hint and sat back, appearing as relaxed as she did.

Cain stared at the mirror and smirked. Whoever was on the other side thinking they were in charge was about to find out differently. To show how worried she was, she closed her eyes and thought of her few days away with Emma.

❖

Annabel Hicks watched Cain from the other side and waited for Kyle to finish putting together his case that he swore would lead to Casey's arrest and conviction. She knew from experience not to count on that, but maybe the new guy had gotten lucky in the year he'd been at it. She wasn't hungry but thought Barney would love to serve a bonanza of crow when he was done.

"Ma'am, if you're ready," Logan North said, holding the door for her, "Agent Kyle is ready in the conference room."

She entered and sat at the head of the table, then waved them on. The explanation of facts was concise and made sense, but it was missing some connections to tie it all together.

"I'm anxious to see how you get a conviction from this because, on the face of it, you've got some holes," she said when Kyle was done.

"The finishing touches are waiting in interrogation room five, but we'll start with Casey. I'll begin the questioning while my team finishes serving the warrants that were issued earlier."

She nodded and dismissed everyone but Kyle. "I'll be sitting in to observe, but it's your show."

They had to sit down before Cain opened her eyes and acknowledged them. Kyle put down a series of pictures and tapped his finger on the first one. "Do you recognize these guys?"

"The guy on the left—I'm not sure about the other one," she said as Muriel looked on.

"If you're going to play the stupid card, this is going to take forever, but we'll end up in the same place," he said, raising his voice. "You broke this guy's nose, so I'm sure you know him."

"Martin III? That's him?" Cain asked, shrugging.

"So you know him?" Annabel asked.

"He put his hands on someone I care about without her permission, then tried to attack me, so I broke his nose. He sued me and lost, and Ms. Verde sued him and won. It's not all that complicated, but we don't have a relationship."

"Cut the bull. These guys work for you," Kyle said, showing her another picture.

"They do? I don't think that's right, and I'm sure I've got a good reason aside from their bad manners," Cain said, and Annabel's gut clenched when Cain tapped on her chin as if thinking about it yet obviously toying with them.

"Let's see how funny you'll be when we finish searching the locations we have warrants for," Kyle said.

"So you're keeping us here while you conduct some kind of scavenger hunt?" Muriel asked. "Are we free to go?"

"Ms. Casey, if you can be somewhat patient, we'll get through this as soon as possible," Annabel said to Muriel, and Cain just spread her hands and shrugged again. "Thank you. I appreciate your cooperation."

She pointed to the door and Kyle followed her out. "What?" he asked.

"Let's go." She called for her car. The warehouse that Kyle's team was searching wasn't that far away, so they headed there. "This is the crux of your case, so if it's not here, she walks."

"Sir, it's all there," one of the agents said when they arrived. "We had to take the supposed owner of the place into custody to get in. He was bitching and trying to bar our entrance."

The open space, as well as all the side offices, was full of crates and boxes with the labels of different liquors. "It's all here?" she asked, confused by the amount of product and the time it'd taken to accumulate it.

A man walked up and offered her his hand. "Agent Hicks, I'm Agent Jake Benton, ma'am, and this is my partner Agent Bradley James. We arrived a few months before Agent Kyle and set up our undercover operation to make contact with Casey and her family." Bradley shook her hand as well. "We started in Atlanta to establish our business contacts."

"Yes, ma'am. This appears to be everything we sold her. She knows us as Jake Kelly and Bradley Draper. We started doing business with Casey through the two surrogates she decided to go with so this represents millions of dollars of product we purchased from the manufacturer and left them unstamped. Each box, though, has been embedded with a location chip."

"So you sold her the boxes, and she stored them here and hasn't moved any of them?" she asked.

"What are you getting at?" Kyle said.

"If, as we suspect, she's a bootlegger, why not move any of this to whoever she's selling it to?"

"We analyzed the money, but that was a dead end," Jake said. "But you're right in that the boxes haven't moved. She does, though, have a reputation for cautiousness."

"The transponders haven't been removed?" she asked.

Jake shook his head. "We've had this place and her two guys under constant surveillance since our first sale."

Bradley moved in and opened a box, making it fall to the ground from his forceful yank since he'd expected it to be full. It was empty, as were the next ten he picked up. A frantic search to the back of the space yielded the same thing. Every single one of them was empty.

"Who owns the building?" she asked the agent who'd bragged about subduing the guy.

"He said his name was Jonas Belson, ma'am."

"As in Senator Jonas Belson?" she asked, walking outside to see where Jonas was. The guy she'd met at a dinner honoring law enforcement was handcuffed in the back of a car. "So one of the buyers was his son?" she asked, but no one answered. "Where is he?"

"We picked up Belson's kid and the other one before we nabbed Casey," Kyle said. "They were our next interviews."

After releasing the senator, Annabel read through the file on the way back. She wanted to gut Kyle for going over her head for this operation because, while the product had made some revenue, they were still in the red. If none of the money was recovered, Kyle's little party would cost the bureau a minimum of three million dollars.

Jonsie and Marty had obviously spent some of the money from their sales on a good time and flashy cars, but Kyle and Jake had no idea where the rest was, since a search of both their homes had yielded no clues. Annabel was informed that the two young men were indeed waiting on them, and the biggest surprise was that they hadn't asked for an attorney.

She walked in and stared at Kyle when he started to say something. "I'm not going to waste my time on trying to play games with either of you idiots."

"Hey," Marty said and laughed.

"Shut the hell up," Jonsie said with an expression that gave Annabel the impression he thought he'd skate no matter what happened.

"One time I could attribute to the thrill of the quick score," she said, putting down the picture of them handing over the money. "Twice I could almost understand, but you two got greedy, didn't you?"

"You were buying from an undercover agent so we got you. You need to think fast and make the right choice to save your asses," Kyle said.

"You bought from Jake Kelly," she said as the video of their transaction came on the screen. "Who'd you sell to?"

"Don't say a word," Jonas said, coming in. "Get out," he told Annabel and Kyle. "But don't go far, Agent Hicks. I'd like a word about how I was treated today."

Annabel walked to the room where Cain and Muriel were waiting. "I apologize for taking so long."

"What exactly is going on?" Muriel asked.

"A little while longer, Ms. Casey." She didn't want to stay and have Muriel bog her down with questions. Kyle was waiting outside, but some of his cockiness had disappeared. "Are you here to knock some more square pegs into round holes? You may not like Casey, but if this is what you have to shut her down, make sure to validate her parking ticket on her way out."

"Ma'am, the senator is ready for you," Logan said.

"What's it going to take to make this go away?" Jonas asked.

"They need to come clean as to who they were selling to," she said, sitting across from them. "You're caught, with plenty of tape and evidence to back it up, so the only way out of our net is to serve up a bigger fish."

"Get on with it," Jonas said, slapping his son on the back of the head.

"Marty met this guy who wanted in the business but couldn't get the first part done. We put up the first money and sold it to him, tripling our cash," Jonsie said as fast as he could get it out.

"Who was it?" Kyle asked.

"I only know him as Big Chief," Marty said softly, appearing as if he might cry.

"Big Chief?" Kyle asked, sounding as upset as Marty.

"Excuse us," Annabel said, thinking she wasn't going to like whatever came next.

"Wait. What did he look like, and where did you meet him?" Kyle asked.

"He was an old skinny guy with a broken nose. I met him at the doctor's office when I was laid up with the same thing."

"Okay, what?" she asked Kyle outside.

"Big Chief was killed way before that kid could've met him. Whoever was posing as Big Chief has to be working for Casey."

"Check with the doctor and see if you can find him," she told Kyle before heading back in. "So you sold to Big Chief. What else?"

"That's it," Jonsie said.

"I read the transcripts—you said you were buying for Cain Casey."

Marty perked up, but Jonsie seemed to deflate. "It was the only way we thought Jake would deal with us."

"But we totally did it on her orders," Marty said.

"The concept of the big fish is backup, Mr. Williamson. Do you have proof?" The way his eyes moved around meant he was trying to fabricate some. "Where's the money?"

"That's our money," Jonsie said.

She sighed and stood. "Senator Belson, you might want to retain an attorney and get in touch with Mr. Williamson's father. As for *your* money, unless you hid it well, it's gone. We've searched every possible location you two had access to, and it's not there."

Annabel took a few deep breaths in the hallway before facing the two Casey women. "Did you get all the nails you'll need to crucify me, Agent Hicks?" Cain asked as she brushed her pants off as if the office had somehow dirtied them.

"You're free to go for now, but please don't leave the city."

"I'm taking a short trip with my girlfriend, so if you're going to charge me—go ahead. If not, keep watching and wishing."

"The two gentlemen in the picture," Muriel said, taking something out of her briefcase. "Here's the restraining orders we filed after they made threatening comments following Emma Verde's settlement hearing. When you talk to them, make sure they give you their copies."

"You just now remembered this?" She held up the papers.

"I knew there was a reason they didn't work for me, so thank God for the lawyer in the family. She always keeps me on the straight and narrow."

The Caseys walked out, and Cain stopped when she saw Kyle. "Sorry to disappoint you, extra Special Agent Kyle. If you need something to cheer you up, come by the pub and I'll buy your guys a round, since they're fixated on liquor."

"This isn't over," Kyle said, and Annabel cut him off.

"Keep an eye on this one, Agent Hicks. He might be a problem," Cain said, smiling at her, and then she was gone.

"Now maybe you'll understand what I first told you," she said to Kyle. "She's certainly unique, and smarter than your average thug, but then thug was your word for her."

❖

"Does this happen often?" Emma asked Cain when she finally got home with Muriel.

"Not that often. Agent Barney Kyle wanted to impress his boss with a case he thought would be a cinch, but nothing in life is simple. At least, it's never been that easy for the federal government when it comes to my family."

"What did he think you did?" Emma was sitting on Cain's bed while she finished packing the bag Therese had started for her.

Cain told her the highlights of Barney's case and who had ended up in custody. Jonas Belson had known better than to try to frame her for his son's greed without exposing himself, so all he could pray for was leniency for a first-time offender. Marty's father wasn't as willing to let it go, but FBI surveillance video didn't lie.

"Are you sure you want to go? The feds don't often knock on my door, but it has a way of changing your perspective if you've never seen it happen."

"Do you need to talk to anyone else before I start modeling swimwear?" Emma responded.

"Just Billy. Then I'm all yours," she said, and she smiled when Emma walked up to her and put her hands on her ass.

"You're all mine now, but I want you to clear your workload so you're not thinking about anything but us."

❖

They walked down together, and after a small kiss from Cain, Emma went with Therese and Marie to the den. Cain's main crew was waiting in the office, and she couldn't remember the last time they were all smiling like this.

"You all look happy."

"Da would've been the first one to be in here laughing his ass off that this worked," Billy said, throwing his arms around her. "Not that I doubted you, but who would've thought the feds were this stupid? It's not every day you end up with a warehouse full of booze courtesy of the federal government."

"Not exactly true, Billy," Muriel said. "All that cost us two Corvettes and a couple of high-priced call girls. Your idea of giving to charity boggles the mind, Cain."

"I believe in throwing good things out into the universe so good things come back to you. We did teach these young men a new business and bankrolled their success. This time karma was incredibly generous because of all our good deeds." She poured them all a drink from one of the bottles Jonsie and Marty had bought from Jake after she'd indirectly introduced them. "To a new era, one that's built solidly on the foundation the Casey family's built." They all lifted their glasses and drank.

"Can you break it all down so we can be ready for whatever comes next?" Merrick asked, and Cain knew it was because of her cautious nature, but that beat carelessness.

"Our two charity cases were looking to get back at me for Marty's broken nose and bruised manhood that he then had to pay Emma for, so Billy and I arranged for him to meet Big Chief. Cousin Colin sent two guys from California to fill the role of that asshole and his driver." She waved Billy on.

"Marty and Jonsie started small, buying from Jake at cut-rate prices that were too good to be legitimate, and they in turn sold to us. They were smart enough to increase their orders, pumping up their profits, but every shipment came with a little something extra Bryce found for us."

She nodded and laughed. "We reboxed and kept buying, storing the original boxes in Belson's warehouse. The real-estate mogul wannabe didn't keep track of his places, and neither did his son. After our last buy, I had you and Billy go by Marty's and get our money back. I mean, who in the hell keeps that much money under the bed?" Billy had brought home the ten duffel bags full of cash that represented most of their money, aside from the cars and the guys' partying.

"Where were the two geniuses when you made a withdrawal from their stash of cash?" Muriel asked.

"Brandi Parrish's girls were happy to pick them up in a bar and give them enough memories to hopefully last them their entire sentences." The famous owner of the Red Door in the Quarter hadn't asked any questions when she'd handed the money over. "Now all we have to do is be extra careful with Barney Kyle and his little band of misfits. I played him, and I wanted him to know it, so he's going to double down like Marty tried to do."

"We got this, so get going," Billy said. "Emma's waited long enough."

"Thanks, brother. I'm proud of you, and so is Da. I'm sure of it."

"You saying that means everything to me, so go be happy. I'll take care of things while you're gone. Don't forget to tell Emma what happened, and since this went so well, I know you'll come up with the right solution for her."

"Nothing like a hint that's like a two-by-four to the face."

CHAPTER TWENTY-NINE

Emma waved to the surveillance team as their floatplane left the Lakefront Airport. It was late afternoon, but Cain promised the trip wouldn't take that long, and she was right when they landed an hour later on the shores of Alabama.

The beach house was more of a small, isolated cabin, which Emma explored as Cain got their bags. "I love it," Emma said, glancing out at the perfect beach as their ride took off again. "Is it yours?"

"It belongs to an old friend, but he only likes to use the main house a couple of miles up the road," Cain said as she started unbuttoning Emma's shirt. "I like the solitude of this place, but I don't mind sharing it with you."

Emma smiled at the subtle message. She was the first and hopefully the last to share this space with her, and it made her want Cain naked as well. Whoever owned the place had cranked up the air-conditioning and lit the fireplace, so that's where they'd start.

"I think I owe you one from this morning, mobster."

"Your credit is good with me, lass, so we'll get to that," Cain said, picking her up so she could wrap her legs around her. "But right now I can't wait to touch you."

She'd gone from inexperienced to someone who got wet when Cain looked at her like she wanted to devour her, and she wasn't about to complain. Cain laid her down and touched her like she'd break if she didn't use a light touch. It was maddening, but it was driving up her need to be loved, so she finally pressed Cain's hand to her breast when she skimmed over her hypersensitive nipple.

"I want you," she said, barely able to get the words out, and screamed when Cain gave her what she wanted. "So good," she said when Cain filled her up.

She clawed at Cain's back as she moaned from the pure pleasure of the tempo Cain had set. It was hard and fast, and she could sense the orgasm starting to build and was desperate for it. "Don't stop," she ordered, grabbing Cain by the shoulders.

"Come for me, lass," Cain whispered in her ear in that low-pitched voice that cut right through her. "I love you."

That was all it took to make her let go. No matter who Cain was, or how many people wanted her for whatever reason—Emma belonged to her. That truth would last a lifetime no matter what happened.

She reached down and put her hand between Cain's legs while she was still over her with her fingers still inside her. "I love you too," she said as she didn't show the same patience as Cain had and touched her hard and fast. Cain kept her eyes on her face, and she could see how much she wanted her, so she almost laughed when she stopped.

"You're coming, but not like this," she said, getting Cain flat on her back.

Emma was tentative at first, but she put her mouth on her and tried to do the same thing Cain had done to her that morning. She almost stopped when Cain said "fuck" loudly enough to be heard outside, but kept going until Cain seemed to melt into the floor.

"Who knew my clumsiness would pay off this big?"

❖

They got dressed a few hours later and walked the beach under the rising full moon. It was the first time Emma had seen Cain this relaxed in her bare feet and shorts, and she tightened her hold on her arm.

Cain had told her about her busted door and trashed apartment from the FBI's search for some large sum of cash and liquor. Why they'd think she had it was almost funny. "Did they think I kept that much money in my underwear drawer?" she asked, and Cain laughed.

"They're trying to make you run to do the right thing," Cain said, stopping and sitting in the sand.

"What do you think is the right thing for me?" She sat on Cain's lap and brushed Cain's hair out of her face.

"Me."

"Good answer, mobster. It keeps me from having to get rough with you. The door can be fixed, and you can help me put everything back where it belongs. None of that is important." She could see the blueness of Cain's eyes even in the dark, and she loved the warmth in them.

"What if I offer something better?"

"Like a maid or something?" she said and shook her head.

Cain reached into her pocket and took out a key. "You might think this is a kneejerk reaction to what happened, but I figured something out this morning."

"What?" Emma asked, taking Cain's hand and pressing the key between them.

"I have a finite number of mornings in my life, and I don't want to waste another one not waking up with you. I want you to move in with me."

"Like into your house with your family? How are they going to feel about that?"

"They're going to welcome you into our family and love you, but not as much as I do. You can think about it if you want, but I meant what I said. I want to share my life with you."

"Yes," she said, wanting it as much as Cain evidently did. "I'd love to if you're sure."

"I'm as sure of this as I am that I'm all yours," Cain said and kissed her.

"Then let forever begin, my love, and all that comes with it. I'll take the good and the bad, the happy and the sad, as long as I get you."

"Wish for something that's not yours already, lass, because that's a given."

"Your mother was right. You're not one to pass up a good thing," she said and smiled.

"You can celebrate it with a drink out of those old family glasses you like so much."

"You've got a date," she said, kissing Cain.

"You do too, for as long as my heart beats."

About the Author

Ali Vali is originally from Cuba and has frequently used many of her family's traditions and language in her stories. Having her father read adventure stories and poetry before bed as a child infused her with a love of reading, which is even stronger today. In 2000, Ali decided to embark on a new path and started writing.

Ali lives in the suburbs of New Orleans with her partner of thirty-one years, and finds that residing in such a historically rich area provides plenty of material to draw from in creating her novels and short stories. Mixing imagination with different life experiences makes it easier to create the slew of characters that are engaging to the reader on many levels. Ali states that "The feedback from readers encourages me to continue to hone my skills as a writer."

Books Available From Bold Strokes Books

Between Sand and Stardust by Tina Michele. Are the lifelong bonds of love strong enough to conquer time, distance, and heartache when Haven Thorne and Willa Bennette are given another chance at forever? (978-1-62639-940-2)

Charming the Vicar by Jenny Frame. When magician and atheist Finn Kane seeks refuge in an English village after a spiritual crisis, can local vicar Bridget Claremont restore her faith in life and love? (978-1-63555-029-0)

Data Capture by Jesse J. Thoma. Lola Walker is undercover on the hunt for cybercriminals while trying not to notice the woman who might be perfectly wrong for her for all the right reasons. (978-1-62639-985-3)

Epicurean Delights by Renee Roman. Ariana Marks had no idea a leisure swim would lead to being rescued, in more ways than one, by the charismatic Hudson Frost. (978-1-63555-100-6)

Heart of the Devil by Ali Vali. We know most of Cain and Emma Casey's story, but Heart of the Devil will take you back to where it began one fateful night with a tray loaded with beer. (978-1-63555-045-0)

Known Threat by Kara A. McLeod. When Special Agent Ryan O'Connor reluctantly questions who protects the Secret Service, she learns courage truly is found in unlikely places. Agent O'Connor Series #3 (978-1-63555-132-7)

Seer and the Shield by D. Jackson Leigh. Time is running out for the Dragon Horse Army while two unlikely heroines struggle to put aside their attraction and find a way to stop a deadly cult. Dragon Horse War, Book 3 (978-1-63555-170-9)

The Universe Between Us by Jane C. Esther. Ana Mitchell must make the hardest choice of her life: the promise of new love Jolie Dann on Earth, or a humanity-saving mission to colonize Mars. (978-1-63555-106-8)

Touch by Kris Bryant. Can one touch heal a heart? (978-1-63555-084-9)

A More Perfect Union by Carsen Taite. Major Zoey Granger and DC fixer Rook Daniels risk their reputations for a chance at true love while dealing with a scandal that threatens to rock the military. (978-1-62639-754-5)

Arrival by Gun Brooke. The spaceship *Pathfinder* reaches its passengers' new homeworld where danger lurks in the shadows while Pamas Seclan disembarks and finds unexpected love in young science genius Darmiya Do Voy. (978-1-62639-859-7)

Captain's Choice by VK Powell. Architect Kerstin Anthony's life is going to plan until Bennett Carlyle, the first girl she ever kissed, is assigned to her latest and most important project, a police district substation. (978-1-62639-997-6)

Falling Into Her by Erin Zak. Pam Phillips, widow at the age of forty, meets Kathryn Hawthorne, local Chicago celebrity, and it changes her life forever—in ways she hadn't even considered possible. (978-1-63555-092-4)

Hookin' Up by MJ Williamz. Will Leah get what she needs from casual hookups or will she see the love she desires right in front of her? (978-1-63555-051-1)

King of Thieves by Shea Godfrey. When art thief Casey Marinos meets bounty hunter Finnegan Starkweather, the crimes of the past just might set the stage for a payoff worth more than she ever dreamed possible. (978-1-63555-007-8)

Lucy's Chance by Jackie D. As a serial killer haunts the streets, Lucy tries to stitch up old wounds with her first love in the wake of a small town's rapid descent into chaos. (978-1-63555-027-6)

Right Here, Right Now by Georgia Beers. When Alicia Wright moves into the office next door to Lacey Chamberlain's accounting firm, Lacey is about to find out that sometimes the last person you want is exactly the person you need. (978-1-63555-154-9)

Strictly Need to Know by MB Austin. Covert operator Maji Rios will do whatever she must to complete her mission, but saving a gorgeous stranger from Russian mobsters was not in her plans. (978-1-63555-114-3)

Tailor-Made by Yolanda Wallace. Tailor Grace Henderson doesn't date clients, but when she meets gender-bending model Dakota Lane, she's tempted to throw all the rules out the window. (978-1-63555-081-8)

Time Will Tell by M. Ullrich. With the ability to time travel, Eva Caldwell will have to decide between having it all and erasing it all. (978-1-63555-088-7)

Change in Time by Robyn Nyx. Working in the past is hell on your future. The Extractor series: Book Two. (978-1-62639-880-1)

Love After Hours by Radclyffe. When Gina Antonelli agrees to renovate Carrie Longmire's new house, she doesn't welcome Carrie's overtures at friendship or her own unexpected attraction. A Rivers Community Novel. (978-1-63555-090-0)

Nantucket Rose by CF Frizzell. Maggie Jordan can't wait to convert a historic Nantucket home into a B&B, but doesn't expect to fall for mariner Ellis Chilton, who has more claim to the house than Maggie realizes. (978-1-63555-056-6)

Picture Perfect by Lisa Moreau. Falling in love wasn't supposed to be part of the stakes for Olive and Gabby, rival photographers in the competition of a lifetime. (978-1-62639-975-4)

Set the Stage by Karis Walsh. Actress Emilie Danvers takes the stage again in Ashland, Oregon, little realizing that landscaper Arden Philips is about to offer her a very personal romantic lead role. (978-1-63555-087-0)

Strike a Match by Fiona Riley. When their attempts at matchmaking fizzle out, firefighter Sasha and reluctant millionairess Abby find themselves turning to each other to strike a perfect match. (978-1-62639-999-0)

The Price of Cash by Ashley Bartlett. Cash Braddock is doing her best to keep her business afloat, stay out of jail, and avoid Detective Kallen. It's not working. (978-1-62639-708-8)

Captured Soul by Laydin Michaels. Can Kadence Munroe save the woman she loves from a twisted killer, or will she lose her to a collector of souls? (978-1-62639-915-0)

Under Her Wing by Ronica Black. At Angel's Wings Rescue, dogs are usually the ones saved, but when quiet Kassandra Haden meets outspoken owner Jayden Beaumont, the two stubborn women just might end up saving each other. (978-1-63555-077-1)

Underwater Vibes by Mickey Brent. When Hélène, a translator in Brussels, Belgium, meets Sylvie, a young Greek photographer and swim coach, unsettling feelings hijack Hélène's mind and body—even her poems. (978-1-63555-002-3)

A Date to Die by Anne Laughlin. Someone is killing people close to Detective Kay Adler, who must look to her own troubled past for a suspect. There she finds more than one person seeking revenge against her. (978-1-63555-023-8)

Dawn's New Day by TJ Thomas. Can Dawn Oliver and Cam Cooper, two women who have loved and lost, open their hearts to love again? (978-1-63555-072-6)

Definite Possibility by Maggie Cummings. Sam Miller is just out for good times, but Lucy Weston makes her realize happily ever after is a definite possibility. (978-1-62639-909-9)

Eyes Like Those by Melissa Brayden. Isabel Chase and Taylor Andrews struggle between love and ambition from the writers' room on one of Hollywood's hottest TV shows. (978-1-63555-012-2)

Heart's Orders by Jaycie Morrison. Helen Tucker and Tee Owens escape hardscrabble lives to careers in the Women's Army Corps, but more than their hearts are at risk as friendship blossoms into love. (978-1-63555-073-3)

Hiding Out by Kay Bigelow. Treat Dandridge is unaware that her life is in danger from the murderer who is hunting the woman she's falling in love with, Mickey Heiden. (978-1-62639-983-9)

Omnipotence Enough by Sophia Kell Hagin. Can the tiny tool that abducted war veteran Jamie Gwynmorgan accidentally acquires help her escape an unknown enemy to reclaim her stolen life and the woman she deeply loves? (978-1-63555-037-5)

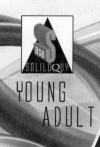